A Scandalous Lady

She forced herself to look up into his face, and oh, crikey, wished she hadn't. The bloke was even more handsome than she'd first judged and did not do her fantasy justice. Raindrops slid off the brim of his hat to soak his shoulders, turning the gray to black. A shadow of whiskers darkened his sharply angled jaw and chin and surrounded a nicely bowed mouth too unsettling to dwell on. The bridge of his nose was straight as a dagger blade, unmarred by the telling bump she so often saw on those prone to brawling, the tip rounded, the nostrils nicely flared. Unfashionably short sideburns looked freshly trimmed, as did the coal black hair pulled back behind his ears and secured at his nape. And his eyes . . . God's teeth, the man had glorious eyes. Spiky lashes swept out above irises the color of mist on stone, and long hooded lids drew down at the corners in a sensual curve that made her think of how a man might look at a woman waiting in his bed. . . .

Other **AVON ROMANCES**

RACHELLE MORGAN

A Scandalous Lady

AVON BOOKS
An Imprint of HarperCollinsPublishers

This is a work of fiction. Names, characters, places, and incidents are products of the author's imagination or are used fictitiously and are not to be construed as real. Any resemblance to actual events, locales, organizations, or persons, living or dead, is entirely coincidental.

AVON BOOKS
An Imprint of HarperCollins*Publishers*
10 East 53rd Street
New York, New York 10022-5299

Copyright © 2003 by Rachelle Nelson
ISBN: 0-06-008470-7
www.avonromance.com

First Avon Books paperback printing: April 2003

Avon Trademark Reg. U.S. Pat. Off. and in Other Countries, Marca Registrada, Hecho en U.S.A.
HarperCollins® is a registered trademark of HarperCollins Publishers Inc.

Printed in the U.S.A.

10 9 8 7 6 5 4 3 2 1

For my sisters and brothers: Crystal, Jay, Molly, Kevin, Cornell and Matthew, who always make me feel as if I've never left home, no matter how long I've been gone; and for Scott and Conrad, who are always in our hearts.

For my beautiful niece, Sarah Greuel, whose friends don't believe her Aunt Rachelle is a famous author. For Meg Ruley, who encouraged me toward "exciting new worlds."

Annelise Robey for being my sanity and support. I don't know what I would do without you!

And always, for my husband and kids, because they are my everything.

Prologue

San Francisco, California
1887

It had been a deception of such magnitude that even the queen of cons couldn't comprehend the feat. One brother's betrayal against another, four lives torn asunder, two little girls stolen from their family—

And Faith Jervais had been one of them.

A salty Pacific breeze blew in from the ocean, where forgotten memories of waves crashing against jagged rocks became reality. Aniste Jervais-Justiss stood upon the terrace, leaning against the wrought-iron railing overlooking the water. Even her name didn't fit. She'd been Honesty McGuire, daughter of the greatest con man in the West for so long that she still had trouble comprehending that she was, in truth, Aniste Jervais, joint heiress to the greatest shipping fortune in the country. How did one adjust to the fact that her entire life as she'd known it had been a lie?

She closed her eyes and tried to absorb all that she'd missed while she'd been away. Sixteen years, she thought. Sixteen years since she'd stood in this spot, felt the cool, balmy air caress her face, breathed in the redolence of marine life, coastal mint and eucalyptus, and her favorite fragrance, lilac, growing profusively in the gardens beneath her. Sixteen years since she'd been taken from it all by a man with greed in his heart and vengeance in his soul. How often had she dreamed of this place, without understanding why? Without knowing its significance?

Then again, she and her sister had only been children when it all began, a plan hatched by a devious uncle to load his pockets, no matter how innocent the victims or how grave the sin. While she'd grown up traveling the West with Deuce McGuire, rooking the gullible, conning the cons, she'd never once suspected that the man who'd raised her, loved her, and taught her everything she knew, the man she'd always believed to be her father, hadn't been her father at all. And she never would have known differently if not for his death and one man's dogged determination to uncover the truth.

As if the thought of him could make him appear, her bedroom door opened, and he stepped inside. Honesty would have known it was him even if she hadn't turned around. It had been that way since she'd first met Jesse Justiss back in Last

Hope, Colorado, the ability to sense his presence before she saw him. Her entire existence seemed to narrow down to pure feminine sensation: tingling nerves, quickening pulses, giddy delight. And even after all these months, the sight of his rugged frame and windswept blond hair, so incongruous among the dainty white lace and porcelain bric-a-brac, still took her breath away.

The door shut softly behind him. He leaned against it, crossed his arms over his broad chest, and gave her one of those hooded examinations that always turned her bones to mush. "What are you still doing awake, wife?" he asked.

Wife. Another thing she still found hard to believe. Honesty glanced back to the ocean lest he see the longing in her eyes. "Just thinking."

"I'm not sure I like the sound of that," he said, joining her on the terrace. "Every time you think, I wind up in trouble."

She gave him a playful swat to his shoulder. Grinning, he caught her against him with one arm around her waist and drew her against his chest. Honesty leaned against him, welcoming the solid strength at her back as together, they gazed upon the ocean where moonlight danced upon the curling waves. How could she ever have gotten through the last few days—the last few months—without him?

"So what were you thinking about?"

"I never in my wildest dreams would have thought my life would turn out like this." Discovering herself the long-lost heiress to a shipping fortune, meeting her true father, a man she'd never known existed, and learning that she had a sister out there somewhere. How did someone forget her own twin? "And I can't help but wonder about Faith."

Her gaze turned to the picture on the nightstand beside the king-size canopy bed. It was a miniature-size replica of a portrait that hung in the library downstairs—her father, asleep down the hall; her mother, buried long ago, and a pair of identical blond little girls, one returned, the other . . . "What if it's been too long? What if we can't find her?"

"We'll find her—wherever she is. I give you my word."

She well knew that Jesse never broke his word. Still, she wished she had his confidence. She couldn't forget that someone's clothes had washed up on the bay after the abduction of herself and her twin sister, and obviously they hadn't been hers. "But what if it's been too long? What if we're far too late?"

"She's a survivor, darlin'. The same blood runs through her veins as yours." He pressed a kiss to her brow. "If you ask me, you're worrying for nothing. She's probably married to some upstate bluestocking, has a passel of kids tugging at her skirts, and is living high on the hog."

"I hope you're right, Jesse." Honesty sighed as she stared at Faith's young likeness. "I hope you're right."

Chapter 1

London, England
1887

The blow came swiftly and suddenly, a sharp crack of flesh against flesh that snapped Fanny Jarvis's head back and knocked her off her feet, onto the solid rock floor.

"This is all you brought me, you worthless piece of rubbish?"

She barely heard him. Her ears rang, her head spun. Blimey if he didn't split her lip again, too. Only half a lifetime of mastering her own actions kept her from pressing her hand to the broken flesh or to her stinging cheek, or give any other sign that he'd caused her discomfort. Weakness of any kind was not tolerated by Jack Swift.

Fanny braced her palms against a smear of

mud on the floor and pushed herself slowly up to her knees. She hoped she wouldn't throw up. The way her stomach was colly-wobbling, it was a distinct possibility.

Aware that the rest of the band watched her from various corners of the antechamber, Fanny swallowed the sharp taste of disgrace rising in her throat. She dragged one foot under her for support, then the other. Every last one of the lot darted glances in her direction—a couple played dice, one whittled, the others drew or sewed or sharpened their knives—but not a one came to her defense or her aid. Not that she would have accepted it anyway. Being the only female in a league of boys had not earned her special treatment for the last ten years; she'd not expect that to change now. As usual, she was on her own, and she would die before letting them see her brought to her knees.

Once again on her feet, she brushed back a screen of wet, tangled hair that had fallen across her eyes and faced the keeper of the band. Most times, Jack was a decent fellow, and any woman would tell you he was a handsome one. Wavy, whiskey brown hair touched his collar, thick eyebrows of the same shade winged above his eyes, and trimmed sideburns reached the hinge of his jaw. His skin was clear and his teeth straight, and fancying himself a gentleman of means, he liked to dress the part. This eve he sported his favorite—if not faded—gold vest over the only white shirt he owned, the one with ruffles at the collar and cuffs. A black serge coat lined in fur fit snugly about his shoulders. His breeches matched his coat and his shoes—the fancy black ones with the faux-silver buckles—had been polished to a high shine.

But under the dandyish layers of a man known commonly on the outside as Gentleman Jack waited the quicksilver temper of Jack Swift, the most cunning thief on two continents.

"There's hardly anyone about this eve, Jack," she softly explained, bowing her head in a subservience that grated against every nerve in her body. "With the season nearly over, most all the gents worth bilkin' have left." Jack must know that. He prided himself in knowing every peculiarity of the noble classes. He could cite the moment the first lords and ladies arrived in London each spring to attend their fancy parties and balls, and the last to leave the city each July.

Crikey, even if they were in the midst of the season, no one with their wits about them would venture out in such miserable weather. It had been raining since dawn, a steady pouring that overflowed sewage ditches and turned potholes into cesspools. Fanny spoke none of her thoughts aloud, of course. Excuses would only enrage him more.

He turned away from her to examine the evening's pickings piled at the corner of the supper table: a drawstring purse, suspiciously light, two leather wallets, three gold pocket watches.

The moments dragged on like lead pipes across concrete as he counted the swag in each billfold. Her heart pounded so hard that she feared he could hear it. Sweat dampened her palms. Her hands clenched and unclenched. She hid them in her pockets before he took note of her nervousness, and prayed he'd be quicker about counting the spoils so she could escape.

Finally, he tossed the last billfold upon the table and turned to her. "I think you are holding out on me, Fanny."

His eyes, deep-set chips of jade known to as easily entice a trollop as freeze a pugilist in his tracks, narrowed to slits. She'd seen more than one man look into them, then tuck his tail between his legs and run. At this moment, Fanny knew exactly how they felt. "I'd never do that." Only a fool would think he could cheat Jack Swift and get away with it.

"Empty your pockets."

Fanny's fingers tightened around a precious chunk of sweet cake that she'd swiped an hour earlier, nearly severing it in two. If he learned that she'd slacked in her duty for even a second, there would be the devil to pay. At the time, with her stomach pinched tighter than Queen Victoria's corset, Fanny couldn't bring herself to care a whit whether or not Jack Swift lost his temper. She'd lain in wait in the alley, her eyes trained on the coffeehouse across the street instead of the pub on the corner. It was crucial to get there the instant the light was snuffed, else you wound up clawing your way amongst dozens of anxious scavengers eager to claim the eve's bounty.

Now, beneath his brittle glower, the victory she'd felt in reaching the rubbish barrel ahead of the pack turned to throat-closing dread.

"Have you gone cloth-eared, Fanny? Empty your pockets!"

She flinched at his tone and forced herself forward. Her legs felt like wood, and a despised sob rose in her throat as she reached into the outer pocket of her coat and laid the evidence of her detour onto the table. Every muscle in her body tightened in preparation for another blow as he stared at the misshapen crust.

"You disappoint me, Fanny. Do I not feed you, clothe you, provide shelter over your pitiful head?"

"Aye, Jack."

"Then why, when I ask only one small task in return, do you defy me?"

"I did not defy ye—"

"Did you not?" He swept his arm across the table. Coins spun through the air and pinged to the floor; a watch chain caught on the back of a chair while another skittered toward the blackened stove at the far end of the room. But it was the sight of her precious chunk of sweet cake dropping into a bucket of stagnant water that made her heart pitch.

"Had you gone to the wharf as you were told, you would have brought back more than this paltry amount. Instead, you deemed it more important to stake out the bloody pastry shop. Need I remind you what happens to those who do not earn their keep?"

Anger bubbled up inside Fanny. "I did not defy ye, Jack," she insisted with strained calmness. "I waited outside Jorge's for hours, but nary a soul came out of the tavern."

"Then get back and wait some more. And don't let me see you back here until you've got something worth bringing me."

He turned away from her. Fanny hesitated a moment before taking a cautious step backward. Then another. And another. Only when she was safely out of his reach did she turn on her worn heel and flee.

The tunnels wound beneath the city, home to rats and vermin, thieves and beggars, and she raced through them with an ease born of nearly a decade of practice. Dripping water echoed through a darkened area to her right, the sharp odor of kerosene mixed with mildew clung to the crumbling walls, and the stench of sewage permeated through every crack and crevice. At the southernmost passage, Fanny swung right, then pushed open a steel door and slipped into an antechamber she'd claimed as her own years earlier. A moth-eaten scrap of wool was folded in half on the floor next to a crate missing three of its slats. The precious stub of a candle sat atop the crate, and a tiny window embracing the silhouette of a low-hanging moon crumbled high up on the stone wall.

Fanny dropped to her knees beside her pallet. Her muscles started to tremble. Tears of pain and humiliation at being set down in front of the band slipped from the control she'd fought to maintain. She swiped at her cheeks impatiently, hating the weakness of tears as much as the cause, and winced when her fingers brushed across a bruise Jack's fist had left behind. If she were a man, she'd not have stood there and taken the hit; she'd have popped him back a good one. Let him see how it felt to get knocked on his arse.

Well, she'd not bear it forever. Jack didn't know

it yet, but one day she'd leave this place. If it took her last breath, she would. She'd find herself a snug little cottage in the country where the spring chill didn't settle in the stones and refuse didn't layer the floors. Food would be bought fresh at the market and served on platters, not dug up from the bottom of a slop barrel. And she'd wear fancy clothes that fit her instead of rags swiped off an untended clothesline, unfit to dust with. And people would call her by her given name. She closed her eyes and let the sound of it fill her mind. *Faith.* She hadn't heard it spoken in so long that it surprised her that she still remembered it. Mark it up to another thing Jack Swift had denied her. Said it sounded too uppity, and he'd not give a worthless urchin any cause for putting on airs. Aye, one day—

Oh, who was she foolin'? Fanny's shoulders slumped. She'd never get away from Bethnal Green, never live in a nice place or eat decent food or wear fancy clothes, never be called anything but "Fanny," as if she were the hind end of someone's mistake. If she tried leaving, Jack would track her down and turn her in. He'd threatened to more than once. And when the coppers learned what she'd done—

"It's about time ye showed up!"

Her heart stopped at the unexpected voice coming from a figure that popped into the room. It took her only a second to recognize the shaggy-headed, baggy-clothed teenager, but that one second seemed to last two lifetimes. "God's teeth, Scatter, ye gave me fright!" She wiped her eyes quickly lest he see her weeping like a babe.

"Where ye been? A feller could starve t' death waitin' on the likes of you." He leaped up and caught an overhead pipe, then hung from it by his knees. "Did ye bring me anything?"

"Don't I always, ye li'l beggar?"

Fanny withdrew a half loaf of bread she'd hidden in a low, inside pocket, broke off a chunk, and handed it to Scatter. He stole it faster than spit on a stick and shoved it into his mouth. Like most of her fellow knucks, he had the look of a street rat stamped all over him—gaunt features born of too few meals, too much trouble, and far more misery than a boy his age should ever know. He claimed not to know his parents, but he had the look of gypsy stock. Black, stringy hair, thick brows, dark eyes, and a sharp nose. Hell, he could be the long-lost heir to a foreign throne for all either of them knew. What Fanny did know was that he'd attached himself to her almost from the minute he'd landed his skinny arse in Jack Swift's band. Though six years her junior, he was the closest she could claim to family. She often thought of him as a younger brother, and had made it her duty to watch out for him. Why, she had yet to figure. He was as useful as a sore tooth.

"Zounds, Fan—what 'appened to you?"

She ducked her head, though too late to hide Jack's handprint on her face. "None of your bloody business."

"Jack popped you again, didn't 'e?"

She saw no point in denying it and gave a short nod.

"Does it hurt?"

"He's done worse." Fanny reached under her

pallet for a tattered black rucksack that she'd swiped fair and square from a sotted seaman who'd been generous enough to leave it unattended. In the distance, she heard Jack's voice rise in displeasure. She felt sorry for his latest victim. "What's got him in such a temper?" she asked Scatter as he all but inhaled what constituted the day's meal.

Scatter licked crumbs from his fingers. "Charlie got tumbled t'day down at Hanover Square."

Fanny snapped around in surprise. "Charlie *what*?"

" 'E tried to rook a copper and got pinched."

"A copper! Did he lose his mind?"

Scatter only shrugged.

"He didn't squeal, did he?"

"Wouldn't surprise me none if 'e did," the boy said. " 'E always was a gutless bloke."

Fanny shoved her leather case into the rucksack. "He can't be too gutless else he wouldn't have fanned a fox."

"That weren't gutless, that was stupid."

She couldn't argue that. She turned away, reeling from the news. Good God, how had Charlie made such a stupid call? Knucks were trained from the moment they joined Gentleman Jack Swift's band on how to sniff out a patrolman, since not all wore the trade brass-buttoned uniforms and round-topped hats. No, some dressed the part of a dandy to catch the unsuspecting in the hopes that they'll spill the whereabouts of their cohorts. Others blended in so well with their surroundings that you couldn't tell one from a market-monger.

But Charlie Topp was no green dipper—he'd been with the band near as many years as her and Scatter and knew the tricks of the police. So what had he been thinking to bilk a bobbie?

She turned back to stuffing her pack with a change of clothes, a brush with most of the bristles broken off, and as an afterthought, a ragged old Phillip Goldsmith doll she'd carried around with her for as long as she could remember. If she didn't bag a decent purse this night, there would be no coming back.

Well, at least she knew what had Jack in such a vile mood. Best just do as he said—at least he'd given her a good reason to keep clear of him. She looped the strap of her bag over her head so it crossed her front and hung high against her ribs.

"Where ye goin'?"

"Out."

"Now? It's rainin' cats and dogs."

"Do you really think that matters to Jack?" Scatter knew as well as she that if she didn't find a decent mark this night, there would be no supper for the week. Or worse, she shuddered, he'd decide that she'd outlived her usefulness and put her out on the streets where, as he'd often told her, she'd really learn the meaning of earning her keep. Aye, a bit of rain was a small price to pay.

He flipped off the pipe and onto his feet with the enviable nimbleness of youth. "Then I'll go with ye."

"You'll do no such thing." The last thing she needed was a snot-nosed fourteen-year-old tugging at her coattails. Besides, Lord only knew how long she'd be out tonight—or if she'd even be coming back. There was no sense in both of them catching their deaths. She reached for a dry, moth-eaten seaman's cap and pulled it over her head. "Just stay here—I'll be back as soon as I can."

"You the baron?"

Seated at a back table in a Thames-side tavern, Troyce de Meir glanced up lazily at the man who'd come to stand before him. George Feagin fit the description he'd been given down to the letter. Barely five and half feet tall, pudgy from his fingertips to his forehead, with thick sideburns down his jowls and a blackened wig that sat slightly askew on his reputedly balding pate.

He snapped the lid shut on the timepiece cradled in his hand and slipped it into the pocket of his waistcoat. "You're late."

"That I am," the tradesman boasted with a flamboyant grin. "A pretty little moll down at The Headless Woman just wouldn't let me out of her arms." He flipped his coattails out behind him and settled his ponderous weight into the opposite chair.

Troyce dismissed the boast with a minimal smile that concealed his irritation. Obviously Feagin didn't regard their meeting worthy of punctuality—or apology. Not a good sign. Then again, what had he expected? Two weeks he'd spent in London, making the acquaintance of a variety of prospects, and his situation was beginning to appear as grim as it had the day he'd returned to England a few months earlier.

"Have you brought the goods?" Feagin inquired in a conspiratorial whisper.

Grimacing, Troyce slid a rolled parchment

across the surface of a table scarred by a century of sweaty iron tankards, spilled ale, and cigar burns. Feagin tore the scroll from its sleeve, carelessly unrolled it, and slapped a recently abandoned tankard from the next table upon its curling edges to weigh it down. Beads of brew slid down the metal stein and soaked the aged paper.

Bloody hell.

While Feagin studied the documents, Troyce leaned back in his chair, his gaze sweeping Jorge's Tavern. The atmosphere reminded him faintly of his time on the shores of Maine, where he'd spent the last eight years. Odors of fish, sweat, beer, cigars, must, and mildew had ingrained themselves over the years into the pocked-wood walls. Dockworkers, seamen, and characters of undistinguishable yet shady pursuit filtered in and out of the riverside tavern. Not exactly the establishment Troyce preferred to conduct business, but neither would it benefit him to have every nob in London learning that the third Baron of Westborough was desperate.

The minutes ticked on with no reaction from his companion. Word about town had it that George Feagin had made a substantial fortune in risky ventures. That fortune was the only reason Troyce had deigned to meet with the tradesman. That, and the dismal fact that he'd been the only one to exhibit even the slightest interest in Troyce's enterprise.

He signaled for a second brandy from a blowsy barmaid with unnaturally red hair and a come-hither smile born of years of practice. Her ample hips swung to and fro in blatant invitation as she brought a bottle to his table, and a generous slice of cleavage commanded his full notice when she leaned over to fill his cup. There was nothing like a lush and willing woman to distract a man from his troubles, he thought, tempted to take advantage of her unmistakable offer and lose himself in her abundant charms. Unfortunately, regretfully, the last thing he needed at this moment was a distraction.

"She looks genuine."

Troyce dragged his attention back to Feagin, bent over the sketchings. "She's genuine, all right," he said, promptly forgetting the maid. "One of Queen Isabella's *Armada de la Guardia* and a war galleon of the Treasure Fleet of 1622. She was fished out of the Mediterranean over fifteen years ago."

"What kind of repairs are you looking at?"

He tossed back a swallow of the bitter swill that passed for brandy. "Complete renovation of the deck, replacement mainmast and topmasts, and canvases."

"She suffered heavy damages then."

Troyce shrugged as if the work was no more substantial than replacing the thatches on a cottage roof. Only the blisters on his hands and the lint in his pockets conveyed the truth. "A sufficient amount as a result of the storms and cannon fire, but not irreparable."

"How long before you can have her seaworthy?"

"With a dependable crew of laborers, three or four months."

"That'll give me time to secure a buyer."

"Buyers I have in abundance. What I need is capital to make the repairs."

"Yes, five hundred pounds' worth, I'm told." Feagin frowned.

"It'll draw ten times that much at auction," Troyce said. Of that, he was certain. The galleon had already garnered the interest of King Alfonso XIII of Spain. Troyce saw no reason to inform Feagin that massive repairs had already been made to the hull, or that those renovations had sorely depleted the de Meir coffers. Once the ship was restored, it would go to the highest bidder, and his present problems would be solved.

"We'll split the profits seventy–thirty," Feagin finally said by way of agreement.

"Forty–sixty," Troyce corrected, wincing as Feagin crumpled his father's sketchings into a roll.

"I'm financing the work."

"I'm doing the work, and it's my ship."

Feagin sat back and pondered the bid. "Fifty-fifty or no deal."

Troyce inwardly bucked at the terms, but much to his dismay, he didn't see that he had much choice. Yes, buyers he could recruit for the finished product; no one seemed inclined, however, to purchase damaged goods. And thanks to the horrid state of affairs left to him by his father, there was no longer any money available to invest in this venture, which reduced him to two options: marry a wealthy woman or raise the money himself. He'd be damned if he'd put his title on the auction block. Not that he carried any particular fondness for it, but it and his pride were all he had left to call his own.

With a single, decisive nod, Troyce agreed to Feagin's terms. A pouch of coins marking the initial investment, arrangements for the distribution of additional funds and a later view of the progress concluded their business. Then Troyce left the tavern while his new partner stayed to celebrate with the barmaid.

Outside, he lifted his face to the rain, sucked in a draft of clean moist air, and smiled. Even the gloomy weather couldn't dampen his suddenly chipper spirits. Feagin might not have been a top-of-the-line choice, but all in all, the meeting had proved more profitable than Troyce had anticipated. For the first time since his father's death, the burden he'd been carrying lifted. He gave the purse a light toss and his grin broadened at the familiar jangle. Despite the unconventional pact, the ship his father had loved with his last breath would be restored, the future of the barony would be secured, and he . . . well, he'd escaped a fate equal—nay worse—than death.

"Any luck yet?"

Heart leaping into her windpipe, Fanny whipped around and nearly fell back on her heels. "Damn yer eyes, Scatter, I told you to wait in the tunnels. What are ye doing out here?"

"Someone gots t' watch out for ye."

As if the fourteen-year-old offered much protection, she silently scoffed.

Still—and she'd pluck herself bald before admitting it—she welcomed his presence. She'd been crouched in the alley for hours with no company save for the aches in her joints. It got bloody lonely sometimes.

While Scatter hunched down against the wall, Fanny's attention slid back to the tavern she'd been watching across the street. A pair of prostitutes loitered on the corner, calling out bawdy suggestions to a gent hanging out the window of a passing hack. Chimney smoke, sewage fumes, and damp mist collided into a myriad of vaporous odors that were both repugnant and embracing, and as much a part of her existence as the damp wool-spun coat, sackcloth shirt, and patchwork trousers plastered to her skin.

She swiped the moisture gathering on her freezing cheek, drew her soggy coat more tightly about her shoulders, and suppressed a shiver. Crikey, it was colder than a ditch digger's bum out here. The weather didn't help any. What irony that, to keep a roof over her head, she was stuck crouching in the rain.

Silence settled around them as thick and eerie as the London fog rolling in from the Thames, save for the clop of hooves on the slick cobble-stoned street as the hack rolled passed the mouth of the alley. Habit had Fanny shrinking back into the shadows. Not that she had any reason to worry about being seen—no one with all their druthers about them would venture out on such a dismal night. No, it was being caught by the bobbies—or worse, the Bow Street Runners—that had her heart slamming against her ribs. They patrolled the streets religiously, their sole mission in life to harass those simply trying to make a living.

The news of Charlie's fate made the risks of her own situation all too real. Only swift feet, clever thinking, and a survivor's instinct had kept her from the clutches of the law for over a decade, but if it could happen to Charlie Topp, what's to say it wouldn't happen to her?

Beside her, Scatter blew on fingers visible above the gloves he wore, the digits cut out at the knuckles for freer movement. "Zounds, Fanny, where is everybody?"

She wondered the same thing. Even on the slowest of nights, pickings had never been this slim. And there was no returning to the tunnels without full pockets. Jack had made that perfectly clear.

All she needed was one loaded bloke.

As if in answer to a prayer, the door to the tavern blew open. Both Scatter and Fanny went instantly alert when a large, looming shadow moved out onto the walk and paused beneath the awning. *Crikey, he's a tall one*, Fanny thought. The top of his hat nearly brushed the wooden frame, the span of his shoulders blocked the doorsill. He lifted the cape of his dark greatcoat around his jaw, glanced down the street, then up.

A gasp tore from Fanny's throat, and she reared back as lamplight hit on a face nearly as familiar to her as her own.

"Do ye know 'im?"

She wagged her head. "Never seen 'im before." Not in the flesh, anyway. But in her dreams . . . oh aye, she knew him. She knew the length of every layer of his coal black hair and the regal arc of his brows. She knew the sunburst design of his silvery eyes, the exact angle of his nose, the precise cut of his cheekbones. And she knew that his mouth, though severe in appearance, was soft and infinitely gentle upon her own.

" 'E looks like trouble," Scatter remarked. "A pence says 'e's a Robin."

"He's no runner." She could smell an investigator a mile off.

No, this man was . . . well, as goosey as it sounded, he was her prince of dreams.

Fanny gave herself a mental shake and flicked the silly notion away. Fantasies did not come to life, figments of the imagination did not take on substance, and princes did not appear out of the darkness of night, no matter how many times she might have wished for it to happen. The gent simply bore an uncanny and extraordinarily eerie resemblance to her dream prince, nothing more.

The explanation steadied her shaken composure somewhat and allowed her to settle down to the business of observation. The tailored nip and tuck of his knee-length coat, quality footwear, and the proud posture marked him as a man of means. When he dropped a familiar bulky object into his front pocket, she knew she'd struck pay dirt.

" 'E's a left kick," she told Scatter, noting the purse's destination. She twisted her hair into a roll and piled it atop her head, covering the mass with a weather-beaten knit cap. "Hook and snatch," she said, choosing one of their most effective team methods. "Catch him at the corner before he picks up a lift."

A hand pressed on her arm when she pushed herself to her feet. "Get off the crook, Fanny. He's alone. We don't work alone."

Fanny narrowed her brows and jerked from Scatter's hold. "Clear off, ye little moll-buzzer. I've been fanning blokes like him most of me life."

"Maybe, but I gots me a bad feeling about this one."

She hated it when he started blathering his hocus-pocus rot. It always made chills pop up on the back of her neck. "That moldy bread's what's givin' ye a bad feeling. Now let's go 'fore he gets away."

"Why him?" Scatter persisted. "Just wait'll someone else comes out. That mark's dangerous."

Fanny couldn't agree more. But she was cold, she was soaked, and she was weary down to the marrow. It was him—or no one. "Are ye with me or not?"

A worried frown creased Scat's forehead, but he nodded anyway, then sprinted along the length of the alley toward a hedgerow to the right of the tavern. Fanny ducked low and watched his progress with one eye, while keeping the other on their mark, who remained beneath the awning in wait. Since there were no horses about, Fanny decided that he'd either sent a stableboy around for his carriage or he was waiting for a hired cab. Either way, they were running out of time.

Noting Scatter's apprehension, Fanny felt a moment's guilt for pushing the lad into a trick. Then she consoled herself with the fact that she'd given him a choice. Truth tell, she didn't need a partner to notch a job. She never had. But pairing up often made it faster and easier, not to mention cleaner.

After Scatter rounded the back of the tavern, he popped his head above a rock wall, giving Fanny her cue to begin closing in. Scatter, as the "snatch," would snag the mark's attention while Fanny acted as the "hook" and relieved him of the thick purse she'd seen him stuff into his left pocket.

No sooner did Fanny cross the street and maneuver herself into position than a second man emerged from the tavern, calling, "Westborough, you forgot your sketchings."

And Fanny froze in alarm. Bloody hell— *Feagin*? What was *he* doing here? Dread crept through her veins like a deadly spider. Wasn't this just her rotten luck! Just last week, Scatter had made the mistake of breaking into one of Feagin's warehouses and got caught picking the locks on his safe-room door. Scatter managed to escape, but there was no doubt in Fanny's mind that Feagin would recognize him.

No wonder he'd had a bad feeling.

She tried to catch Scatter's attention, tell him to call off the operation, but with his head bowed as he crept along the stone wall, he failed to take notice of her.

And then, it was too late.

Chapter 2

In the manner of a thousand heists before, Scatter jumped over the stone wall in front of his mark. If he was surprised to find two of them instead of one, he gave no sign. He shrank into himself and offered his hat in the age-old pose of the downtrodden. "A pence for the poor, suh?"

The stranger peered down at his bent head, and Fanny couldn't be sure of it from the distance, but she thought she saw him frown. It was not him who concerned her, though.

It was Feagin.

She quickened her pace, hoping to reach Scatter before he revealed himself. While the gent reached for his pocket, as if to grant Scatter's request, Feagin was not inclined toward such generosity. He shoved Scatter against the chest so hard that it threw him backward.

"Get back, you sniveling leech."

The stranger's head snapped around. "Feagin, what the hell are you doing?"

"Damned beggars. 'Tis the third time this week that they've come a panhandling. 'Tis getting so decent citizens can't even walk the streets without being molested."

To Fanny's astonishment, the stranger wedged himself between Scatter and Feagin. "He's but a child."

"He's a bloody nuisance. Not a one of them are worth the skin it took to cover their bones."

Cold-hearted bastard, Fanny thought. Not that she was surprised. She'd had dealings enough with Feagin and his ilk to know charity and kindness were as plummy to them as burrs in their bums.

She moved faster, urgency driving her the last twenty feet despite the stitch developing in her calf and the lack of air in her lungs. She finally reached the men, bumping into one, then the other. Years of ingrained reflexes took over as she brushed through them, and fleet hands slipped into their coats for the night's pickings.

"John, what mischief are ye about this night?" she dramatized. "Mum's worried sick!" She grabbed Scatter by the arm and shoved the bounty into his coat.

Then she pulled him behind her and turned to face the men. "Thank ye for finding me brother, kind sirs. I'll just see that 'e gets home." She twisted around and prodded the boy away from the men.

"Not so fast."

One broad hand landed on her shoulder, another on Scatter's. Fanny froze. Her throat constricted, sparks shot through her veins.

She glanced warily behind her and found her view blocked by a solid wall of chest. Grosgrain fabric the color of charcoal stretched across its breadth. A spicy, masculine scent curled through dampness, smothering the stench of the West End, teasing her senses. Her gaze worked its way up the row of togged buttons on his gaping greatcoat, past a silvery vest worth a week of meals, over a plain ivory shirt, to the base of his throat. Nothing but smooth, bare skin lay beneath the starched linen collar. Glimpsing that tiny wedge of nudity seemed more intimate than if she'd caught the gent stripped down to nothing.

Fanny swallowed over the sudden tightness in her throat. Up close he was more powerful than he'd appeared from afar. He stood at least six feet in height, a mere four inches taller than she, but the span of his body far exceeded hers, making her feel small and fragile and oddly vulnerable.

She forced herself to look up into his face, and oh, crikey, wished she hadn't. The bloke was even more handsome than she'd first judged and did not do her fantasy justice. Raindrops slid off the brim of his hat to soak his shoulders, turning the gray to black. A shadow of whiskers darkened his sharply angled jaw and chin and surrounded a nicely bowed mouth too unsettling to dwell on. The bridge of his nose was straight as a dagger blade, unmarred by the telling bump she so often saw on those prone to brawling, the tip rounded, the nostrils nicely flared. Unfashionably short sideburns looked freshly trimmed, as did the coal black hair pulled back behind his ears and secured at his nape. And his eyes. . . . God's teeth, the man had glorious eyes. Spiky lashes swept out above irises the color of mist on stone, and long hooded lids drew down at the corners in a sensual curve that made her think of how a man might look at a woman waiting in his bed. . . .

"My purse, *s'il vous plaît*."

Dumbly, she glanced down at the hand he held toward her, the palm unexpectedly callused. Palpable tension emanated from the scrawny body behind her. "What purse?" The words came out surprisingly strong considering that it felt as if she were shoving them through a pinhole.

His lip quirked as if he found her false ignorance amusing. "The one you lifted from my pocket."

His voice held the hint of an accent that didn't match his aristocratic appearance. Not French, though he obviously spoke the language, but something more exotic—and hauntingly familiar.

Before she could place its cant, Feagin cried, "Why, the little thief got my watch, too!"

Fanny squealed as her collar was seized and she was hauled up against Feagin's rotund chest.

"You think you can steal from George Feagin?"

Spots swam before her eyes as the odors of fish, cheap cologne, and the merciless grip on her collar threatened to choke the life right out of her.

Scatter charged out from behind her, eyes afire, hands outstretched. "Let 'er go!"

"Why you little—hey, I know you! You're the

weasel I caught breaking into my warehouse!"
With a tight hold still on Fanny, Feagin made a
grab for Scatter with his free hand.

"No!" Fanny angled herself between the two
and shoved Scatter with all her might. "Run,
Scat!"

"Damn your eyes!" With an enraged growl,
Feagin swung his arm upward, and Fanny
flinched, bracing herself for the backhanded blow.

It never came.

Shocked, she glanced up and saw that the dark
stranger had seized Feagin's wrist in midswing.

"Strike again, and I'll break your hand," he
said, his tone so deadly that chills broke out along
her spine.

Fanny had not a single doubt that he meant
what he said.

Neither, apparently, did Feagin. His face suddenly paled, and he laughed, more a sound of rattled nerves than humor. "You wouldn't dare."

"I'd more than dare." The stranger smiled. "I'd
take great pleasure in it."

"You're making a grave mistake, Westborough.
I'm not certain I wish to deal with a man whose
loyalties lie with riffraff."

"Then I shall relieve you of the uncertainty. We
no longer have a deal."

If Feagin thought he'd had the upper hand with
his implied threat, the man he called Westborough quickly burst the illusion. Eyes bulging,
complexion ruddy, he sputtered in disbelief,
"You'd call off a profitable venture over a pair of
thievin' guttersnipes?"

"I never conduct business with men who can't control their tempers." He released his grip on Feagin's arm and stepped back. "Now, I suggest you unhand the youngster and take your leave. I'll see your coin returned to you on the morrow."

The tradesman's jaw dropped. "You *need* me, Westborough."

His expression never wavered. "Not that badly."

The two men stared at one another for several seconds, one coldly calm, the other blazing mad.

"You will regret this," Feagin finally spat. "Both of you." After dropping his grip on Fanny's collar, he spun on his heel and headed for one of two hacks that, at some point during the altercation, had drawn up at the curb.

And Fanny knew that if ever there was a time to save herself, it was now. She hadn't survived the last ten years in London's underworld by dawdling about. And yet, as much as she willed it, she couldn't seem to tear herself away from the sight of her dark prince, standing in a halo of lamplight, watching Feagin's hack pull away, his shoulders tense, his hands fisted. And there was something in his eyes . . . a bitter disappointment that reminded her of the times she'd held opportunity in her hands only to watch it combust before her very eyes.

Why? Why would he have come to her defense?

She shook her head, thoroughly befuddled. Hard as she tried, she just couldn't wrap her mind around the fact that a complete stranger—one of such obvious high-knobbed breeding—would not only protect her from the likes of George Feagin, but that he was willing to break some sort of arrangement because Feagin tried to hit her. She'd never heard of such a thing!

Only when the first hack disappeared around the corner did he finally turn to her. "Well, my young bandit, it seems that you and I have some unfinished business."

Though cordial in manner, his tone carried a parlous undertone and eyes that only moments ago reminded her of midnight sins now held all the warmth of a cemetery slab. Even a half-wit would understand that he held her to blame for his loss.

Well, to hell with him. She never asked him to take up for her. "Some other time, guv. I gots me more important things to do." Wrapping her pride around her, she spun on her heel.

He caught her by the sleeve. "Not quite yet, my sticky-fingered friend. Now, I have asked you once, I shall ask you only once again. My purse, if you please?"

Fanny couldn't say if it was that oddly familiar cadence of his speech, or the steely warning hovering just below the surface of civility, but she was beginning to feel terribly uneasy. She swallowed over the knot of dread creeping up her windpipe. "I don't have it."

His lips curved in a lopsided grin that she might have found charming under different circumstances.

"You'll understand if I don't believe you."

That brought her up to her full height. "Are ye calling me a liar?"

"I have called you nothing. However, this night has been quite trying thus far, and my patience is wearing thin, so perhaps you should reconsider your answer."

"I told ye, I don't have yer bleedin' purse."

He studied her a moment—actually, challenged seemed a more apt description. His eyes, gray as polished pewter, bored into hers, as if trying to decide if she spoke the truth. She couldn't deny that she filched the pockets of those who had more money than they could count. She would even admit to an occasional evasion of the truth.

But she never lied.

"All right, if this is the way you want to play . . ."

Fanny gasped as his hands shot out and began vigorously patted her hips, her waist, her rib cage. "Get your filthy hands off me, ye rotten bugger!"

"Not until I—" Whatever he'd been about to say came to an abrupt halt when his hands landed just below a part of her anatomy that she often wished had never developed. His dark brows shot up, then narrowed into a V. "Well, what do we have here?"

She almost blurted, "Breasts, you idiot!" but he spun her around before the words formed and whipped her cap off her head. She grabbed for it and missed. Her hair tumbled around her shoulders in riot of tangled curls. Fanny went rigid, mentally preparing herself for the worst.

But he didn't tear at her clothes, didn't grope her body.

Instead, with a gentleness she'd never imagined existed, he tipped her chin into the dim light of the streetlamp and searched her features.

A queer, swampy feeling spread through Fanny's middle, as if she were sinking into a pit of warm molasses. She knew she should fight it. Struggle to pull away. She couldn't. His eyes, shot with the same silvery tint of his vest, pulled at her, drew her in, held her motionless.

Never in twenty years had she given any thought to her own appearance, but that was before she saw her own reflection in the mirror of his eyes—the dirt-streaked cheekbones, matted hair, ratty clothes. A deep flush scorched her face, and the longer he studied her, the more cheap and worthless she felt.

"Well I'll be. . . ." he said in awe. "You're naught but a girl!"

Fanny blinked. He'd only just now figured that out?

"What's your name?" he demanded.

She jerked her chin from his grasp. "Queen Victoria, ye loggerhead, now bugger off."

"Tut, tut. Such language, Your Royal Majesty." Laughter resonated in his deeply lyrical voice. "I wonder what your subjects would think were they aware their sovereign speaks with such *savoir-faire*?"

She pressed her lips tightly together. She'd been manhandled enough for one night and by crikey, she'd not take it from this gaumless muck-a-muck. "If you're through pawing at me," she ground out, "I'll thank ye to let me go."

"Indeed? And I'll thank you to return my property."

The grin he gave her was so boyishly disarming that she wasn't even aware that he'd grabbed the strap of something much more personal and private than body parts. "Give me that!" She grabbed for the rucksack holding her most treasured belongings, but he hoarded it to his front as if he were a flask-nipper who'd just discovered the last drop of rum in England.

"You had your chance."

Seething, she watched helplessly as he plundered the canvass bag. A second later, he withdrew a leather kit that housed a pair of palm nippers, a widdy for sliding locks, and a set of bar keys. His gaze sought hers in question; Fanny held her breath.

"Tools of the trade?"

She tried to think of some pithy response, but her tongue seemed stuck to the roof of her mouth.

The gent finally released his hold on the strap and sighed. "It's not here," he muttered to himself.

Clutching the rucksack tightly beneath her coat, Fanny immediately stepped back out of his reach. She couldn't breathe when she stood so close to him, and her heart forgot to beat right. "I told ye I didn't have it."

"Where is it then?"

She refused to answer.

"You passed it on to your mate, didn't you?"

Again, Fanny refused to answer. She stood in stony silence, staring at a spot past his shoulder, waiting for him to tire of his bullying and let her go.

"All right, if this is the way it is to be, then so be it."

The flickering hope that he would release her crumbled in the next instant when he wrapped his hand around her arm and started leading her toward the second hack, where a silent, regally uniformed footman stood holding open the door.

Fanny dug in her heels. "Wait—what are ye doing?"

"Keeping the streets of London safe from impertinent thieves."

His jaw was set in a determined frown, his stride was sure and swift. The panic she'd held under such tight control began to unravel through her veins and claw at her throat. "What do you mean?" Her voice dropped and trembled. She could hardly keep up with him. "Where are ye taking me?"

"Someplace where you can't cause any more trouble."

Newgate!

Stories told late at night in the darkness of the tunnels by knucks who had spent months—even years!—trapped behind the stone walls came at her in a rush. Of bodies shrunken from starvation and illness. Of cries of the convicted and insane, and worse the hopelessness of freedom forever denied. . . .

Fanny slammed her elbow between his ribs then took off. She didn't wait to see if he followed, she just ran, ducking into alleys littered with broken carts, crates, and foraging pigs, slipping through wrought-iron fences and crossing yards strung with clotheslines. Images of Newgate loomed up before her like wraiths in a nightmare. She'd not go to prison. She couldn't. She had bigger plans for her life than to spend it rotting away in some dank cell.

She should have known escape would not come easy. His arms were too long, his reflexes too swift, and the night had gone poorly from the outset. He caught up to her after only a few hundred yards, seized her around the waist, and lifted her off the ground, hitching her backside against his hip as if she were a sack of feed. Her breaths came out in harsh gasps, sobs snagged at the back of her mouth. She pounded his wrist, as angry at him for catching her as at herself for being caught, but it was like beating a chunk of iron. "Let me go, ye bloody oaf! Let me go or I'll—"

"Scream? Be my guest."

Oh, she wanted to. The scream built in her throat, choking off what air she'd managed to take in. But she held it back, knowing as well as he did that it would only serve to call every bobbie in the district down upon her head. "You've got no proof against me."

"I felt you. That's proof enough for me."

He'd felt her? Oh, God, Jack was right then, she was losing her touch! He'd told her often enough over the last year, and it had been all she could do to prove him wrong.

Certainly she could deny taking this bloke's money to her heart's content, but who would the coppers believe? A respectable gentleman or a street rat? Fanny wilted in defeat, knowing the answer to that.

They rounded a corner, and the tavern came into sight. Once they reached the horse-drawn cab, she knew it would only be a matter of moments before she forfeited any chance of escape. "Please, sir." Fanny had never begged for anything in her life, and even now, the words felt as if they were being ripped from her throat. "Please, just . . . just let me go. I can't—I won't—go to prison."

"I have no intention of taking you to prison; however, you have cost me two hundred pounds and an important alliance, and I am not a man to take such offense lightly." His stride never broke. "If you want my money so badly, you will have to earn it."

Earn it? Her gaze flew to the lamplight ladies watching him carry her across the street from their corner post. Outrage blazed through every pore. "I ain't lifting me skirts for *no* man."

"Lift your—" He came to a startled stop, let her drop to her feet, then spun her around. "Let me assure you that I have no intention of having you"—his gaze swept her ragged trousers and ill-fitting coat—"lift your skirts as they are. Some men may harbor adolescent preferences, but I find women much more to my liking than children."

Children! He thought her a *child*? Her spine stiffened. "Just how old do ye think I am?"

He angled his head and studied her a moment. "Thirteen—no, too tall. Fifteen, then, perhaps sixteen, even. Still too young for my tastes."

So insulting was the notion that Fanny almost declared her true age until it occurred to her that a measure of safety lay in his misconception. "What do ye want from me, then?"

"Simple. You shall come to work for me in my home."

"Doing what?"

"Well, I was going to suggest stableboy, but under the circumstances, housemaid seems more appropriate."

Her mouth fell. "Ye want me to be a . . . a *servant*? In yer *house*?" Of all the things she'd expected him to say, this was not one of them.

"Do you prefer the alternative?"

"But I don't know nothin' 'bout being a servant!"

"It's not as difficult as you might think. Millie, my housekeeper, will teach you everything you need to know."

But what if she couldn't be taught? What if she messed it up? Perspiration beaded above her lip, but Fanny didn't voice her doubts aloud. A lesson learned long ago with Jack—never let your enemy know your weakness. "What'll me duties be?"

"To see to the comforts of my home. No more, no less."

Fanny blinked back tears of relief. If he was trying to ease her fears, it was working.

"The position shall pay a half a sovereign a week—"

Her eyes widened and her mouth fell. "A half a sovereign? A week? All for *me*?" That was . . . she mentally did the math . . . ten shillings! Even on a good day she couldn't recall bringing in that much, not once Jack took his share!

"Eventually, yes. According to my figures, your debt to me should be paid off within the year. If at the end of your term you wish to remain in my employ, and your work is satisfactory, we shall discuss a permanent position if that is your desire, as well as an increase in your wages."

It seemed too good to be true. And usually when things *seemed* too good to be true, they were. "*Why* are ye doing this?"

To his credit, he did not insult her by pretending not to know what she meant. "Because I see no gain for either of us in sending you to a cell."

" 'Course not. Why should ye when you can indenture yerself a workhorse instead?"

"I prefer to call it an investment in honest labor," he parried with a smile.

"Oh, crikey, if things ain't bad enough, I'm being nobbled by a bloody reformist."

His bark of laughter drew the attention of the prostitutes on the corner. Both took turns regaling Fanny with ear-burning advice on how to best please the man in their midst. Fanny shuddered; Westborough merely smiled at them.

"Now," he turned to Fanny, "you may come with me willingly or not. The choice is yours. But be aware that your decision will mean the difference between a pleasant outcome—or not."

Fanny looked first at the hack, where the footman waited, his face impassive, as if this were not the first time he'd witnessed one of society's sons chasing through the streets of London after a runaway, then at the lamplight ladies, then back at the gent. He'd given her a choice: Newgate or him. Hadn't she always dreamed of leaving Bethnal Green? Escaping Jack Swift? Experience cautioned her that any man who associated with blokes the likes of Feagin could not be trusted. And yet, she could not forget that he had done something that no one had ever done for her before.

He'd defended her.

Resigning herself to what she hoped was the lesser of two evils, she said, "I'll go willingly."

"Wise choice." He gave her that crooked smile that she was beginning to detest, bowed, and swept his arm into a low arc toward the open door of the hack. "After you, Your Majesty."

Wise choice? Somehow Fanny doubted that.

As the hired coach rolled down Mile Road out of London, Troyce studied the creature sulking across from him, cocooned up to her neck in a lap robe he'd found beneath the seat. A girl, certainly, though it hadn't been so obvious at first. He blamed it on the layers of baggy clothing, the dockside mist and poor lighting. The moment his hands came into contact with a pair of very unladlike breasts, he'd realized his error.

Even now, with the dimmest of light seeping into the carriage, he wondered how he hadn't known right off. Features like hers could never be mistaken for those of a lad. Lush lips, pinched cheeks, wild hair of an undistinguishable shade barely to her shoulders ... There was a dark smear along her jawbone as well, whether caused by smut or bruise, he could not say. But one thing was glaringly clear—she had not been leading a life of either ease or comfort.

If anyone asked him to explain why he was bringing her to his home instead of simply turning her over to the authorities, he'd not be able to give them a logical answer. He was not normally prone to bouts of sentimentality. Or insanity.

And it was insane. He'd searched high and low

for someone willing to invest in the restoration of
La Tentatrice, a venture that promised to replenish
the once-sizable de Meir fortune, only to throw
the opportunity away. And for what? A pocket-
swiping vulture with a piss-poor attitude? He
had not a farthing to his name, yet here he was,
dragging home another mouth to feed. And he
had to find a way to raise two hundred pounds by
morning.

Two hundred pounds. Where was he going to
come up with that, and by morning no less? Every
cent he'd made over the last eight years laboring
on the docks of Maine had gone to pay his father's debts, and still it hadn't been nearly
enough.

By all rights, he should be furious at her for
costing him the only chance he'd had to save what
was left of his inheritance. No one would blame
him if he'd had her gaoled.

Except, he'd seen something in those big doe
brown eyes, an undisturbed innocence, a wild
desperation to escape her fate. . . .

Heaven knew he understood that feeling.

Troyce brought his arm up along the back of the
seat, his curiosity of her gnawing at him. "Are you
hungry?"

She shook her head, though she did not look at
him. Her attention remained fixed on the passing
scenery; what she could possibly find so interesting in the expanse of darkness that stretched beyond the rain-spattered window, he couldn't
begin to guess. She was scared, though. Her fear
betrayed itself in the tight set of her jaw, hunched
shoulders and the hands clenched around the

folds of the blanket. She'd be a fool not to be scared. But she was here, and that said a lot for her character.

"You've not asked where we're going."

"Does it matter?"

"No, I don't suppose it does." He could be taking her to the wilds of Northumberland, if he had a mind to, and she would no doubt find it preferable to prison.

Indentured workhorse. He hated the tag she'd given to their arrangement, hated that she thought of herself as such. He'd seen the miserable souls during his stay in Maine, brought in from the holds of ships to enslave themselves for a year, two years, even more just to pay for their passage. But as much as he loathed the title, he could hardly deny that it fit. He couldn't pay someone to perform the work Westborough Manor desperately needed to become functional again; the only staff left of twenty-seven servants were loyal Millie and Chadwick, and both had agreed to remain on for the simple compensation of food and shelter.

And so, he'd taken advantage of an opportunity provided him by a gumptious cutpurse.

He felt her watching him out of the corner of her eye and arched a brow. "Is something amiss?"

"Ye don't talk like a Brit."

"I'm only half-Brit."

"Is that like a half-wit?"

He chuckled, pleased that she hadn't lost her spirit over the night's events. "That's a matter of opinion, I suppose." His grandfather was certainly convinced that he'd gone dotty eight years ago, for no Englishman with any sense would relinquish the promise of a fortune for the beckoning of distant shores. "There are some who consider my American blood quite exotic."

"American. I should have known." In the darkness he couldn't see her sneer, but he heard it. And he felt it.

"That offends you?"

"Actually, I don't give a whit one way or the other. I just never heard of no American nobleman."

"What makes you think I'm noble?"

She frowned as if she didn't know how to react to his teasing, and fell silent. Troyce leaned back, listening to the rain patter on the roof of the two-seat carriage, the rhythmic creak of churning wheels, and waited for her to ask the questions he could almost hear whirring in her mind. She reminded him of a woodlands badger, and like any creature of the wild, she would lash out when cornered, claws and teeth bared, before retreating to safety. All one needed was a bit of patience to lure her out of her nest.

He bit back a smile when her curiosity finally got the better of her.

"So what are ye?" she asked, her tone bordering on belligerence. "A duke? An earl?"

"Nothing so lofty as that. I am merely a baron. Troyce de Meir of Westborough, at your service."

He inclined his head and a parody of gallantry, and was rewarded with a faint rising of color in the chit's cheeks. Troyce wished he knew what it was about her that drew him so. She was but a child, one of the many street urchins that haunted the alleys and taverns in search of unsuspecting fools used as pigeons to line their pockets, far too young to interest him, yet he found himself intrigued nonetheless. There was just something so . . . vulnerable about her. No doubt she'd club him a good one if he ever voiced his thoughts. She didn't strike him as the type who took kindly to having her weaknesses known.

"That's certainly an impressive set of wares you keep hidden beneath your coat," he said. "How long have you been engaged in such a fickle line of work?"

The question took her off guard, and a moment passed before Fanny realized that the wares he referred to weren't her body parts. "Long enough." It seemed pointless to deny what he already knew.

"And how many times have you been caught?"

"I ain't *never* been caught."

"Till now."

She pressed her lips tightly together.

"Are purses all you take?"

She pinned him with a warning glare. "You're a nosy bloke, ain't ye."

"Simply curious. There aren't many who dare steal from me."

She supposed not. He didn't strike her as a man anyone easily swindled.

Well, long as they didn't get too personal, she decided that it wouldn't hurt to answer his questions. "I've filched a few watches. A bit of jewelry." She shrugged, at once ashamed and proud of her ability. "Just depends on the person." And how much they had to spare.

And how much Jack demanded.

"I'd be interested in a demonstration of your method."

Fanny straightened in amazement. "You want me to *show* you?"

"We have a bit of a journey ahead of us. It might help pass the time. I expect you to return it, of course."

She couldn't believe her ears. She'd shared her tricks, of course, but mostly to green kids new to Swift's band. Never to a grown man.

Never to her prince of dreams.

She licked her lips, strangely nervous about touching him. It hadn't bothered her before, but then, she hadn't given it any thought before, either. "I just . . . distract the mark . . . then slip me hand into 'is pocket—"

"Distract him, how?"

"Most times with a nudge. Or a bump." Crikey, why'd he ever bring this up? "Sometimes I pretend I've lost something, like a pet or a bonnet. Or I pretend like I've met 'im before . . . like you." She gazed into the swirling mist of his eyes. "First time I saw ye, I had this feelin' that I knew ye from someplace."

"Where?" he whispered.

It didn't occur to her not to tell him. Lost in his eyes, she spoke the secret of her heart. "Someplace far, far away, where flowers grow wild in the fields and the smell of the sea is strong in me nose. The sun never stops shinin', and music never stops playin' . . ."

And then, she couldn't speak at all. Flutes and harps and violins. Sunshine clear to her toes. The glorious spice of birch and clover and . . .

Man.

Fanny yanked herself back against her seat, her breaths coming in short gasps. She hadn't meant to . . . she never should have . . . she was only supposed to . . .

Stunned, she glanced down, and his timepiece was tightly clasped in her hand. Oh, God. Fanny closed her eyes and damned herself a thousand times.

"You are quite adept." He cleared his throat and reclaimed his watch. "I didn't feel a thing— this time."

If only she could be so lucky. Her fingers tingled clear to her elbows. She curled her hand into a ball and pressed it against her stomach, disturbed by the sensation. "Ye really felt it before?"

"In a sense. Actually I felt more of a brush against my . . . hip."

She glanced away, and mumbled, "I'll be sure t'remember that."

He leaned back in his seat and tucked the watch back into the slit in his vest. "Perhaps you would like to send word to your mother of our arrangement."

Fanny tensed, the remark hitting a tender chord. "I have no mum. She died when I was very young."

A heartbeat passed, then he said, "I'm sorry."

Paltry words, yet oddly, he sounded sincere, and she drew comfort from that.

"The lad who was with you, then. The one who escaped."

Scatter. Fanny shut her eyes. She hadn't let herself think of him since he'd padded the hoof out of harm's way. He'd be back at the tunnels by now, with the baron's purse, no doubt getting what for from Jack over her whereabouts. He'd worry when she didn't fall in behind him, but that couldn't be helped. She didn't dare try another escape now; the baron would have the coppers on her tail faster than she could say Golden Jubilee and she'd not risk bringing trouble down on the rest of the band.

"We could send him a message if you wish."

And let Jack get wind of her flight? That was the last thing she needed. Crikey, when he learned that she'd left him high and dry, there would be the devil to pay. No one left Gentleman Jack's band and got away with it. She had no idea where the baron was taking her, but it wouldn't take long for Jack to track her down. He'd send out a few of the boys asking about her at the police stations—that would buy her some time anyway. Time to put some distance between him and herself. Time to plan how she was going to get herself out of this mess . . .

"Ain't none of his business where I am," she finally said. " 'E knows his way home, and that's all that matters." As soon as she figured out where she was going, and if it was safe, she'd get word to Scat. Somehow.

"Is there not anyone you wish to get word to?"

An unbidden image of a distinguished gentleman, bowing his head in grief, and a young girl in pale blond braids, took Fanny by surprise. A surge of longing rose up inside her, so swift and strong, that she had to shut her eyes against it. She hadn't thought of her father and sister in years.

Why she'd think of them now didn't bear examining. "There's no one."

There hadn't been in a long, long time.

Fanny pushed the memory away and once again stared absently out the window, hoping to put a stop to the endless tide of questions.

"You look weary. Perhaps you should rest now," he suggested.

She searched his eyes in the dimness. What was his game? It wasn't human for a fellow to be so kind. Not in her world, where only the cutthroats and stone-hearts thrived. But then, she wasn't in her world anymore. She was tumbling headlong into the unknown with a man of equal mystery. A man of position, of power, of prestige. Should she fling herself at his feet in gratitude or throw herself from the hack and take her chances? She didn't know, and the confusion troubled her as much as anything. She was used to making split-second decisions.

Though she didn't mean to obey his order to rest, she closed her eyes anyway just to keep him from carrying on further conversation. How she managed to fall asleep with the coach jouncing hard enough to shake her teeth loose she couldn't begin to explain. But she must have dozed off at some point, for the next thing she knew, the hack had gone still.

Fanny blinked, then lifted her head from the side of the coach. A horse snorted. A harness jingled. She glanced around the misty darkness, and realized that they'd left the clatter of the city far behind. Fields of glistening grasses stretched for miles in each direction, broken by jagged silhouettes that she suspected were woods. Crikey, how long had she been asleep?

She leaned over to peer out the opposite window. It had stopped raining, but the wet pane gave her a somewhat distorted view of a stunning three-story red brick house lit by bell-shaped lamps attached to the veranda posts. White shutters flanked the profusion of windows, and a white front door bore a large black wreath in its center, silent testimony that this was a house of mourning.

"Where are we?"

"Radcliff. My manor house outside of London."

"You live here?"

"Only during the season. We'll spend the night here and leave for my country estate in the morning."

His country estate. A frisson of unease set her heart to quickening. She barely remembered a time when she hadn't lived in London, and the thought of leaving the city she'd called home for most of her life scared the wits out of her. "Is it far away?"

"A half day's journey, more or less." With a twist of the handle, the door to the hack flung open on oiled hinges and he stepped out only to duck back inside. "Oh, and I have only one rule, Your Majesty. There will be no stealing from me again—ever—or I promise you, prison will sound heavenly in comparison."

Chapter 3

The cryptic warning lay thick in the air long after the baron walked away from the cab. Fanny's first impulse was to tell him what he could do with his "agreement"; had he been any other bloke, with less control over her future, she probably would have.

But as she watched his long-legged stride eat up the distance to the front veranda, she was seized with a sudden desperation to call him back. Tell him that she had changed her mind, that she wanted him to take her back to London this instant.

It was nearly too dark to see, the only light coming from a pair of black lamps attached to the columns flanking the steps, and soon he was little more than a shadow among shadows. There he waited, silently beckoning her, one hand on the door handle.

Fanny frowned. What was this, some sort of trick? Surely he didn't expect her to walk in like some grand lady of the manor. Never in her life had Fanny of Bethnal Green been allowed to enter a house of the ruling class, much less do so through the main entrance. How did one react? Should she insist on entering through the back door? Accept the invitation? Turn tail and run?

She had never been a coward, but in that moment she sure felt like one. She swallowed heavily. Her heart pounded erratically. Her hands went damp and started to shake.

This is foolish, she told herself. The boys in the band would laugh themselves goosey if they could see her now, crouching in the carriage like some timid mouse.

She sucked in a deep breath for courage, licked her lips, then forced herself out the hack. She took one small step toward him. Her heart picked up pace, slamming so hard against her breastbone that she could hardly breathe. She felt as if she were being challenged to do something reckless. Daring. Absolutely forbidden. And he, the baron, was just waiting for her to take that first step into his territory so he could give her a good cuffing for her insolence.

Her gaze shot to his hands again; one lay curled loosely at his side, the other rested on the long brass grip that served as a knob. He looked harmless enough, and yet, she couldn't shake the feeling that if she walked through that door, her life would never again be her own. Heart pounding, palms sweating, she took a second step. Then a third. Her legs seemed to have developed a will of their own as they carried her toward him, almost as if he were reeling her in by an invisible string. She didn't understand this power he had over her, but neither could she find the will to fight it.

Finally, she mounted the steps and stood at his level. Crikey, he smelled good. Like the sea and the wind and distant memories that were both comforting and distressing. She raised her gaze to his and lifted her chin, defying her weakness, him.

His lips twitched as if her qualms amused him and he gave a slanted nod, whether of mockery or approval, she couldn't be sure, but strangely enough, it calmed her nerves a bit.

Then, with a click of the handle, the door opened beneath his hand. The baron offered her a slight bow. "Welcome to my humble abode."

And Fanny gasped.

Long ago, when she was still gullible enough to believe that fairy tales came true, she would fancy herself walking through a palace on the arm of a dark and handsome prince. That the prince stood beside her, guised as a baron, was staggering enough. But even her wildest dreams never came close to the reality of Radcliff.

Humble abode? The place was a bloody palace! The foyer alone was as big as the common room of The Headless Woman inn! And no dirt floors, here, no sir! Instead white stone marble rimmed in black paved the entrance, so polished that she could see the reflection of her shabby shoes. Brass sconces with perfect tapers hung on walls paneled with dark wood on the bottom, papered from waist to ceiling in green velvet. Several lit candles cast a serene glow on the gilt-framed stag hunt and earth-toned landscapes that had been hung at precise intervals. Second nature had her mentally tallying up the value of her surroundings. "Crikey, guv, ye must be rich as Midas!" she whispered in awe.

"Don't let these trappings fool you; I am far from wealthy."

Either he was the most humble gent she'd ever met or he was hopelessly blind. The wall sconces in the foyer alone would feed the band for months!

"Ah, so the prodigal son has finally returned."

The melodic greeting reached Fanny in the same wavelet as a powerful scent of roses. Even as the pressure built, she knew she'd not be able to control the—

"Achoo!"

Flushing from the roots of her hair to the tips of her toes, she slanted a glance up at the baron, and found him looking at her with arched brows. "Sorry," she mumbled, feeling as if she'd just cursed in a cathedral.

He nodded, then slid his attention toward the woman descending the flying staircase connecting the two levels. She looked every inch how Fanny thought a lady ought to, all graceful gestures, flawless skin, and glossy black hair braided down her spine.

"Devon, this is a surprise," the baron said. "I thought we were meeting at Brayton Hall in the morning."

"Circumstances changed my plans," she replied in a mezzo lilt.

"What circumstances?"

"Nothing to concern yourself over, darling."

As she came closer to take his hands and accept the kiss he pressed to her cheek, Fanny's heart tumbled at the familiarity between the two. Was this the baron's lady? He'd not mentioned a wife. Then again, why should he?

Another tickle swelled at the back of her nose. Her eyes watered and her face grew hot as she tried to rein in the uncontrollable and wholly bothersome reaction to certain fragrances. But even sheer force of will could not contain the sneeze. Fanny twisted at the last moment and buried her nose in her coat.

"Dieu vous bénit," she heard the baron say.

When she turned back around to accept his blessing and offer another apology, she found the lady watching her through narrowed eyes. Fanny clutched the folds of her coat tighter around her, keenly aware of the threadbare condition of the shirt and trousers she wore beneath.

"Who is your friend, West?"

"Oh, yes. Devon, meet—" He leaned down, and his warm, brandy-laced breath caressed her ear. "You never did tell me your name."

A moment passed before Fanny recovered from the disturbing sensation of his whisper against her skin. Of course she'd have to give him her name; she couldn't very well let him introduce her to his lady as Queen Victoria.

"Me name—" The Cockney accent of her environment slipped unwelcome into her speech. Maybe it was the impervious lift of the lady's brow, or the nearly imperceptible sneer of her mouth, or maybe it was the opulent surroundings that drove home an awareness of where she'd come from, and where she was now.

Whatever the source, it struck her suddenly that this was no place for the likes of Fanny Jarvis, notorious knuck. Maybe, just maybe, this was her chance to rise above the sewage fumes and vermin. No more huddling in the freezing rain, waiting for marks. No more skulking in the shadows to avoid the coppers.

No more Gentleman Jack Swift.

From the recesses of her soul, the blossom of a memory unfurled. Of a little girl with plaited saffron braids and boundless spirit. A girl she'd long lost hope of ever seeing again. And in a single, defining moment, the innocent child she'd once been beckoned to the jaded adult she'd become. "*My* name is Faith." She tipped her chin decisively. "Faith Jervais."

From this point forward, Light-Fingered Fanny, as the boys in the band had taken to calling her, no longer existed.

As if sensing the newborn strength in her decision, the baron smiled. A flash of dimple in his left cheek, a spray of creases at the corners of his eyes. A warm and unexpected glow spread through her breast at his approval.

"Devon . . ." he dragged his gaze away, "meet Faith Jervais. Faith, may I present my sister, Lady Devon de Meir Heath, Duchess of Brayton."

His sister? Well, that explained their familiarity with each other. The swell of relief that the lady was not his wife slipped into her system so quickly that it caught Faith unprepared. Why their relationship would matter one way or the other, she couldn't begin to guess.

Nor did she want to speculate.

Looking closer at Lady Brayton, however, the resemblance did become more noticeable. Both were strikingly fine-looking folk, sharing the same dark hair, sloping features, and patrician postures. Faith wasn't sure where "duchess" ranked in the nobility chain but the way the woman carried herself, she suspected it was pretty high up there.

The baron set his hat on a narrow cherrywood table, hung his coat upon a tree, leaving him clad in impeccably tailored coat and dove gray trousers. "Miss Jervais will be joining my staff."

The glow instantly vanished when his sister gasped. "Troyce, you cannot be serious!" She shuddered delicately. "She smells abominable, and I do believe I see her hair crawling."

The blood drained from Faith's face, then rose again, swift and blazing at the implication. "Why you . . ."

A tight grip on her arm held her from charging forward. "Faith . . ." he warned.

"I do not have bugs!" she cried.

"Calm yourself." His tone suggested she'd best obey him, and he addressed Lady Brayton with the same authority, "Have a care, Devon. I realize that she looks a bit worse for wear at the moment, but Millie will see that she is made presentable. Millie!"

A short, heavyset woman in a white mobcap and a somber gray robe appeared in the entryway, holding a candlestick. She was seventy if she was a day, and had obviously been roused from her bed.

"Yes, milord?" came the housekeeper's monotone query.

"Miss Jervais requires a meal, a bath, and suitable clothing, *s'il vous plaît*."

"I do not have bugs," she repeated to him, hating the tears of humiliation stinging her eyes. "I don't smell, neither!"

He spun her toward the maid by the shoulders and gave her a gentle push. "Go with Millie. She will see to your comforts."

The housekeeper curtsied, then guided Faith by the arm toward a doorway. Faith cast one last glare at the baron's insufferably rude sister before allowing herself to be led away.

Once out of earshot, Devon rounded on him. "Troyce, have you gone mad? What do you mean, bringing that filthy creature into this house?"

Troyce slid his attention from the doorway into which Millie and Faith had disappeared. Only a blind man would have missed seeing the deep wounding in her eyes at the welcome she'd received from the Duchess of Brayton. Only the respect he'd always held for his sister compelled him to explain at all. "I'm short on household help, and she has agreed to work for me. It's as simple as that."

He headed for the library to quench a sudden craving for a nightcap. He should have known that he would have a shadow.

"What did you do, drag her out of the Thames?"

She had no idea how close her guess, Troyce thought, reaching the sideboard. "She encountered a bit of trouble outside a tavern on the docks, and I offered my assistance." He uncapped a fluted decanter. "And that's the end of it, Devon."

Heeding the warning in his tone, her own pitch dropped to a more courteous level. "Tell me that you at least made an appearance at the Countess of Haversley's ball before embarking on your little"—she flipped her hand— "errand of mercy."

A healthy dose of the last of his father's Napoleon brandy spilled into a crystal goblet. "I had a more pressing engagement."

"Yes, I can see that. Gallivanting from pub to pub, consorting with riffraff, dragging that filthy . . . guttersnipe into your home like a common Samaritan . . ."

Troyce turned to look at his sister with thinly concealed impatience. At thirty-one, a year older than he, she was still a strikingly beautiful woman. Glossy black hair neatly braided, flawless ivory complexion, and trademark blue-gray eyes of a de Meir. . . .

Unfortunately, the vibrancy had gone out of her years before. So, apparently, had her compassion. "Would you have preferred I left her to fare on the streets?"

"Better there than here! Heed my words, brother, she will rob us blind."

The remark had Troyce throwing his head back with laughter. "Oh, but Devon, dearest, have you not heard? There is nothing left to rob."

"Which brings us back to my point. The season is nearly over, West. By this time next week all of the eligible ladies will have been betrothed."

"I can only hope."

She all but stamped her foot. "How do you ex-

pect to make a successful match when you contin-
uously avoid opportunities to find a suitable
wife?"

Troyce barely restrained a sigh. "I've told you
before, I have no interest in taking a wife—suitable or otherwise."

She stiffened her spine and sniffed in displeasure that plainly said that she didn't appreciate
his mocking a topic near and dear to her heart.
Namely, seeing him tied to an heiress.

"You are being unreasonable—not to mention
derelict in your duties. It is well past time you settled down and set about securing a legitimate
heir."

"As opposed to an illegitimate one?"

"Do not even jest about that!"

Troyce fought the urge to rake his hand through
his hair and laughed instead. "For God's sake,
Devon, I have been in London barely a fortnight,
and already you are trying to arrange my schedule as well as my life."

"And you have been back from America over
three months and have made no attempt to ingratiate yourself into society."

"I have no desire to ingratiate myself with anyone."

"What of your responsibility—"

Any sense of humor he found in their sibling
banter disappeared. "My only responsibility,
thanks to our dear feckless father, is to see to it
that the people who now entrust me with their
livelihoods do not lose everything they have
spent their lives working for."

"Then marry, for God's sake!" She swept further into the library and propped her hands upon the desk. "Find yourself a wealthy, virtuous maiden, fulfill Grandfather's terms, and be done with it. I can personally recommend several ladies of impeccable breeding willing to exchange their doweries for your title and good name. Arrangements such as this are made all the time. It's business."

Troyce turned away from her imploring examination and nursed his brandy. As much as he hated to admit it, his sister's reasoning was sound. But everything within him rebelled at conducting such business. He'd learned long ago that the only fate worse than marriage was marriage to the wrong woman. He only need look at his parents' union as example. His father had spent his life trying to please his mother, and look where that had gotten him. Troyce had no desire to repeat the mistakes of Charles de Meir.

Aye, he would have to marry someday. Produce an heir to carry on the barony. He accepted that. But God's teeth, he was barely thirty. Hardly a relic yet. If and when he took a bride, it would be a woman of his choosing, at a time of his choosing. And it certainly would not be one of those vapid, socially ambitious twits Devon and their grandfather would foist upon him given half a chance. Just the thought of being anchored for life to some *la noblesse saisir la fille* made him shudder.

No, the woman he took to wife would be impulsive and exciting. Independent and quickwitted. Courageous and uninhibited. If he chose to take off for Africa or Ireland or aye, even back to his beloved America, his lady would be eager and willing to go with him. And she would not care if he bore a title or nay, nor would she hold him at fault for pursuits considered unacceptable to society. His friend Miles often mocked him for holding such high standards. But Troyce cared little. She was out there somewhere. He simply hadn't met her yet.

"You haven't heard a word I've said," his sister accused.

Troyce brought the glass to his mouth and paused. "All of England can hear you, Devon. I'm hardly an exception."

"Then you agree that marriage is the best solution."

For whom? "Has *Grandpère* put you up to this?"

"Don't be ridiculous. I haven't spoken to the man in years."

"Then why this haste to see me wed?" he challenged. "One would think you, of all people, would respect my decision not to marry."

Devon turned three shades of pale, and Troyce could have kicked himself for the careless remark. Never before had he thrown his sister's folly in her face. Never before had he broached the subject of her youthful indiscretion with her husband's brother. Never before had he judged her for throwing her heart away for the sake of duty. Hadn't she suffered enough? "Devon, forgive me. I shouldn't have said that."

But she'd already turned away. As he watched her wander aimlessly about the room, trailing her fingers along an intricately molded mantel, fidgeting with the globe of a fringed lamp, re-arranging a carved set of chessmen on a gaudy Hepplewhite table near one of the crown-backed sofas, it struck him then that everything she did was just that way. Aimless. Without purpose. Movement just for the sake of movement.

Maybe he should be grateful that his sister was passionate about something, even if it was the demise of his bachelorhood. He couldn't remember the last time he'd seen her this alive, this animated. How often had he wished for a glimpse of the bold, vivacious swashbuckler he'd grown up with? The one who used to command the helm of their imaginary pirate ship and take no quarter? The one who used to slide down banisters and sword-fight with him in their father's study? The one who used to laugh—just for the joy of laughing?

But now, in typical Devon de Meir—correction: Devon Heath—fashion, she tipped her chin and stared at him through stony gray eyes. "The last thing I wish to do is see you repeat my mistakes, Troyce. If I saw any other way out of this situation, I would seize it in an instant. Unfortunately, I do not see any other choice. Father's debts are no closer to being paid off today than the day you arrived, and we are running out of time."

Troyce clenched his jaw. He well knew the consequences of his inherited pecuniary obligation; the demise of his personal fortune, the dissolution of the de Meir holdings, the loss of the family's ancestral estate, and the fate of villagers who depended on the Baron of Westborough for their livelihoods. He certainly didn't appreciate being reminded of his failures, and by his own sister at that. "I told you that I would see the situation remedied and I shall do so. Once I secure an investor for *La Tentatrice*—"

"You have spent months trying to find someone feebleminded enough to pour money into that ship to no avail. Why can you not at least consider other alternatives? You would have a fortune at your disposal if only you will swallow that blasted pride of yours."

Pride? She thought it *pride* that kept him from bowing to their grandfather's whims?

Damn. If only it were that simple.

"That fortune you speak so highly of comes with strings. I will not be controlled—not by him, not by you, not by anyone."

It was the one thing he'd always taken pride in, being an authority unto himself. Of being in control of his own actions and reactions. Everything he did, he did by design. He lived the way he wanted in the manner he wanted. No one told him what to do unless he allowed it. He maintained a good sense of humor because it kept him sane and he smiled often because it pleased him to smile. He took risks because he liked not always knowing the outcome; sometimes he was disappointed, and sometimes he was pleasantly surprised.

But in the last three months, the ability to control his own life had begun slipping away bit by excruciating bit, chipping at his masculine vanity, crippling his sense of self-worth . . .

No longer did Troyce feel as if he captained his own destiny. In three short months, obligations and duty had forced him to leave a country he'd called home, sacrifice the modest fortune he'd spent years amassing, accept a title he'd loathed since childhood, and return to the place that had always made him feel like a prisoner.

The only bright spot since returning to England had come in the form of a sharp-tongued blighter who'd managed to surprise and delight him when he'd least expected it, and now, even that small pleasure was being whittled away.

A rap on the door created a welcome diversion from his troubling thoughts. Troyce raised his head toward the door just as Millie walked in.

"I beg your forgiveness, milord." The housekeeper dropped a slight curtsy toward Devon. "Milady."

"Is there a problem, Millie?" Troyce asked.

She hesitated a moment, then said, "Maybe you should judge for yourself, milord."

He turned to Devon, relieved at the timely interruption. "Dear sister, as invigorating as I find these conversations with you, it seems my presence is required elsewhere."

She looked as if she would argue further, but seemed to reconsider. "Very well," she sighed. "But do not think this discussion finished."

"I wouldn't dream of it."

As he followed Millie out of the drawing room, he wondered at the housekeeper's apparent distress. In all the years she'd worked for the de Meir family, he'd never once seen her anything less than calm and composed. That she would summon him for any issue spoke of a matter of great importance.

The minute he entered the kitchen, he understood.

Faith sat huddled in the corner of the pantry, shoveling mouthfuls of leftover stew into her mouth with a spoon, clutching a chunk of bread in her fist. Her hair was still a snarled mass, and she wore the same grubby clothes she'd been wearing since she'd accosted him in London. A quick survey of the kettles steaming on the stove explained her unchanged condition, but why was she eating off the floor?

He threw a questioning glance behind him at Millie, who lingered at the doorway, wringing her hands. She shrugged in silent, helpless response and shook her head. Troyce discreetly flicked his hand, permitting the housekeeper to leave them. After she'd backed out of the kitchen, he took a cautious step toward his young charge. "Faith?"

She glanced up. The moment he looked into her startled eyes, he was hit with a discovery that stole the breath from his lungs—this was no street-wild waif. This was a very angry, very bitter, very wounded young woman.

And he was in for the undertaking of his life.

"What are you doing?"

A flush crept across her cheeks. "She gave it to me. I didn't steal it."

"It pleases me to hear that, though I had not presumed otherwise." He kept his voice calm, patient, gentle, as if trying to tame a wild animal. "But you need not sit upon the floor. Eat at the table." She'd catch her death; a draft tended to blow in beneath the doors, and with her hair still damp from the earlier rains, she would be doubly susceptible to illness.

"The table?"

"Yes, like—" *any normal, civilized human being* "like the other servants." He held out his hand to help her to her feet.

She shrank back against the wall. Her arm curled tighter around the bowl, and her expression went guarded. Never a man prone to soft emotions, the unaccustomed tenderness flooding his chest took him by surprise. "No one will take your food, Faith," he assured her with quiet gruffness. Good God, what kind of life had she lived, where she didn't sit at a table, and feared the theft of a meal?

A myriad of emotions flittered across her face. Mistrust. Apprehension. Suspended belief. Until, at long last, the fight return to her eyes. Lips pursing, she lifted herself off the stone floor in one fluid motion. Then, she tipped her chin and swept past him with a grace that would have done the Queen Mother proud.

And abruptly tossed her bowl onto the butcher-block table in the center of the room. Brown gravy spattered the surface. "Keep your bloody food, Baron. I don't want any favors."

A second later, she'd vanished out of the kitchen.

Troyce remained hunched down near the corner, too astonished by her behavior to speak, too baffled over what he might have done or said to scold her.

Then, a reluctant smile toyed at his lips. God, the girl was proud. She cowered, but she didn't cave. She stole, but she didn't beg.

Oddly enough, there was something to be admired in that.

It was two o'clock in the morning before Faith was finally released from Millie's brutal ministrations and led down to a room in the servants' wing on the third floor. Her skin had been nearly scrubbed raw, her head smelled as if she'd doused it in the pit of a coal mine, and her stomach ached for want of the stew she'd left behind. The bed she lay on was a far cry from her pallet in the tunnels. Six inches of soft ticking cushioned her body from the drafty floor and a pillow with a genuine slip-cover felt like a cloud under her head. Across from her, Millie snored loud enough to jostle the dead while her granddaughter—Lucy, Faith believed was her name—tossed restlessly in her cot. It felt strange sleeping in a room with two women when most of her life she'd shared living quarters with a dozen boys.

She clutched her ragged doll close to her, and stared at the fancy molding joining wall to ceiling. Never had she slept in such a fine room, never felt such soft, clean fabric against her skin.

And yet, she was so homesick she could hardly bear it.

She missed the unruly noise of the band as they gambled on a roll of the dice, argued over chores, or yelled in triumph when one scored big. She missed her antechamber with its rattling pipes, concrete floor, and ratty pallet. But most of all, she missed Scatter. A tear slipped down the side of her nose, and she brushed it away. Why there'd be such an empty longing in her heart for the little leech she couldn't figure. He'd been nothing but a thorn in her side since the day he'd turned up in Jack's band.

Aye, it was utterly mad that she'd pine for the life she'd left behind. How could she miss Bethnal Green for even a moment? God's teeth, what did she have to mourn? She'd dreamed all her life of escaping poverty; she had that chance now thanks to the baron.

Except, for all its shabbiness and chaos, the tunnels had been home to her for nearly ten years. At least there, she was accepted. She knew what the rules were and what to expect.

Here, she knew only a vast isolation. A bone-deep aloneness. Here, she was completely out of her element.

What had she gotten herself into? Living with a woman who hated her on sight and a man bent on making her his bondsmaid?

His image filled her mind and the leaden feeling inside her intensified. Oh, God. She couldn't believe he'd caught her eating off the floor like a dog. She'd never been so humiliated in her life. Even the servants knew better behavior than she did. Bowing and scraping and calling the hoity-toities by their proper titles. He'd never understand that in the real world, manners didn't exist, and something so simple as eating at the table got a bloke tumbled.

She ought to resent him for expecting her to be something she wasn't. For dragging her here

against her will. Forcing her into agreeing to live
in his fine, fancy house and clean up his muck and
obey him without question. She ought to tell him
what he could do with his bloody claims of *honest
employment*.

But despite it all—his judge-and-jury arro-
gance, his sister's holier-than-thou haughtiness—
a part of her was so bloody grateful to him that
she could hardly bear it. If not for the baron, she'd
no doubt still be waiting on a soggy street corner
like a two-bit strumpet, waiting for crumbs. Or,
and it made her cringe to think it, rotting away in
a dank, dark prison cell. *What makes you think I'm
noble?* He could easily have hauled her off to
Newgate, but he hadn't. Instead, he'd brought her
into his home. Given her a true-blue job—even if
it was indentured servitude—a clean bed, clean
clothes, a clean start.

Why? What did he want from her? He'd said
maid service, but no one extended such a kindness without expecting something greater in return. He'd also said he had no intention of making
her lift her skirts. Ha! She believed that like she
believed man could fly. He was a man, a nobleman, and an *American* at that. She knew their
kind. Once he realized she wasn't as young as
he'd first assumed, he'd reveal his true colors.
They all did.

Well, she wasn't about to stick around and wait
for it to happen.

She raised her head from the pillow. Millie
snored on, dead to the world, and Lucy had finally settled into peaceful oblivion. She drew the
soft cotton nightgown she'd been given over her

head and started to shove it into her rucksack, then stopped. *Do not steal from me.* It was the nicest thing she'd ever worn, and she hated to part with it, yet she'd not give him any more reason to come after her than he already had. She got the feeling that the baron was not the sort of man to spout empty promises.

With one last, wistful glance, she carefully folded the gown and laid it on the pillow. It took only a few minutes to find her own clothing, and she recoiled at the stench. Just the thought of the stiff, filthy clothes against her clean skin made her want to vomit, but there was no help for it; the set in her rucksack was just as bad. She'd not leave with anything she hadn't brought with her.

Faith dressed quickly and without a sound. With the rucksack looped across her shoulder, she crushed her hair and wrestled the too-silky curls under her hat, then tiptoed toward the door. Where she'd go and what she'd do, she had no idea. Going back to Jack was out of the question; she'd burned that bridge. He had three unbreakable rules: don't get caught, don't squeal, and don't run away. She'd already committed two out of three. If she went back, they'd find her carcass floating in the Thames.

She supposed she could attempt a position as an orderly at the hospital—except, she couldn't stand the sight of blood. Applying as a governess was another possibility, but she'd need references, and she didn't think petty thief would be the ticket.

Sadly, she really wasn't qualified for anything besides picking pockets. It might not be a respectable means of making a shilling, but she knew every technique in the book. More, she was bloody good at it—even the baron thought so. And as long as she could filch, it kept her from living on the streets. Not such a bad prospect if there were more ways for a woman in her twentieth year to make a living than prostitution. . . .

Well, first things first. Get out of the house. Make her way back to London. Find Scatter. She'd take everything else one step at a time. At least the decisions would be her own.

She stepped out of the room and looked up one side of the hallway and down the other. The house was dark as pitch and quiet as a tomb as she made her way down the first flight of steps to the second floor. Solid wall waited behind her, a short, blackened corridor stretched ahead, and she could make out a dip in the floor where the main staircase would take her to the front door. A high sense of risk stole through her veins. Any moment she expected Jack Swift to fling himself into the foyer, barge up the steps, and drag her out of the house by the hair. Surely by now he knew of the incident at Jorge's. . . .

Well, all the more reason to pad the hoof.

Ten years of creeping stood her in good stead as she made her way toward the staircase. The soles of her shoes were thin enough not to squeak on the hardwood floor, and her clothes were dark enough to blend well with the shadows. The baron no doubt rested behind one of the closed doors on either side of her, and if he caught her, she'd be hard-pressed to explain what she was doing, skulking about at this time of night.

She made it to the top of the steps without incident and blew a breath of relief between her lips. She was just about to begin the long descent to the main floor when the sound of a door opening below froze her in her tracks. A wedge of light spilled onto the foyer floor. A long shadow crossed the foyer.

Faith pressed herself against the wall. She glanced behind her toward the back set of stairs; too far to make it back safely. Ahead, beyond her stretched a dark passageway, more doors on either side. Which were occupied? Which were empty? Damn this house! Damn herself for not mapping out the place earlier—not that she'd had time; everything had happened so fast that she'd not had a chance. She was paying for that now.

Footsteps approached the stairs. Faith flipped herself around a corner, opened the closest door, and found herself in a cavernous room. A huge four-poster bed dominated the floor. A quilt-covered chest acted as a footboard. A scroll-topped secretary and one overstuffed chair commanded a corner. There was not a single place to hide.

The rhythmic beat of heavy heels in the hallway grew louder. She raced to the window beside the secretary and twisted the clasp. After several seconds of struggling, the pane finally slid up. The footsteps stopped outside the door. Glancing first left, then right, Faith saw what she was looking for and threw her left leg over the sill at the same moment she heard the door latch click.

She hadn't thought there could be any worse humiliation than when the baron had caught her eating off the floor like a stray cur.

She'd been wrong.

Chapter 4

A dark and handsome prince should find a lady stitching delicate samplers on a drawing room divan. He should find her seated primly at a gleaming pianoforte or strumming the strings of a lute. He should find her gliding gracefully across a ballroom floor.

He should *not* find her hanging upside down from a rose trellis two floors off the ground.

"My, my, Your Majesty, you are quite full of surprises," came his mirth-filled observation from the window directly above her where he leaned over the sill.

Fighting against gravity, Faith tried to curl upward in an attempt to salvage a measure of dignity and felt the trellis give another inch under her ankle. Falling back in defeat, she almost wished it would fall. Better to be buried in thorns than face another mortifying episode before the baron.

Unfortunately, she would not be spared.

"You wouldn't by chance be trying to run away, would you, Highness?"

"Do I look like I'm running?" She sneezed, then cursed the reaction to the roses that had first caused her ungainly slip, then no doubt given her away. So much for her clever escape.

"Actually, you look like you're about to break your crown. Come down from there, Faith."

"I can't," she almost whimpered. "Me foot 'as gotten stuck b'tween the slats."

She couldn't be sure if he chuckled or sighed. Maybe both. The first touch of his hand around her ankle sent a shock of lightning coursing down her leg. Faith jerked; the trellis quivered.

The baron muttered a mild curse that echoed across the lawn. "I can't seem to get a secure grasp to pull you up, so I'll have to come down. Stay put, I'll have you untangled in a jiffy."

Stay put? Crikey, where did he expect her to go? She'd already discovered that she wasn't strong enough to pull herself up and untangle herself, else she would have done so long before he'd discovered her hanging like a sea monkey from the fragile wooden ladder.

Several minutes later, she felt his presence below and sought out his lean figure. Little more than shadow seemed to appear at the base of the trellis. Then a dim curl of moonlight brought him into mellow focus. She watched him bend down and pluck her stocking cap from the ground, where it had dropped beside her pack. "Why, I believe you've lost your tiara!" Even in the tip-turned darkness she could see his eyes twinkling as he swung her limp wool cap back and forth from his forefinger by the brim.

She clenched her teeth together. "Just help me down."

"Please?"

She glared into the laughing gray eyes and ground out, "*Please.*"

He chuckled, then grabbed hold of the braces of the trellis, and after giving it a shake to test its sturdiness, began to climb.

And she began to sneeze.

And sneeze.

And sneeze. Her eyes watered, her nose ran.

"If you keep doing that, we're both likely to take a tumble."

"I can't help it. It's these bloomin' flowers." His weight seemed to dislodge every ounce of perfume in the blossoms.

"Ah, yes, the roses. My sister is very fond of them, as was my mother. 'Tis unfortunate they don't agree with you . . ." His eyes became level with hers. "Wouldn't you say?"

If she weren't so afraid of him taking her with him, she'd have shoved him off the trellis. As it was, the blood was draining straight to her brain, and her leg was beginning to ache from being stretched beyond its limits. All she wanted was to feel solid ground beneath her feet once again—even if that meant being the brunt of Westborough's humor.

He climbed another two steps until her upside-down body was faced with his right-side-up bum.

Never in her life had she given a thought to a man's backside, but the sight of this one, with its low snug curve shrouded in velvety dove gray, made her mouth go dry, her head swim, and strange sensations rise up her middle.

"Hold me about my waist so that you won't fall."

Hesitantly, Faith released the hold she had on the trellis to circle her arms around his stomach and back. No coat padded his form, just a simple shirt made of thin cotton separated the soft flesh of her arm from the hard plane of his belly.

Another step upward jarred the trellis. Her grip tightened about him, and she buried her nose against his thigh. The scent of roses vanished, replaced by the potent scent of heat and serried muscle. Crikey she liked the smell of him. So strong. So solid. So . . . manly.

She was dimly aware of his fingers prodding her ankle above her shoe and the instep of her foot. He cursed several times as he loosened the strings of her shoe. "Blasted thorns. Ah, yes, I think I've got it. Can you work your foot loose?"

She twisted her ankle one way, then the other, and to her surprise, her foot slipped from its moorings.

"That's a girl," he praised. "Now hold fast while I step down."

Oh, aye, she thought, tightening her arms about him in pleasure. She was barely aware of the smooth descent until she heard him chuckle.

"You can release me now, we've reached the ground."

Her eyes snapped open. Her head jerked back from his leg.

He braced her against him with one arm crossing her back and the other hand cupping her thigh. A hot iron to her flesh could not have burned a deeper imprint.

It took a bit of acrobatic maneuvering to set her upright. Standing on her feet at last, Faith's knees felt weak as pastry dough, and her instincts blared a warning to step away, put some distance between him. But with his arm lingering around her waist, holding her close to his powerful frame, thigh to thigh, breast to chest, she could do naught but stare into the eyes fixed on hers. Her mind went numb to all but the musky scent and male heat of the body pressed against hers.

A bit of moon peeked out from behind the clouds sliding across the sky, giving her a glimpse of his darkening pupils. More perfect features had never been created on a man. A sloping jaw, shadowed in whiskers. Smooth, firm mouth, temptation incarnate. And most compelling, eyes like the sea, which seemed privy to the deepest secrets of her soul.

What did he see when he looked at her? Could he see the wild street urchin, abandoned by her family? The foul pocket-thief, desperate to survive? The lonely young woman, lured by delusions of being a lady?

Then his eyes narrowed. All traces of amusement left his face. "What happened here?" With the same unexpected gentleness as he'd shown before, he tipped her chin toward the light of the waxing moon and brushed his thumb across the discoloration in the hollow of her cheek, and the world stopped along with her heartbeat. "Who did this to you?"

Faith blinked. The question seemed to come from a tunnel.

"Did someone strike you?"

The murderous rage in his eyes took Faith off guard, as if given the chance, the baron would kill whoever touched her. Rip him apart with his bare hands. He might not be as bulky as some or as robust in frame, but there was no doubt in her mind that with his lean and wiry strength, he could brawl with the best of them.

"Maybe I scraped it against the wall." It wasn't a lie. Exactly. Jack hadn't done more than bruise her pride. It was more a twist to divert the truth, she told herself. Not to protect Jack Swift. She did it to protect herself. Somehow she knew that if he learned Jack had struck her, he would hunt him down, and though the knowledge filled her with unaccustomed tenderness and bittersweet shame, she didn't want Lord Westborough knowing the extent of the depths to which she'd sunk. Bad enough she was already labeled a guttersnipe and thief.

"Oh, Faith . . ." The tender stroke of his finger against her cheek was nearly her undoing. "What am I going to do with you?"

Hold me close. Tuck me into you heart. Make me yours. "Let me go," she found herself whispering. "I'll get ye back yer money somehow, I swear I will."

His hand dropped slowly, as did his lashes, shuttering his thoughts. "I can't do that, *cherie.*"

She almost wept. "Why not? It ain't as if ye

need the money—crikey, two hundred pounds is a drop in the bucket to gents like you!"

"We have an agreement, Faith, or have you forgotten?"

"T'hell with our agreement!" she cried recklessly. Then, aware that she might be treading on dangerous ground, she took an instant step backward and put herself out of his reach. "Ye might as well summon the magistrate right now because I'd rather spend the rest of me days in Newgate than step foot inside that house again."

"You don't approve of Radcliff?" The sweep of his hand encompassed the opulent surroundings.

Approve? Crikey, it was everything she'd ever dreamed of! "T'ain't nothing wrong with it."

"Then what is it, *cherie*? Is prison so much more preferable to working for me?"

If he'd demanded an explanation, she could have kept up her guard. But the infinite gentleness in his smoky tone broke through her reserves and sent her defenses crumbling. "I don't belong here," she whispered, her voice as raw as her fear. "I don't belong here at all."

"Neither do I. But it seems that we both must make the best of our situations."

She'd half expected him to laugh off her angst, or at the very least, scoff at her for being a silly twit.

She hadn't expected him to understand.

"Come," he commanded, taking her by the hand. "Everything will look brighter in the morning."

As they turned away from the trellis, the baron stopped and bent low. When he raised up, he had her pack and hat clutched in his hand. The cap he returned to her, but the rucksack he slung over his shoulder. "I think this should remain in my safe-keeping for a while."

Faith couldn't find the will to protest. It wasn't as if she'd be needing the tools anytime soon.

He guided her across an overgrown courtyard and through a rust-hinged gate to a side door that opened into the kitchen. Her rejected bowl of stew still lay on the worktable where she'd thrown it earlier. She stared at it wistfully as they passed but said not a word.

She followed him up the stairs in dull obedience. When they reached the landing, she started toward the room she'd been assigned, only to be brought to a firm halt.

"No you don't, Faith." Gripping her arm, the baron inclined his head toward the door of the room in which she'd used to make her escape. "You'll sleep with me tonight."

For a second, Faith wasn't sure she'd heard him right. She had been awake for nearly two days straight. Her mind was dull and her body numb with fatigue. But as she replayed the words in her mind, there was no mistaking them. "Over me dead body, baron. I'll sleep in me own bed."

"Your bed is wherever I decide it is."

She'd known it would happen. She'd known he would show his true colors; she'd just convinced herself it wouldn't happen so soon. "I won't sleep with ye, baron. I won't be no one's whore."

"Whore? Good God, where do you get such ideas? The fact is, Faith, you tried to escape before working off your debt to me, and I can no longer trust you not to escape again. Therefore, I plan to keep my eye on you every moment—even if it means tying you to my bedpost—until our agreement is fulfilled."

And in that moment, she hated the Baron of Westborough with every beat of her heart. How could she for a moment have been fooled into thinking she was safe with him?

With one last glower, she yanked her wrist free and entered his room, the very same one she'd used to climb out the window. The irony didn't escape Faith. The bed seemed to have increased in size. Her first thought was to flee, but there was nowhere to go. Nonetheless, she lingered near the door, her arms wrapped around her middle. The baron made his way toward the hearth. She watched in surreal detachment as he knelt before the stone mouth and fed it wedges of wood. So this was how it was to be then? A hundred pounds of flesh for two hundred pounds of coin? The price for her crimes? The punishment for her sins?

She'd known she should not have trusted him at his word.

Maybe she should be flattered that he would .deem her body worth even a farthing of that. But all she felt was bone-deep resentment and soul-licking terror.

She would fight him, she decided, mentally scouring the room for a weapon. She didn't want to hurt him but if it meant—

"There's an extra quilt on the chest. You may sleep on the bed or the floor, it makes no difference." He lifted himself up and away from the fire now flickering in the grate. "But be aware that I am a light sleeper. I will hear you if you try to leave."

Her brow furrowed in confusion. "I don't understand."

"'Tis half past three o'clock in the morning, Faith. I am weary to my bones, and we must be ready to leave in a few hours."

What? He wasn't going to punish her?

He rounded the side of the bed, seeming to forget her presence. Dizzying relief washed through her. She slumped back against the wall, her knees too weak to hold her, and closed her eyes. She couldn't believe he would spare her.

Then she opened her eyes and caught him pulling his shirt from his waistband.

"Ye ain't taking off your clothes!"

He paused. His eyes crinkled at the corners. "'Tis the natural order of retiring." Then he drew the shirt over his head and discarded it into the round-backed chair by the secretary.

And for the first time in her life, Faith swore she was about to swoon. He was neither brawny nor scrawny. Instead, his build seemed in perfect proportion to his height. Wide-shouldered, deep-chested, long-waisted and long-legged, not an ounce of spare flesh marred the beauty of his body. He was simply corded muscle and tightly stretched skin, the deep, rich hue of dusk.

Faith had been raised among boys of all ages and had seen countless number of men in all manner of dress—and undress. But not a single member of the male species compared to the Baron of Westborough. Not a single one aroused her fascination as he did. He looked sleek and sinuous and more irresistible than she ever dreamed a man could look. She could easily imagine him besting a Nordic warrior as waltzing across a ballroom floor. Watching him, the fluid play of bone and sinew, the purposeful gestures, the smooth and somehow deliberate dance of motion, captivated her. Intrigued her.

Tempted her.

Her nails cut into her skin as she clenched her hands. The urge to let her hands roam across his bare chest, to explore the hard wall of his torso became nearly unbearable. A line of fine dark hair extended from his navel to the waistband of his gray, form-fitting breeches.

The warmth in her veins rose to a blazing wildfire. She felt feverish and dizzy. The air in the room seemed to disappear. How easily it would be to cross the distance between them, climb into that four-poster bed, lift her skirts as they were, and let him tumble her.

And become the one thing she'd sworn on her mother's soul never to become.

His fingers adroitly released the buttons on the front placket and Faith's eyes slammed shut. She heard the squeak of bed springs, two muted thuds on the floor as he removed his boots, the rustle of material. A sudden picture of him sitting on the bed wearing nothing but skin appeared in her mind, the image so clear he might as well have stripped down to nothing before her very eyes.

The room went silent, save for the pop of firewood nearby. She cracked open one eye, then the other. He now stood by the bed, folding his britches. Much to her relief, and disappointment, he wasn't naked as she'd expected. Instead, a pair of loose cotton underdrawers covered him from waist to knee.

He opened a large valise and withdrew a simple white shirt. Rather than covering up his bare chest as she hoped, he tossed the shirt at her. "Put this on."

Faith caught the garment on sheer reflex and gaped at him in astonishment. Take off her clothes?

"Remove them, or I will remove them for you."

Ah, so that was his game. Bastard. The baron had no wish to bed her. He only wanted to lord over her. Bring her to heel. Humiliate her. She pursed her lips, summoned her pride, and reached for the top button of her coat.

And Troyce was entranced.

Never in his life had he been so aware of a female. So sensitive to her sound, her presence, her scent. He told himself only the worst of scoundrels would look. Good God, she was hardly more than a child on the brink of womanhood. Yet he couldn't stop himself from watching if his life depended on it. Morbid fascination kept his attention fixed on her as, with her back to him, she kicked off her shoes and shed her coat. Her hair was shorter than was conventional, just past her shoulders, and firelight danced in loose curls of saffron and amber. The coat sailed toward one of the chairs in front of the hearth, hit the back, and tumbled to the floor.

Then she began unbuttoning her shirt. If she was aware of him spying her, she gave no sign.

She kept her head down, and he imagined her gaze focused on the buttons as she slipped them through their corresponding holes, her fingers long, tapered, graceful in their task, stirring his fantasies, fanning a heat in the room that already seemed suffocating.

Once the fasteners were dealt with, she shrugged out of the ratty garment, not bothering to hide her figure from his prying eyes as she bared her shoulders, her back, her waist.

And Troyce nearly choked on his own shock. He'd seen undernourished before; working on the coast made him privy to all manner of characters who disembarked ships from all over the world, the promise of a future paved in gold destroyed by misery, illness, and starvation. Yet no amount of experience prepared him for the sight of Faith's emaciated figure. He could count every joint in her arms, every vertebra in her spine, every rib in her torso. When she turned slightly and raised her arm to shove it into the sleeve, he realized that only her breasts had been spared starvation. They were full and proud and high, seemingly too heavy to be supported by her fragile frame.

His loins tightened. His blood thickened. His brain kicked into carnal gear.

And in that brief moment, one thing became starkly apparent.

She was hardly a child.

Feeling her glare burning holes into his skin, he glanced up from her beautiful breasts and met her over-the-shoulder stare unflinchingly, hoping none of the lascivious thoughts parading through his mind were visible to her. With near-defiant purpose, she shoved her arms through the sleeves, poked her head through the neck opening, and covered her nudity. The sleeves dangled past her fingertips, and the tail of his shirt kept her bottom half concealed as she then peeled away the stiff britches and kicked them away. What he could see of her legs told him that they were just as thin as the rest of her, yet delicately turned at the knees and ankles, and her feet were small and slender.

"There. Are you happy now?"

The sheen of tears in her eyes made him feel like England's most depraved cad. How could he put her through this humiliation? He hardened himself against the sympathy and the desire. "Almost."

He plucked the divested shirt and britches off the floor and threw them into the fire.

"What are you doing?" she cried, racing toward the hearth as the rags burst into flames.

"Ridding you of those hideous garments once and for all."

"You had no right!"

"I have every right. You are in my employ, and I'll not have people thinking I cannot care for my own people."

She glared at him for several seconds, her doe brown eyes growing almost black. Her chest heaved, her fists clenched. "I hate you, Baron."

His heart fell, and his chest went suddenly hollow. "I know you do." He left her to stew by the hearth, knowing that if he stood there much longer, he'd give her a reason to really despise him. "Good night, Faith."

Moments later, he lay on his stomach between

the sheets, his pillow beaten into submission beneath his head, his fist curled against the bedcovers. Faith had taken the quilt from the chest and was spreading it on the floor in front of the fire. Pity, he thought, when there was so much room beside him. So much *empty* room.

This was absurd, this damnable desire for her. He could hardly deny it when the proof of that desire throbbed hot and rigid between his belly and the mattress. What he didn't understand was how. Or why. Aye, she promised to be a comely woman, but he'd known many a comely women in his day; not a one of them aroused him to such a degree.

So what was it about a scrawny wisp of a cutpurse that kindled his passions and tied his emotions in knots? Devon was right; Faith would no doubt rob him blind the instant he turned his back. And if there was one thing Troyce could not abide, it was a thief.

The wisest thing would be to cut his losses and take her back to London where he'd found her. Or at the very least, find her a position in another household where she'd not pose such a temptation. And yet, from the moment he'd laid eyes on her, he could not bring himself to turn his back on her. It felt too much like abandonment.

So instead, he'd brought her not just into his home, but into his very bedchamber, where he could be sure she'd not escape.

As he drifted off to sleep, he did so with the scent of roses strong in his nostrils and a strangely disturbing contentment deep in his heart.

* * *

"What do you mean, you lost her!"

Scatter flinched in spite of himself. Jack didn't raise his voice like he normally did, and Scat almost wished he would. Hollering would ha' been much easier to block out than the frozen gravel of his tone. He clutched his hat in his hand, rolled the brim, unrolled it again, over and over. "After we bilked the pair of gents over by the docks, one of 'em got Fanny and took 'er away in some fancy coach."

"Who took her?"

"Don't know, Jack. I ain't never seen the bloke before."

"Then find out!" He slammed his fist down on the tabletop and sent a pile of coins from the gent's pouch rolling helter-skelter. "I want to know where she is, and who she's with."

His nod felt wooden, as if his head had suddenly gotten too bulky for his neck. "Aye, suh."

"And Scatter, do not return without news."

Again, he forced himself to nod. Zounds, why couldn't Jack just be happy with the money he'd given him? He was so tired. He'd hidden in the old shoemaker's shop for hours and hours, waiting for Fanny to meet up with him like she'd done hundreds of times past.

But she'd never shown.

So he'd gone back to the tavern. He wasn't sure what he would do if he found her there, but he knew he couldn't just sit around waitin'. Him and Fan, they'd been mates for a long time, and a mate didn't just leave a mate.

At least, that's what he'd always thought until

he'd seen her get into the hack. She wasn't struggling either. She looked almost like she'd wanted to go away. And he remembered all the times she'd talked about gettin' out of the band, of leavin' Bethnal Green.

Still, Scatter couldn't believe his eyes, couldn't believe that she would have just left him. He'd always thought she would take him with her.

He followed the cab as far as he could, but he'd never been no good at running for long ways. He'd tuckered out just outside of the city, watching the fancy cab with its fancy bloke inside, take her off. He'd had a bad feeling about him from the start, and now he knew why.

With no place left to go, he'd returned to the tunnels.

Now, with Jack's orders pounding in his ears, he left again, scared he'd not find her. But more afraid he would.

Chapter 5

Morning came quickly, and the house awakened with a bustle of activity that left Faith's head spinning. She had no idea what to do with herself or what duties she was supposed to be performing. They were readying for the journey to Westborough, that much she knew, but her attempts to help only seemed to cause more harm than good. She was scolded by Millie for packing sacks of flour and sugar in the same crate; cursed at by Lucy, a gel near the baron's age and fairer of coloring than Faith, for not properly wrapping the candlesticks, and banished from the drawing room by Lady Brayton for covering the furniture with good bed linens found in an upstairs pantry instead of oilcloths.

She wanted to help, but she knew nothing of being a maid, and every attempt to learn was met with scorn. Feeling out of place and out of sorts and completely out of her element among all the gleaming brasses and rich velvets and polished oaks, Faith wandered about the ponderous house, unable to shake the thought that she had made a dreadful mistake taking this job. Put her in the rookeries of London, and she could tumble with the best of them; put her in a fine house like Radcliff, and she felt as useful as a sixth toe. As soon as the baron discovered how completely useless she really was, he'd turn her over to the authorities.

She hadn't seen him this morning, as he'd been gone before she awoke, and for that, at least, she was grateful. She'd seen far too much of him last night. Even now the memory of his lean and sinuous body sent heat creeping up her neck. How much was due to lingering anger at his high-handedness and how much at her own response to him she didn't want to examine too closely. She could only hope that he'd not force her to continue sharing his chambers once they reached his country estate. She'd not be able to withstand the torment. The man had an uncanny knack for sending her emotions spinning. He seemed to find the most degrading experiences of her life amusing. And though he had a glorious laugh, she didn't like that laughter being at her expense.

Determined to find something to keep her mind otherwise occupied, Faith had just grabbed a crate of baking goods intended for one of the fancy black carriages waiting out front when a floor-throbbing crash shook the foundation beneath her feet. She dropped the crate and sprinted up the flying staircase.

A man old as Moses stood in the center of the hall, scratching his head, staring at a leather-wrapped trunk that barred a bedchamber doorway at a cross angle. He let out a stream of curses in a cadence so familiar that Faith almost wept.

" 'Aving a bit o' trouble, are ye?" The missing consonants and misshapen vowels of her upbringing filled her mouth and bridged the air between them like a dear friend.

The old man straightened and spun about, pinning her with a curious stare. His silvery hair, what was left on his head, stuck out every which way. "Who ye be, moll?"

"Fan—Faith Jervais, the new maid." Even now the name she'd been born with felt foreign to her ears, but like everything else lately, she figured she would adjust to it with time. "And you?"

"Chadwick, 'is lordship's man."

At last! A possible ally!

"Well don't jus' stand there, moll. 'Elp me get this bit of fluff back in its box before 'er ladyship 'as me flogged."

Relieved to finally be of use, Faith didn't hesitate. She situated herself between the doorframe and the fallen trunk. One of the hinges was bent, and fabrics of all shades and textures scattered from the broken lid to the glossy, hardwood floor.

"I best find me some tools to repair the latch."

Faith nodded. After Chadwick left, she knelt on the floor in a puddle of slippery, fuzzy, and gauzy fabrics that would make the queen herself drool. Faith plucked a bony contraption from the mound and it spread out before her. It looked like a falcon's skeleton. "God's teeth, how does this even

go on?" Her imagination took wing, and she giggled. She knew women wore them under their
clothes to enhance their figures, though she
couldn't imagine why. Who would purposely
truss themselves up in something so stiff and
tight? No wonder the duchess was always in a
snit.

She dropped the stays and began folding shifts
and skirts, petticoats and shirtwaists, piling them
neatly on the floor until the old man returned to
repair the trunk. Most everything was in shades of
gray, black, charcoal, or pewter—sad, somber colors that made Faith think of the wreath on the
door and wonder who had passed away. Then,
near the bottom of the spillage, a splash of color
caught her eye. She couldn't help a delighted gasp
of surprise. It was a silk gown the brilliant red of a
cardinal's wing and the most beautiful thing Faith
had ever laid eyes on. She shook it out and held it
up to the starched front of her maid's uniform.
Thanks to the baron's audacity in pitching her
clothes in the fire, she'd had no choice but to accept one of Lucy's castoffs. The bodice was too
tight and the hem too long, but it was still the
nicest outfit Faith had ever felt against her skin.

Until now.

She ran her fingers across the ivory lace trim-
ming the neckline of the dress—she assumed it
belonged to Lady Brayton—and stroked the shim-
mery panels of the skirt. She sighed in bliss. What
would it be like to own such fine clothes? To live
in a fancy house such as this and have folks greet
you with half curtsies and address you with
pretty titles like "my lady" or "Your Grace"?

Faith slowly rose to her feet, the dress falling in glorious crimson ripples down her apron. "Why, how do you do, sir," she said in her best blue-blood imitation. "Oh, no, milord, I'm afraid I shall be too busy enjoying myself to dine with you this evening, but thank you for asking.

"Red flatters the roses in my cheeks?" she flipped her hand in a "pshaw" gesture. "Oh, your earlship, you are too kind!"

Letting her imagination take flight, she pressed three fingers to her heart and batted her lashes. "Me? Oh, but Your Grace, you've certainly collected a bevy of admirers much more beautiful than I!"

She dropped into a deep curtsy, "I am flattered, Your Highness, but I cannot possibly accept." She smiled coquettishly and whispered, "You see, I am to dance with the Baron Westborough."

Faith giggled and swirled around. It didn't matter if she'd mucked up the proper form of address, she didn't care. In her pretend world, she could be as improper as she wanted and the masses loved her anyway for the beauty, the grace, the privilege, and wealth—qualities she didn't possess in real life. And in her pretend world, she could renounce a prince for a baron who would smile his blinding white smile, take her arm in his, and lead her across the room. Ladies and gentleman of the highest order would recede like a confidence man's hairline. And she would feel like the princess of her mother's stories as he twirled her around the floor—

"*What* in heaven's name do you think you are doing?"

Faith stopped in midwhirl. At the sight of the duchess glaring down at her, she crumpled the gown and tried to hide it behind her back. A deep blush burned into her cheeks.

"I asked you a question, and I demand an answer."

What could she say? That for the space of a few moments she'd completely lost her mind? "The trunk fell. Your man went to fetch some tools to mend the latch, and I was repacking your clothes. . . ."

"Is that what you call it?" Lady Brayton asked with an imperious lift of her brows. She sauntered closer to Faith, her arms crossed, her eyes condemning. "How a woman of your questionable . . . charms, shall we say, convinced my brother into bringing you into this house, I cannot imagine. But what do you think Lord Westborough would say were he to learn of the liberties you've taken with my personal belongings?"

Faith was so unsettled she could hardly form a coherent thought much less a full sentence. For the life of her, she couldn't think of a single thing she'd done to earn this woman's animosity. They didn't know each other from Adam. "I don't know, mum."

Her porcelain-pretty features contorted into a mask of rage. "Do not ever address me in such a vulgar manner. You shall only address me as Lady Brayton or 'Your Grace,' *never* again as mum. Is that understood?"

And something inside Faith snapped. In the last twenty-four hours, she'd been bullied, intimidated, and threatened. She'd been torn from the only

home she'd ever known and thrust into a world
into which she'd been disdained, belittled, and
shamed to her core. She would not take it anymore.
"I understand you perfectly, Your Grace. And *you*
will address *me* as Faith or Miss Jervais. Never
again as guttersnipe or louse. Is *that* understood?"

As Faith stalked off, shoulders squared and
spine stiff, she might have been satisfied at the
shocked look on the duchess's face if she wasn't
so deuced angry.

And humiliated.

She wished the ground would open and swallow her whole. To be caught in her moment's
whimsy by the lady of the house. How completely, utterly degrading. Better Chadwick had
caught her. Or Millie. Or even Lucy.

No, it would have been just as bad, for even
among them she ranked lower than an egg-
thieving weasel.

God's teeth, she hated this place. She hated its
people—the way they walked, talked, looked at
her as if she were slime on their pristine boots.
They dropped their drawers the same way she
did. So what if some of them were made of silk.
Did that make them better than she?

Lord Westborough was probably laughing
right along with them. He probably thought her a
witless clod. Or worse, a foolish dreamer. Damn
his eyes for bringing her here.

Damn her own soul. She wanted to be just like
them.

The ledgers shut with such force that the heavy
velvet portieres draping the window rippled.

Troyce leaned back in his chair, pinched the bridge of his nose, and sighed. He'd spent half the night and most of the morning studying the estate records he'd brought with him from Westborough. The numbers carefully scribed on the pages hadn't magically bred for the better overnight; if anything, they looked more dismal now than when he'd first looked at them three months earlier.

Bloody hell.

He pushed the chair away from the desk and strode toward the window overlooking the courtyard. The rosebushes desperately needed pruning, vines choked the hedges, and weeds had overtaken the beds. His mother would be horrified if she were alive today to see the condition of her beloved garden. Appearances had meant everything to Caroline de Meir.

How had it come to this? When he'd left eight years ago, the barony had been thriving and prosperous. Or so he'd thought. According to the ledgers, it had been in a downhill spiral for nearly two decades.

Finding an investor for *La Tentatrice* should have been the perfect solution. He certainly hadn't expected everyone in London, from blue blood to sot-head, to avoid his petition—or worse, laugh him out of town. Granted, fronting the funds for the old relic was a risk, but could no one except him see its potential? Repaired, the galleon would bring in a fortune! More than enough to settle his father's massive debts, provide for the villagers, and secure the barony—and all without bowing to the Viscount of Beckham's terms: to marry a wealthy, virtuous woman of noble birth.

Unfortunately, only he seemed confident of the venture. Only he could see the diamond in the rough.

Then again, only he had his freedom at stake.

Rubbing his tired eyes, Troyce withdrew his timepiece. Instantly, Faith popped into his mind. He swore he still felt the heat of her touch upon the gold casing.

What a contradiction she was, he thought, shaking his head. Instinct told him that under her pitiful facade lay a strength of character. A boldness tempered. He couldn't explain this curiosity to peel away the seasoned layers, to uncover the gem beneath. Except that his father's blood ran through his veins, and with it, an insatiable preoccupation with restoring objects to their raw and natural beauty. Given time, patience, and care, he imagined Faith might grow into quite a beauty herself.

He returned his watch to his pocket, then gathered the estate records and stacked them neatly into a bound leather valise. Beyond the doors of his study, he could hear Millie calling out orders to the rest of the staff in preparation for the journey to the coast. Knowing that the enterprise was under her capable direction, Troyce blocked out the sounds and mentally ran through the remainder of his schedule for the morning—a meeting with his best friend Miles, another with the banker to extend the delinquent notes, a visit to Feagin's warehouse to pay back the investment money . . .

His train of thought came to a screeching halt at the sight that appeared in the doorway. For a moment, he could do naught but stare.

Faith?

She'd been sleeping peacefully when he'd left his bedchamber this morning, and knowing that today would be as taxing on her energies as the day before, he hadn't wanted to disturb her. But by God, he'd had no idea he'd been harboring an angel in disguise! Perhaps angel was stretching it a bit, for no angel could stir a man's senses to such a rousing pitch.

The transformation was astounding. Gone were the rags she'd worn since the moment he'd met her, and in their place was a crisp, starched uniform of light gray. He'd always thought the outfits drab and unflattering, just as his mother intended, but the gown only served to complement Faith's slender figure. The breasts he'd been so admiring of last night bulged against the snug white apron front, and the narrow skirt molded to the shape of her legs. Even the pallid shade seemed to complement her coloring. Unlike most English misses who coated themselves in creams and shrouded themselves in layers of clothing to protect the lily whiteness of their skin, hers had been darkened to the shade of honey by exposure to the sun, giving her a raw, earthy loveliness that he found refreshing and eminently desirable. She wore no mobcap, and the morning light streaming through the window behind him glowed in her hair, bringing out fiery highlights that matched her temper.

Where was the wild urchin who'd swiped him

blind on a London street corner? The intrepid sea monkey he'd rescued from a rose trellis the night before? The malnourished vixen who'd incited his pity and his admiration and aye, even his lust?

At last he recovered his astonishment, and said, "Good morning, Miss Jervais. I trust you slept well?"

"Well enough."

Taken aback when she strode boldly into the room, a basket of folded white cloths on her arm, he asked, "Is there a purpose to your invasion of my study at such an ungodly hour?"

"Millie told me to drape the portraits and pack your essentials," she declared with a defensive tilt of her chin.

"Indeed?" He sat on the corner of the desk and bit the inside of his cheek. "Most would request permission from the lord of the manor before barging into his private domain."

She ignored the reprimand, which amused him all the more. "I don't remember you asking my permission before dragging me from my home."

"Aren't we in a cheery mood?" he taunted.

"Do I have your permission to enter your lair, Baron Dragon?"

Baron Dragon? He grinned, knowing she hadn't meant it as an endearment. Most gentleman in his inherited social circle would have her flogged for such impertinence, but Troyce liked the fact that she didn't simper around him, calling him Lord Westborough. It made him feel more . . . human. He hadn't felt like that since leaving America. "By all means, *votre majesté*, carry on with your duties."

Anger flared in her eyes at his continued mockery of their first meeting, and Troyce felt a curious thrill that he could incite such a reaction in her. If she insisted on calling him "baron" in that defiant manner that set his blood to pumping, then turnabout was certainly fair play.

But instead of rising to the bait, she averted her face, and he found himself faintly disappointed. Why did he gain such pleasure in teasing her? Why converse with her at all? She was naught but a servant, working off her debt. And a cheeky servant at that.

He returned to his task of packing the records he would be taking back to Westborough and pretended that she was not distracting him. Not an easy feat when she seemed to delight in creating as much noise as possible. Dragging chairs across the floor. The furious swipe of a cloth. The abrupt clunk of knickknacks.

Troyce hid his grin behind his hand. Something certainly had her riled, and my, she was glorious in a temper. He watched her from beneath his lashes as she mounted a stool near the granite, floor-to-ceiling fireplace. The swish of gray skirts against her bottom as she wrestled with draping a cloth over a picture frame. And what a lovely bottom it was. Not plush and snooty as were many he'd glimpsed in his bachelor years, or low and flat from being pressed against a tuffet all the day long. No, Faith's bottom featured a midway curve that flowed gently from her spine to her thighs, and flaring hips, the perfect width to cradle a man's loins. The ribbons of her apron framed her lower figure like a gift, and he was caught with a sudden urge to tug on the ribbons and slide off the wrapping. . . .

In an effort to redirect the dangerous path his thoughts were taking, he reached for the stationery box on his desk containing his waxes, seals, and quills, and added it to the valise. "Has my sister grown accustomed to you yet?"

She hesitated a second too long. "I have much to learn."

Troyce didn't miss the troubled expression that flashed across her face before she brought it under control. "What happened?"

"Nothing." She stepped off the stool and dragged it to the next portrait. "She is merely teaching me my duties."

He could well imagine how Devon was teaching her.

Very rarely did he question his own actions, but now he had to wonder. Had he made a mistake bringing her into his home? Sentencing her to a year or more with himself and Devon at Westborough? God knew, neither of them were easy to work for. Devon alone had gone through four servants in the last three months, with her sharp tongue and exacting perfectionism. And he, well, it had been said that he often demanded more than he gave. Perhaps he'd inherited more of his mother's traits than he wanted to acknowledge.

Still with no friends and no family to rally around her and protect her, Faith was undoubtedly better off with him than if he'd left her on the streets. At least she'd have a warm bed to sleep in and decent food in her stomach.

Besides, she owed him. Greatly.

His conscience mildly appeased, he told her, "I'm certain that you'll catch on quickly." He crossed the room and removed the contents from the safe hidden behind a portrait of the second Baron of Westborough. Troyce had inherited his father's piercing gray eyes, passion for the undiscovered, and a crumbling estate built on a foundation of debt, but little else.

"Is that your father?"

"Aye, it was. Troyce de Meir, second Baron of Westborough."

"You were named for him, then."

He nodded and Faith watched him shuffle through the papers in his hand, as though searching for one in particular.

Troyce. His name filled her mouth, rich, smooth, like a warm chocolate pastry. It was a strong, strapping name, one a man could wear with dignity. "Why does no one call you Troyce?"

He paused and grinned at her. "You just did."

And Faith's stomach colly-wobbled. She kept waiting for the baron to mention the night before in his chambers, to taunt her with the power he'd wielded over her, but he didn't. The longer he avoided it, the more relieved and anxious she felt. He acted as if neither of them had stripped before the other—or at the very least, as if it was of no importance. No doubt it meant nothing to him, but she was not accustomed to a man seeing her nude, and part of her couldn't help but wonder what he must think of her.

Hell, why did she even care? She'd gotten along just fine for twenty years without his opinion, and she'd get along another twenty. "You didn't answer my question. Why does no one call you by your Christian name?"

He shrugged. "They did in America. Here, you're recognized only by the title you bear, so with the exception of my intimates, I am called West or Westborough."

That struck her as sad, though she couldn't explain why. It probably meant nothing, just some oddity of the upper class he belonged to; nobles had lists of social etiquette as long as the Thames. He didn't seem particularly troubled that no one called him by his Christian name. Yet there was something in his tone of voice, an edge of bitterness, that made her believe that few were allowed close enough to this man to be awarded such a privilege. Or maybe it was the way he diverted conversation with quick-witted quips. Almost as if he used humor to keep himself aloof.

So who was Troyce de Meir? The unconscionable gaoler? The charming rogue? The reluctant nobleman?

She strolled down the line of portraits, each one framed in burnished brass, as much to put some distance between them and collect her slowly fizzling thoughts as to discover what kind of man she was working for. The gallery boasted likenesses of ladies in high-collared, wide-panniered gowns, and gentlemen with stiff cravats choking their necks. "Is this the rest of your family?"

"Aye. Most of them are distant relations on my father's side—aunts, uncles, cousins. We hardly know one another, but my mother always insisted on putting them on display for company."

He sidestepped, closing the gap between them until their shoulders were nearly touching. The scent of him surrounded her, potent, inviting. She barely heard the names he recounted.

"And this stodgy old goat is *mon grandpère*," he said, pointing to portrait of a stern but distinguished gentleman with familiar gray eyes. "Oliver de Meir, sixth Viscount of Beckham and first Baron of Westborough. He was once a French merchant, you know." At the surprised lift of her brows, he went on, "It's true. He came to England when he was a young man—only a few years younger than I—and earned himself the barony for service to King Edward; later, he pleased the king again and became a viscount; the barony, as his subordinate title, was given to my father at his birth as a courtesy."

The baron hailed from common stock? She never would have guessed! Why she'd been under the impression that the Westborough aristocracy had been in existence for centuries she couldn't say. Perhaps it was the pride in which the baron carried himself, or the way he seemed to blend so well with the upper class, as if it was in his blood. "What was your title at birth?"

"I didn't have one until my father died six months ago, then I inherited his and became the third Baron of Westborough. And when the old man dies, I will no doubt be cursed with the superior dignity of becoming the seventh Viscount of Beckham."

"How dreadfully confusing."

"I agree wholeheartedly. Quite unnecessary, too."

She envied him the ability to trace his lineage back through the generations. He knew his father and his grandfather. He knew his cousins and uncles and the rest of his family. She knew far too little.

And far too much.

"If you hate the titles so much, why don't you just refuse them?"

He looked amazed that she would ask such a question. She probably wouldn't have been so bold in her curiosity if his disdain for his lineage wasn't so obvious.

"It doesn't work that way. Once earned, the titles are passed down from generation to generation, except in rare cases when our Sovereign is feeling generous and creates a new one. It is the obligation of a nobleman to care for those under his protection."

"Where I come from, we take care of ourselves."

"Ah, so that explains why you sent off your friend—to protect yourself."

The mention of Scatter—by indication if not by name—caught her off guard. She'd tried not to let herself think of him, of how she'd left him behind, of how much she missed the pesky little beggar. "Of course. He'd have only landed me in prison."

"Instead he landed you here."

Aye, he did, Faith thought. And at the moment she didn't know whether to thank him or strangle him.

Orders being barked outside the study served to remind Faith of her purpose in the room. The last thing she needed was for the duchess to catch her idle. Nothing she did seemed to please the woman as it was; not that she'd ever tell the baron that. . . .

She reached into the basket and withdrew a square of oilcloth, then positioned the stool just below the stern visage of the sixth Viscount of Beckham. As she climbed upon the stool, the baron moved to her side and reached for the drape.

"Let me give you a hand with that."

"I can do it myself."

He pulled the cloth toward himself. "It will go a lot faster with my help."

She pulled the cloth back. "As you so *kindly* remind me, I am the one working off a debt." And the faster she could get that done, the sooner she would have her freedom back.

Again he pulled on the cloth. Again she pulled it back. Back and forth they went, each jerking the oilcloth away from the other until one solid tug threw Faith off-balance. She floundered on the stool, waving her arms like a duckling to keep from falling.

In the end, it served no purpose.

She fell against him, throwing him off-balance, and both tumbled to the floor. With the wind knocked out of him, it took Troyce a moment to realize what had happened.

What he'd *made* happen. A yearning to feel Faith's body against his had been haunting him ever since she'd bared her naked body to him the night before. Perhaps the accident hadn't been such an accident at all.

He knew the instant Faith had come to the same

conclusion. Her body stiffened, her brown eyes darkened. "You did that on purpose!"

He couldn't help it. He grinned.

Anger sparked in her eyes. She struggled against him. Reflex took over. His hands tightened on her upper arms. "Faith, wait—"

Whatever he meant to say lost its importance when she fell back against him. Desire slammed through Troyce's midsection like cannon fire. One look at her startled expression told him that she was as shocked by the contact as he.

Her hair had come loose from its tidy coiffure and fell on either sides of their faces, creating a shield of filigree amber and gold, fire and ice. Her eyes, seconds ago hard and flat, grew soft and round. The air simmered. He felt himself growing warm, stuffy in his jacket, his collar choking him. God, those eyes, that face. Was there ever a maid so pretty?

She had the most beautiful skin. Not pallid like so many English misses, but smooth and golden and nearly flawless, save for the purpling bruise on her jawline. The sight of it in the broad light of day sent another stab of anger. He didn't believe her story last night any more than he believed her claim of being Queen Victoria. There was also a scar above her lip, a tiny lightning bolt that made him think of stormy nights and sultry air and sweaty skin. He rolled his lips inward. His chest went tight.

And when her gaze dropped to his mouth, the self-control he'd always prided in himself slipped another notch. Her brows dipped with puzzled curiosity, as if she'd never seen a mouth before.

Troyce heard the warning go off in his brain but ignored it as, of its own volition, his hand moved toward her cheek and his head lifted off the floor. Just one kiss, was all. Just one taste . . .

"Is this a private party, or can anyone join?"

Troyce and Faith snapped toward the inquisitor in the same second his best friend's grinning face appeared mere inches from his own. Troyce let his hand drop, and the back of his skull thumped against the carpeting and he cursed the oblivion that enshrouded him from everything but Faith. "Damn it all, Miles . . ."

His grin widened. Crouched on all fours beside them, he inclined his head toward Faith, who remained atop Troyce, her features frozen in shock. "Aren't you going to introduce us?"

Snapped from her spell, Faith scrambled backward off Troyce. Her knee caught him between his thighs. Troyce gasped, cupped himself, and swung one leg over the other as pain ricocheted through a stiff and highly sensitive portion of his anatomy.

Faith cried out and instantly crawled to his side while Miles, the damned scoundrel, fell back on his arse and burst into peals of hilarity.

"Quit laughing, you buffoon!" Faith scolded him. Turning to Troyce, her hands fluttered above his lower half, but she didn't seem to know where to touch him. "Oh, God, Baron, did I hurt you?"

Spots danced before his eyes. Beads of cold sweat broke out on his brow. He was afraid to move, afraid to breathe. Struck with a sudden and all-too-realistic insight of how a horse might feel being gelded, Troyce could do no more than singe the air with dockside vulgarities.

"Damn it, stop swearin' and answer me! Are you all right?"

Her concern penetrated the painful haze befogging his brain. "Quite all right, *cherie*," Troyce assured her through gritted teeth. "Just give me a moment."

"Ah God, what a lark!" Miles roared with laughter.

Faith glared at him. "I cannot believe that you think this is funny!"

He only laughed harder.

"Faith," Troyce said, "that guffawing jackanapes over there is Lord Miles Heath, my soon-to-be *former* best friend. Miles, this is Faith. She has recently joined my staff."

"Indeed?" Miles said, bringing his mirth under control. Cobalt blue eyes that had melted female hearts all over the world glittered with lingering amusement as he leaned over and took Faith's hand in his own. "You always did have impeccable taste in servants."

A becoming flush rose in Faith's cheeks when Miles lightly kissed the tips of her knuckles, and an odd sense of possessiveness gripped Troyce's insides. "And you've always been notorious for your bad timing."

Irritation made his tone harsher than it should have been. In truth, Troyce supposed he should be grateful that only Miles had caught him and Faith in such a scandalous position. Anyone walking by could have seen him flat on his back in the middle of his study floor, Faith atop him, her skirts hiked up to her knees like a common tart. Rumors would have flown, and the chance he'd wanted to give her for a respectable living ruined. And it would have been all his fault. What the hell had he been thinking?

Kissing Faith, that's what he'd been thinking. If he were honest with himself, he'd admit that he'd been thinking about a whole lot more than kissing her. What man wouldn't, with the lushness of a comely woman's breasts crushed against his chest, her shapely legs entwined with his, her sweet lips mere inches from his own . . . ?

Heading off the thoughts before they spun into a direction best not traveled again, Troyce forced himself to sit. A cramp seized his gut; his world went from pitch-black to blinding white. In that instant, he didn't see how the morning could get any worse.

Then Devon walked in.

Chapter 6

"**T**royce, I simply must speak to you about that—good heavens!"

Three sets of eyes turned as one toward the doorway where Devon stood, Lucy behind her, both wearing identical expressions of shock.

"*What* is going on here?"

Troyce knew how it must look—himself sprawled on the floor, Faith, hovering over him, her hair mussed, her cheeks flushed, and Miles all but slobbering over her hand.

"A small mishap, Devon, nothing more." He rolled to his side, pushed himself off the floor, and struggled to his feet. At least his stomach had settled and the sharp throbbing in his groin had subsided. There was still a lingering tenderness, but his equipment didn't seem to have sustained any permanent damage. He was lucky he hadn't been crippled. "Faith, perhaps you should see if Millie needs any assistance in the kitchen."

Nodding vigorously, she marched past Devon, out of the study. As if sensing that her presence was not required, either, Lucy followed, leaving himself, Miles, and Devon alone in the room.

The air went thick with tension. A near-violent electricity swirled between his sister and his best friend, a storm of disquiet. The two shared a past, he knew, as childhood friends and sweethearts. There was a time when he even thought they'd marry. But their parents had had more influence over his sister than he'd thought. Neither Devon nor Miles had ever discussed the events of that night eight years ago, nor had he ever pressed for details; whatever had happened between them to drive Miles to America and Devon into the arms of Miles's older brother was between the two of them.

But neither had been the same since.

The dense silence finally broke when Devon hissed, "What is *he* doing here?"

"Miles is here at my request."

Her face went ashen, and betrayal glittered in her eyes, so brilliant and wounding that Troyce had to look away. It was hell when a man was forced to choose between his best mate and his only sister. "Was there something you wished to discuss with me?"

"Another time, perhaps. This room has developed a decidedly foul odor."

And she followed in Faith's wake.

"She's hasn't changed a bit, has she? Still has

her nose so far up in the air that she'd drown if it rained."

Troyce would have disagreed if it wasn't so true.

"I appreciate you coming by on such notice, Miles," Troyce said.

"If I'd have known you had feisty beauties falling from the ceiling, I'd have been over much sooner. I've always fancied strawberry blondes."

Realizing from the description that he was referring to Faith and not Devon, Troyce turned to his friend. Lord Miles Heath boasted much to interest the ladies. Blond good looks, a sizable bank account, and more charm than devil on his best day. It was not uncommon for those of the fairer sex to make utter fools of themselves to gain his notice. "Cast your eyes elsewhere, mate, she is far out of your league."

"Oh-ho, so that's the way of it!"

"The way of what?"

"You're taken with the chit yourself."

"Don't be absurd. She's a servant."

"Since when has that stopped you?"

Troyce thought of his short liaison with Lucy a decade ago, and of other dalliances with chambermaids during his misspent youth, both in England and abroad. His mother had been horrified by his womanizing, but his father had seen no harm in it. Nor had Troyce. Sowing oats he'd called it. But those women were different, they'd played the games before and knew the rules. Faith didn't have that advantage. Aye, she was a servant, and considering his history, it probably shouldn't make a difference to him. Yet the thought of indulging himself with her to satisfy his own sexual appetites seemed somehow—sacrilegious. "She's an innocent."

"She didn't look so innocent a few minutes ago." Miles dropped into the seat of a Hepplewhite chair, hooked one leg over the arm, and folded his arms behind his head in a typically ungentleman-like pose. "Where on earth did you find such a gel?"

"Outside Jorge's. The cheeky chit picked my pocket."

After pouring fresh coffee from the server and spiking both cups with a dose of brandy, Troyce went on to tell his friend of the meeting with Feagin, up to and including his nasty abuse of Faith and her young companion. It never occurred to him to hide his activities from Miles. They'd known each other since birth; their coastal properties joined on the westernmost tip. Miles had accompanied him to America after that last horrible row between him and his father and grandfather. With the exception of what had transpired between his friend and his sister, there was nothing the two didn't know about each other, no secret that hadn't been shared, no adventure that hadn't been experienced together.

But for the first time in their lives, after he'd explained Faith's appearance in his life and his subsequent falling-out with his investor, he wished he'd kept his mouth shut.

"Good God, West, just make her return the money!"

"I tried. She claimed not to have it. I suspect she passed it on to her young cohort."

"Then make her get it back."

Why didn't he? It would be the most logical solution. Bloody hell. America had made him weak. Or England had made him daft. Better he started worrying about his own predicament than squander time pondering his newest serving girl. Easier said than done if he could just erase the picture in his mind of her defending the scamp. "I fear the money is long gone."

"Has it occurred—never mind."

"What?"

"Nothing. 'Tis none of my affair."

"You've not hoarded your opinions to yourself before, Miles. Pray don't let yourself be stopped now."

His friend turned to him, visibly debating with himself. "All right," he gave a decisive nod. "The situation strikes me as a bit too convenient. A seemly chit accosts you outside a tavern, robs you of your last farthing before it's even grown warm in your hand, then allows you to drag her off the streets into your home. . . ."

"What are you saying?"

"Has it not occurred to you that perhaps your pretty little wench may have planned the entire charade?"

"That's ridiculous, Miles."

"You are not without reputation."

"And you are being overly cynical. Even if she had known me, she could not have known that I would bring her to my home instead of turning her over to the authorities. She is what she is."

"Aye, and that's what worries me. We're no longer callow boys, West. We know what it's like to scrape bottom. We've tasted despair and been embroiled in desperation, or have you forgotten the early days?"

"Of course I haven't forgotten." Hell he'd been young and full of himself, so cocksure he could conquer the world in a day. Learning that the world fought tooth and nail had been a nasty awakening for himself and Miles.

"From what you've told me, the gel's spent most of her life on the streets. She's a survivor, West. I'd bet my last farthing that she's learned how to use the talents God gave her well, just as we did. She would not be the first pretty wench to try and lure you into a compromising situation for her advantage."

Again, it was on the tip of his tongue to refute the charges being cast against Faith, but as much as Troyce wanted to dismiss them, a seed of doubt had been planted. What if Miles was right? Had Faith plotted the whole scenario? And if so, had he simply been in the wrong place at the wrong time, or had he been marked a pigeon from the start?

It was hard to believe Faith guilty of such duplicity. She was too . . . outspoken. Straightforward. But comments she'd made seemed to support the charge: his being "rich as Midas," her seemingly casual interest in his lineage. . . . As Miles had pointed out, she was a street survivor. That made her wiser to manipulation than the average gel.

Well, if she thought to use him to better herself, then she could think again. His father had fallen into that trap—married a woman who wanted him for his position and fortune after she'd lured him into compromising her reputation. He'd been too besotted by her to notice. And if Faith thought to rook him out of a fortune, she'd soon learn the error of her ways. He no longer had a fortune to rook.

"Your point is well taken. But I didn't invite you here to discuss Faith."

"Then what did you invite me over to discuss?"

"Real estate."

He handed over a velum slip, which Miles scanned, eyes growing wide in astonishment.

"The deed to Radcliff?"

Both were well aware that the paper was nearly priceless. Privately owned town houses were a rarity in London, and to possess a deed bespoke of a prestige that far exceeded the title.

"You've long coveted property closer to the city."

"Aye, but Radcliff?"

"I need the money, and I'm running out of options," Troyce stated without preamble.

"Isn't this a bit extreme?"

"Until I find an investor, I can't repair the ship, which means I cannot pay the taxes on any of the family holdings, so I will lose them to my father's creditors unless I sell. And I'd much rather you have Radcliff than let it revert to the crown."

"I've offered to invest in *La Tentatrice*, Troyce."

"If she belonged only to me, there is no one I would trust more. But I'm sure you understand why I can't accept your generous offer."

"It is extended to you, not *her*." Venom dripped

from that one word, reminding Troyce of the pain his sister had caused to his best mate.

"Be that as it may, Devon holds half interest and she would never forgive me if I entered into an agreement with you."

"Then for God's sake, let me at least lend you the money to settle your father's debts."

"If I were confident that I could pay you back, I might consider it." Miles had accomplished what he set out to do in America—made himself incomparable in fortune and power. Troyce had never wished for their friendship to be tarnished because of it, and so never called upon his friend's good fortune or generous nature to bail him out of trouble. "But you and I both know that there are no guarantees that Westborough can be salvaged, or that *La Tentatrice* will sell, and I will not compromise our friendship."

Miles held up the sheaf of papers and cocked his head. "Is Beckham aware of this?"

"I don't feel the need to inform my grandfather. Radcliff belonged to my father, not him, and I've never held any attachment to it."

At length, Miles's sigh of resignation conveyed that he considered himself a carrion preying on a dead carcass. What he couldn't seem to understand was that Troyce would be glad to rid himself of the house where his father had drawn his last breath. To him, it signified nothing more than a last, desperate extravagance to please a mother who would never be pleased.

"How much?" his friend asked.

Troyce quoted the figure he'd arrived at, enough to pay off Feagin and settle the enormous balance of his father's debts, as well as provide a small household stipend once they moved back to Westborough.

With a stiff nod, Miles agreed on the amount and scribbled his signature on the sheets of paper Troyce presented. After he took his leave, Troyce picked up the promissory note and his copy of the signed bill of sale.

First, the loss of two hundred pounds and an investor for his ship; now, he was giving up his London town house. Bloody hell, what was he to lose next?

"Did you enjoy making a spectacle of yourself with his lordship?"

Her heart racing faster than an Ascot thoroughbred, Faith spun around so quickly that the tray of silverware she'd been instructed to pack scattered across the floor. Had her nerves not been so highly strung from the scene in the baron's study, she would have heard the footsteps approaching from behind. Crikey, not even a full day away from the streets and already her senses were dulling.

She knelt and began plucking utensils off the polished floor. "Bugger off, Lucy, I've got work to do."

"Yes, I saw you at work." She laughed. "I also saw the way you looked at him." She sauntered deeper into the dining room and stood at the table, trailing her fingers along the surface. "You're wasting your time, you know. Men like Lord Westborough care nothing for a woman's sensibilities, they care only about getting them into their beds."

"Lord Westborough has no interest in bedding me."

"Either you are the stupidest chit I've ever met or the most naive. For reasons I cannot fathom, his lordship fancies you. But do not fool yourself into thinking his interest will gain you any advantages. You're fresh duck, that's all. You can throw yourself at him, flaunt yourself before him, seduce him till the crows molt. But it will not change the fact that he's nobility, and you're nothing but a common scullery maid. He will amuse himself with you, nothing more."

"Really? And how would you know what amuses the baron?"

"Because I've been one of his amusements."

Faith longed to swipe that superior smirk off her face. "Yes, I can see that you would be."

Her pallid face turned three shades of red, and if looks were daggers, Faith would have been sliced to shreds. "Mock me if you will, but mark my words, 'tis I who will be laughing in the end, because when the time comes, Lord Westborough will do his duty and marry a lady of breeding and *you* will be left with nothing save a broken heart and the shame of his bastard in your belly."

With that parting remark, Lucy spun on her ankle and walked out of the dining room.

Faith remained on the floor on her knees, her fingers clenched around the hilt of sterling silver serving spoon. What she wouldn't do for five minutes—just five minutes—alone with the uppity little she-cat in a back-street alley. . . .

Crikey, first Lady Brayton, then her maid. The two must come from the same bloody pod. Well, t'hell with them both. Fanny Jarvis of Bethnal

Green would have stomped both women's arses into a mudhole by now.

But she wasn't Fanny Jarvis anymore.

And she was for certain not in Bethnal Green.

For the rest of the morning, she threw herself into the task of loading baggage into a pair of gleaming black carriages parked in the front drive. When Millie declared all in readiness, they set off.

The carriage ride was much the same as the last one, with Faith scared. Excited. Resentful. Grateful. Too many conflicting emotions to sort out. Only the company had changed. Instead of the baron, the elderly housekeeper snored in the seat across from her. Behind them in a second carriage, Lucy rode with Lady Brayton, who Millie had announced would be staying the summer at Westborough Manor, much to Faith's dismay, and returning to the city for the Queen's Golden Jubilee. It was an enormous event, a pickpocket's dream. Nobility from all over the Continent were planning to attend.

Unfortunately, she'd not be attending any events. As the baron seemed to delight in reminding her, she'd made her choices—more or less—and for better or worse, she was stuck with them.

For now.

Faith supposed she should think of this as the grand adventure she'd so often dreamed of, the chance to leave her old way of life and begin fresh somewhere else. Maybe even become . . . respectable. Unfortunately, her day had been one extreme after another, and all she could think of was that she hadn't been out of the city in almost two decades, and the realization that not only was her "adventure" taking her from everything familiar, but it was also taking her closer to the point of no return.

And so, as the coach jostled along rutted paths and through the wide-open country, she purposely kept her mind blank and her body numb rather that try to imagine what awaited her at the baron's "country estate."

The day drew on, and as the coach rolled across flat, grassy lanes dotted with tall leafy trees and short, clipped hedgerows, she found herself absorbing the sights and sounds and smells of the countryside, as far removed from the rookeries of London as she'd ever been. They passed prosperous farms and elegant mansions, quaint villages, and slapdash marketplaces, and once, even, a summer fair in a roadside park, where lasses danced gaily and young gents dodged between them, tugging on their ribbons, while others raced horses to impress them.

Scatter would have loved this, she found herself thinking as she watched the festivities from the window. The sights and sounds, the sense of adventure mixed with the simple freedom of being a boy. He had often regaled her with stories of his time in Sherwood Forest, living off the land, outwitting the traveling peddlers, imagining himself some sort of Robin Hood, except in stealing from the rich and giving to the poor, he pocketed the gold himself, claiming he *was* the poor. Like herself, he'd lost his innocence too young and gained harsh wisdom too soon.

Refusing to mourn over what could not be changed, she rested her head against the coach and tried not to dwell on the past, the present, and, most especially, the uncertain future. But as the coach rolled past the festivities, Faith spotted a sweet young couple strolling hand in hand a good distance away from the crowd. The girl looked like a princess bride in a flowing pink gown, a wreath of summer flowers on her head, and ribbons trailing her skirts from the posy in her hand. And the dapper gent seemed so besotted as he looked down at her, laughed at something she said, then popped a kiss on her mouth.

A spot of envy took roost in her middle. For one brief moment, her mind rolled back to that moment in the baron's study. Never in her entire life had she badly wanted to be kissed by a man. Her cheek tingled where he'd touched it, her body still burned where it had been pressed against his. . . .

She was twenty years old, near as she could remember. She had never been kissed, never been courted, never been romanced. But it hadn't stopped her from dreaming. An honorable and noble prince, dark of looks and strong of heart . . .

Faith shook the image away. The fairy-tale dreams of her childhood had been shattered by the harsh realities of London underworld. There was no room for such nonsense in the tunnels. The best she could ever hope for now was to seek out a modest, respectable living, as far from Jack Swift and Bethnal Green as possible. That meant staying in his lordship's good graces. No more lipping off. No more challenging his authority. Like it or not, he owned her until she paid off the bloody two hundred pounds she'd swiped. Even though he couldn't prove that she'd taken it, all that was needed was his word. Who would the courts believe? A member of English nobility or a Bethnal Green guttersnipe? She knew the answer to that.

Aye, a wise woman would stick with her tiny dreams. Lucy was right. A man like Lord Westborough would never give a street rat like her a second glance. No one would.

Even her own family wanted nothing to do with her.

Chapter 7

"Let's take a look at what we've got," Jesse Justiss announced to the room.

Honesty stepped back to allow her husband space at the table. He dumped an armload of items onto the polished mahogany surface of her father's dining room table: newspaper clippings from the *San Francisco Chronicle* featuring the abduction of the Jervais twins and the search for culprits, photos of herself and her sister, maps of California and the surrounding states, and reports of the investigation.

Jesse bowed over the table, his weight braced on one leg, and bent his head to study the collection amassed over sixteen years. Her father Anton and her cousin, Alex, followed suit. Both were impressive men, not nearly so impressive as her husband, but their fair coloring and strong features would still turn the head of any woman.

A sense of *déjà vu* hit Honesty as she watched the three of them, a feeling that she'd seen men gathered here before, heavy into discussions that held no interest to a pair of inquisitive young girls. The image of her sister filled her mind then, so stark and detailed she felt as if she were seeing her in the flesh. She was riding in a fine coach pulled by four horses across a vale of blinding greens—

"The house is here," Anton said, pointing to a spot on the map.

The image disappeared.

Honesty grabbed for it, but it was like trying to catch a whisper. Shaken, she moved to her husband's side and clasped his hand.

"And the cemetery here," Anton continued. "It's the last place the girls were seen together."

Her gaze met Alex's across the table, then Alex looked quickly away. She knew he still felt guilty for not watching them during their mother's funeral. "I wish I could remember that day. I feel like it would help."

"You were only four years old," Jesse said.

"One cannot expect a girl of such tender years to remember such an early incident," her father added consolingly. "I've heard that the mind will block out traumatic events but memories can return when the person is of greater strength and stability to handle them."

A look of intense sorrow passed across her cousin's eyes so quickly that Honesty wondered if she had imagined it. She had never considered her years with Deuce McGuire traumatic. He might not have had the wealth and respectability of Anton Jervais, but he'd been a good father who'd doted on her and made her laugh and kept her safe to his last breath. "So it's possible that I will recall my abduction."

"Anything's possible," Jesse said.

"Do you think Faith remembers?"

"I cannot imagine she does," Alex gruffly said, "else she would have found her way back to us as you did."

Neither spoke of the high possibility that she might not have been *able* to return. It was not a point any of them was willing to consider at this moment. "It could be that she is attempting that as we speak," Honesty said.

"It's as I said, anything's possible," Jesse repeated.

When his eyes lit on her and lingered, Honesty blushed. They'd spent the entire night celebrating what Jesse called the beginning of the rest of their lives. Her body was sore in places she hadn't known could ache and still she wanted him.

As if sensing her rekindled desire, he winked, then turned back to the table. "In the meantime, we're going to turn back the clock and collect every piece of information we can find. Anton, I'm aware that your brother Phillipe was behind the abductions. What I don't know is why. Anything you can tell me might shed some light on who he might have hired to take the girls."

"My wife's family was not supportive of our marriage. I had spent my entire life building ships, as had my father, and his father before that. Her family thought she'd wed beneath her and made our lives quite . . . difficult. After the girls were born, it got worse. They even threatened to take Aniste and Faith from us. So we thought it best to leave France. I'd heard of the opportunities to be found in America, so we boarded a liner for California. It was here that I built Jervais Shipping. Phillipe arrived a year or so after that with Alex here, who was barely ten at the time. He'd lost his mother on the voyage, and my wife took him under her wing. I put Phillipe in charge of one of the warehouses." He stepped away from the table to stare out the window at the ocean in the distance. "I knew almost immediately that it wasn't working out. He and I got into many arguments over decisions he was making about my company without my knowledge, and he accused me of being a stubborn Frenchman who knew how to build but knew nothing of business. He claimed that if it wasn't for him, Jervais Shipping would have failed. I should have fired him then, but he was my brother, newly widowed, with a young son to support, and my wife . . ." His voice cracked. "My beloved Cossette was dying. I suppose I turned a blind eye." Anton shook his head. "Phillipe had made no secret of his desire to own Jervais Shipping, but I had no idea the lengths he was willing to go to get what he wanted."

A flock of long-beaked white birds flew past the bay windows, and a sailboat drifted out of the harbor, its canvasses billowing in the wind. Snippets of the story Anton had told last night at supper came back to Honesty. She could only imagine what anguish her father had suffered when he'd discovered his own brother was responsible for stealing—and presumably murdering—his two daughters on the day of his wife's burial.

"According to the police reports, Deuce McGuire wasn't the only suspect in the girls' abduction. A second man was believed to have been involved."

"That's right," Alex concurred. "There were a great many people at the funeral that day; we were all suspects at one time or another. But since a positive identification could not be made, the abduction of both girls was laid on McGuire."

As if aware of how uncomfortable it made Honesty to be talking of the man she'd been so fond of for sixteen years in front of her, her father added, "It was also hoped that when McGuire was found he might reveal the identity of his accomplice."

"Except he had no accomplice to his knowledge." Jesse scanned the letter Deuce McGuire had left behind for Honesty to find. It had taken her and Jesse months to unravel the riddle and track down the "flowing stones of time." "He only mentions being hired by someone who promised him wealth beyond his wildest dreams. McGuire took Honesty, that's a fact. But he never once mentioned Faith, nor can I find anything to substantiate his involvement in her abduction, which leads me to believe that there was a second man involved." Jesse slid a yellow-edged photograph out of the pile. "Does either of you recognize this man?"

"His name was Frances Capshaw," Anton announced, glancing on the image. "His friends called him 'Cappy.' He worked in the shipyards, but we let him go after we discovered that he was selling cargo on the black market."

"Is this the man who took Faith?" Honesty asked, looking at the picture over Anton's shoulder.

"I think it's a strong possibility," Jesse said. "Phillipe must have known the risks in taking the girls himself, so he had to hire someone to keep his hands clean. I've spent years tracking criminals. One of the easiest ways to throw the scent off your trail is to split the gang. I think Phillipe arranged for Capshaw to take one, McGuire the other. Once the ransom was paid and the girls returned, they would split the money and disappear."

"Except my fath—Deuce spoiled the plan when he learned that Phillipe had no intention of returning me alive."

"Exactly. Which leads me to believe that McGuire had been nothing but a pawn all along."

"What makes you think Cappy was the second man?" Alex asked.

"Someone would need to take the blame. Who has better motive and means than a disgruntled employee? I've not been able to find a single connection between McGuire and Phillipe, but my gut tells me we'll find one between Capshaw and McGuire."

"Well, what are we waiting for?" Honesty cried, hope rising inside her for the first time since she'd discovered her sister missing. "Let's talk to this Cappy fellow!"

"Unfortunately that's not possible. He was killed in a brawl a week after the abduction," Alex said. "Several witnesses will attest to it."

No! Oh, God. Oh, God.

"I also believe that's why the case was dropped

for so long; Since McGuire seemed to have disappeared off the face of the earth, the only other viable suspect had been killed, and with the girls believed dead . . ."

"How will we find out if he was responsible for taking Faith now?"

The silence in the room became deafening. The men looked at each other, as if the answer might be found in one of their worried expressions.

Finally, Alex said, "Uncle Anton, do you remember hearing rumors of his involvement with a woman around the time he was caught selling the cargo?"

"Yes, yes. A woman of ill repute down near the wharf. Alice Moore was her name, if I remember correctly."

Honesty wasted not a second in seizing her shawl from the back of a chair. A flick of her wrist sent Jesse's hat sailing toward him. "Let's go, then."

"Where the hell do you think you're going," he asked, catching the Stetson.

"To the docks with you. If we can find this Alice person, she might be able to tell us something."

Alice Moore was not the type of woman that inspired hope. She had the look of a small barge that had ridden through one too many storms. Her hair was an odd mix of sunset red and royal purple, and hung in coarse shanks down to her knees. She had washed-out green eyes with bags down to her cheekbones, a bulbous nose, and three chins.

And Honesty had never been so glad to see anyone in her life.

It had taken them the entire morning and a small fortune to track her down. The shanty they found her in reeked of stale sex and onions and beer. The only pieces of furniture in the room were a bed that Honesty wouldn't have sat on if her life depended on it, a shredded chair with stuffing bulging out from the tears in the horsehide, and a table bearing a soot-crusted lamp. There was a charred black cookstove in the far corner with a cast-iron skillet that hadn't been washed in who knew when, and a slanted wooden cupboard with no food in sight.

She and Jesse crowded together on a bench at the table. Honesty had never thought of herself as a snob. After all, she'd spent half her life living in everything from tents to train cars to brothels, some places so pathetic as would have offended a stray dog. But never had she been exposed to such filth, and she was careful not to touch anything but her husband.

"McGuire . . . McGuire," Alice said, tapping her finger against her cheek. "I don't know. Been a lot of men in my life. Not sure I could recollect one from the other."

"Maybe this will jar your memory." Jesse held out a shining gold piece and her eyes lit up.

"I think it's coming back to me now. . . ."

She reached for the coin, but he snatched it back. "Not till you answer our questions."

She fell back in the chair with a pout, and Honesty swore the house shook. "He was some Irishman that used to come around now and again. I haven't seen him in years."

"What was his connection to Cappy?"

"Cappy?"

If not for Jesse's restraining arm across her waist, Honesty would have come out of the chair at her pretense of stupidity. Up until now, she'd kept quiet and still while he "interviewed the subject." But she was fast reaching the end of her patience.

"Frances Capshaw. We know you were involved with him."

"So what? I been involved with lots of men."

"So, we also know that Cappy did some work with two gentlemen: McGuire and Phillipe Jervais. Tell us what you know about their business with a little girl."

She went suddenly quiet, and her eyes darkened before she dropped her gaze to her lap. "I don't know nothing about no little girl."

And Honesty snapped. "You're lying." Even her husband's arm couldn't stop her from rising off the bench and storming toward the woman. "Let me tell you something, Mrs. Moore," she hissed in her rolled face. "I've spent most of my life living with people who would eat you for breakfast. We know she was here." Just the thought of her sister in this hovel made her stomach turn. "Now tell me what you did with her, or I promise you, you will regret it."

Drawn back into herself, she glanced around Honesty's shoulder and pleaded to Jesse for help. "Can't you do something with this she-cat?"

" 'Fraid not. She's one mean interrogator," he replied, beaming.

Realizing that she'd just signed herself onto a losing battle, Alice blurted, "I got rid of her! On a ship."

"What ship?" Honesty demanded, her hands on the arms of the chair.

"I don't remember the name. Just some ship in the harbor. Climbin' Christophers, I only had her with me a few days, and she was driving me daft. Kept staring at me with those deer eyes—"

"When?"

"A couple days after Cappy kicked the bucket. McGuire ran off with his share of the money. When Cappy found out, he met Jervais at the tavern and told him he was going to spill if he didn't come up with some tuppas real quick. Next thing I know, Cappy's dead. A couple of the boys said a fight broke out in a tavern, and he got caught in the middle. If ya ask me, Jervais done him in."

Jesse nodded, as if the news didn't surprise him. "That's right about the same time the hunters started after Deuce."

"Why didn't you just turn the girl over to the police?" Honesty pressed. "You had to know she belonged to someone."

" 'Course I knew. It was all over the papers. I knew if I got caught with her, they'd think I nabbed her so I took her to the first ship in the harbor and convinced one of the fellows I knew aboard to take her with him."

"How did her clothes end up in the water?" Jesse asked.

"I was taking her up the plank when she started

crying because she'd spilt something on her dress, so I ripped it off her and threw it into the bay. Later on, it washed up and she was pronounced dead. And my problems were over."

Honesty narrowed her eyes on the smiling face. "That's where you are wrong, Alice. Because if we don't find her safe and sound, your problems have only just begun."

They lost a week poring over shipping logs and manifests in every office of every shipping station in San Francisco. Anton used his considerable power in the city to commission the records, and to Honesty's admiration, often worked with them late into the night. She was learning so much about the man who'd sired her, and for the first time in sixteen years, realized that though her life had gone on in blissful ignorance, his had stopped the day his wife and girls were taken from him. And she desperately wanted to give him back some of what he'd lost, to try and make up for the sorrow that had rested deep in his heart for so many years.

Hope was waning, though, that they would be able to find the name of the ship and its destination, until one day, a small entry in the captain's log of the *Queen Victoria* caught their notice. "Several weeks into the journey, a young stowaway of near four years was found in the hold. Couldn't speak. Upon interrogation of the crew, one of the seaman confessed that his sister had just died, and that he was taking the child to relatives. . . ."

"Do you think he was talking about Faith?"

"I think it's a distinct possibility. Right now, it's the only one we've got."

Honesty fell against her husband. "Oh, God, Jesse, she could be anywhere."

He tipped her chin up, kissed her nose, and grinned. "Anywhere in *England*."

Chapter 8

The sleepy barony of Westborough lay in the Downs directly between the thick woodlands of West Sussex and the bare and arable view of East Sussex, with the English Channel to the south and the wilder landscape of the Weald to the north. Clumps of beech and ash held in their embrace a village that had birthed itself from Westborough's womb at the foot of blinding green hills, then encroached upward on the gently swelling slopes.

Horse hooves clattered in a hollow rhythm as Troyce guided his black steed across the stone bridge stretching toward the estate. A gusty wind whipped at his coat, bringing with it the tang of limestone cliffs and the briny scent of seawater. Before him, the manor house itself loomed against the azure sky like a sea captain's widow, tall, proud, lonely, a centuries-old sentinel for way-ward ships crossing the Channel. She stood three stories high upon the summit of a chalk-faced hill that dipped its base into the Channel. Notched turrets flanked her north and south walls, and ivy had taken control of the western walls, leaving the quarried white stone of her pediment bare to the elements.

The journey had been uneventful. Lonely even. Troyce had often found himself wishing for the banter shared with Faith on their first carriage ride. Of course, the lord of the manor would never share a coach with a female servant, and so she had ridden in the company of Millie while he had ridden on horseback, alone.

He was suddenly nervous about her reaction to his home. He probably shouldn't have taken her to Radcliff first; no doubt he'd given her false ex-pectations. At the time it had seemed a more pru-dent decision than making the long journey to Westborough. Though easily a half day's ride in good weather, the same couldn't be said in the dark of night and under such gloomy conditions, and he'd suspected that she would run the first chance she got.

It seemed his instincts had been right on the mark.

An image of her royal pain in the behind hang-ing by her pant hems from the trellis like a sea monkey the night before had him chuckling.

At least there were no trellises at Westborough.

A crunching against the oyster-shell drive drew his attention to the lavish pair of landaulets bear-ing the Duke of Brayton's crest, each drawn by a matching set of black Percherons. Troyce swung out of the saddle of his own mount just as Chadwick, his steward, valet, and groomsman all rolled into one, set the brake of the first carriage near the gate of the low stone wall surrounding the manor. The lines of weariness around the old man's eyes and increasing stoop of his shoulders concerned him.

"How are you faring, Chadwick?" he asked, noticing as well the addition of gray in his rumpled pepper black hair. Though he suspected he only stayed with him out of concern that his advanced years would hinder employment elsewhere, he still appreciated Chadwick's loyalty.

"Well as can be expected, milord." His gaze strayed to the manor house.

"We've got our work cut out for us, don't we?" Troyce said.

"Aye. 'Twill take an army to set the place to rights."

As to that Troyce could not argue. It would take an army, and he'd had only one old man, one old woman, and a saucy thief. He left Chadwick to see to the horses and met Devon just as her footman was assisting her from the first carriage. Lucy emerged after her, and Troyce pretended not to notice the coy smile she sent his way. Thank God she had transferred to Devon's household during his absence. He was getting too old to be dodging the attentions of a former bed partner. In that, Lucy left no doubt that if given the least encouragement, she would willingly resume the relationship from their distant past. It was not an inclination Troyce shared.

While Devon directed the unloading of her trunks, he wandered to a second, more modest but no less comfortable landaulet, where another footman had already opened the door and was handing Millie down the step. Then the second passenger appeared behind her and Troyce's heart stumbled.

He'd thought her lovely this morning, but in the broad light of day, she was nothing less than glorious. She'd tucked her hair beneath a mobcap, but a few stray wisps flirted against her cheeks. And her eyes, such a sultry contract against her red-gold hair, positively shined.

He closed the few paces between them and the scent of her, warm sun and innocent wonder, wrapped around his vitals.

Unaware of his reaction, she stared at Westborough with open-mouthed shock. "*This* is your country house?"

"I'm afraid so."

"Crikey, guv, ye never told me ye lived in a castle!"

Troyce almost choked. A warmth invaded his chest, and he had to bite the inside of his cheek to keep from smiling. Leave it to Faith to give this decrepit heap of stone and debris such a fanciful description. It had once belonged to some nobleman of status—Troyce had long since forgotten who—before being awarded to his grandfather by the king. "Pray, do not be too impressed by this monstrosity; It's naught but a hand-me-down."

Hand-me-down? *Bloody hell*, Faith thought, reverting to old habits, *I wish someone would hand me down a palace by the sea*. She was lucky to get clothes that fit decent! Never, in all her imaginings, had she reckoned on the baron owning half a bloody country. Not only did the lands surrounding the enclosed outer yard stretch for miles, but the building seemed to go on forever as well. Fifty rooms, at least! And there were turrets—turrets carved of real stone on either side with notches in the bulwark, a cathedral-high entrance, and windows en masse. It was a home fit for a fairy-tale princess. The only things lacking were a moat and a drawbridge. "It's so . . ."

"Remote? Maudlin? Uninviting?"

"Big," she finally said.

"Aye, it is."

Faith licked her lips and smoothed the narrow panel of her borrowed skirt. She waited for him to say more, to ease the anxiety curling through her veins. Instead, he simply watched her with that same unnerving manner that threw her senses off-balance and set her nerves afire, eyes twinkling, lips twitching, as if he knew a secret that she didn't. Though she tried not to, she found her attention straying to him more often than was wise. The weather was fine, the sun warm, and a blustery breeze blew in from the Channel. Beneath his coat, his white shirt billowed and flattened against his torso, a taunting reminder of the strength that had lain beneath her hours earlier. And she decided then that there was only one way to describe the third Baron of Westborough.

All man.

And he watched her as if she were all woman.

"I wish you would not stare at me that way, Baron."

"What way?"

"Like a falcon after a mouse."

"First a dragon, now a falcon . . . do you truly think of me as such a beastly predator?"

She didn't know what to think of him. She only knew that when he was near, her heart thumped a giddy rhythm and her thoughts scattered like dandelion seeds in a gusty wind.

Just when she thought she couldn't endure a moment more of his scrutiny without erupting into flames, a feminine call from the direction of the carriages drew his attention. He backed up a pace and hooked a thumb in his waistband. "Well," he cleared his throat, "I should leave you and Millie to your duties. You'll summon me if you need anything."

She barely managed a nod and silently begged him to go away.

He twisted on his heel, took a step, then stopped. "Oh, and Faith?"

She looked at him askance.

"We have an agreement. I trust that you will honor it."

There was no humor in the reminder. In fact, Faith thought it carried a veiled threat. Her heart dropped. She averted her eyes and, resigning herself to her lot for the next year, gave her pledge with a simple bend of her head. No matter how desperate her bid for freedom, she valued her own vows; she would not try to escape again until her debt was paid.

Satisfied, he brought two fingers to his hat brim in a mock salute, then strode with long-legged confidence toward the first carriage, where the duchess waited impatiently, a frilly parasol shading her delicate skin from the coastal sun's harsh rays.

Faith released a breath of relief and waited for her heart to start beating normally before she reached into the boot for one of the numerous pieces of baggage cramped into the space. Crikey, her knees felt like pudding, and her hands were shaking worse than leaves in a summer storm. Stupid girl. What was the matter with her? Hell, she'd bilked some of the most influential gents in London and never felt this rattled.

Shaking off her unsettling responses to him, Faith grabbed several bags and followed Millie through the arced doors. The instant she stepped inside, she knew she'd be earning every penny of her sentence.

"Oh, lud," Millie breathed, coming to a slow stop. " 'Tis worse than I imagined."

Faith supposed that compared to Radcliff, the interior of Westborough Manor did leave a bit to be desired. The entrance hall was a cavernous room unto itself, with archways that opened into a dining hall to the left, a common room to the right. Gray-brown dust coated every surface, and cobwebs had strung the walls together. *Do not steal from me.* She didn't know why he was worried about her stealing anything—there was nothing left of worth to take. No candlesticks, no pretty bric-a-brac, no portraits—only faded silhouettes on the walls where frames might have once hung—and very little furniture to speak of.

Still, there was something enchanting about the

dusty old place. All it needed was a good dose of spit and polish, and the place would soon be fit for the queen Herself. "How long has it been since anyone lived here?" she asked.

"Not since the old lord took ill and moved us all to London four years ago." They were the most words the housekeeper had spoken to her in one sentence since they'd met. "I knew I would have a job ahead of me, but this . . . I don't even know where to start."

Faith hoped Millie wasn't looking to her for direction. She knew as much about keeping a home as she did about proper behavior.

Then, on a firmer note, the housekeeper stated, "Well, nothing gets done standing about. The place needs airing and Her Grace and his lordship will be wanting a hot meal and baths right off. I'll check the pantry and send Lucy to market. You fetch water, stock the coal bins, and start opening windows." She wiped a gloved hand along the silty surface of an oblong foyer table then brushed her fingers together with a moue of distaste. "Then we'll see to scrubbing this sty."

Faith spent the first couple of days in Westborough sweeping and scrubbing, hauling and lugging until her hands were raw and her back ached so badly she could hardly stand upright. She labored from dawn to dusk, and often before and beyond. Never had she worked so hard or been so tired. And yet, there was a soul-deep sense of pride when she completed a task and the woodwork gleamed or the floors shined.

One thing she could say without a smidgen of

doubt—she felt more comfortable here amid all the grit and grime than among the shiniest of golds in the baron's London house. The castle— as she'd come think of Westborough Manor—was a massive estate on the edge of the English Channel, remote and forgotten. The interior reminded her of the kind she'd seen in a Greek picture book she'd once found in a rubbish pile. There were dark stone columns throughout the house—in the entrance hall, the lord's study, and the ballroom. Faith thought that a coat of whitewash would brighten up the place, but she didn't dare suggest it.

As she grew more acquainted with her surroundings, she realized that while parts of Westborough held a flavor of the very old, other sections appeared very new. She longed to hear of the manor's history but there was no one to ask. Everyone made it quite clear that they only tolerated her because their lord had ordered it. Even Chadwick, the one ally she'd managed to find, seemed not to have much time to spare for her. Having grown up in a place where her skills were respected and her experience sought after to train the new nippers, being placed at the bottom of the rank, in a role of which she knew nothing, left her feeling lacking.

And so, she kept her distance, remaining with the servants yet apart from them, working alone, eating alone, and much to her boundless relief, sleeping alone. She'd been given a room to herself in the hall with the other hired help, with a bed, a chair, a chest for clothes, and a small stove to chase away the chill.

It was a simple, contented life, she supposed, if not a bit lonely, and she found herself thinking of Scatter and the rest of the band more often than she should. Some of the boys would not trade their way of life to save their skins, but there were a few others, including Scat, who would give their last pair of shoes to live in a place like Westborough.

In the brief moments she could claim for herself, she would sneak up to her favorite room high in the north tower and the only one that didn't echo every sound. Windows had been set into a rounded wall that overlooked the cliffs and a view of the sea beyond so awe-inspiring that it had taken her breath away the first time she'd seen it. She'd stared out the window for a good quarter hour, watched ships crossing the Channel and waves crashing against the cliffs, her heart lodged in her throat, feeling at once humbled by its might and nostalgic for a distant home she'd left long ago. And so, she returned every chance she could, drawn to the sight by a force she neither understood nor examined.

High above, on the domed ceiling, tiny painted cherubs fluttered around a beautiful, reclining lady in pink silk and lace that reminded her of her mother. There, with no one to spy on her, Faith would practice the graces she'd thought forgotten.

Hard as she tried, she couldn't rid herself of the memory of Lady Brayton's contempt when she'd caught her twirling in the halls of Radcliff with her red gown. If for no other reason than to spite the duchess, Faith was determined to one day become something grander than an aristocrat's scrub maid.

And that meant shaking herself loose of her Bethnal Green roots.

Ten years had past since she'd left the orphanage, but when she concentrated really hard, she could still hear Vivette, one of the older girls in the home, instructing her and the other children on proper speech, behavior, and manners in her lightly accented French until the headmistress found out and ordered her to stop. She'd been self-educated and soft-spoken, and like so many of the others, orphaned too old to adopt. Her grandest hope was to become a governess.

It had been her voice that captivated Faith more than anything, bringing her back to a time and place that was both soothing and painful. Still, Faith was grateful for the lessons and sought to emulate what she'd been taught, allowing herself to pretend that she was indeed a grand lady of the manor.

And every now and again, she'd swear the angel-lady above would smile upon her.

Then the day arrived when, in the midst of scribing her name on the window with her finger, she'd seen him.

Troyce de Meir, third Baron of Westborough, her master gaoler and prince of dreams, navigating the rocks on the cliff, making his way to the shore beneath. Giddy breathlessness overtook her. He was nimble on his feet, and a powerful form against the backdrop of blue sky and moss-blanketed crest. The wind whipped at his loose shirt and raked blustery fingers through his hair, much as she often longed to do herself.

Then just as quickly as he appeared, he vanished. What beckoned him down there? She wondered. She was tempted to follow him, just to learn where he disappeared to.

Just to be close to him.

Rattled by the dangerous turn of her thoughts, Faith fled the tower room and made her way through long stone hallways and back stairwells to the main floor. It was a goosey thought to want to be close to a man who'd hijacked her into thralldom.

But if she thought to escape him, she soon discovered there was no escape from the third Baron of Westborough.

She was down on her knees in the common room, scrubbing grime off the floor, muttering to herself . . . "a team of plow horses . . . grow crops . . ."

"Are you speaking to anyone in particular, Faith?"

She spun around and her heart dropped to her toes. He looked as if he'd just awakened. There was a sleepy cast to his eyes and a lazy saunter to his stride. "I said, this place is a pigsty, Baron. The dirt is thick as a village field."

"I imagine so. It has not been lived in for many years."

"Millie said as much. It will take weeks to make it livable."

"Then it's a good thing you have an excess of

weeks," he quipped, and left the room with a jaunty grin that threw her heartbeat into a tizzy.

Once he was out of sight, Faith flattened herself against the wall, shut her eyes, and pressed her hand to the thudding beat beneath her breast. Crikey, what was the matter with her? Her skin burned, her nerves leaped. She felt as if she was coming down with a fever or something. Except, it only seemed to strike when the baron was about.

Disgusted with herself and determined to rid herself of the curious ailment, she pushed away from the wall and forced her feet to carry her to the kitchen. The thousand and one chores that had been heaped upon her would surely keep her too busy to dwell on him.

When she reached the kitchen, she found Millie standing at the table, breathless and holding her chest. Faith dropped her armful of buckets, dust rags, and tins of polish. "Millie? What's wrong?"

The old woman wilted against the table.

"Oh, Lord . . ." Faith hurried to her side and guided her into a chair. The smell of pigeon dumplings, browning bread in the huge oven, and cinnamon-flavored rice pudding boiling atop the stove reminded her that the midday meal would soon be served.

What on earth was the matter with Millie? Her glazed eyes and pale face told Faith that she was in pain. Faith didn't do well with pain. "For God's sake, where is Lucy?"

Millie gasped and gripped Faith's arm. "Gone . . . to the village."

It figured. Like herself, Lucy had no secular role, but as Millie's granddaughter and because she had been with the family the longest, and worked as a housemaid since she was a young girl, she laid claim to the more desirable duties of serving meals and acting as Lady Brayton's maid.

As a lower servant, Faith had been assigned to scrubbing floors, emptying chamber pots, and washing dishes. Both were to share such tasks as candle-making, polishing silver, and hanging laundry. Faith quickly learned that Lucy felt herself above such tasks and therefore made herself scarce. It was not a pattern of behavior that garnered respect. Especially now.

"I'm going to get the baron." He'd only just left. He couldn't have gotten far. . . .

The bony hand clutched her arm tighter. "No, please don't tell his lordship."

"You need help, and he'll know what to do."

"He'll boot me out on my arse without a pension, that's what he'll do." She grabbed her chest again.

"I'll get Lady Brayton then."

"No!"

"You're hurting, Millie. You need help." Under any other circumstances, Faith wouldn't have dreamed of going to the duchess if her life depended on it. But it wasn't her life that concerned her at the moment. It was Millie's.

A moment passed before she could find the strength to speak again, and when she did, her voice was thready and moist. "I'm begging you, Faith, say not a word. This will pass, it always does."

"This has happened before?"

"A time or two. Neither Her Grace nor His Lordship can ever find out. I'll lose my position, and I'm too old to get hired on elsewhere."

Since Millie couldn't be a day younger than seventy, Faith reluctantly had to agree. That she retained a position in Westborough spoke highly of its lord. "How long have you been with the baron?"

"Since he was a babe. Thirty years this past May."

"That's a long time to be with someone. Surely he'd not send you away because you're feeling poorly."

"Then you don't know him very well. He tossed Cook out on his ear just for serving spoilt turbot."

Faith couldn't imagine the baron being so heartless. Not when he'd gone out of his way to make her as comfortable as possible under impossible circumstances. But how could she be so certain of the character of a man whom she'd known less than a week? Lord knew she was hardly a good judge of first impressions. She'd thought Jack Swift a savior. "Tell me what I can do then."

Millie blinked as if surprised that anyone would offer, much less Faith.

"You're not strong enough to sit upright much less work, and I can't stand by and do nothing. Tell me what needs to be done."

"The table must be set. The meal served. The wine poured."

"I'll take care of it. Do you think you can make it up to your room by yourself?"

After a moment's hesitation, Millie nodded.

"Then go upstairs and rest."

"If you're certain you . . ."

"I am. If anyone asks after you, I'll tell them you're counting linens or something."

Finally, Millie shuffled up the back stairs.

Once Faith was assured that the housekeeper had made it to her room without incident, she looked about the kitchen. The pan on the stove boiled over, steam poured from beneath the lids of another. Loaves of bread sat whole on the table beneath towels, while others remained in the oven, and a stack of plates waited on the corner. Faith decided Millie must have been carrying them into the dining room when the attack occurred.

Pulling her sleeves up to her elbows, she headed for the stove, and after removing the pans and taking out the bread, she fetched the pile of plates. She hadn't a clue what she was to do, but crikey, how hard could it be to feed a pair of aristocrats?

Chapter 9

It was a complete catastrophe.

The moment she stepped into the dining room and saw Lady Brayton and the baron waiting to be served, her fingers turned to butter and her legs to dough. She tripped over the edge of the carpet, and the plates slid off one another. Even Faith's juggling act could not stop them from crashing to the floor.

Her heart stopped and her mouth fell as she stared at the broken plates at her feet. Slowly, she dared to look up at the baron, who watched her with that secretive and unsettling twinkle, then at Lady Brayton, who wore her usual scowl.

"For heaven's sake, Faith, can you be any more clumsy?"

"I'm sorry, mu—Your Grace," she said, blushing to the roots of her hairline. She dropped to a crouch and began picking up the pieces of stoneware.

"Where is Millie?" Lady Brayton demanded.

"She's occupied elsewhere." Having gathered as many shards as she could reach without crawling under the table, she got to her feet. "Dinner will be served shortly."

"In one piece I hope."

Faith bobbed her head in what Troyce suspected was her version of a curtsy, then took the broken dishes away with her.

"This ought to be interesting," the duchess muttered after she'd left the room.

Troyce glared at his sister. "Stop it, Devon."

"Stop what?"

Being such a virago.

Faith's reappearance with a fresh set of dishes saved him from answering. She set the plates on the table, and he noticed that her hands trembled. He hated seeing her unsure of herself. It was obvious that she knew nothing of the role which he'd thrust upon her, and as such, it fell on him to guide her, "Perhaps you could serve the wine while we wait for our meal," he gently suggested.

"Uh . . . of course." She bent low and teased him with her faintly floral scent. "Where is it?" she whispered.

Troyce smiled and pointed to the cabinet three paces away. She lifted her brows, and he had to grin. *Yes, Faith, I'm perfectly capable of getting it myself, but that's what I've got you for.* She'd said herself that she knew nothing of being a servant; how was she to learn what was expected of her if he did her work for her?

She sighed and fetched the half-filled bottle of red wine from the sideboard. Then she set it on the table in front of him.

And there it sat.

Troyce looked at the bottle. Devon looked at the bottle. Then both looked at Faith.

"Surely you don't expect us to pour," Devon cried.

Faith immediately whisked the bottle off the table. As she struggled with the cork, Troyce saw a disaster in the making and relieved her of the bottle. "I've got this. Why don't you see to dinner?"

She all but ran out of the dining hall. A few minutes later, she returned, hands hopping on a printed serving bowl. It fell to the table. Then she left again, and returned again, another hot plate in her hands and a basket of bread dangling from the crook of her arm.

She caught on this time, and after removing the plate's cover, plopped a mound of scorched rice pudding onto his plate. A serving of pigeon dumplings followed.

Troyce picked up his fork. "*Merci.*"

"What was that, West? Did I just hear you *thank* a *servant*?"

"In my house, common courtesies are practiced at all times, with all people."

He thought he saw Faith's lips twitch as she filled the spoon and stretched her arm across the table to Devon's plate. And the sight so took him aback that for a moment, he forgot who and where he was. 'Twas like a glimpse of a sunbeam after months of cloudy skies, and his spirits suddenly lightened.

Catching her eye, he winked at her. She startled. The serving fell short of its mark and pigeon dumplings slid across the table and into Devon's lap.

Devon leaped to her feet and, arms akimbo, stared at the sliding red stain on her gray crepe skirt. "Oh, for God's sake!"

Troyce's brow lifted.

Faith's mouth went slack. "Your Grace!" She raced around the head chair to Devon's seat and reached for the dumpling in her lap.

Devon batted her hand away. "Don't touch me, you . . . you . . . just don't touch me."

"I'm sorry. It was an accident."

"Of course," Devon countered shortly.

Faith bowed up and looked as if she was ready to hurl herself across the table and scratch his sister's eyes out. "Faith, don't concern yourself. It's about time she wore a bit of color to relieve that damnable mourning gray."

His attempt at levity seemed to work, for her shoulders relaxed a bit. She even gave him a half grin that had him grinning in return.

"I've obviously misjudged your newest servant, brother dearest," Devon retorted when Faith left a moment later. "She's not only reckless and impertinent, she's completely incompetent."

Troyce sighed and snapped a week-old newspaper open. It would be a long, long summer if Devon kept up her complaints against Faith. She seemed to have a new one each day. "Don't be so harsh with her. She's trying, and her heart is in the right place." *Her heart, and everything else*, he thought, remembering her body against his. Though weeks had passed since he'd felt her sinuous curves atop his frame he could recall the moment as if it had only been yesterday.

"For heaven's sake, this is the reason help is not hired without references." She dabbed at a spot of sauce on her skirt. "If it were up to me, the chit would have been dismissed the day she darkened your doorstep."

"It's not up to you, is it?"

"Do you not see it is only a form of manipulation?"

Rare anger kindled in his blood. He narrowed his eyes at her over the top of the London *Times*. "If you are so displeased with her, you could always go back to your husband."

"And leave you alone with that London alley cat? I know her kind. She has designs on you, Troyce, and as long as she can gain your sympathy she'll think above herself."

"Enough!" His hand slammed down on the table so hard that the goblet jumped and tilted. Bloodred fluid pooled on the hard wood surface and streamed toward the edge. "Faith is my concern, not yours, and I'll not have you casting aspersions on her every time she turns around."

"Well." She sniffed. "I should have known you would take up for her." Carefully she folded her napkin and set it beside her untouched plate. "Very well. If you are so insistent on championing the chit, I cannot stop you. But you cannot be so blind not to see that she holds a *tendre* for you. Unless you intend on breaking the poor mouse's heart, I suggest you do something—and do it quickly—before she destroys the entire manor."

A *tendre*?

How absurd. Though the idea that Faith might fancy him, even a bit, created a warmth around his heart, he knew she could hardly stand the sight of him. She only tolerated him because she had no choice.

Troyce sighed again. "What would you have me do, Devon? Take her back to London and dump her on the closest street corner where she'd no doubt be forced to steal—or worse—to survive?"

It was a frightening thing to see his sister's eyes light up. "Actually that's not a bad idea."

"Judas Priest, Devon!"

"No! Not London—send her to Radcliff!"

Oh, hell. He'd known this moment would come, and now that it had, he squirmed like a ten-year-old caught peeking under the chamber maid's skirts. "I can't do that."

"Of course you can! It would be the perfect solution. Westborough might actually be salvaged, and she would still be under your protection—or whatever it is you feel you owe her. I would even be willing to send one of the maids from Brayton Hall to train her."

How charitable, he thought dryly.

Still, the time had come; the confession could not be put off any longer. "I sold the town house."

The hall fell so silent that he swore he could hear her heart stop.

"You what?"

"I sold the town house. To Miles Heath."

She looked as if he'd just plunged a dagger into her heart. "How could you even consider selling our family's property to that reprobate?"

"Radcliff was expendable—Westborough is not."

"But why him? For God's sake, Troyce if you had to sell the house, I'm certain you could have found another buyer!"

"Not on such short notice." Her silence was condemning, and his mild temperament snapped for the second time in just as many minutes. "Stop looking at me as if I've committed a mortal sin. I'll not let my people starve so you can feed this animosity you bear against Miles."

The chair screeched against the stone floor as she shot to her feet. "You dare lay this at my door? What of you, Troyce? The solution has been within your reach all along, and yet you willingly choose to ignore it." She shook her head at him and tears swam in her eyes. "I shall never forgive you for this."

And she stalked out of the dining hall.

For a moment, Troyce thought about going after her, but decided against it. His anger with her was still too fresh, too raw. They would no doubt wind up quarreling again, and God's teeth, he didn't want that.

He set his glass upon the table and strode out of the dining hall, down the hallway, and out the back terrace. He started for the well-worn path leading to a monstrous shelter built in the cove where the galleon was housed, but stopped just

shy of the chalky-limestone cliffs that dipped into
the channel. Any other time, he would have gone
directly into the boathouse without a second's
hesitation and sweated out his mood with back-
breaking labor. But the thought of facing his fail-
ure in mammoth proportions had his gut twisting
into knots. Instead, he turned to the Channel and
stared out to sea.

What was he to do with his sister? Aye, he knew
of the rift between Devon and her husband, so
he'd not objected when she asked to spend the
summer at Westborough. To be truthful, he'd been
feeling so guilty about not being there when she'd
needed him most that he'd latched onto a chance
to spend time with her.

But he'd not be able to endure months of her
shrewish temperament. It reminded him too
closely of his mother's nature all the way up to
her death ten years earlier. If this was the manner
in which she behaved toward her husband, it
was no wonder Ross spent most of his time hunt-
ing.

He cursed himself for the uncharitable thought.
In truth, though she was a termagant of the highest degree and at times frustrated him beyond
measure, he'd learned over the last three months
how to deal with her. He simply rode out the
storm until it blew its course.

If only the rest of his problems were that easy to
solve.

Faith watched him pace the cliff line, obviously
troubled. His shoulders were slightly bowed, one
hand rested on his hip, while the other rubbed at

his chin. She could hardly help overhearing the argument between the baron and the duchess; the stone walls of the castle acted as a cave, echoing every sound.

She didn't want to be the cause of a rift between brother and sister, and yet, it warmed her heart to hear him defend her.

She went back to scraping the burned dumpling sauce off the stove.

"Well?"

Faith glanced up at Millie. "What are you doing up? You're supposed to be resting!"

"I've been resting so much my bones are melting into my mattress." She lowered her ample figure onto the bench at the end of the table, and Faith brought her a glass of water. She still looked alarmingly pale.

"How did the meal go?" Millie asked.

Faith had never lied before in her life, and she knew if she tried now, Millie would detect it right off. But neither could she bring herself to admit what a disaster she'd made of a simple meal. "I learned much about stain removal," she brightly invented.

Millie's eyes softened. "That bad, was it?"

To Faith's utter shame, the tears she'd locked deep inside sprang to her eyes. She ducked her head and nodded. "Worse."

Millie chuckled. "If we are going to remain in this house together, there are a few things you need to know about working for nobility. They must always be served and serviced promptly. A well-trained staff makes the lord and lady of the house look in control of their holdings to others.

'Tis important should anyone get it in their minds to take what does not belong to them."

Faith flushed, remembering how many times she'd taken what hadn't belonged to her, but Millie didn't seem to notice.

"After setting out the meal, you move discreetly to the corner of the room. Keep the glasses filled and the plates moving. Of course, our larder is not as well stocked as it should be, so we must make do with two courses, but that cannot be helped. Do not speak unless you are spoken to and always with the proper form of address."

The instructions went on, and on, and on, until Faith thought her head might explode: Don't use the main staircase, always use the servants' steps. Keep your person and your surroundings neat and tidy at all times. Curtsy. Bow. Scrape. Kiss their bloody rings or hems or whatever else they want you to kiss. . . .

"What makes them so much better than us?" she finally asked.

"Not better, just different. 'Tis a great responsibility that weighs on the shoulders of the highborn. They work with the monarchy to set our laws and see to our country's safety. They also provide for and protect the tenants on their lands, using their considerable wealth and prestige. And 'tis a great amount of pride to the lower born to serve their master or mistress well."

Pride? The way it sounded to Faith, it took a great amount of humility, and she wasn't sure she had enough of that to sustain her for the next year.

"Aye, you've instructed me well, Millie, and I will try. I cannot promise more than that."

" 'Tis all I ask."

"So what's next?"

"Has Lucy returned?" Millie asked.

"I haven't seen her since this morning."

"Then you'll have to see if Her Grace needs assistance with her toilet."

"Her . . . toilet? Crikey, anything but that!"

Millie looked horrified. Then she burst into laughter.

"Oh, dear, I probably shouldn't have said that."

Millie struggled to contain her impetuous burst of mirth. "Nay, you shouldn't have."

One good thing seemed to have come of Millie's infirmity, at least—she felt at last that she had a friend in the house. "It's just that she makes me feel so . . ."

"Lacking?"

Faith nodded. Crikey, put her in the rookeries and she could tumble with the best. Put her in a place like Westborough Manor, and she felt like a bull in a china shop.

"I know she can be difficult at times, but try not to let her distress you."

"Why does she dislike me so much?"

" 'Tis not you. She treats everyone the same way." Millie picked up a paring knife and started slicing the greens off a pile of carrots. "Her Ladyship wasn't always so difficult. She used to dance about this place like a Russian ballerina, swordfight with His Lordship in the gardens, sail down the banister on her bum—"

Faith choked. She couldn't imagine the graceful, elegant, hoity-toity Duchess of Brayton riding down a banister. "What happened to make her such a shrew?"

"Life, I expect. She married the duke, took on the responsibilities of her station, and just plain didn't laugh as much—unless she was with Master Edward, God rest his wee soul."

"Master Edward?"

"Aye, her son."

"She had a child?"

"Oh, aye. He was the sun and the moon in her eyes. She rarely even used a governess, which caused no little scandal, I'll have you know. Losing him was the last straw, I think. She hasn't been the same since."

Faith wanted to ask how she'd lost her child, but the entrance of the lady herself put an end to the conversation. One look at her hard eyes and pinched mouth told Faith that she'd caught enough of the conversation to warrant guilt.

"Have the two of you nothing better to do than gossip between yourselves?" she asked tightly.

"Aye, my lady," Millie replied, shooting to her feet and giving the duchess a slight curtsy. Then she shuffled away from the table.

A strained silence fell between Faith and the duchess after Millie left the kitchen. Faith debated on whether or not to apologize for discussing such a private subject behind her back, then thought better of it. The way her luck ran with this woman, she'd no doubt find herself with her foot in her mouth.

"Where is Lord Westborough?" the duchess finally asked.

Crikey, how was she supposed to know? Was she now his keeper as well as his servant? "I think he's down by the water."

"Working on that ship, no doubt."

Faith nearly didn't catch the remark, it was so softly spoken. "I'll fetch him for you, Lady Brayton."

And before the woman could object, Faith seized the opportunity to escape her presence.

He wasn't on the shore, where she'd seen him pacing, nor had she run into him on the way to the cliffs. Recalling the mention of a boathouse, Faith searched the area for a building, but saw nothing save the carpet of green clear to the line of woods in the eastern horizon. Ahead of her, craggy rocks descended to the white sands below. It was an awe-inspiring sight. Waves crashing into a jut of rocks. The soaring of gulls in the sky. The vast enormity of water. In her mind's eye, she saw wharves filled to brimming with sailors and dockmen, blanched canvass sails rippling in the winds, two little girls squealing in delight at a horde of barking creatures below. . . .

Faith gave a swift shake of her head to dislodge the image. Scanning the shore, she spotted a curious incongruity in the coloring, where white limestone faded to gray, then back at the waterline. As the wind shifted, she heard a raspy sound that had nothing to do with nature.

Brows dipping, Faith stepped over the edge of

the cliff and noticed a narrow wearing in the
scrubby grass. She gathered her skirts close to her
thighs and, careful of her footing, made her way
down to the base of the cliffs. A briny wind
whipped her mobcap off her head, and had it not
been for the ribbons loosely tied around her neck,
it would have gone sailing into the sea. She let it
ride on her back as she strode the distance toward
what she now realized was an opening in the
rocks.

And inside the opening, someone had built a
door.

It screeched in protest as she pushed it halfway
open. Darkness met her on the other side.
"Baron?"

Her voice echoed.

She pushed the door open fully. Her eyes
slowly adjusted to the darkness. Faith stepped inside and realized that this place was not so different from parts of the castle. The walls were moist
and cool and holders with unlit torches lined a
path that led to only God knew where.

Again, the raspy noise came from somewhere
ahead. Faith found a box of matches tucked beside the holder. After lighting the torch, she followed the path toward the sound and found
herself standing once again at a closed door at the
top of a set of stone steps.

Her heart thundered in her breast as she slid the
bar up. The door opened easily into a cavernous
room filled with light from a large mouth at the
other end that fed into the channel. It smelled of
raw, shaved wood. Burning oil and fresh varnish
and the sea.

And in the midst of it, resting easily on the water, was the most glorious creation she'd ever seen.

She stared up in openmouthed amazement at the ship. Its sleek lines, swollen girth, ribbed bulwark. Kinship and repugnance swirled inside her and a vision of a young girl in the belly of a vessel, and men—so many—rough, crude, completely without morals, flashed through her mind so quickly she wasn't sure if was a dream or a memory.

And then she saw him.

Faith's heart stopped beating for several seconds before it started pounding again an erratic beat. Oh, crikey, he was a beautiful man. Naked from the waist up, bowed over a wooden object on the deck. His midnight hair was tousled and stood in spikes atop his head. A sheen of sweat glistened on his smooth, sun-darkened skin, causing her fingertips to tingle, and the corded muscles flexed with each movement as he drew a measuring tape across a boxlike unit.

As the first time she'd seen him nude in his bedchamber, an excitement filled her veins, much like the one she felt when honing in on a loaded mark. A hum of the senses, a fever in the blood. For a woman who was beginning to yearn for something more than a disreputable lifestyle, those were dangerous things to feel. Indecent. Wicked. Feelings that made her think of the women on dockside street corners.

He glanced up then and spotted her. Faith went stock-still, frozen as if she'd been caught swiping a bloke's purse instead of admiring his flawless form. Could the baron see how her nerves jumped just looking at him? Did he have any inkling of his effect on her? Crikey, she hoped not. It would be the crowing humiliation.

Averting her gaze from his penetrating study, Faith focused her attention on the ship. An intrinsic feeling that she should know all the names gathered in her mind, yet it seemed a feeble grasp at knowledge. "So this is where you spend all of your time."

"As much as I can. Not as much as I'd like."

He rose from his crouched position on the deck, the motion sheer poetry, and for a moment she could only stare at him. Waves of awareness bathed her veins.

"So what do you think?"

I think I'm going to swoon. I think you are the most magnificent creature on earth. "Are you building it?"

"Rebuilding it." He cast a frown at the half-constructed rail around the deck. "Or trying to, at least. I seem to have reached a standstill."

"I had no idea you possessed such a talent."

It was praise such as he'd not heard in more years than he could remember. Troyce captured it, held it close to his heart. "Shipbuilding and restoration is a passion of mine. My father taught me as much of the craft as he knew. The rest I learned on the shores of Maine."

"Is that what you were doing in America?"

"Aye. For eight years. I'd probably still be there if my father hadn't died." He paused to glance around the cavern. "I felt close to him in here. In there"—he pointed to the manor—"we were strangers, but in here . . . we were father and son."

She strolled toward the bow and ran her hands lightly on the freshly sanded bulwark. "What's her name?"

He looked at Faith in surprise. Not many women realized that a ship was a woman in itself, to be pampered and cherished and guided with a firm but loving hand. She was the shelter on the stormy sea, a carrier to mysterious and exciting new lands. But Faith understood, and the affinity she seemed to share with him stirred a forgotten piece of his soul. "*La Tentatrice*."

"*The Temptress*."

The way she translated the galleon's name sent a frisson of desire straight to his groin. "I didn't realize you knew French."

"There's a lot about me you don't know."

He couldn't disagree with that. Faith was a mystery wrapped in layers. Just when he thought he had her pegged, he'd learn something new to blow his theories out of the water.

"Why *La Tentatrice*?" she asked, appraising the vessel.

"My father named her," he said, making his way off the deck and down the steps. "He loved ships." Reaching Faith's side, he continued, "I was with him the day he raised this one from the sea. You should have seen the look on his face. One would have thought he'd just discovered the lost city of gold. He would spend months sanding, painting, and polishing each one until they glowed, then when he was through with his renovations, he'd sell them to the highest bidder."

"If he loved them so much, why did he sell them? Why didn't he just keep them?"

"It wasn't the object he loved as much as the process. He loved taking things no one deemed worthy of saving and restoring them to their natural, raw beauty. Perhaps that's why he fell in love with my mother. She was a commoner who had come to England as a young woman. My father saw her and fell in love. My *grandpère* nearly had apoplexy when he announced he planned to marry her—he said he hadn't kissed the king's ballocks so his only son and heir could throw it all away on some American out to better herself. But my father was stubborn, and he married her anyway."

"And they lived happily ever after."

"On the contrary. She was everything my grandfather had predicted. She went through the fortune, flaunted her newly acquired title, and once she bore him his heir, she all but left him to pursue other interests. He turned to his ships, and she, of course, objected to the time he spent on them as well. 'Gentlemen do not engage in such a common trade,' she'd tell him. But it wasn't a trade to him, it was his passion, or perhaps his escape."

"My father loved ships, too."

The remark took him by surprise. She never talked about her family. "Did he?" he asked nonchalantly.

"I remember little ships all over his study. On the walls, on the shelves, on the tables. One time my sister and me were playing hide-and-seek and I knocked over one of the models. We tried to fix it but . . . it was beyond repair."

Her smile, small and unsure, even a bit wistful,

took his breath away. He wanted to ask how a girl with a father who collected ships and a sister who played childhood games wound up in London's underworld but knew she'd never tell him. Instead, he asked, "Is there a purpose to your visit?"

She shook herself from whatever past had absorbed her and replied, "Actually, yes. Lady Brayton is looking for you."

"Did she say why?"

"No, milord. She just sent me to find you."

In a rare moment of generosity, Jack had once told her that her curiosity was one of her finer qualities. But as Faith huddled with her ear against the door of the baron's library, she decided that it was an attribute she could do without.

"My red dress is missing," the duchess said.

"Bloody hell, Devon, you summoned me away from my work to complain about some piece of feminine frippery?"

"It's not frippery, West! It's an expensive silk gown, and I think your little maid took it."

Silence fell, and Faith stiffened.

"You cannot make such a serious accusation without proof," the baron said, his voice low and flat.

"She was snooping through my trunks at Radcliff."

"That proves nothing."

"Perhaps not, but I've not had a problem with thievery until *she* arrived." A pause . . . "What do you really know of that girl? You told me yourself that you found her on the docks . . ."

Her voice faded as if they were moving farther

into the room and the rest of the conversation became indistinct, but Faith was beyond listening anyway. She rested her head against the wall beside the library door and stared unseeingly at the intricate carvings of a column near the split staircase. She'd heard enough to know one thing. Lady Brayton thought her a thief. A sense of foreboding crept through her veins as she realized she'd made herself a formidable enemy in the baron's sister.

And there didn't seem to be a bloody thing she could do about it.

Chapter 10

The days blurred one into another, and Faith found that she'd developed a routine of sorts. Rise before dawn, stock the coal bins, put the bread on to bake. The duchess had forbidden her to serve meals, much to her relief, and the task had fallen to Lucy. The girl didn't bother hiding her displeasure, either. Still, Faith managed to ignore her, even though it went against her nature. Back on the streets such behavior would have made her appear weak; here at Westborough, it was simply an act of survival.

And so, she consigned herself to helping Millie, who continued to instruct her on the ways of being a proper servant. Faith was tempted to tell her that she didn't plan on being a servant any longer than she had to but kept her silence. With the exception of Lord Westborough, Millie was the only person within the house who deigned to treat her civilly, and she had no wish to make an enemy of her.

She had enough of those already.

When Millie no longer needed her help in the kitchen, Faith would tidy up the main rooms, then tackle one of the unused rooms with broom and rags until it glowed. It was mundane and back-breaking work, but it kept her busy.

She rarely saw the baron, which was probably for the best, and did her utmost to avoid the duchess. It should have been an easy feat consid-ering the size of Westborough and yet, every cor-ner she rounded, Her Grace seemed to be waiting on the other side, no doubt hoping to catch her in some act that would send her away.

As hard as she tried to forget the woman's accu-sation, it pounded in Faith's head. She'd had plenty of opportunities to clear not only Radcliff, but Westborough of every valuable object within and without its walls. Her promise to the baron and the threat of prison would not allow her to steal, though, no matter how tempted she was at times. And it bothered her more than she wanted to admit that the duchess thought so little of her. And so, she began to think of Lady Brayton as a Bow Street Runner, to be avoided at all costs. It helped to lessen the tedium and lighten the stress brought by her unfounded charge.

But by the time she entered her third week at the castle, as she'd come to think of Westborough, she was beginning to climb the walls. She longed for the challenge of skirting danger. The daring in outwitting the outwittable. The unpredictability of what each day would bring. Even the pretense of evading Robins, the discovery of new rooms or the occasional thrill of finding a hidden panel where she imagined coming across a treasure chest of coin to buy off her debt did nothing to alleviate the hollow, restless feeling inside her.

The walls slowly began to close in on her more and more until Faith thought she'd suffocate. She wanted out, if only for a few moments, to regain her bearings, to catch her breath, to escape this wooden identity that seemed to wrap itself around her.

And so, she was grateful when she entered the kitchen late one morning and found Millie fit to be tied. "Where is Lucy with that mutton?" She sat at the table, peeling potatoes. Both had agreed that as long as she did not tax herself, she could remain downstairs and no one would guess her health was still fragile. "I sent her to the village hours ago, and she still hasn't returned."

It didn't surprise Faith.

"Would you mind going to the village to see if you can find her?"

"I don't mind at all." Seizing on an excuse to leave the house, Faith quickly fetched her shawl from the back of a chair and all but ran out the door.

The day was balmy and the sky as clear as she'd seen it in a month of Sundays. Thick, fluffy clouds meandered across the expanse of powder blue. Fields of clover and black-and-yellow wildflowers stretched into woods of beech and ash. Faith knew that the village lay just beyond the woodlands but decided against taking the shorter, more pollinated route across the fields. Though she

knew supper could not be started without the
meat Lucy was to bring, 'twas too grand a day to
cut short the first stroll she'd been permitted since
leaving London.

Instead, she walked along the edge of the cliffs,
her gray skirts swishing around her ankles, a gentle breeze playing with the ribbons of her mobcap.
She dragged the hat off her head, lifted her face to
the sky, and simply enjoyed feeling the sun on her
face. Turning, she could see the manor house
looming high above, the shimmering waters of
the Channel to her left, and beyond, the distant
shores of France. Before her stretched a grassy,
flowerless vale of green.

She laughed for the sheer pleasure of laughing,
and the sound at once startled and thrilled her.
She could not remember the last time she'd felt so
free. No duchess to accuse her of wrongdoing or
lying in wait for her to err, no Lucy glowering at
her from behind her mistress's skirts, no baron to
confuse her emotions and send her senses into a
turmoil.

Aye, she was still under his command, but oh,
for a few minutes to herself, with nothing but the
fresh sea air and sunshine to keep her company,
she could endure anything.

The land began to slope and turn inward. The
sight of the first cottage took her by surprise, as
she wasn't expecting to find homes so far away
from the village, and she fell in love with it the instant she set eyes upon it. It mattered none that
the thatches bowed into the crumbling walls, or
that it was badly in need of chinking. Nor did it
matter that weeds had overtaken the herb garden

to the side and the circumference of the foundation. She did not even care that the door hung at a cockeyed angle courtesy of a broken leather hinge.

Before she realized what she was doing, she had pushed open the front door. Dust motes swirled as if angry at the disturbance. There were two woven chairs sitting before a river stone hearth, a dust-thick rug between them littered with toys. Several tables and cupboards had been set against the walls, and benches and a round table displaying a vase of dried and brittle flowers marked the dining area. A curtained doorway at the far end of the cottage suggested a sleeping room.

But what beckoned to her most was the boundless amount of love she felt within the crumbling walls. The kind that endured generations. Familiarity. Security and a kinship beyond explanation.

She imagined a beautiful lady baking pies at the table. A handsome man seated in one of the chairs, smoking a pipe while two little girls played with their dolls on the rug in front of the fire. . . .

Who had it belonged to? Why would anyone abandon such a charming home?

Reluctantly, Faith drew the door shut, then left the tiny cottage by the sea. Strolling farther down the hill, she spotted several more cottages, all in similar states of disrepair, chimneys broken, thatches gaping, walls bowing inward. Surrounding them were fields that had one time borne wheat or corn but now lay fallow. She called upon any stories she'd heard in the tunnels, and decided that, since the homes had been constructed so close to the manor house, they'd probably once belonged to farmers or fishermen, gamekeepers or laundresses, and every trade in between. No doubt they, like she, longed for the fresh air and sunshine not found in the confining walls of the castle.

Laughter trickled from one of the lowermost cottages, first feminine, then masculine. Then a pair tumbled out the door and Faith came to an abrupt standstill. "Well, I'll be a bloomin' . . . !" Lucy? So *this* was where the wayward wench spent all her time!

She seemed unaware of an audience as she danced about the bearlike man with dirty blond hair braided at the temples, taunting him with swishes of her hips and bouts of laughter.

The man lunged for her and scooped her off the ground by the waist.

Anger such as Faith had never known surged within her. While she'd been working her fingers to the bone inside the manor house, scrubbing and polishing and lugging and toting, Lucy had been squandering her time dallying with one of the local serfs.

"Lucy!"

The girl spun around, shocked. The man, just as shocked, dropped her to her feet.

"What are you doing here?" Faith demanded.

"Visiting an old friend," Lucy replied, recovering her surprise. "And you? What brings you so far from his lordship's clutches? Has he tired of you already?"

She would not let this cheap bit of rumpled

skirt rile her, Faith told herself. "Millie sent me to fetch you. You were supposed to bring mutton for supper."

"I guess I had other things on my mind." The lascivious glance she slanted toward her companion left no mistaking what sort of *things.* "Perhaps you should stick around. Learn a few tricks. Goodness knows, a scrawny spinster like yourself needs all the help she can get if she's to capture the baron's notice."

Fanny of Bethnal Green would have ripped out the girl's tongue and fed it to the rats.

Faith of Westborough Manor would not stoop to that level. With a dignity she'd not known she had, she tipped her chin and calmly stated, "Your grandmother has been feeling under the weather lately. If you can tear yourself away from your gentleman friend here, I'm certain she would appreciate your help."

"Who are you to order me about, you impertinent little wench?"

"You know what, Lucy? I've tried to be decent to you, and I've tried to work with you, I've even tried to ignore you, but I've about had my fill of ye." She felt the speech she tried so hard to perfect start to slip away but was too angry to care. "Now, unless ye want yer activities here made public, ye'd best hie yer plump li'l arse back to the manor house and give yer grandmum a hand."

"How dare you threaten me!"

"There are two things ye should know about me, Miss Lucy. I don't waste words on threats. And I never make a promise I can't keep."

Knowing that there was still the mutton to fetch, Faith turned her back on the pair and started down the hill toward the village. If the task were left up to Lucy, the baron and Lady Brayton would not get any supper tonight, and somehow the duchess would make it seem Faith's fault.

What's more, the gel had managed to ruin the first good morning Faith had had in weeks.

Her mood soured even further when she finally arrived in the village. Faith's steps slowed and she took in her surroundings with a mix of horror and disbelief. The village, if it could be called that, consisted of cottages in worse shape than those on the outskirts. A marketplace lined out in two rows of perhaps a dozen two-story buildings made of stone with broken windows and sagging roofs, housing everything from pubs to a livery to a butcher shop. Refuse littered the gutters, rubbish had been piled against the walls and left to rot. Worse, people lived amid this. Not many, but she spotted a few peeking out window sockets and staring at her from front stoops.

A group of scraggy children played in a mud-hole nearby, oblivious to whatever filth had been dumped there. Two women wearing dresses that hug on their frames were picking through a pile of rotting apples in a cart. A man emerged from the pub in the center of town, stepped into the street, and in full view of everyone, relieved himself.

Faith spun around, shut her eyes, and covered her mouth to keep from spewing. She thought she'd left such crude behavior behind in London. Obviously, poverty existed all over England.

She'd just never expected to find it here.

How could Lord Westborough permit such filth? How could he allow his own people to live in such squalor?

How could she stand by and let it continue?

"I would like a word with you, milord."

Troyce glanced up from the estate books to the summer squall blowing into his study. Her stiff tone and the scathingly formal manner in which she addressed him did not bode well. He tucked the quill into the holder beside the ledgers, and lifted one brow. "Only one?"

"I have just returned from the village. The place is slovenly, the buildings are ready to fall over, and the people are little more than unkempt drunkards with nothing better to do than lie around like a heap of rocks. I've seen corpses with more energy!"

Troyce bent over the books again. "That's enough, Faith."

She was too angry to heed the warning in his voice. "How dare you hide yourself away with your books and your ship and ignore the plight of those people!"

"Miss Jervais, you are treading on dangerous ground."

"You call yourself a nobleman. You are no better than the tenement owners in London."

"Cease!" He shot up from the chair and rounded the desk, eyes blazing, veins throbbing.

The last week had been horrendous at best—his row with Devon, a broken mast on the ship, another missive from one of his father's creditors threatening him with debtors' prison if he did not clear the account by the end of month . . .

The last thing his already strained mood could endure was criticism by a bloody London thief. "Who do you think you are to talk to me in such a manner?"

She raked him up and down with scorn. "No one, obviously. Just a lowly servant to a highborn master with no care to the plight of his people."

"You have been in this house only a few weeks and you dare make judgments. I suggest you remember your place lest you find yourself in a position far worse than they."

It got so quiet that Troyce could hear a feather fall. Part of him wished he could take the words back. Another part of him was glad he'd said them. He'd given Faith more leeway than he even allowed some of his closest comrades—her performance here proved that if he did not remind her of the boundaries, she'd overstep them. Just as his mother had done.

Just as Devon had warned.

Still, the hurt in her eyes was not easily dismissed.

She shook her head, and disillusionment filled her face. "How could you do that, Baron? How could you let those people—*your* people—live that way? I thought you were more honorable than that."

He turned away and stared out the window, unable to endure the accusation in her eyes. Aye, he understood her outrage. But that did not give her leave to throw his failures in his face.

"When was the last time you went to the village?" she asked. Her tone was strained, but the angry courage she had unleashed upon him seemed to have deserted her.

He clenched his jaw. "Six weeks ago."

"Then surely you must have seen the inhuman condition in which those people live."

"I saw." The first time he'd been to the village, he'd been just as shocked, just as appalled as Faith. He'd gone to speak with several business owners regarding rent owed. Since the village had been built on Westborough lands, each business owner was a tenant in his own right, and as such was beholden to pay a small rent, which hadn't been done since the onset of his father's illness and his move to London.

Nothing could have prepared Troyce for the sight that met his eyes. The place looked as if it had been pillaged by revolutionaries. He'd traveled halfway around the world, seen everything from royal palaces to newly birthed settlements and yet, in all his journeys, he'd not seen such neglect and destitution.

And on his own lands no less.

But the villagers had made it brutally clear that they wanted nothing to do with the Baron of Westborough, old or new. "What do you expect me to do, Faith?"

"You could help them!"

He spun around and slapped his hands on the desk, upsetting a bottle of ink. "Don't you think I haven't tried? They loathe me. They want nothing from me and would just as soon burn me at the stake as welcome my help." Collecting his emotions before they got out of control, he straightened his spine and shuffled stacks of papers away from the spreading pool of ink. "Short of running them out and burning the place to the ground, there is nothing I can do for them."

"You could bring them here. Put them to work and let them earn a decent living. God knows there's plenty of work to go around. At least they'll be fed and clothed while their homes and businesses are being rebuilt."

"And who, do you propose, will finance all this *rebuilding*?"

"You, of course! It's your village! You're the bloody baron, it's your responsibility!"

"There is no money, damn you!"

Silence dropped upon the room like a concrete slab. Troyce slammed the open ledgers shut, then gave his frustration free rein and swept his arm across the surface. Papers, ink bottles, quills, books—all flew off the desk and slammed into the bookshelf built into the adjacent wall. Troyce raked his hand through his hair, then drew his palm down his mouth. He couldn't believe he'd blurted out such a personal and private matter to a mere serving girl.

"What?" Faith sat down. Hard. At any other time, her open-mouthed shock might have been comical. "You're . . . poor?"

He winced. "As a church mouse."

"But—the house in London—"

"Is no longer mine. I sold it along with everything else of value. There is nothing left."

"Why? How?"

The unabashed disappointment sent a pinch of apprehension careening through him. "How does anyone become poor? Excess spending, pitiful harvests, poor management. My father did not always make sound business decisions, Faith. He allowed himself to be manipulated until his assets were overextended beyond salvation. And we—myself, my staff, and my tenants—are all paying the price."

"What of Lady Brayton? Could she not help?"

"Devon is completely dependent on her husband's charity. Other than granting her a small allowance that barely covers her personal necessities, Ross remains in full charge of their treasury."

Troyce didn't know why he was sharing such personal information with a woman he'd met less than a month ago, and whom he wasn't even sure he could trust. Not even Miles and Devon, whom he'd known his whole life, were aware of how deeply dire the situation had become. Yet talking to Faith seemed to relieve some of the burden he'd been shouldering alone since returning to England and seeing the horrible mess he'd inherited.

"Surely there must be something you can do."

"There was."

He saw the events of the last few weeks clicking into place in the pointed silence that followed.

"Feagin," she finally said.

"Yes, Feagin. He was to invest in the galleon. Once sold, it would bring in more than enough money to save our sorry hides." And he'd surrendered that opportunity.

For her.

"I can help you."

The declaration, earnest and bold and so very . . . *Faith*-like, caught him off guard. That she would even offer touched him to the core. He laughed but it held no humor. "Unless you've a fortune at your disposal, I do not see how you can help."

"I don't have money, but I know money."

He could only imagine her experience, and he'd not support the estate with ill-gotten gains. "I appreciate the sentiment, Faith, but—"

"I *can* help you! There are ways to extend and to increase. It's true that it's too late in the season for a wheat crop, but we can still begin tilling the ground for spring, sow garden seeds, herd sheep, repair cottages."

"And you know how to do all these tasks?" What a London pickpocket might know of planting wheat or herding sheep, he couldn't imagine. Then again, he wouldn't have imagined she'd know anything about ships either.

"No, but I'm sure that you and your tenants do, and what we don't know we can learn. The people just need a little kick in the bum to get them going."

"We? Since when did this become a partnership, Faith? As you so crudely reminded me, those are my people out there—why do you care what happens to them?"

"Because I've been where they are, in places where there is no hope, no purpose, and no pride. And by God it sickens me to see that which I detest in myself."

"You have pride!"

"Perhaps now. But there was a time when I

didn't. I was four years old when my mother died and my father sent me away. I lived in a house for orphans until I was ten. You cannot know what that was like, Baron, to simply go from never wanting for anything to not even knowing where your next meal is coming from."

His lip twisted in wry grin. "You'd be surprised."

"Then maybe you would understand. We worked. We slept. We ate when we were lucky. We went through the motions of living, but not a one of us believed we'd ever get out. One day a man caught me pilfering a loaf of bread from a local baker. He promised me that I'd never go hungry, never be cold again. And I was young enough and desperate enough to believe him. He'd given me hope. At that time I had no idea that hope comes with a very a high price."

He almost asked how high a price she'd paid, but decided that some things were best left unknown.

"Where's your father now, Faith?" he asked instead.

"I don't know. I don't even know if he's alive anymore."

"Have you ever thought of looking for him?"

"What for?"

"To ask him why. To tell him how you feel."

She rose from the chair and strode to the window, saying nothing. She seemed so far away, lost in some past he couldn't see, and it was all he could do not to take her in his arms and make her past disappear.

Just when he was sure she wouldn't answer,

she said, "I'll admit to giving it a bit of thought over the years. But in the end I decided it wasn't worth the heartache if he rejects me again."

"But maybe he wouldn't," Troyce told her softly. "Perhaps your father regrets what he did."

Her shoulders stiffened, her eyes went shuttered, and he knew that he'd pushed too far. "Then that's his loss, isn't it?" With the grace of a ballerina, she pivoted on her heel and impaled him with a determined stare. "If I can help you, I ask two things in return. The first, a cottage on the outskirts of the village. The one highest on the cliffs."

He could not believe he was even considering accepting the help of a woman who might very well be plotting to use him to further her own agenda. But Faith had proven herself industrious and clever. She'd taken on more than he'd ever expected without complaint. And if confessing the extent of his woes had accomplished anything, it had made clear that any designs Devon insisted she had on him, on the estate, or on the Westborough "fortune," were for naught. There was no fortune. Not anymore. Did he have anything to lose? "I know the one. It shall be yours. Your second request?"

"My freedom."

A crossbeam to the chest could not have taken him more by surprise. "No."

"If I can put your village to rights, I will have earned it!"

"You will have earned it when you work off your debt to me, and not one day sooner. Do you understand me?"

"Perfectly." And with a completely blank expression, she marched out of the room.

Troyce glared at the door she shut behind her, his chest feeling bruised and hollow. He'd granted her the cottage she wanted, but her freedom? No, absolutely not. It was the only thing he had that bound her to him.

Chapter 11

There were times when Faith wished she'd think before she spoke.

She stood at the edge of the village, hands on her hips, and surveyed the daunting task she'd set for herself. She hadn't been able to sleep last night. Her mind twisted and turned over the condition of Westborough, over its liege, over her own commitment and his refusal to grant her freedom. Damn his eyes for denying her that.

On one hand, she was still so angry with the baron that she could spit. On the other, she couldn't forget the despair in his eyes when he'd confessed to being poor as a church mouse. That he wasn't able to help his people obviously ate at him. For a man of his station, of his determination, it must strike a blow to his pride not to be able to provide. And it made even worse the fact that she, in part, was unwittingly responsible for that. He'd had the answer in his grasp and because he'd stood up against Feagin for her, he'd lost the chance.

Well, she could not give him back the money he so desperately needed, but her work on the village might serve to assuage some of the guilt she felt for adding to his troubles.

And in the end, she would have the cottage. Her own home, within her own grasp, where the spring chill didn't settle in the stones and refuse didn't layer the floors—just as she'd wished for so long. Best think of what she'd gained, not what she'd lost. A home of her own wasn't much, but it was a beginning. At least she wasn't in prison, even if it did feel as though she were working off a sentence. Best just do so, pay her debt.

But where did she start? With the barren fields? The collapsing cottages? The hovel of a market-place?

The people, she finally decided, picking up the pair of buckets she'd brought. The mission she'd set for herself was not one to be undertaken without help and who better to recruit than those who would benefit the most?

"Hallo the town!" she called, reaching the collection of cottages that marked the beginning of the village. "Is anyone about?"

Not a soul stirred. Even the dogs lying alongside the dirt road were too lazy to bark.

"Is anyone here?"

Again, no one made any effort to greet her. Though it was still early, surely people would be up. Then it occurred to her that perhaps they were awake and were simply not receptive to strangers.

Well if that was the way it was to be, then so be it. They'd realize soon enough that she did not pose any threat.

She marched down the hill to the first hut, set her buckets and donned a bibbed apron and pair of leather gloves she'd wheedled out of Chadwick. Then she dropped to her knees and began clearing weeds from the side of the house. If she alone had to attack the village one house a time, then that's what she would do.

"Lassie, what the hell are you doin'?"

Startled, Faith glanced up at the bear of a man standing in the doorway, scratching himself. God knew how many days' worth of beard covered his face, his matted hair hung down to the middle of his back; his clothes looked as if he'd been wearing them since the beginning of time. She spotted the two children she'd seen playing in the mudhole the day before peering at her curiously from behind a rotting cart with one broken wheel.

"Pulling weeds. When I'm through, the ground can be tilled and a garden planted. The vegetables will help sustain you through the winter."

"Be gone with ye, wench. I like my weeds just where they are."

She pinched her lips together, gathered her buckets, and moved to the expanse of patchy grass and clay earth at the front of the house. "Then I'll just start to work on your yard. Do you perchance have a rake or pitchfork?"

"Yer the new skirt from the big house, ain't ye?"

She should have expected they would hear of

her arrival. "Yes. Faith Jervais." She stuck out her hand. "And you are?"

"Getting mighty riled." He made no attempt to return the greeting. "Now I've told ye once to leave. Don't make me tell ye a second time."

What did he think he would do, beat her? "I'm trying to help you, sir."

"I don't need your help, and I don't want it." He narrowed his beady eyes at her and took a threatening step forward. "Now take your buckets and be gone!"

Since the man was three times her size and dangerously cranky, she decided not to push her luck. "All right, as you wish, but don't think I won't be back."

And she moved on to the next house. This time, she knocked upon the door and introduced herself and her intentions first. The door was immediately slammed in her face.

There was no answer at the fourth cottage, and at the fifth, she received the same reception as from the others from an old crone who shook a gnarled cane in her face. "I don't need your help, either. Now get you're skinny arse off my property!"

"It's my understanding that this property belongs to Lord Westborough."

"Not anymore." And again, a door slammed in her face.

Huffing a frustrated breath, Faith crossed the road, irritated at the people's reactions. She would have thought they'd be more grateful that someone from the manor house was offering to help them. Instead, they treated her as if she were trying to peddle them the black plague. What did they think, that she planned to rob them?

She stopped abruptly at the front of one of the nicer-kept cottages and frowned. *Was* that what they thought? How could they have known of her old occupation unless someone had told them?

The baron. He was the only one who truly knew of her past.

And she'd been stupid enough to confirm it.

But why? Why would he try to sabotage what she was trying to accomplish here? It made no sense, when he would be the one to profit from her labor.

Well, if that was his intention, she'd be damned if she'd let it happen. She wanted that cottage, by God. She needed to get out of that castle, away from the accusations of his sister and the disturbing effect the baron himself had on her.

Resolved, she marched up to the front door of the next cottage, rapped her knuckles on the splintered wood. An old man who resemble Chadwick so closely as to be his brother answered, and as before, the instant he saw her, started to shut the door.

Faith slapped her hand against it. "I would not do that, sir," Faith said, standing her ground. "I am here to help you clean up this hovel, and I will not take no for an answer."

He scanned the other houses, whose occupants lingered in their doorways watching her with scowls on their faces. "It doesn't seem that anyone is pleased to have your help, lass."

"But it pleases them to put out buckets to catch

the rain because the thatches are falling in? It pleases them to hear their children crying at night because they've no food in their bellies? Well, it doesn't please me. Like it or not, I'm here to work, and I'm not going anywhere until I'm done."

"What's in it for you?"

"A place I can be proud to call my own." Directing her voice to the rest of those within hearing range, she said, "A place you can all be proud to call your own! Now you have a choice, either help me or get out of my way. Either way, I will not leave this place until it is set to rights."

He'd vowed to himself that he would not visit the village today, not spy on Faith. He had too many other duties to attend to let himself become distracted by the gel's crazy delusions. He and Chadwick were planning on finishing the repairs on the windmill and rechink the ovens in the bakehouse, both of which would take most of the day.

But in spite of his resolve, he found his duties carrying him farther away from the manor and closer to her. With an ax in the scabbard, he guided his horse through the forests north of the village boundaries. He told himself that Millie would need wood once the bake ovens were completed, and that the best oaks grew near this stream. But when he saw Faith in the distance, he knew he was only lying to himself. The house had felt empty since she'd begun her project, the days twice as long. He'd secretly been hoping for a glimpse of her, just to assure himself that all was right, that she'd come to no harm.

His heart beat faster, his blood flowed hotter. She'd donned a ragged pair of trousers no doubt borrowed from one of the village boys, and an oversize shirt that swallowed her frame. And still, she was so pretty she took his breath away. Using a tined garden tool to rake at the weeds that had overtaken a patch of earth beside the old counselor's office, she attacked the ground with an obsessive zeal, without a soul in sight helping her.

What drove a woman to such mad—and futile—extremes?

He shook his head in bafflement, purely amazed that she who had nothing would give so much of herself. And to the most ungrateful lot of souses he'd had the misfortune to meet.

Let her. She'd learn. She'd tire of her wasted efforts soon enough.

But she didn't.

Each day for the next week she returned to the village again and again. After her morning chores at the manor house were completed, she would make the two-mile hike along the shoreline for the village, toil until near dark, then return to the manor house to assist with supper and sleep.

And each day for the next week, Troyce grew more and more concerned. If anything, she looked worse now than the day he'd brought her to Westborough. Her hands were chapped from harsh soaps, her face drawn, her features thinner, and the shadows under her eyes stark against her tanned skin. Was she even eating? Troyce didn't think so, and he blamed himself. He never should have consented to this scheme. He above all knew how fruitless it was. At the same time, he couldn't find it in his heart to deny her something that was so obviously important to her.

But neither could he allow her to continue working herself into an early grave.

With a sigh of surrender, he returned to the manor. After a quick trip to the boathouse, he once again mounted his horse and wheeled him in the direction they'd just traveled. But instead of guiding his horse toward the outskirts, he headed straight for the bloody village.

Troyce didn't think it was possible, but the place looked even more dismal now than when he'd first set eyes upon it nearly four months earlier. Though signs of Faith's labors were everywhere—rubbish piled neatly on the side of the road, carts overloaded with broken furniture, trails of water leading in and out of buildings from where she'd been hauling buckets—his own failures were more apparent. The barren fields, paupers' huts, the dearth of activity . . .

Wasn't that just the rub? Away for eight years learning to rebuild things, and he couldn't rebuild his own life.

Unable to bear the sight, he looked away and clicked the horse forward. His heart thudded against his ribs as he closed the distance between the outlying farmlands and the village itself. A festering stench rose from the corral, making Troyce wonder when it had last been cleaned. No wonder she thought him such a monster.

The stillness alerted him that his presence had been noted. Troyce braced himself, knowing what would come even before the first stone caught him between the shoulder blades. The second hit him in the back of the head. Soon, he was being pelted from both sides by hand-sized pieces of his own land.

Still, he kept his posture straight and his gaze trained ahead. He was no stranger to the villagers' welcome; he'd endured it several times in his initial efforts to meet with them and discuss how they could work together to save Westborough.

Then, as now, the situation seemed to have surpassed discussion, but he refused to let them run him off his own lands. And so, steeling himself against the pain of rocks nicking his flesh and the shouts of disdain searing his soul, Troyce continued down the center roadway, his thoughts focused on finding Faith.

He never saw the one that dropped him to his knees.

Faith was pushing a wheelbarrow overloaded with debris from what had once been the baker's shop when the shouts of the crowd gathering at the end of the village drew her notice.

She glanced up and spotted a rider. She recognized his broad-shouldered frame at once, and her heart gave a traitorous leap at the sight of the baron heading in her direction. What was he doing here?

And what were those things flying in the air around him? Her eyes narrowed as she tried to make them out when suddenly, the baron jerked in the saddle and keeled sideways.

The grips of the wheelbarrow slipped from her hands and the load toppled. "Baron!" Grabbing her skirts in both hands, she tore down the street.

The crowd began to converge, and terror surged through her veins like frozen fire.

"Get away from him! Get away!" She shoved herself between foul-smelling bodies until she reached the center of the mass. There her baron lay facedown in the mud and muck. Faith dropped to her knees, heedless of the shouts around her. She rolled him over. Blood seeping from a cut above his eyes made her stomach roll, and a haze of anger blurred her vision. "What the bloody hell 'ave ye done to 'im, ye sorry sons of Satan!"

She ripped a portion of her underskirt and wiped away the mud and blood. "Baron? Can ye hear me? Open yer eyes."

Thick sooty lashes fluttered, then lifted. Faith wilted, never so relieved to see those silvery gems in her life. "There ye are . . ."

She smiled, and the darkness that had been Troyce's world suddenly brightened. "Faith . . ." He smiled back, a weak effort. With the sun shining behind her, her curls looked like a halo. Her brown eyes shone with a suspicion luster, as if she were fighting tears.

She brushed something soft across his brow. "Are ye all right?"

"Not so highborn now, am I?" he whispered.

"Oh, ye bloody fool." She laughed. But it was sad laugh, not the kind he'd often hoped to hear coming from her. "What are you doing here?"

I missed you. The thought slapped him like a fierce wind on the open sea, stealing his breath. Troyce closed his eyes lest she read the emotion in them, and struggled to sit. His world spun like a child's toy. His head pounded with the fierceness of a warrior's drum. He clutched the side of his head as if that would dull the pain and pointed toward his horse. "I brought canvass. For the windows."

"Where did you get—" Her face snapped around to the bundle tied to the back of his saddle. "You took them from your ship, didn't you?"

"They weren't being used."

"Oh, Baron . . ." She started to caress his cheek, then drew back as if remembering where they were.

And who surrounded them.

Troyce didn't need to look into their faces to know what he would find; they'd made it perfectly clear when he'd ridden through town. Condemnation. Disdain. Utter and absolute hatred.

"Someone help me get him on his horse," Faith ordered.

Not a person moved.

"He brought coverings for your windows to keep out the rain."

Still, no one moved. In fact, the tension in the air only seemed to intensify, and a sliver of apprehension embedded itself at the back of Troyce's neck.

"He's trying to help you, can't you see that?"

"Faith, let it go," Troyce said, gathering his strength and his bearings. "I can manage on my own."

"Where was his lordship when the crops failed two seasons in a row?" Someone called out from the crowd. "Where was he when we needed timber for the fences?"

"Too busy slippin' his hands up some muck-a-muck's skirts, I'll wager," someone else cried.

"Off hobnobbin' with the hoity-toities, that's where he was," another chimed in. "Forgettin' all about the little folks what put supper on his table."

"We don't want his bloody help," a bear of a man spat.

"Then you are fools, every one of you," Faith hissed in his defense. "He alone has the means to give all of you a fresh chance. Though why he'd do it, I can't imagine. You've certainly done nothing to deserve it."

"He abandoned us!"

She looked them up and down with undisguised loathing. "You abandoned yourselves."

Faith had no idea how she managed to get him on the horse. He was swaying so badly on his feet that she feared he would lose consciousness. Somehow, he put his foot in the stirrup and with her shoving his backside, swung his leg over. No sooner was he in the saddle than he slumped forward.

She'd never ridden a horse before and didn't think now was the best time to learn. Instead, she took the reins and walked beside the animal, hoping it wouldn't give her any trouble. If the baron fell off, she had no idea how she would get him back in the saddle.

It took nearly thirty minutes to reach the manor, and in all that time, the baron didn't stir again until the horse came to a stop at the front gate. "Stay here and don't move. I'll be right back."

Faith was afraid to leave him, but there was no possible way she'd be able to get him into the

house without help. Several minutes later, Lady
Brayton was following her outside. Against
Faith's orders, the baron had dismounted, and
stood leaning heavily against the animal's flanks,
his hand cradling the right side of his head above
his temple.

"What happened?" Lady Brayton cried, rushing to his side. "Good heavens, you're bleeding."

He pushed himself upright, and though he was
steadier on his feet than he'd been before, his face
was an alarming shade of gray. But Faith was so
grateful to see him alert that her legs went weak.

"I fell from my horse, Devon. Don't concern
yourself." The look he cast Faith's way warned
her not to gainsay him.

"I'll get some water and rags," Millie said, then
rushed toward the kitchen.

With Faith on one side, Lady Brayton on the
other, they supported his weight into the house
and led him up the stairs to his room.

Faith had never been in the master's chambers
before, since the task of cleaning the lord's and
lady's rooms had been delegated to Lucy. The
room was large and airy, decorated in shades of
rich burgundy and gray the same shade as his
eyes, with a heavy, masculine wardrobe, two
trunks, two thick-cushioned chairs, and a massive
four-poster bed fit for a king.

Or a prince.

He sank onto the mattress and ordered Lady
Brayton to leave him, which she, of course, ignored. Faith stayed back near the door, out of the
way, wringing her hands and fighting the instinct
to comfort him. But she knew it would not be al-

lowed. Lady Brayton would strangle her before letting her near the baron, and Faith was in no position to challenge her.

But as she watched the duchess fuss over him like a mother hen, the realization struck her of how dearly Her Grace cared for his lordship. The two might grouse and disagree, but the bond between brother and sister could not be mistaken. Seeing it, feeling it, made her remember a time when she'd shared the same sort of bond with her own sister. Faith's throat tightened, and the hollow ache she tried to ignore whenever she thought of Aniste—or *Honesty* as she'd dubbed her during their childhood—settled in her breast. They'd been so little, alike in so many ways and close as peas in a pod, but Honesty had always been the more vibrant of the two.

No wonder their father had chosen her sister over her.

Spotting her lingering in the doorway, Lady Brayton frowned, then shut the door, banning her from the baron. She was not allowed near him for the rest of the day, and worry for him was driving her mad. Finally, near dusk, Lady Brayton left his room.

"How is he, Your Grace?" Faith asked, rising from the hallway floor just as the duchess shut his door.

"What are you doing here? Haven't you caused enough damage?"

"Me?"

"I don't care what my brother said happened, his horse didn't throw him. West learned to ride before he could walk. I know that he went to the village, and I also know that he wouldn't have gone there if hadn't been for you."

Every word seemed to take nicks out of her flesh. "I'm sorry." She could hardly get the words passed the lump of anguish lodged in her throat.

"Sorry? You could have gotten him killed!"

Faith didn't know what to say. How could she deny what she knew to be true?

"If you want to waste your time and risk your life on that bloody village, then so be it, but do not jeopardize my brother's. Until he is in a better position to provide what they need, he will not be returning. In the meantime, you just . . . stay away from him, do you hear me?"

As if to drive the edict home, Lady Brayton locked the baron's door and pocketed the key, then marched past Faith down the hall.

Faith stared at the door for several long moments, before turning away. Back in her own room, she paced the floor. The duchess was right. It *was* her fault the baron had been hurt. If she hadn't been so damned insistent on fixing the problems of the lands, he never would have gone to the village, and they never would have stoned him.

Why had he gone there?

Why had he decided to bring the canvasses, knowing what sort of welcome he would receive?

She managed to obey Lady Brayton's order for all of an hour before digging out a familiar leather case from her rucksack, which she'd confiscated while loading the carriages for the journey to Westborough. Even though she hadn't thought she'd have need of her tools again, it still belonged to her.

Returning to the baron's room, she knocked softly on the door. "Baron?"

No answer. She knocked again. "Lord Westborough?"

Still no answer.

Her blood beginning to run cold, she extracted a set of false keys from her kit and wedged them, one after another, into the keyhole. On the fourth try, she heard the familiar click of the lock releasing. Absently tucking the case into her apron pocket, Faith let herself inside.

He stood by the window, the moonlight casting his face in half shadows, so much like the first time she'd seen him under the lamplight in front of a London tavern that her heart skipped several beats. Then she'd thought him her prince of dreams.

Now, she knew he was only a man.

A remarkable, foolish man.

"Troyce?"

He turned, saw her, and looked back out the window.

She took a bold step forward. "I thought you were resting." Another step. "How are you feeling?"

With a brief and slanted glance over his shoulder acknowledging her presence, he answered, "My head hurts like hell, but I'll live."

"This is not the first time they've turned on you, is it?"

His silence said it all.

Anger rose inside Faith, swift and blazing. At him for being so foolhardy. At the villagers for being so cruel. At herself for causing it in the first place. "Why do you allow it?"

"Because they're right. I did abandon them. Like father like son." He laughed a humorless laugh that ended on a groan.

Instantly, Faith was at his side. The swelling above his temple seemed to have abated, but the cut had been deep, and he'd no doubt carry a scar. "Oh, Baron, I'm sorry," she said, reaching up to touch the knot, then drawing back at the last moment lest she cause him pain. "Can you forgive me?"

"For what? You had nothing to do with this."

"I feel like I did."

"Oh, Faith." He brushed a damp curl from her cheek with his finger. "Their contention has been an issue long before you arrived, and it will be dealt with, I promise you that."

She could hardly think when he touched her. Her heart jumped. Her mouth went dry. "What will you do?"

"I will finish what you began. I refuse to let them drive me away any longer."

A flash of fear mingled with the pride in her expression, and Troyce's heart soared. Unlike Devon, she didn't scold him for his decision. Instead, she understood his inability to give up. To let them win.

"Lady Brayton will not be pleased if you go back to the village."

"Lady Brayton is my sister, Faith, not my mother."

"She worries over you."

"I'll admit that it's nice to know that someone worries over me, but I'm a grown man. I make my own decisions."

"Even at the risk of your own life?"

"Are you worried for me, too, Faith?"

Slowly she looked up at him, and he lost himself in her eyes. Every emotion she felt was reflected there. Fear. Hope.

Desire.

"Yes," she whispered. "I couldn't bear it if something happened to you."

His resistance slipped. God, to hear her say that he meant something to her was like receiving a gift. He took a step toward her. She watched him closely, but she didn't move. Her lids grew heavy. Her lashes fell, dark crescents against her cheekbones. Then she licked her lips, and the ache he'd been nursing in his head all afternoon took a downward shift. The top of her head came just below his chin. Faith was not exactly petite, nor was she overly tall. But next to him, she seemed so small. So fragile. So defenseless. It could have been her being pelted with stones. It could have been her on the ground.

Aware that he was flirting with danger, he traced the edge of her jaw with his fingertip. "God, you are so beautiful." A man could drown in those eyes of hers, and her skin . . . it wasn't pallid like so many women, but fresh and healthy and natural. His fingers traced their way to her mouth. He should leave her alone. But he couldn't. She'd haunted his thoughts, tormented his dreams . . . he could hardly sleep at night for wanting her.

Her lips parted under his caress and Troyce lost all sense of reason. He dipped his head, paused, then settled his mouth on hers. There was hesitance and then a strange resignation as her mouth softened beneath his. Ah, God, she tasted good. Like the heat of sunshine. Like the mystery of moonbeams. And simply like Faith. He slid his tongue across her bottom lip, once, twice, gently so as not to frighten her. He had no idea how much experience she had with men, but from her awkward and timid response, he guessed little or none at all. The thought pleased him immensely.

His patience coaxed a response. She tasted him back, the feel of her tongue meeting his so sweet, so tentative that his chest swelled to the point of bursting.

He'd never known that simply kissing a woman could be so arousing. It took every ounce of willpower he could summon not to thrust his tongue into her mouth, shove her skirts up to her waist, and bury himself inside her. His manhood strained against the front of his breeches, his blood crashed through his veins likes waves in a tempest.

Instead, he held himself tightly in check, his hands remaining around her delicate jaw, his tongue stroking her mouth until his entire body trembled with the effort of holding back.

A whimper penetrated the haze of desire. She brought her hands up between them and pushed at his chest.

He drew back, his brows furrowing. "What is it?"

"I can't . . ." She shook her head.

"You can't what?"

"I can't do this."

"You can't kiss me?"

"I fear it would not stop with kissing."

"Would that be so bad?"

"Aye. I will be no man's whore, Baron, not even yours."

"I don't want you to be any man's whore, Faith. Most especially mine." His dropped to a husky pitch. "Intimacy between a man and a woman who desire each other need not be vulgar or distasteful. Quite the opposite is true—it can be immensely pleasurable."

"In your world perhaps, not in mine."

"Has no man ever made love to you, Faith?" He brushed the pad of his fingers across her kiss-slicked mouth. "Has no man ever feasted upon those succulent lips, buried himself in the glory of your softness? Has no man ever brought you to the highest of heights?"

Every word he spoke, every touch he bestowed, surrounded her in dreams she'd long forgotten to dream. Of being loved. Of being wanted. "You wish to make me your lady, then?"

His shock might have been comical to Faith if it weren't so heartbreaking.

"I wish to be with you," he said carefully. "Why tarnish something so rare and special with something as confining as marriage? We shall simply enjoy each other. If the time comes when one of us is no longer pleased with the other, we would be free to seek our pleasures elsewhere."

What if she didn't want other options? What if she just wanted him?

Faith stepped back from his dizzying nearness and folded her arms about her waist. "So you want me to be your mistress."

"No, I want you to be my lover."

"I see no difference."

"A woman becomes a man's mistress for reasons of security, both personal and financial. With us, there would be no compensation, nor gifts in exchange for services. And our relationship would be completely unrelated to our other arrangement."

"And what would you call me?"

"I'd call you my grandest hope, my deepest desire, my dream come true. What say you, Faith? Will you be my lover?"

For a long time, Faith couldn't say a thing. Was that all she was to him? A body in which to seek his pleasure until someone better came along? She was torn between feeling flattered that he wanted her and hurt that that was all he wanted from her. *He will amuse himself with you, nothing more.*

Well, just because she was in danger of losing her heart to him did not mean she must submit her body to him as well.

"It's a tempting offer, Baron, but it's not enough. I can't deny that I am attracted to you, but I want more out of life than to be some handsome lord's lover."

Bloody fool that she was, she wanted to be his lady.

Chapter 12

By the end of the week, Faith wished someone would just dig her grave and be done
with it. The baron had stuck to his word and returned to the village each day with her. Together,
they worked side by side, each unconsciously
watching the other's back. The villagers had been
both amazed and fearful when he'd walked
boldly into their unofficial territory the next day,
and rather than singling out any of the instigators
for punishment, simply unbuckled the roll of canvass from the back of his saddle.

His tone brooked no protest when he tossed the
canvass to the ground and ordered a young
woman standing nearby to begin cutting squares
for the broken windows. The next day, he hitched
an old plow to his horse and gave the reins over to
the bear of a man, silently commanding him to be-

gin tilling his field. The man, whose name Faith discovered was Bear of all things, glared daggers at the baron but he did not disobey.

On the third day, a team of children were sent throughout the village to gather every nail they could find, and a team of middle-aged adults were instructed to salvage boards and brick to repair the holes weather had created in the walls of buildings. The old crone was given the task of stripping branches Faith and Troyce hauled in from the forests so that thatching could begin the following day.

In all that time, not a word was spoken between Lord Westborough and his tenants—not of the stoning, not of the four years of unpaid rent, not of his eight-year absence. A fragile truce seemed to have been made, almost as if that day had never happened, and Faith could not have been more relieved.

Or more exhausted.

She dragged her weary body up the back steps to the kitchen, thankful that the day had finally ended, yet dreading the chores still ahead. She couldn't find the strength to raise her head much less scrub floors; even breathing seemed too much a chore. Between taking over so many of Millie's tasks, and her work in the village, she recognized that she was reaching her breaking point. But short of quitting there was nothing else she could do. There wasn't a quitting bone in her body. And she wanted that cottage.

Some good did seem to come from keeping busy to the point of exhaustion, though; it left very little time to dwell on the baron's proposal. Not once had he either mentioned it or made another untoward move on her. But hard as she tried, she could not forget those few moments in his chambers. The feel of his mouth, the heat of his body, the touch of his hands. Never in her life had she felt so beautiful, so wanted. Like the princess of her mother's long-ago stories. And the temptation to take him up on his offer would nearly consume her.

Then she would remember Lucy's remark of being an amusement, and her mind would conjure an image of the lamplight women in front of Jorge's, and reason would return.

Reaching the top step, Faith would have missed the basket if she hadn't stumbled over it on her way through the door. When she bent to move it out of her way, heavenly aromas poured forth from beneath the wicker lid. Honey and clove ham. Fried apples. Baked bread that smelled fresh from the oven. Faith dropped to her knees, her mouth watering, her hand paused over the lid. A gluttonous haze clouded her vision and she was certain that if she opened the lid, she'd find chunks of coal put in there as a joke. A very wicked, very cruel joke.

But she couldn't walk away without knowing.

She flipped the lid.

And nearly died.

Inside, the aromas took form in very real lumps wrapped in white cloth and the smells were so powerful she nearly wept. How could someone leave something as beautiful, as wonderful as this on the back porch, all by itself? Treasures like this shouldn't be left alone; they should be cherished. Savored. Treasured. Faith touched one warm lump, caressed it like she would a cloud, fearing it would disappear. Hunger pinched her stomach, temptation mottled her brain. The urge to hook and snatch and pad the hoof with her bounty knotted itself through every aching muscle in her body.

Do not steal from me.

I've not had a problem with thievery until she arrived.

And then, suddenly she knew why the basket had been left here.

He was testing her.

The basket—it was Eve's apple. Temptation calling. Sin incarnate.

Gritting her teeth, she rose, let herself in through the back door, and let it slam behind her. She'd not take something that did not belong to her. No matter how hard it was to resist.

He didn't know if he wanted to strangle her for her stubbornness or applaud her for her willpower, misplaced as it was. Never in a million years would Troyce have imagined that she would have rejected his gift, or that doing so would cause her such anguish. The longing on her face when she'd opened the basket would have made a grown man cry.

He let the drape fall and left his chambers. He was growing increasingly concerned for her health. Each day she seemed to get thinner, dropping weight she could ill afford to lose. According to Millie, she didn't eat enough to keep a sparrow alive and now, even when faced with fare she'd obviously wanted, she refused it.

Was she punishing him?

Bloody hell, why had he ever made such an indecent proposition to her? If she'd been a lady of society, he wouldn't have dared offend her with such an offer. To possess her body, he would have had to give her his name. And he wasn't prepared to give that to anyone. Not yet.

Still, that was no reason for Faith to starve herself.

It was time to take matters into his own hands.

He entered the dining room, and when Lucy arrived to serve the evening meal, he instructed her to send Faith to him.

She appeared in the doorway a few moments later. "You sent for me, milord?"

"Aye." Troyce waved to a chair at his right. "Join me this evening, will you?"

"I don't think Lady Brayton would approve of a servant dining at the master's table."

"Lady Brayton is not feeling well this evening and has decided to dine in her rooms."

"It's nothing serious I hope."

"Nothing that will not pass in a few days." Even the vague reference to a woman's monthly courses had Faith blushing to the roots of her hair. "Sit. What Lady Brayton does not know will not hurt her."

When Faith continued to hover in the doorway, he said, "It was not a request Faith."

Finally, she lowered herself into the chair adjacent to him and clasped her hands tightly in her lap. Her eyes darted about the room in obvious discomfort. But that she didn't put up more of a protest bespoke of her weariness. The shadows under her eyes looked like bruises.

From one of the dishes Lucy had set before him, Troyce dished up heaping portions of roasted quail, boiled potatoes, and a slice of apple pie and set it before her. "You will not leave this seat until you have eaten every bite off this plate. The larders are beginning to run low, so I will not have it wasted."

He felt like a bloody heel when her eyes went damp. "Why are you doing this?"

"Because you are too thin."

"You are too gallant."

"I meant no offense. But I'll not have everyone believing that I starve my servants." He took a sip of his brandy-laced coffee, a pleasure he'd picked up in America that would have horrified his mother if she were alive to know of it. "Since you have rejected my gift, I have no recourse but to insist you eat with me."

"Gift?"

"The basket."

She looked puzzled. "That was a gift?"

"What did you think it was?"

Faith did not dare tell him that she suspected it a test of her trustworthiness.

Or a bribe to get her into his bed.

Jack had always known her greatest fear, of winding up on a street corner. And the baron knew how petrified she was of going to prison. Could he have somehow discovered her greatest weakness—that of food? Was he using it to lure her? To punish her?

"Eat before it gets cold," he said, gesturing toward her plate with a fork.

Ever conscious of the first time she'd been caught eating in front of him, Faith forced herself to pick up the utensils. To place a bite of food in her mouth. To chew slowly.

"You've been working too hard on my behalf, Faith."

"It's been on my own behalf as well, milord." Surely he hadn't forgotten his promise of the cottage. It was even more important now than before that she put some distance between them.

"Be that as it may, I only wanted to express my gratitude with the basket. You will take tomorrow for yourself, as well."

"No, thank you."

"I insist. You need to rest, and it's time Lucy and Millie share some of the workload."

Faith's promise to Millie burned on her tongue. Though the woman was much improved, it had been barely a fortnight since her attack, and she had not yet regained all of her strength. But rather than concede to his orders, she changed the subject. "Is it true that you fired a cook for serving bad fish?"

"Millie has been filling your ears, has she?"

She couldn't lie, so she remained silent.

"Suffice it to say, Cook's demands exceeded his talents, so I released him. It was a mutual agreement. He is happily employed with another, much more prosperous household."

She picked at her food and watched him from beneath her lashes as he ate along with her. His expression gave not a hint of his thoughts, and the guessing was worse than not knowing his motives.

"Are you adjusting well to your life here in the—castle?" His eyes twinkled.

Faith almost choked on a potato. She sucked down a drink of water from the goblet set before her, and once she'd caught her breath said, "Aye, I'm adjusting well enough."

"Good. I feel better knowing that you're settled in before I leave."

She glanced up, startled.

"You're leaving?"

"In the morning. For London." His eyes darkened with what might have been anxiousness before he masked the emotion. "I have a business engagement that I must keep."

Take me with you! She wanted to cry. *Don't leave without me!*

"I want you to stay away from the village while I'm gone."

"I cannot!"

"You can, and you will. It's too dangerous. The tribes may have quieted, but I still do not trust them, not to the extent of allowing you to continue working without me beside you."

"But there's still so much more work to be done."

"Be that as it may, I forbid you to go to the village during my absence. No motley lot of rioters is worth risking your safety."

She would have reminded him that it hadn't been her safety at risk, but his high-handed manner made the point insignificant. "How dare—"

"I dare." He wiped his mouth with a linen napkin, dropped it beside his plate, and got to his feet. "Do not defy me on this, Faith."

Why you arrogant . . . She swallowed roughly, and asked, "When will you be back?"

"A day. Two at the most." He brushed the side of her cheek with his finger and smiled. "I trust you will still be here when I return?"

It was only later that Troyce realized she hadn't answered.

Troyce was beyond being disappointed.

He wanted to hit something.

The minute he'd set eyes on the overdressed, overslicked, overpompous jackanapes, he'd known his last chance for salvation had gone straight down the cesspit.

Gentleman Jack Swift.

What a damned waste.

He had oily opportunist written all over him. Flashing wads of money. Boasting of connections he could not possibly have. What's more, the ass didn't know a bow from a mast. Why he'd claimed interest in the galleon, Troyce couldn't begin to guess, but it became perfectly clear that even the last-ditch effort of discreet inquiries he and Miles had been sending out were not paying off as he'd hoped. Was his dream so unworthy, so ridiculous that it would attract only the lowest of life-forms?

Troyce bellowed at a passing hack, wanting only to get out of the rotting cracker box of a city; he longed for the open country, the salty air and drafty stones of Westborough with a fierceness that surprised him.

The hack clattered on by, churning wheels spraying London muck all over his breeches.

Oh, bloody hell . . . !

He brushed ineffectively at the spatters on his thigh and with a disgusted curse, stormed across the rain-soaked cobblestones toward the river.

Forget hiring a hack, he thought in disgust. The way his luck was running, the coach would wind up cracking an axle and he wouldn't get home at all. He veered toward a livery located in the better part of the city, known to rent decent horseflesh. En route, he passed dockside hawkers huddling beneath misshapen umbrellas, waiting for hardy souls braving the rain to take interest in their stands. Laborers screamed profanities at one another as they struggled to load cargo into a waiting ship.

Finally, he reached the livery. While he waited for a horse, his mind turned once again to home. The term struck an odd nerve. Never before had he called Westborough home; never before had he felt so anxious to go back. He'd spent half his life trying to escape the shackles it represented.

Now he couldn't wait to return.

To Faith.

A restless hunger churned inside him every time he thought of her. He felt as if he'd been away from her for months instead of mere days, as if half of him was missing by leaving her behind. She'd brought life into his heart and into his home. Chased away the gloom and dreariness. He looked forward to each day, wondering what antics she might get up to and what secrets she might reveal about herself. What delights he might discover if he could ever convince her to share his bed.

Troyce frowned. He tried not to think about her rejection, tried to understand why she would not consent to being with him.

She wanted him, just as he wanted her. He saw it every time their eyes met, every time they came near one another. He would catch her looking at his hands, his mouth, and he knew she remembered that kiss in his chambers with every bit of clarity that he did. Even now, the mere memory had the power to drive the temperature around him up a few degrees. And yet, for reasons he didn't comprehend, she thought that being with him made her a trollop.

Or was it that she knew of the temptation she posed and was holding out for more than he was willing to give?

The groom approached, interrupting his thoughts, and handed him the reins to a saddled gelding that would take him to the outpost where he'd stabled his personal mount. Troyce sent the groom away with a gold piece for his trouble and led the horse out of the livery. A man shouting near the docks snagged his notice. Troyce ignored him, mounted the horse, and would have passed right on by had a small yelp not cut through his dulled senses.

He snapped back around and spotted a familiar figure in a worn macintosh shaking his finger at something on the ground. Then he drew back his foot and kicked. A second yelp erupted at the same time Troyce noticed the small form huddled between two barrels that reeked of fish. The reins dropped heedlessly from his fingers and before his brain gave the command, he slid off the horse.

". . . you worthless piece of baggage! Didn't I tell you not to show your face around me until you brought news?"

Just as he drew his booted foot back for another strike, Troyce's fingers clawed over the man's shoulder and spun him around. "Is there a problem here, Swift?"

"This is none of your affair, Westborough. Move along."

Déjà vu hit him then and his mind spun back to the moment he and Feagin had engaged in a similar . . . discussion . . . in front of Jorge's Tavern. Troyce told himself not to get involved, to get back on his horse and just go home. But before he could stop them, the words slid from his mouth in stony determination. "I'm making it my affair."

Swift made the worst mistake he could have made in that moment. He put up his fists.

Troyce heaved a sigh. Then he doubled up and slammed his fist into Swift's pretty face. The bloke fell like a sack of grain.

" 'Zounds, guv! You just dropped Jack Swift!"

"Aye, I did." He shook out his fist. "I've been wanting to do that all morning." He turned to the source of the small voice. Recognition hit both of them at once. "So we meet again, mate," Troyce said, taking in the ragged clothes, the grimy face, dark eyes, and stringy black hair visible from beneath the cap.

Scatter's mouth fell. "You're . . . 'im!"

He couldn't believe it! Hell, he'd turned over every brick in London looking for the bloke who'd taken Fanny, but the chum had disappeared into thin air. Then, of a sudden, he shows up on the docks? What famous luck!

Scatter glanced around. "Where's Fan? Is she with you?" It would save him a whole lot of trouble if she was. If he could find out where Fanny was, Jack would finally let him go back to the band! He'd been living on the docks so long he'd almost forgotten what the tunnels looked like.

"No, she's not with me."

"What 'ave ye done with her?"

"Calm yourself. She's quite safe, and I'll venture to say, she'll be overjoyed to see you."

"Ye know where she is?"

"Aye. Come along. I'll take you to her." He started to walk away, then a thought struck. "What ever happened to the coins the two of you pilfered from me?"

The boy's expression turned wary, reminding him so much of Faith in that instant that his heart swelled. "Have no fear, lad, I just want to know what you did with the money."

The boy slid a cautious glance toward the prone figure on the ground. With a devilish grin, Troyce crouched beside Swift, dug through his pockets for the wad of notes he'd taunted him with during their earlier meeting, peeled two hundred pounds worth off the stack, and dropped the rest upon his chest. *Let the carrion feed.*

Moments later, with the boy secured in the saddle, Troyce asked, "Is there anything you need before we leave? We won't be coming back."

The lad shook his head. "I just wanna see Fanny."

"Aye, I know the feeling." He'd just put his foot in the stirrup and was preparing to mount up in front of the boy when shouts from a group of passengers fresh off a nearby ship spooked his mount.

Troyce took a moment to calm the horse, then he glared at the crowd. The old familiar sight of an American cowboy hat bobbing up and down with the crowd moving along the wharf caught his notice. The owner materialized with a woman in a red gown and black cape at his side. Their heads were bent close, hers just below his chin. The man held his coat over their heads to protect them from the rain, his arm circled the woman's shoulders protectively, possessively, improperly. There was nothing exceptional about the pair except that watching them made him think of the way Faith fit against him.

Then the woman looked up.

Troyce drew back in surprise. Faith?

No. It couldn't be. His eyes were playing tricks on him. So the woman had the same amber-hued hair. So her jawline was the same delicate slope, and her nose tilted in the same adorable manner. It couldn't possibly be Faith huddled in the shelter of another man's—an American's—arms. Faith was tucked sixty kilometers away at Westborough Manor.

Wasn't she?

My red dress is missing.

His heart picked up pace and prickles of trepidation climbed up his spine. He ducked beneath the horse's head and stepped forward to get a closer look just as her companion pulled her closer. She leaned into him the exact same way Faith had leaned into him that night in his room and let him tip her chin up with his finger.

Then the American kissed her.

On the mouth.

Troyce felt as if he'd taken a mainmast to the sternum. His breath left his lungs in a rush. His knees buckled. Every caution delivered to him over the last couple of weeks came back at him in biting sequence:

She'll rob you blind!

Isn't it coincidental . . . ?

. . . form of manipulation . . .

She had designs on you . . .

The man flagged down a passing hack and once it stopped, they climbed inside.

What the hell would Faith be doing in the city with an American? Who the hell was he? And what in the hell did he think he was doing kissing her?

Well, by God, he was going to find out.

"Stay here," he barked at the lad. Then he started toward the vehicle, only to hit a crowd of seamen spilling off the docks, engaging in bawdy revelry. Jumping on the balls of his feet, he tried to keep the hack in sight. When it pulled away from the curb, he tried pushing his way through, but even a man of his size was no match for a dozen brawny, barrel-chested sailors.

He spun on his heel and sprinted to his horse.

* * *

"Feeling better now, darlin'?"

Honesty laid her head on Jesse's sturdy shoulder and sighed. "I will. I'm not much of a sailor, I'm afraid." The train ride from San Francisco to New York had been stuffy, but tolerable, but the six-week journey across the Atlantic, then up the Thames had not agreed with Honesty in the least. Her stomach still hadn't settled from the trip. "I don't think I've ever been so glad to feel land beneath my feet."

Jesse chuckled. "We should be at the hotel soon. You'll feel better once you've had some rest."

"I'd really rather start searching for Faith." It had been the only thing that kept her going when she'd been so sick she didn't think she'd survive another day aboard her father's ship.

"I promised Anton that we'd wait until he finished his business on board. He wanted to be with us when we talked with the Scotland Yard investigators."

"Do you think they'll be able to help us after all this time? She might never have even been to London."

"We'll know soon enough. This is the best place to start, though, Honesty. And if Scotland Yard can't help us, I've heard that London boasts one of the best detective agencies in the world. They call themselves Bow Street Runners."

"Surely they can't compare to Allen Pinkerton's men."

"Of course not," Jesse boasted, "but they come mighty close."

Shouting outside the carriage interrupted their

joint spurts of laughter. Jesse swiveled in the seat
to peer out the side of the coach.

"What is it?" Honesty asked.

"Just a pair of fools tearing down the middle of
the road on a horse."

"Do you think they're after someone?"

"Either that or someone's after them."

She grinned at the irony. "There seems to be a
lot of that going around."

"Looks like they're not going anywhere now."

Despite her lingering nausea, curiosity had Honesty twisting around to peer out the other side of the
coach. Instantly she spotted the riders he'd been referring to, one man, one boy, both bellowing profanities at an army of dockworkers blocking their way
with a crate large enough to house the Alamo.

The frustrated desperation on the man's face
touched a cord of sympathy inside her. And in
that instant, she knew that he, like herself, was after someone.

"I hope he finds her," Jesse said as if reading her
mind.

She looked at her husband as he settled back
down into the seat. "What makes you so sure that
he's after a woman?"

"Because the only thing that can make a man
curse like that is a female."

Troyce didn't even let the horse come to a full
stop before vaulting out of the saddle and racing
into the house.

"Faith!" He stormed through the entrance hall,
heedless of the mud he was tracking on the clean

stone floor, or the child dogging his steps. "Faith, where the hell are you!"

Millie appeared in the doorway, her face wreathed in puzzled concern. "Is something wrong, milord?"

"Where's Faith?"

"She went to the village. I expect her back anytime."

That defiant little—"How long has she been gone?"

"Since early this morning, milord."

Troyce cursed. It was past dusk. Thanks to the crowd on the wharf, he'd lost track of the carriage she'd been riding in, so the only way he knew to find out for sure if she'd been the woman he'd seen was to return to Westborough. If he found her here, and the staff could vouch for her, he'd know he'd made a mistake. If she wasn't here . . .

"Do you wish for me to send someone after her?"

"I'll go myself." He spun around and nearly ran Scatter over. "Millie, the lad needs a meal, a bath, and suitable clothing—oh, and someplace to sleep. See to it, if you will."

"Oh, lud, another one?"

Troyce returned to his horse and left for the village. And if Faith knew what was good for her, he would find her there.

But he didn't.

Night fell, and with it, what little control he'd managed to retain on his temper. He recognized that he was fast venturing beyond rational action, yet he couldn't rid himself of the vision of her in the other man's arms, lifting her face for his kiss, riding away with him.

He didn't want to believe it. Didn't want to think she would betray him or that he could be so deuced stupid to have let it happen.

But the truth he'd stubbornly tried to deny was, Faith Jervais—if that was even her name—was a product of the London underworld, a street survivor. Her submissiveness and cooperation had simply been a ploy to throw him off her true intent.

Whatever the hell that was.

A slow burning fury continued to simmer inside him as he entered the village, and by the time he finished questioning the tenants, his mood had grown dark as the thunderclouds rolling across the blackening sky. No one had seen her since that morning when she'd announced that she planned on rounding up stray sheep. Clever thinking—a perfect excuse that would leave her free to make the trip to London, meet her lover, and be long gone before anyone knew what hit them. And no one would be the wiser. And he, fool that he was, had given her carte blanche to roam at will.

A drop of rain all but sizzled against his skin as he veered his horse toward a shortcut through the woods on the off chance he might see her or at least some sign of her passage before the rains wiped out any tracks she may have left. He was probably wasting his time. No doubt she was halfway across the Continent with her American cowboy by now.

It crossed his mind that if she wanted away from him so badly, he should simply let her go. He'd gotten his money back from Swift, there was no longer any reason to keep her here against her will. Yet he couldn't. She still owed him for the trouble, he told himself, kicking his horse into a lope. Two hundred bloody pounds worth of trouble to be exact, and by God he'd get it back if he had to track her to the ends of the earth and take it pound by pound out of her flesh.

Halfway through the woods, a sound startled his horse. It stepped back, danced in placed then lunged forward again. "Easy boy, easy," Troyce muttered, keeping a firm hand on the reins and his eyes peeled for the source. The woods of the low weald were thick with full-leafed beech and maple and holly. Wild hedges and barbed plants grew between them, creating hazards enough for man and beast during the daylight; but in full darkness, the trail became even more treacherous.

Again the sound came, almost a bleating, causing the horse to pull its forelegs off the ground. Its ears flattened against its head, his eyes rolled back. It took all Troyce's strength to keep the animal from bolting. Again, he searched the trees, the ground, the area around the trunks.

And there he saw her, lying on her side on a bed of leaves at the base of a pale-barked beech. In the space of a few seconds he took in the sight of her. Muddy skirts. One shoe missing.

Tear stains on her cheeks.

Nearby, a lamb cried plaintively.

"Sweet Jesus . . ." he whispered.

The anger that had been driving him faded, replaced with raw fear. Was she . . . ? He couldn't think the word without a cold chill spearing his heart.

He dismounted and after securing the nervous horse to a low limb, strode on silent feet toward her, the leaves muffling his footsteps. The lamb backed away when he crouched beside her, close enough to see the even rise and fall of her shoulder.

He closed his eyes, relief making his bones weak. "Faith," he called softly. When she didn't stir, he touched her shoulder.

She shot up so fast it threw him backward. Eyes wide, she scrambled back, grabbing at the ground for a convenient weapon—a broken limb—and wielded it before her like a club.

Troyce regained his balance, and slowly unfolded his body. "Faith, it's me." He held his hands out. "It's Troyce."

Recognition reached her eyes. She dropped the club, and with a half sob, hurled herself into his arms.

His first thought was that one of the villagers had taken their bitter resentment out on her. "What happened?" he demanded, shoving her back a step for a cursory examination. "Are you hurt? Did they touch you?"

She shook her head, then launched herself back into his arms. "I didn't think anyone would find me," she said, her words muffled against his coat. Small fingers pressed into the back of his neck, slender curves fit against his rigid frame.

Troyce steeled himself against the wave of tenderness threatening to engulf him. He wrapped his hands around her shoulders and pushed her back. "What the hell are you doing out here?"

"I was looking for—" She immediately searched the surrounding area. "Where's the lamb?" Spotting the frightened critter, she scooped it up and cuddled the lamb close to her. "There you are, you little wretch!" She lifted him until their noses were nearly touching. "Do you know how much trouble you've caused?"

Her smile softened the scolding. "I was rounding up sheep. One of the women in the village owns a spinning wheel—I thought if we could gather some of the strays, we might have a shearing party. That's when I heard this little fellow bleating." She scrubbed his cottony head with her fingers. "I went looking for him, and I must have wandered farther than I thought, because then I couldn't find my way back. All the trees looked the same, I think I was going in circles. Then it got too dark to see anything, so me and this little fellow planted ourselves by the closest tree. I must have fallen asleep."

She sounded so convincing. So honest . . .

"It's quite embarrassing really," she said, a becoming flush coloring her cheekbones. "I knows the streets of London like the back of me hand, but put me in the wide-open country, and I'm helpless as this little blighter."

As always when she was nervous or upset, she fell into the street cant of her upbringing. That, more than anything kept him from falling under her spell. "You expect me to believe that you spent the entire day and half the night looking for sheep?"

She took a long time in answering. Then she looked up at him, her brown eyes bottomless pools of heart and soul. "Actually, I think . . . I must have been waiting for you."

Chapter 13

There was something potent in the silence that followed. Something alive, electrical.

She looked pitiful, hair a sopping stream of amber. Dirt under her cheekbone. Clothes lank and torn on her slender frame. Like a ship in storm-tossed sea, mast listing, rigging shredded, canvases limp.

And still she was so damned desirable she made his chest hurt. How had it come to this, that he could be more aroused by a drowned street rat than the most beautiful ladies in England? He saw her at her best and he wanted her. He saw her at her worst, her most unappealing and still, he wanted her. He saw her in the arms of another man, wearing a gown that belonged to his sister.

And still . . .

He wanted her.

"God damn you, Faith, what kind of game are you playing with me?"

Her brows drew into a V, she shook her head.

Then she opened her mouth as if to answer but he cut her off. "You say you were waiting for me. What of your friend?"

"What friend?"

"The one I saw you with earlier." With each question pelting her like stones from the villagers, Troyce took a step forward, driving Faith backward. Betrayal coursed from every pore. "Where is he now, Faith? *Who* was he? Your lover? Your accomplice? Both?"

"What are you talking about, Baron? I haven't been near a single soul since I left the village this morning."

"Did you leave Westborough lands?"

"I may have," she answered carefully. "How far does Westborough go?"

"To London!"

Her eyes widened. "Your estate reaches all the way to London?"

"No, I mean, have you *been* to London?"

"Of course I have. I lived there over half me life!"

She was playing with his questions, twisting the words. "Today! Yesterday! Anytime in the last week!"

"Why would I go to London? How would I even get there?"

"Just answer the damn question!" He had to know, had to hear it from her own mouth . . .

A birch tree at her back prevented her from retreating any farther. Her eyes blazed, yet her voice was unnaturally calm. "No, milord, I ha' not been to London today or yesterday or anytime in the last week. I ha' not been to London since the day you put me in your carriage and brought me to your home."

As if to punctuate her claim, thunder cracked overhead, a bolt of lightning split the sky.

Troyce glanced up, then back down at Faith, who wore the same defiant expression she'd worn the day he'd caught her picking his pocket. If he let himself, he could easily fall under the same spell now that she had wrapped around him then.

But he refused to let himself be played the fool a second time. "Get on the horse. There's a storm blowing in, and I've no wish to get caught in it." He'd been caught in one since leaving the city, one of such violent turbulence that it would put a typhoon to shame.

"You don't believe me."

He didn't know what to believe. He wanted to trust her—badly. He'd known he was bringing a petty thief into his home, but he didn't want to think he'd been harboring a liar this whole time as well, someone who could be so devious as to sneak around behind his back, plotting who-knew-what transgression against him.

But he'd seen her.

Hadn't he?

Was she the woman he'd seen in London, embraced in another man's arms? The evidence piling up against her had grown more damaging by the minute. No one had seen her since this morning. No one but a lamb could support her story.

She could have made it there and back, same as he had.

Or had she truly spent half the night in the woods, lost, scared, alone?

"Tell me this, if I'd have found my way to London, why would I have come back here?"

He hadn't thought of that. There was certainly nothing holding her here. Of course, the chap she'd been with could have abandoned her, he supposed. Or he could have sent her back to Westborough to bide her time. . . .

"I don't know what it is you think I've done, Baron, but let me make one thing clear—I don't lie. I don't make promises I can't keep, and I don't say things I don't mean. If ye can't believe that, then t'hell with ye."

She started past him. He seized her by the arm and pulled her to him. Instant awareness sizzled between them, born of anger and confusion and, aye, he admitted, raw jealousy. "I thought that you'd left," he blurted.

"What?"

"When I returned from London and you weren't here, I thought you'd left. I couldn't find you." He didn't tell her of the woman he'd seen, didn't tell her that he'd nearly been driven insane with jealousy. "I was worried."

"You were worried about me?"

She sounded skeptical, and he couldn't blame her. "I thought the villagers might have hurt you."

"Are you saying you believe me?"

He didn't answer for a long time. He wasn't sure he knew how. If she hadn't been the woman in London, then it meant that, although Faith was telling the truth, he was seeing her face in other women. If she *had* been the woman he'd seen, it meant that she'd rejected him for someone else. Either way, she was coming to mean more to him than she should. Rattled, he released his grip on her and stepped back. "Aye, I believe you." He sighed, knowing even as he said it that he was probably the biggest fool in England. "Now get on the horse before I do something we'll both regret." Like kiss her sense-less, show her who owned her, brand her in the most primal way a man could brand a woman.

Whether she allowed it or not.

She looked as if she would defy him but to her credit seemed to decide against testing the limits of his control. Wise choice, he thought, watching her approach the horse. He was holding on to it by a thread as it was. Troyce had never considered himself an irrational man, yet the feelings rolling inside him were anything but rational. And if he didn't put some distance between them now, he wasn't sure he could hold himself accountable for his actions.

A pouring rain kept them company on the way back to the castle. With the lamb tucked beneath her coat, Faith rode behind him, holding herself as stiff as she dared without falling off the back of the horse.

She felt like a fool. For getting lost. For being so glad to see him. For thinking he'd actually cared.

He was furious with her, that much was clear. Part of her couldn't blame him. She had dis-obeyed him by going to the village after he'd for-bidden it. Aye, for that he had a right to be angry.

But another part of her could not understand what the bloody hell he'd been ranting about. He didn't strike her as a lunatic, but his accusations were hardly the ravings of a sane man. How could he have thought to have seen her in London—with someone else, no less—when she hadn't been anywhere near the city in nearly a month? It made no sense. No sense at all.

He'd said he believed her, though. She supposed she should take comfort in that. Except she didn't think he meant it. The knowledge stung. For in the back of his mind, distrust lay like a sleeping giant, ready to be wakened at any given moment.

How could she take comfort in something so fickle?

By the time they reached the manor house, both of them were soaked to the bone. The baron guided the horse straight through the double doors of the stables. Inside, it was warm, dry. The scent of horseflesh and leather lay thick in the air. Piles of hay lay in the corner, as inviting to her weary body as a feather-stuffed bed.

"Go on up to the house and get yourself dry while I put up the horse."

"I'll help."

"I can do it myself, Faith."

"And I said I'd help." Maybe she was testing fate by staying near him when he so obviously wanted to be rid of her, but if he hadn't found her, she'd be spending yet another night of her life sleeping outside, exposed to the elements. For that, if nothing else, she owed him her gratitude. "It's the least I can do."

By the time Faith had put the lamb in an empty

stall and latched the gate, the baron had already removed the saddle from the horse. She dragged the wet blanket off the gelding's back and laid it over a sawhorse to dry.

They worked in strained silence, he removing the gear, she rubbing the animal's hide with a rag. She wanted to ask him how his trip had gone, why it had taken him so long to return. The house had never felt so big as when he was not in it.

She'd missed seeing him make his way to the boathouse each morning, his powerful frame outlined by sky and sea. She'd missed catching him in his study, worrying over his ledgers. Most of all, she'd missed working by his side in the village, sweat dripping from his brow, clothes sticking to his back, muscles flexing as he wielded a hammer or ax.

By going to the village, she'd only wanted to feel closer to him. She hadn't counted on losing her way back. So she'd done the only thing she could think of.

She'd sat down to wait.

She'd fallen asleep.

And she'd dreamed. Of storybook princes and castles and evil dragons. Of the sun and the sea and a place far away. Of a dashing man and a little girl and a graveside that held ghosts that wouldn't stop haunting her.

Ho-ne-sty, come out come out wherever you are . . .

Faith clenched her eyes shut. Honesty had never come out.

And she'd been sent away.

Faith shook the dream away. She hadn't thought of that day in years, hadn't let herself think of the sister she once loved, the father she once adored. Why it would become so vivid now, she didn't want to know.

With the horse dried and brushed, there seemed to be nothing else to keep her in the stables. She hung the rag over the top of a stall and decided to see if Millie knew what she could feed the lamb until it could be reunited with its mother. But when she reached the double doors, she couldn't bring herself to leave with so much unsettled between herself and his lordship. He didn't trust her, she knew that, and maybe, he had just cause. But he'd come after her anyway. "Baron?"

He glanced up. Rain dripped from a curl of hair over his forehead, moonlight cast the sharp angles of his face in mystery.

"Thank you for looking for me." No one had ever come looking for her before. Not even Jack. He'd have found her by now. Apparently she was as disposable to him as she'd been to everyone else in her life.

"Did you think I would just let you run off?"

"No one else would have cared."

At that, she dashed across the saturated lawn to the front steps of the castle and let herself inside. She still couldn't get over the fact that the baron allowed his servants to use the front entrance. She ran into Millie in the entryway, carrying a pile of folded towels. Each day the woman grew stronger and was able to take on more tasks. Still, Faith kept a close eye on her to make sure she did not overtax herself.

"There you are, Faith. His lordship is out looking for you."

"Actually, he found me. He's in the stables now, brushing down his horse."

"He wasn't too happy about you going to the village."

"I know. I found a lamb in the woods," she said to change the subject. "Do we have anything in the pantry that we can feed it until I can get it back to its mother?"

"We might have some milk in the icebox," she answered.

Faith had just started for the kitchen to fetch it when Millie's next words stopped her. "Oh, I nearly forgot—there's a gentleman waiting for you in the kitchen."

"A gentleman?" She hadn't noticed a horse or carriage outside, but then again, nor had she been looking. "Did he say his name?"

Her eyes twinkled. "No, but he seems quite anxious to see you."

He'd found her.

Jack Swift had finally tracked her down. He was the only person with the motive or the means to have located her so far out of London.

Faith's hands were damp with perspiration as she forced herself down the long hall toward the kitchen. She imagined him waiting with courtly impatience, sneering at Millie while she tried to serve him coffee. Toying with his solid gold pocket watch he often bragged had been coughed off a prince.

She realized now that sometime over the last few weeks, she'd grown lax. Fooled herself into thinking that he was part of her past. That she'd not have to face him again. It was a mistake she would pay for now.

Resigning herself to the inevitable, she opened the door.

And gasped.

"Fanny!"

"Oh, my God—Scatter, ya lovely little leech!" He raced toward her, and she caught him in her arms. Crikey, the top of his head reached hers now—had he grown taller? "What are ye doin' here? How did ye find me?"

"The baron brought me."

"The baron? Ye mean Lord Westborough?"

"Aye. Zounds, Fan, ye should have seen him." Black eyes glittered with joy. "He punched him left, then punched him right—" He swung each hand in turn.

"Punched who?"

"Jack! Oh lud, 'twas a sight. We'd ha' made a fortune bettin' on him in the ring."

"Lord Westborough brawled with Jack?"

She sensed his presence and turned. He stood with one shoulder against the doorframe, arms loosely crossed over his chest, hip angled, and booted foot turned outward. Eyes soft as the sea at dawn gazed upon her.

"You fought Jack Swift?" she asked in awe.

Whatever tenderness she'd seen in those misty gray swirls disappeared. "It was nothing. A minor squirmish."

"It weren't even that," Scatter interjected. "He

popped him one right in the smacker and *phlooop*—down Jack went."

"Scatter, I believe Millie is waiting for you outside," the baron said in a tone that brooked no argument.

"They want me to take a bath," Scatter told Faith.

"It's not so bad. You'll get a meat pie once you're clean."

"A whole meat pie? All to myself?"

"You won't have to share it with anyone. And you'll get to eat at the table, too."

"At the table? Zounds, Fan!" He started for the door, then turned abruptly, his brow creased with concern. "You'll still be here when I'm done, won't ye? You won't leave me behind again?"

"I won't ever leave you behind again, I promise you that."

"Good. Cause mates don't leave mates."

"Mates don't leave mates," she whispered.

With her fingers pressed to her lips and her eyes so blurred with tears she could barely see, she watched him walk out the door. Her mind reeled over the fact that Scatter, the closest thing she could claim to family, was here at Westborough. God's teeth, she'd missed the little beggar, more than she ever thought possible.

"I thought you might be pleased to see him again."

"Pleased! Oh, milord, you've no idea." She grinned through her tears. "I can't believe you found him. That you brought him here. . . . Thank you. From the bottom of my heart, I thank you for bringing the lad home to me."

* * *

It was a vision that haunted Troyce in the days to come. Faith so grateful, her face so soft—almost motherly—her love for the waif clear to anyone who looked. He didn't think he'd seen a more lovely vision in his life. It made him want to give her the world on a silver platter. Seize the moon straight out of the sky and hand it to her just to see her eyes light up. It made him want to—

Do exactly what his father had done for his mother.

She has designs on you.

Was that it? Troyce wondered. Faith was perfectly aware that he had not a farthing to his name, but he did have something many girls dreamed of having. A title. Granted, it wasn't much of one, the lowest of the peerage ranks, but it was still a title.

He raked his hands through his hair. Why was he so damned suspicious of her? Why couldn't he just treat her like any other servant in his household?

Why the hell couldn't he stop thinking of her?

He picked up the quill he'd thrown down on the desk, and determined to purge her from his mind. It took several minutes to focus his concentration on the ledgers, and then, he wished he hadn't. The numbers weren't increasing, but they weren't shrinking either. Pence by pence Faith was saving by making do. Replacing coal with peat gathered from the countryside. Trading surplus supplies or labor with the villagers for necessities. She was absolutely amazing in bartering and thriftiness, and again he wondered how she'd come to live such a life.

But it wasn't enough.

If the finances weren't already in such a sorry mire, another of his father's creditors had popped up, demanding a twenty-thousand-pound payment for some bauble his mother had no doubt thrown into the Channel for being the wrong color. But the real clincher was the Notice of Taxes Due he'd received in the morning's mail. He had little more than two months to pay the queen her due, or he would lose everything he'd worked so hard to keep. The noose grew tighter around his throat. The sinking feeling in his stomach told him where to find the answer.

He had no choice anymore.

He would have to find a wife.

Chapter 14

"So which would you prefer, a garden soiree or a summer ball?" Devon asked after breakfast two mornings later.

She was in her element. Give her an event to plan, and she was all aflutter. Normally, Troyce would have celebrated the rare burst of life that lit her eyes. Unfortunately, he felt as if she were simply planning his day on the hanging platform.

"You don't have to enjoy this so much, Devon."

"It is my duty as your sister to see that you are properly betrothed. However, you are not making this easy by refusing every invitation that I've presented to you. So I've decided that if you will not go to society, then society shall come to you."

"I can't afford to host a party, and you know it."

"You don't have to. *Grandpère* is taking care of all the expenses."

"You told *Grandpère?*"

"I had no choice, West. If you are to attract a wealthy, titled maiden, you cannot appear the pauper. Now which do you prefer?"

He would prefer to survive the whole bloody debacle with at least a measure of his pride intact. No one was even supposed to know that he was in the market for a bride. It was supposed to be a simple gathering of their closest, wealthiest neighbors, a discreet opportunity to assess his prospects. "Not a garden party. The last thing I want to do is spend the day smacking a bloody croquet ball all over kingdom come."

"Then a summer ball it is. It will be nice to put the ballroom to use after all these years. Do you remember the parties Mother used to host? Oh, I just loved those tiny bowls of fish she'd place on the tables. Of course, Aunt Phoebe mistook them for finger bowls and Uncle Edward thought they were water goblets and drank four of them."

A reluctant grin tugged at his mouth at the memory. "I remember the time you and Miles—" Troyce caught himself too late. "I'm sorry, Devon."

She tossed her head. "It doesn't matter. Miles Heath means nothing to me." But her hands shook nonetheless as she took a drink of water. "I'm thinking about wearing my red dress."

"Your red dress? I thought you said it was missing?"

"Lucy found it a couple of weeks ago."

"And you did not see fit to tell me?"

"Why would I? You made it quite clear that you care nothing for a lost piece of—what did you call it—feminine frippery?"

He wouldn't have given a flying fig about it if she hadn't been ready to hang Faith for something she hadn't even done. And he hadn't seen another woman in a red dress and thought it was her. Troyce felt his stomach turn.

"Do you think it would be too scandalous if I wore it so soon after father's death?"

He threw his napkin on the table and shot to his feet. "Wear a bloody potato sack for all I care."

He walked outside and saw Faith and Scatter heading down the hill for the village. What a pair they made. Faith so fair and slender and graceful, Scatter so tall and dark and gangling. He thought about joining them; he missed spending his days working with Faith at his side. He missed watching her with the children, grubby urchins that they were, and he missed hearing her explain her ideas to the older ones, cantankerous crones that they were.

Most of all, he missed the way she always looked for him. Their gazes would meet across a street or over a field or under a broken cart, and all the pieces of his broken world would fall into place. She made him feel like a bloody hero.

His throat tightened. He shoved his hands into his pockets and headed for the boathouse. Damn it all, what was he doing? He had no right thinking of her. No right wanting to be with her. No right wishing he could give up everything his father had left him just to have her.

He was to marry someone else.

"Do ye ever miss the tunnels, Fanny?" Scatter asked, his voice echoing across the entrance hall.

He'd been anxious to help her in the castle today, so Faith had set him to the task of replacing the candles in the pewter holders that sat on one of the tables they'd brought in from an unused room.

Polishing the lion's head at the bottom end of the balustrade, she said, "Not so much the tunnels, but I miss the band. How is everyone?"

"Don't know. I ain't been back since ye left."

"What do you mean?"

"Jack wouldn't let me go back till I had news of ye."

The rag paused on the lion's mane. "Where did you live?"

"On the docks, mostly. Sometimes I'd find a building no one was usin', but I'd have to be real careful of the coppers, so I didn't get much sleep. This sure is a big house. I bet a few of the lads wouldn't mind living here."

"Don't think it, Scat. Lord Westborough was kind enough to bring in a few of the villagers to help ready the house for the party, but I don't want to test his generosity." Not just yet anyway. Once he learned to trust her and Scatter, though, she hoped she might persuade him to bring in a few more members of the band.

"Ye want me to start fillin' the lamps?"

"Aye—I mean, yes," she corrected herself. "The oil is kept in the pantry on the other side of the icebox. Do you know where that is?"

Scatter nodded, then tore down the hall. Faith smiled. In the two days since he'd been at Westborough, he'd brightened her days. She finally had someone to talk to, and someone who listened. Someone who didn't judge, didn't accuse, and most importantly, didn't set her nerves a-riot.

Unlike some people she could mention.

She knew she should probably be grateful that she hadn't seen much of the baron since he'd brought her back from the woods. The truth was, though she didn't see him, he was never far from her thoughts. She kept seeing him as he'd been in the stables, his shirt plastered to his skin, his hair in disarray, his eyes shooting fire. He'd been mad enough to skin a cat and yet, he'd also been the most wildly attractive man she'd ever seen.

She still couldn't believe he'd brought Scatter back with him from London. That he would have gone back to her world, just to bring her back a piece of it, still touched her to the depths of her soul. No one had ever done something like that for her before.

Sighing, calling herself the silliest of gooses, she moved up a step to reach the upper railing of the banister. Lady Brayton had left instructions that the entire house was to be spotless by the Friday of next week. Apparently, the party was to be a grand event, a chance for the baron to meet some powerful people. Faith hoped that one of them might be willing to invest in his ship. She knew how much he worried about money. She'd already been informed by Lady Brayton that no nonsense would be tolerated. Fifty or so guests had been invited to Westborough, and while they were there, Faith was to remain out of sight and out of trouble or there would be the devil to pay.

Faith tried not to let it bother her, but there were times when she wondered if she would ever fit in here. Aye, the villagers seemed to accept her well enough. And all the house servants save Lucy had grown used to her, but Lady Brayton . . . she shook her head. She just didn't know what to think of that woman.

Or her brother.

Faith pushed the baron from her mind and moved up another step. Best just to concentrate on her task, for the year would end soon, and she would be free. As she dragged the rag up the banister, she found herself thinking of her life on the streets, of all the times she'd slid down pipe rails in her haste to escape a bobbie.

It seemed years had passed instead of months since she'd been chased. And while she could not say she enjoyed being a target, neither could she deny an odd thrill in the pursuit. The outwitting of foxes. The excitement of running and dodging, leaping and . . . yes, sliding to freedom.

She stared longingly at the gleaming banister. No, she couldn't. She didn't dare. If she got caught, Newgate would look like paradise compared to where Lady Brayton would send her.

But oh, how slick it looked. How damned inviting.

She glanced at the kitchen, then the study door. No one was about. The baron had left hours ago to work on his ship; Lady Brayton had gone to Brayton Hall with Lucy to collect extra bedding for the guests. Millie was napping, and Chadwick had been sent to the village to train a few of the villagers on butlering. No one would ever know . . .

Her heart pounded with the thrill of the forbidden as she raced to the very top of the staircase. Bunching her skirts, she mounted the banister sidesaddle. A smile of sheer delight spread across her face as she started to slide. "Wheeee!" she cried, picking up speed. When she reached the bend in the railing at the landing where the staircase split into wings, she tilted her body to accommodate the slant.

It was in that moment that the front door opened, and in walked Lady Brayton, Lucy, and Chadwick.

Faith's heart flew into her throat but she couldn't have stopped if her life depended on it. The starched fabric of her skirt on polished oak was like butter on a hot skillet, and down she went. Just before she would have hit the lion's head at the end of the railing, she leaped off onto solid ground. The momentum drove her forward and she slammed into Lady Brayton. She had a flashing image of wide-eyed shock and mouths agape before one after another, the group tumbled like a row of dominoes: the duchess fell back against Lucy, Lucy fell back against Chadwick, and all three landed on the floor while pillows and bedding flew into the air like an exploding linen factory.

Faith landed on the floor on her bum, her plain gray skirts and muslin petticoats tangled with Lady Brayton's black crepe gown and frilly underslips. Behind her, cushioning her body from the stone floor, lay Lucy on a mound of blankets, and beside her sat Chadwick, blinking in confusion.

For several long, swollen moments, no one said a word until Lady Brayton, red-faced with fury, sputtered, "You . . . you . . ." She grabbed the nearest object and swung.

Years of quick reflexes had Faith ducking. Instead of sailing harmlessly through the air, the pillow struck Chadwick against the side of his head. And then it burst. Feathers spewed from one end like ash from a smokestack.

At first, Faith was too stunned to react. She saw Lady Brayton clap a hand to her mouth in equal parts horror and mortification; Lucy gasped. Chadwick spat a feather out from between his lips.

Then to everyone's openmouthed astonishment, Lady Brayton laughed.

It started with a tremble of her shoulders, moved to the quaking of her back and then a very unduchesslike snort. Downy white feathers swirled around them, heavens rain, and angelic peals of laughter built into a choir of song. "Oh, Chadwick, forgive me, I did not mean to hit you," Lady Brayton gushed. "I meant to hit her!"

Faith wasn't quick enough this time, and the pillow caught her against the shoulder. Again, goose feathers exploded from the cotton slip.

"All right, I've had about all I can take..." Consequences flew out of Faith's mind as she grabbed a second pillow and swung.

Lady Brayton squealed and threw her arms over her head and her body to the floor; the pillow caught Lucy on the shoulder and knocked her over.

Roaring with laughter, Lady Brayton flung a blanket at Faith and smacked her in the face.

Peeling the shroud away from her eyes, Faith growled, "You think that's funny?"

And the war began.

Pillows, feathers, blankets, even a few articles of clothing were tossed through the air. Chadwick tried his best to break up the fight, Lucy did her best to encourage Lady Brayton, but Faith and Lady Brayton had eyes only for each other as they raced around the entrance hall of Westborough Manor with downy clubs, sometimes using people as shields, sometimes taking well-aimed blows with cries of, "You call yourself a sporting girl, Miss Jervais?" and "Is that the best you've got, Duchess?"

Sometime during the fray, Scatter arrived and Faith found her back guarded from Lucy, who had given up encouraging her lady and had started walloping Faith from behind.

Then as suddenly as it began, it stopped.

The room grew eerily silent.

Faith glanced up; the blood rushed from her face.

In the doorway stood his lordship, looking like thunder in the flesh.

"West!" Lady Brayton whispered.

"What the bloody hell is going on here, Devon?"

"Nothing."

"It doesn't look like nothing to me. It looks like a god damn chicken farm blew up in my hall!"

It was as if someone had just stomped on the moment and snuffed it out.

With unfailing sophistication, the duchess unfolded her lithe figure from behind a potted plant and glided toward the baron. "Then perhaps you should speak to your servants about the proper use of banisters."

The baron looked at Faith, and she blushed to the roots of her hair. Instead of berating her for her mischief, he turned to the duchess, and said, "Indeed. I seem to recall someone who used to love riding down the banisters."

Lady Brayton's chin shot up. "That was a long time ago." She started to walk out of the room and tripped over a pile of feathers. "For God's sake, Miss Jervais, get this mess cleaned up before the guests arrive."

"Yes, Your Grace."

It took only a few seconds for the room to clear of everyone save herself and the lord of the manor. Now she was in for it. Now he would surely call off their agreement and send for a padded wagon to haul her off to Newgate.

"Faith?"

She heard his steps grow closer.

"Would you mind telling me what happened here?"

She couldn't look at him. "I'm, sorry, Baron. This was all my fault."

"Aye, I'm sure it was."

And to her utter amazement, she found herself being plucked off the floor, enveloped in his arms, and swung around in a circle.

"And for it, I owe you a debt I can never repay."

Faith's head spun; feathers dislodged themselves from her hair and landed in his. She blinked, taken aback by the broad smile on his face. "I don't understand."

"Have I told you that you are the most wonderful lady I've ever known?"

Lady? He thought her a *lady*? "But I did nothing—except bowl the duchess over on her arse."

"You performed a miracle." His eyes were damp, and she wasn't sure if he was laughing or crying. "Faith, do you know that that is the first time I've heard my sister laugh in . . . I can't remember when."

Faith could do nothing but dig her fingers into his shoulders and hang on for dear life when he took her for another spin around the entry hall. His laughter, so free, so reckless, rumbled through her veins.

"Tell me what you want."

"I want for nothing, milord."

"There must be something. A new dress? A day to yourself? The moon? Tell me what you want and it shall be yours."

You.

He went still, and for one horrifying moment Faith feared she'd spoken her greatest, most secret wish out loud.

Time seemed to stop as he continued to hold her against him, her chin level with the top of his head, her hands upon his shoulders for balance, her feet dangling off the floor.

And when she looked down she realized why he'd grown so quiet. Three buttons of her gown had come undone. The material gaped, showing the bare, inside swells of her breasts.

And he was staring right at them.

Faith knew she should be outraged. She should demand that he let her go and she should right her clothing immediately. Instead, her nails bit into his shoulders and she watched in fascination as his glorious gray eyes darkened to pitch. He wet his lips with his tongue. A roaring began in Faith's ears. Her breasts went hard, tight against her blouse, swelling, aching.

And then, he kissed her. There. At the seam of her breasts which seemed to have been presented to him in just that state, for just that reason. Faith's heart stopped. She couldn't move, she couldn't breathe. She could only remember. The sensation of his lips on hers. The gentle power of his kiss. The sizzling giddiness swirling through her middle.

And she could only feel. His arms tight around her waist, his chest pressed flush against her breasts, her own blood rushing through her veins.

When she did nothing, not push him away, not demand he release her, not cry out in protest, he kissed her breasts again. Then, with his tongue, he traced a wet path up the cleft, around the top of one heavy globe under the fabric, over to the other breast.

Her head dropped back and her eyes fell shut. She thought she even heard herself moan. His warm, moist breath fanned against her skin and she swore she went up in flames.

"What do you want?"

You, oh God, I want you.

"Tell me what you want, Faith, just say the word, and it shall be yours."

The hungry timbre, the greedy demand, reached past the fog dulling her senses and gripped Faith's sense of reason. She opened her eyes, saw his face buried between her all-but-naked breasts . . .

And wanted to die.

Fully aware of where they were, and what he was doing to her, Faith pushed at his shoulders. Kissing her on the mouth in the privacy of his chambers where no one could see was one thing. This . . . *this* was quite another matter entirely. She could not believe she'd allowed him, the lord of the manor, to . . . kiss her in such an intimate place—right in the middle of the bloody foyer. "Baron . . . please . . . let me go before someone walks in." She would not be able to bear the shame.

He blinked. He looked up. Then he looked around. As if coming to the same awareness, he let her slide down the front of him and he released his hold, but he did not step away. His body, so hot, so hard, so . . . male, called out to the woman in her. "Forgive me, you're right. Such . . . activity should not be conducted in so public a setting."

His voice was deep, husky, and so incredibly sensual. Faith fumbled with the buttons on her blouse. Tears stung the backs of her eyes. Her skin burned. Her throat closed. She wanted nothing more than to leave, to catch her breath, to collect her scattered emotions and her tattered pride. "Such activity should not be conducted at all," she whispered raggedly.

Something in her voice must have penetrated, for he blinked, stepped back, and rolled his lips between his teeth. "You're right. Such activity should not be conducted between us at all." He sounded almost . . . hurt. "However, there must be something you want that I can give you."

My freedom! Give me that, please give me that. She

could not bear to be near him, to feel these wicked, wonderful things she was feeling for him and not be able to have him.

But she held her tongue. He'd made his position clear the first time she'd asked for her freedom, and she had no wish to test his limits. "You already did, milord," her voice trembled. "You gave me Scatter."

"It still does not compare to what you did, but if you insist, we shall call it even."

He bowed, then headed for the staircase.

"Baron?"

He paused with one foot on the bottom step and looked at her over his shoulder.

"Why does Lady Brayton not laugh?"

"Her pain is only greater than her regrets."

"What would she have to regret?"

"Choices." A soul-deep sorrow filled his eyes where laughter had always lurked. "Don't we all regret a few of those?"

The guests began arriving early Friday afternoon, among them, Miles Heath.

Troyce met him at the door of the stables. He and Chadwick, along with a half dozen of the male villagers, had spent the morning preparing the stables and carriage houses for the dozens of horses that would be boarded over the next three days, with Troyce cursing the expense the entire time. Reminders that his grandfather could well afford the expense did nothing to improve his mood, for it only served to remind him that his bachelorhood was fast coming to an end.

"It's good to see you, mate," he told his friend.

Miles passed the reins to Scatter, who led the bay through the doors. "You look like hell."

"I don't want to talk about it."

"She's getting to you that bad, is she?"

"Who?"

"That sweet little morsel of a maid you took under your wing."

His jaw tightened at Mile's reference to Faith. He'd seen her only once in the last week, and the moment had been so brief it might never have happened. Aye, Devon had kept her busy, but he knew she was also avoiding him.

He didn't know what to do about her. He'd offered her what he could, and it hadn't been enough. He'd tried to take care of her, and it hadn't been enough. He'd shown her how much he desired her, and still, it hadn't been enough.

What the hell did she want from him?

"I told Devon about Radcliff."

"That must have gone over well."

"Just don't rub it in her face, Miles. I'd hate to have to kill you."

With more serious subjects said and out of the way, the pair spent the next hour standing outside the stables catching up on politics and current news, who was gambling away his father's money, who had escaped the matrimonial noose, and who had succumbed to it, before Miles claimed weariness and adjourned to his room.

Troyce then spent the remainder of the day greeting new arrivals, some being neighbors he hadn't seen in nearly a decade. Every carriage held at least one bell-skirted, hair-powdered, parasol-toting maiden of marriageable age who began assessing himself and his holdings the minute she stepped onto Westborough soil.

By dusk, all their guests were accounted for and Troyce could put off his doom no longer.

"Good heavens, West, you don't plan to attend supper in that?" Devon whispered in horror when he walked into the house.

Troyce glanced down at himself. His boots were muddy, his trousers spattered, and his shirt soiled. He couldn't resist. "I thought this was a country ball? Do I not look country enough?"

"This is no time for jesting."

"There's always time for jesting." He popped a kiss on her cheek. "You look beautiful, Devon." Her glossy black hair was piled high on her head, ringlets had been artfully arranged to frame her face, and the red in her dress brought out the roses in her cheeks. "None of the men here tonight will be able to keep their eyes off you. Shall I don my cutlass in the event I'm needed to avenge your honor?"

She blushed, and for the second time in as many weeks, her eyes sparkled. "You are such a rogue. Now, please do something with your attire before our guests arrive."

He could have told her that their guests had been arriving all afternoon, but decided not to encourage her flustered nerves.

Instead, he mounted the stairs to his room, trailing his hand along the banister. With each step, the image of Faith he'd tried to hold at bay formed in acute clarity. A slow smile spread across his face at the memory of her covered in feathers.

Like an angel. A bold, vibrant angel, tossed from heaven to give him hell.

Troyce sighed, suddenly tired. Someone had set up a bath in his room, and though he was tempted to spend the evening soaking away his sore muscles in the steaming water, he knew that Devon was expecting him to help her greet their guests. So he scrubbed quickly and after towel-drying his hair, donned the clothes that had been laid out for him on his bed.

Though he admitted that it was quite pleasant being waited on hand and foot, he didn't think he'd ever get used to it. Having someone decide what you would wear, when you would dine, whom you would marry . . .

Jesus.

He sat on the bed and rubbed both hands over his face. Could he really go through with this? Sell himself to a woman? Let his grandfather choose his life-mate? The mother of his children?

Did he have any other choice?

Sighing more deeply, he rose from the bed and crossed the room. He stood in front of the full-length cheval mirror, fumbling with the buttons of his shirt, trying not to think of how empty his life would be, when he spotted Faith's reflection watching him from the doorway. She looked neat, tidy, her formal black maid's gown crisp and pressed, her wild curls tamed beneath a mobcap. And still, so beautiful she took his breath away. "How long have you been standing there?"

"Long enough to see that you've no idea how to button your shirt."

He grinned wryly and held out his arms. His unbound sleeves drooped from his wrists. "It seems I am in need of some assistance."

"Where's your man?"

"Chadwick has taken ill—quite inconveniently, I might add. I'm having a devil of a time with all these fasteners. I fear I cannot manage these on my own."

She snorted. "Leave it to the gentry not to be able to dress themselves."

She entered the room, brushed his hands away, and plucked his father's silver button links from a velvet-lined box. "You smell nice."

Her artless candor surprised and delighted Troyce. "I'm pleased you think so."

"Are you wearing cologne?"

"No."

"Then it must just be you."

"And what does 'just' me smell like?"

"The wind. The sea. The forests at midnight."

He watched her lips move as she talked. God she had a beautiful mouth. Full. Ripe. The taste of her, sweet as summer fruit, still haunted him. "I've not seen much of you these past two weeks," he said gruffly. "You look beautiful, Faith."

"I've been busy."

She pointedly ignored his compliment, but the rising color in her cheeks told him she'd heard it. "Aye, I've seen you with the village lasses, teaching them their duties. It has been a great help to Millie, and much of a relief, I'm sure."

"It's too soon for Millie to be exerting herself," she said.

"Too soon after what?"

Faith's fingers stilled against his chest. Then she sighed. "She has been ill for some time."

Troyce stared at her in dismay. "Why was I not told of this?"

"She made me promise. She feared that you or Lady Brayton would retire her."

"Why would I retire the most loyal housekeeper I've ever known?"

"Then you wouldn't?"

"Of course not. And I'm disappointed that either of you would consider me so heartless."

Faith lowered her gaze, then her chin. "You're right, milord. I was wrong not to tell you. I would have if she hadn't made me promise not to."

Would she? "Have you made any other promises that I should know about?"

"Only to myself."

Troyce wanted to ask what that promise was, but something in her shuttered eyes told him she'd not reveal it to him, so he didn't bother. Instead, he lifted his vest off the arm of a nearby chair and slipped into it. A glance at Faith's dubious expression in the mirror made him frown. "What?"

"May I speak freely, milord?"

"Since when have you required my permission?" he teased her.

"You look like a Robin in that waistcoat."

"A Robin?"

"Bow Street Runner." She moved to his wardrobe and rifled through his clothes as if she'd been born to the task. "Here, try the silver. It will bring out the color of your eyes."

Troyce laughed. "My eyes aren't silver."

"They certainly are. When the sun hits them just right, they glitter like rich ore."

That she would make such a personal observation put a knot in his throat and sent heat shooting straight to his groin. He couldn't remember any woman commenting on his eyes before. "What does a Bow Street Runner do?" he asked, turning around as much to don the vest she held up to him as to hide his unwelcome arousal.

"Well, they spent a lot of time making my life miserable," she grinned.

"No thanks to Gentleman Jack Swift, I'll wager. How did you ever get involved with a fellow like him anyway?"

"I wasn't involved with him. I worked for him. There's a difference."

"I would think you of all people would have more sense than to work for a man like him."

"Life doesn't always give a person such choices," she countered in her own defense.

That was true, Troyce silently agreed. Look at him? He hadn't chosen to be the heir of Westborough. The responsibility had been imposed on him the day of his birth, and all because he'd had the misfortune of being the firstborn son of a nobleman.

"So how did you become . . . *associated* with him?"

She shrugged, and Troyce wondered what she would do if he suddenly tore the mobcap off her head, buried his hands in her hair, and kissed her senseless.

Knock him on his arse with a pillow?

"It's a long story, one I'm sure would not interest you."

The longer the better, he thought. "Humor me."

"Well, do you remember when I told you about the blo—the man that caught me stealing from the pastry shop?"

It took every ounce of concentration Troyce could must to focus on her story and not on the hands brushing his rib cage as she buttoned his vest. "I remember."

"It was Jack. He told me that talent like mine shouldn't be wasted, and he put me to work. I'd been selling matches on the street corners at the time to make extra coin, but go hungry a few nights and see how desperate you get."

He'd been hungry for months, and he was past desperate.

"It was simple," she went on, unaware of his salacious thoughts. "Lift a few watches. Weed a few wallets. My fingers were small and deft. I have a dim memory of a piano, and think I once played. In any case, I was a very good pickpocket. I had my own block by the time I was eleven, a full neighborhood at twelve, and by the time I was thirteen I was teaching the tyros how to bilk. We gave the money over to Jack, and he saw that I had food in my mouth, clothes on my back, and a roof over my head."

She sounded so proud, and in a sense, he supposed she had a right to be. She'd done what she had to and survived. "What he did is against the law, Faith. You could have turned him in."

"And where would that have left the band? Jack wasn't the kindest man in the world, but he took care of us; and at the time, he was all I had."

The last thing Troyce wanted to do was make Faith defend her actions, yet it seemed he'd done it anyway. "What of your father, Faith? If he'd known—"

"He wouldn't have cared," she interrupted in a tone of hard-edged steel.

Though Troyce had been witness to Faith's temper a time or two, the bitterness she carried toward her family surprised even him. "Why do you think he sent you away, Faith?"

She didn't answer for a long time, and just when Troyce thought she'd ignore the question all together, she answered, "I wish I knew."

And there was something so deeply painful in those four little words that it wrenched his heart.

She shook her head as if to clear her mind of a past she didn't want to remember. "He might still come after me, you know. There's still that chance."

"Your father?"

"Jack."

Troyce's lips flattened, and as he stared into the mirror at the lovely young creature beside him, he wished he hadn't stopped with breaking Swift's nose. "Let him try."

He'd not let *anyone* take what belonged to him.

Chapter 15

The ballroom looked like Faith's every image of a fairyland. The chandelier glittered like stars in a midnight sky. The wooden floor gleamed with a high sheen of wax. A four-piece orchestra composed of piano, violin, cello, and harp provided lovely music by composers Faith had never of but admired nonetheless. Ladies, wearing gowns of every color of the rainbow shimmered and shined, were escorted into the room by gentlemen in evening dress decorated with everything from red-and-yellow epaulets on their shoulders to frilly cravats up to their chins. Servants in black livery moved discreetly among the guests bearing silver trays of canapés that Millie and the kitchen staff had spent three days preparing.

Lady Brayton had outdone herself, for a more perfect vision Faith had never seen.

Except she could have done without the roses.

They were everywhere. Roses in every shade and state of bloom—among the candles and delicate lamps, in vases, in wreaths, in bowls ... petals had even been strewn across the tablecloths. They were inside: in the entrance hall, the staircase, the balconies. They were outside: in the courtyard, on the terrace, even in the necessary located beyond the gardens.

Oh, yes, the gardens. No expense had been spared there either. Climbing roses, creeping roses, tea roses, and long-stems. Roses, roses, roses, everywhere.

Faith desperately would have loved to watch the gala from one of the balconies in the ballroom like a few of the other servants did, as it was quite unlikely that she'd ever get the chance to see such a glorious display again. But even there, one could not escape the powerful scent, for like heat it seemed to rise.

Within a half hour, Faith's eyes were nearly swollen shut and watery, as if she'd been crying for a month, and her nose hurt from sneezing so much. She was absolutely, completely, and utterly miserable. And she couldn't help but wonder if somehow, Lady Brayton had chosen this particular form of torture to keep her from wringing even a moment's enjoyment from a night she had worked so hard to help make perfect for the baron.

So she kept to her rooms for the greater part of the night, since the tower room had been converted to a guest chamber, and listened to the sweet, soulful music echo down the stone halls. Never had she felt so alone.

Or so lonely.

No doubt, her prince of dreams was down there among the brightly colored socialites, lathering them with genteel flattery, humoring them with his wit. Faith rolled over on her mattress and pounded the pillow beneath her head while the strains of a waltz formed a halo about her ears. No doubt he was dancing with them, as well. Holding one of those twittering gems in his arms, swirling them about the floor, flashing his charming dimple.

She buried her face in her pillow and screamed. She could not take this! She had to know, even if it blew her to kingdom come. She had to see for herself if he looked as dashing on the ballroom floor as she'd so often imagined he would be. She had to know what he was doing—and aye, who he was doing it with.

Slipping a large square of linen into her apron pocket, Faith slid her mobcap over her hair and marched out of her room. She paused half a dozen times in the hallway to sneeze before she finally reached a section of the house where, not only was she awarded a surprisingly clear view of the ballroom, but there wasn't a single, solitary, bloody rose in sight.

Beneath the west branch of the staircase.

Slowly, cautiously, she crept toward a slatted partition separating her from the open doors of the ballroom. She searched the crowd, seeking one dark head among many, one blinding smile among dozens. She spotted the duchess, standing near a patterned vase, surveying her creation with a small, pleased smile. Wait—wasn't she wearing . . . she was! She was wearing the bloomin' red dress she'd accused Faith of stealing!

Why that—

"Faith?"

She spun around so fast she nearly fell over. "Baron?"

"What are you doing here?"

"Nothing, Milord." He stood in a small wedge of moonlight that shone brightly from one of the many windows set high in the castle walls. The space was small, barely four feet square, and it seemed to have shrunk to half that size. It wasn't exactly a place that could be found unless someone was looking. "What are *you* doing here?"

"Well, I was on my way outside, hoping for a breath of fresh air when I heard the strangest noise coming down the hall. *Achoo. Achoo.*" He smiled.

Faith felt her stomach sink to her toes and the blood rush into her face. Why . . . oh why, oh why, oh why . . . did this man always catch her at her very worst? Suddenly reminded of how she must look, with her swollen eyes and cherry red nose, she made a mad dash past him, knowing if he saw her thus, on tonight of all nights, she would simply curl up and die of mortification.

"Wait, Faith—don't leave. You have every right to admire your handiwork."

His hand burned on her arm. "You don't understand, Baron."

He tipped her chin and she slammed her eyes shut. "Have you been weeping?"

"No, milord."

"Your eyes are puffy—oh. Oh, no." The chuckle

started low in his chest. "Oh, Faith, open your eyes."

She shook her head adamantly. "Come now, open your eyes."

She lifted her lashes a margin. Her gaze lit on his chin first, which carried the merest shadow of whiskers in spite of being shaved only hours before. Then on his mouth, with that crooked smile that warmed her down to her toes. Then to his eyes, hooded and secretive, a spray of creases at the corners.

"Is it the flowers?"

"Please, don't laugh at me, milord."

"I'm not laughing. All right, I am, but not at you. The scent is cloying enough for me, I can only imagine how miserable it must be making you. Is that why you're hiding here under the stairwell?"

"I'm not hiding, it's the only place I could find that didn't reek."

"Well, then by all means, Faith, take advantage of the clean air." Gently he turned her around so that she faced the slats she'd been peering through. The heat of him remained at her back, and the scent of him—of fresh winds and cut grasses and his own male essence—settled around her like a protective embrace. She watched the dancing, and tried to ignore him.

But he wouldn't let her forget his presence. As if she could.

"They're dancing a quadrille," he said beside her ear.

"It's beautiful, isn't it?"

She felt him shrug. "I suppose it is. I don't

think I've ever considered dancing beautiful, though."

"That's because you're a man."

"I consider you beautiful."

She didn't know what to say to that. Beautiful was hardly a term she'd ever apply to herself, but she couldn't deny that when he said it, she could almost believe it. "I used to dream of being a princess."

"Not a queen?"

"You're mocking me." Why had she made such a confession, anyway? He probably thought her a silly twit. Not that she cared what he thought . . . oh, who was she trying to fool? She did care what he thought. She cared too much.

"I'm not mocking you. I'm honestly curious why you would dream of being a princess and not a queen."

"Because queens are usually married by the time they reach the throne. Then they've got the entire country to worry about. They've no time to be courted. But a princess . . . she can spend her days helping people and her nights with her prince."

"And how do you know so much about what a princess does with her days and nights?"

"Because when I was little, my mother used to read this story about a girl. She was very lonely. She used to work from dawn to dusk trying to help people so they would be her friends, until one day, she was so tired she couldn't help people anymore and she fell asleep. Then a handsome prince found her and awakened her with a kiss.

"He made her his princess, and she had servants to help her with her duties so she wasn't so tired, friends around her so she wasn't so lonely, and a prince who loved her and held her each night so she would never have to be afraid of being alone."

The lump in Troyce's throat nearly choked him. He stood stock-still beside Faith, watching her watch the ball through the slats, her gaze wistful and almost . . . lost. It broke his heart and humbled his soul. Here was a woman who dreamed of all he'd taken for granted, coveted all he'd shunned, and longed for all that he'd disdained. He could have told her the unvarnished truth, shattered her illusions. That with all this glitter and gold came responsibilities that could crush a person's soul. That no matter how many servants a person had, the day still ended with a body so tired and sore that no amount of rest would refresh it. And that love never entered the picture when a man took a wife.

Instead, he preserved what innocence had miraculously remained intact despite the rough life she'd led in the London underworld. She gave so much, asking so little in return.

Spotting a vase of orange blossoms in the corner beyond the underwell, Troyce plucked several delicate flowers from the container, and with deft fingers, wove them together. Once he had them circled, he returned to Faith's side and tugged the mobcap off her head.

"What—what are you doing, milord?"

Her hair spilled free to her shoulders, tumbling curls of saffron and amber. "Every girl should feel like a princess at least once in her life." He tossed the mobcap over his shoulder and set the makeshift tiara upon her head. Then, with a deep and courtly bow, he extended his hand and asked, "May I have this dance, Your Highness?"

Faith stared at him in speechless awe. "You want to dance with me?"

"Aye, very much."

"But . . . I don't know how to dance."

"Then perhaps you will allow me to teach you?" She'd taught him so much these last weeks. Of devotion, of determination, and a strange sort of honor where thieves stole but didn't lie and girls dreamed but didn't hope.

With great hesitation, she set her work-worn hand upon his palm and allowed him to turn her so they faced each other. A sympathetic smile touched his lips as he took in her pitifully swollen eyes and reddened nose.

He slowly drew her to him, close enough to feel the heat of her body and nothing else. With one hand holding hers, the other placed at the center curve of her waist, he slid left, back, right, forward, a simple form of dance that resembled a waltz, but left out the intricate steps not permitted within such close confines. Faith caught on once she stopped looking at her feet and let him guide her moves. As he stared into her eyes, and she stared into his, the rest of the world faded to nothing but song and motion, until Troyce could almost believe that the fairy tales Faith had heard as a girl really happened.

"This is scandalous, you know," she said, but she didn't seem to care any more than he did.

"Indeed. But I fear I can't resist. I've always

held a fantasy to dance with a beautiful maiden beneath the moonlight."

"And instead you're stuck with me under the staircase."

"Aye, and it exceeds my expectations."

She came to a stop, and so did he. For a moment, all he could do was look into her eyes. Then her lips. His face lowered, tilted. Their breaths mingled, moist, seductive. "I want to kiss you, Faith."

"You do?" she asked breathlessly.

"Very much." He cupped her jaw, threaded his fingers through her silky hair, and tilted her face to receive him.

The first brush of his lips across her sent bolts of fire shooting through his veins. He brushed her lips again, then settled his mouth upon hers. *Ah, God* . . .

His arm came around her waist and he drew her close, relishing her soft curves against his hard planes. Her hand crept up to his chest, her palms sliding up the front of his coat, blazing a path of heat that would have consumed him if he'd allowed it. Instead, Troyce held himself tightly in check, fearing that any sudden moves, any outward show of the desire she created within him would scare her off. Slowly, leisurely, he glided his tongue across the seam of her lips and nearly moaned when they parted. She tasted of sugar, of spice. Of innocence and of mystery. He wanted to devour her. He wanted to push against the wall. He wanted to bury himself in her hot, sweet folds, again and again, until both were spent with exhaustion.

Instead, he forced himself to draw back, to kiss her cheek, her jaw, her neck.

"Oh, Baron . . ."

"Say my name," he whispered hoarsely against her skin. "I want to hear you say my name."

"Troyce . . ."

"*Faith?*"

They snapped apart like a broken twig, both glancing around in guilty surprise.

"*Faith, where are you? Lucy, have you seen, Faith?*"

"Bloody hell, who is that?" Troyce cursed.

With her fingers clutching his lapels, Faith whispered back, "It's Millie." She started passed him. "I must go."

Troyce gripped her arm, stopping her. "Don't. Stay with me."

"I can't. She'll come looking for me."

"If we're quiet she won't find us."

"She needs me, Baron. I must go." She smiled sadly, then drew her fingertips along his jaw. "Thank you for the dance. I'll remember this night for as long as I live."

And then she slipped from his grasp and hurried down the servants' hall, her orange-blossom tiara bobbing upon her head.

Troyce watched her until she disappeared around a corner.

Then he turned and plowed his fist into the wall.

"You look like you could use this."

Troyce accepted the tumbler Miles handed him

and without inquiring as to the contents, downed it in one swallow.

"Ah, this requires a double, I see."

And Troyce found another tumbler pressed into his hand. Though his first drink of this one was deep, he forced himself to conserve the rest, knowing from experience that getting drunk would served no useful purpose.

"What are you still doing here, Miles?" The dancing had long since concluded, and the guests who hadn't been invited to stay the weekend were beginning to collect their coats and carriages. He'd figured his friend would have long since found himself a secluded spot in the gardens and had his hands up some willing wench's skirt, not sitting in Troyce's study, supporting his mission to drown his sorrows in spirits.

"Scouring the prospects for a bride, same as you. The more scandalous the lady, the better."

Blast Devon's wagging tongue. Soon it would be out all over the country that he'd put himself on the bloody market. "What reason have you to marry? You're not the one about to lose your entire inheritance."

"Someone must support my unscrupulous tastes." He grinned. "Alas, no fair maiden seems taken with my empty pockets."

"Empty pockets? You could buy England ten times over."

"Ah, but I've naught but a courtesy title to impress the lasses."

"It's ironic, isn't it, Miles? You've the money, I've the hereditary title, and neither one of us is worthy enough to claim." It shouldn't bother him; all his life he'd fought against the dictates of his parents and grandparents, shunning the society he'd been cursed with at birth.

Unfortunately, that was before his father had run him and all of Westborough into the ground. And of all those in attendance tonight, the ones who were suitably wealthy and titled enough to fulfill his grandfather's expectations wanted nothing to do with him. Those who did want him had nothing *he* wanted.

Except Faith.

Troyce slumped back in his chair. Gads, the girl was turning him inside out. She was a pocket-swiping princess, who for all he knew was out to lift him of his title as easily as she lifted the coin from his coat. And at the same time, she was earthy and unaffected. She spoke her mind, she didn't hide her feelings, and, oh damn, she aroused him like no other woman. And she looked at him as if he were her personal hero. Her dream prince. It made him want to protect her, cherish her, keep her safe from all the Jack Swifts she'd ever known in her lifetime. "She believes in bloody fairy tales, for God's sake."

"Who believes in fairy tales?"

"The one I want." The one who didn't even come close to fulfilling his grandfather's requirements.

Miles sighed in silent understanding of his plight. "The perfect bride will reveal herself. Give it time."

"Time, I'm afraid, is not something I have in excess. What am I to do while I wait for the 'perfect bride'? Watch my villagers starve? Watch my castle torn from my grasp?"

Miles stared at him. "Your *castle*?"

"Never mind," he grumbled into his cup.

"It'll happen, my friend." He clapped him on the back, winked, and smiled. "You just need to have a little faith."

His gaze slid out the open doors to the gray-clad figure sneezing her way through the throng of departing guests. For once, Troyce decided, he couldn't agree with his friend more. "I intend to, Miles. I intend to."

The house was dark and blessedly quiet for the first time in twelve hours. It seemed to take forever for his guests to leave, and the welcome few who remained had been made comfortable in spare bedrooms in the west wing.

Troyce knew he'd had a bit too much to drink, not enough to be drunk, but enough to know that he shouldn't be skulking the servants' halls. He should just go to sleep, but his sense of reason remained clouded with the same woman who had occupied his thoughts all evening. Nay, all week. Nay . . . for months.

Faith.

Have a little . . .

Oh, aye, just a little. Just enough to rid himself of this gnawing hunger. Once he had her, she'd be purged himself of this deuced . . . obsession he seemed to have developed for her.

The doorknob twisted beneath his hand, and clad in gray breeches and a loose shirt, Troyce stepped out of his room. The floor was cool beneath his bare soles, and a single sconce provided the light guiding him down the hall. Not that he needed light. He needed only to follow his nose. Her scent pulled him to her, and he could have found her in pitch-darkness.

He had not realized how cool it got on the third floor until a draft hit his bare stomach. Faith slept with this chill. The thought disturbed him. A woman with her fire should never be cold.

Tonight, she would not.

Tonight, she would burn for him as he burned for her. The spark he'd felt between them the first time they'd kissed would burst into flames. He'd seen it in her eyes tonight, felt it on his lips and in his blood. She lusted for him as he lusted for her.

Tonight, they would both get what they'd been denying themselves for far too long.

He reached her door and stood, his hands growing damp with unaccustomed nervousness. Should he woo her slowly, tenderly? Or drag her into his arms in the way of a commanding lover? Bloody hell. Why so unsure all of a sudden? It wasn't as if she was the first woman he'd bedded. He knew the ways of pleasing, and he intended on pleasing her as she had never been pleased before. And if she proved a satisfactory lover in return, he would persuade her into becoming his mistress until such time as he sold himself to the highest bidder.

With that decision, he let himself into her room.

The music surrounded her, flowed through her blood and bones, sweeping her away to a world of make-believe, where silks rustled and emeralds flashed. Where women were ladies and men gentlemen resplendent, and her world had merged, if only for a moment, with her prince of dreams.

She felt him now as she had hours before, the steely muscles of his chest beneath her fingers, the heat of his breath against her lips, his mouth upon hers . . .

The door creaked like an old man's knees, and Faith came awake with a start. Her eyes popped open. Her heart stalled. Her fingers clutched the pillow beneath her head. A squeak of the floorboards alerted her that she hadn't mistaken the sound of the door. Who would be stealing into her room at such an ungodly hour? Someone up to no good, certainly. The house was full of sotted gentry, and she'd found herself dodging groping hands more than once throughout the course of the evening.

Should she scream? She wanted to, God knew. The sound became a physical sensation, building in her throat, choking her. Would anyone hear?

Would anyone care?

The faint odors of spirits invaded the room, and she sensed the intruder drawing closer. Her breath was trapped in her chest. She let her eyes shut, hoping that if she pretended sleep, whoever it was would leave.

Another creak. *Oh, God.* She slipped her hand beneath the sheets, searching, seeking. For what she hadn't a clue. Just something to make her feel less helpless. Even the tiniest of weapons would give her some measure of power. Finding nothing, she moved her other hand over the side of the bed and tapped her fingers against the floor, beneath the metal framing. Her fingers brushed against something long, solid, and slender. A handle.

The intruder reached her bedside. Faith didn't give herself time to hesitate; she wrapped her hands around the handle and just as the bed dipped under the intruder's weight, she swung. In the same moment she heard a familiar voice whisper her name, the weapon made contact with a clanging thud.

"Ow, bloody hell!"

"Baron? Omigod!" She scrambled for the matches on the bedside table. His groans of pain told her she hadn't killed him, but she could have done some major damage.

"What did you hit me for?"

The match flared to life and she touched it to the candlewick. "I didn't know it was you!"

"What did you hit me *with*?"

She glanced at the blackened, skillet-shaped object she'd dropped onto the counterpane. "A bed warmer."

"Son of a—that *hurt*!"

She rose on her knees beside him and propped her hands on her hips. "Well, you shouldn't be skulking about in a person's room in the middle of the night!" She reached for his head. "Let me see."

He shielded his head with his arm and shied away. "No."

"Let me see—I don't want you bleeding all over my blankets."

When he dropped his arm, she parted the thick strands of his coal black hair and prodded the back of his skull. "You'll have a goose egg to be sure, but you'll live."

"No thanks to you. If I'd have known this was the welcome I was going to get, I wouldn't have come here."

"You shouldn't have come here anyway."

"I know."

She sat back on her heels and rested her hand on her knees. "Then why did you?"

"Because I couldn't stay away." He slanted his face toward her. "What are you doing to me, Faith?"

How was she supposed to answer a question like that? "You've been drinking." She frowned.

"Aye, a little. Do you want me to leave?"

She fell silent and debated whether or not to answer. He didn't look dangerous. Just lonely. And if truth be told, she was lonely, too. "That depends."

"On what?"

"What you planned on doing when you came into my room."

He was quiet for a moment. A tense heat permeated the air. Faith's skin prickled with a premonition that she'd just entered forbidden territory.

"What if I told you that I planned on making love to you till dawn?" he said.

Her breath caught, her eyes widened. Her pulse began to quiver.

"What if I told you that I can't stop thinking about kissing you?" His slumberous gaze fell to her lips, then dropped lower and her breasts grew heavy with remembered pleasure, her nipples hardening against her thin cotton shift.

"Or that the scent of you . . ." He moved closer, slowly, seductively, grazing her neck with his nose. ". . . drives me mad with desire?"

His lips touched the rapid pulsebeat at her throat. Her lashes fluttered down. Sensations, wild and mysterious, sped through Faith's entire body. His mouth opened against her neck, his tongue caressed the sensitive flesh. And when he suckled, she felt as if her bones were melting.

"Baron . . ."

"My name."

"Troyce . . ."

He lifted himself from the bed and braced his hands on the mattress on either side of her. She knew she should tell him to stop. But the words somehow got tangled in her mouth, and her brain had stopped functioning.

Weightlessly, helplessly, she floated backward, the mattress cushioning her fall.

"What if I told you that I've dreamed of having you naked beneath me. . . ."

He hovered above her, his hands on either side of her.

"Of feeling your soft skin against mine."

His voice was husky, seductive, as, with one deliberate, fluid stroke, he pressed his loins against her womanhood.

"Of sliding inside you . . ."

Every long, hard inch of him moved against her, nothing but her shift and his breeches preventing him from claiming her.

"Filling you . . ."

"Troyce . . ."

Before she could protest, his mouth covered hers in a kiss so hot, so greedy, so wild that Faith's thoughts scattered. Her hand fluttered in midair before finally settling on his chest. His tongue tangled with hers, and she moaned at sheer pleasure of the taste of him. Brandy and chocolate truffles. Rich. Smooth. Completely irresistible. The kiss was long and deep and searching. His tongue thick in her mouth and his body hard against hers.

His hand moved from her cheek to her nape and his fingers clenched in her hair. "Faith . . ." he moaned into her mouth.

She tore herself away and, breathing raggedly, she pressed her hands against his chest. "Baron, stop."

"I can't."

"You must. You shouldn't be here."

He stilled, then drew back.

"I think it's best you go."

"You want me, Faith, as much as I want you." His brow furrowed, confusion swirled in his eyes. "Dammit, why are you denying us?"

"Aye, I do want you, Baron. More than I ever thought it possible to want a man. But I told you before, I will be no man's whore, not even yours. Nor can I be your mistress, or your lover. That's the promise I made to myself."

He didn't move, he didn't breathe. For several long, crackling seconds he simply stared at her. "If I made you my lady, would you have me, then?"

Faith's heart leaped. Her breath caught. It was the brandy talking, she told herself. Or the moment. Whichever, she doubted he was even aware of what he'd said. Even so, if he did remember come morning, she wanted him to know that if his intentions were truly honorable, she would take him. "Aye," she brushed a lock of hair from his brow and smiled tenderly. "I would have you, then."

And Troyce closed his eyes, feeling the bottom fall out of his stomach. They'd been right all along. She didn't want him. She wanted his cursed title.

Worse, he didn't care. He'd give it to her, if he could, just to have her, just to hold her.

He was no better than his father.

He pushed himself off her, away from her, and headed for the door, aware that if he didn't put some distance between them this moment, the self-control he'd always been so proud of was going to snap.

"Troyce?"

"Good night, Faith." With a bittersweet grin, he added, "Sweet dreams."

Chapter 16

He knew she stood behind him without turning around to look. Her scent drifted in the wind, soaked into the sands, saturated his blood. An iridescent moon hung high in the blackness above, and a briny wind blew in off the Channel, but it did nothing to cool the fever raging through his blood. He feared that nothing ever would.

"It's beautiful here," she said at length.

"Aye. My father loved this place. Unfortunately, my mother preferred Radcliff, so we never spent as much time here as he would have liked." He pointed across the water. "On a clear day, you can see the outline of France in the distance."

"Have you ever been there?"

"Often. It's my grandfather's homeland. *Et tu?*"

"I was born there."

"You were born in France?"

"Don't look so shocked, Baron. I wasn't always a pickpocket," she reminded him.

"Forgive me. It's just that you don't sound French."

"I'm only half-French."

I'm only half-Brit.

Is that anything like a half-wit?

"You're angry with me," she said.

"Not with you." Or maybe he was. He didn't know anymore. He kicked a drift of white sand and squinted into the night. Moonlight played with a spray of waves, making the caps iridescent. "I shouldn't have come to your room, Faith."

"No, you shouldn't have."

Knowing that he couldn't explain his actions to her any more than he could to himself, he squinted at a stream of moonlight on the water's surface. "What brought you to England, Faith?"

"A ship," she said, and his heart jumped. He couldn't remember a single time when Faith had joked about anything. She was always so serious.

She strolled down to where he stood at the water's edge, letting the waves roll over his bare feet, and crossed her arms about her tiny waist. "My sister and me . . . we used to play this game when we were little. One of us would hide and the other would go aseeking." The cant of her upbringing slipped unbidden into her speech. "The day me mum died, m'sister was frightful upset, and didn't want to go to the buryin', but Papa told her that he needed us to be brave little girls. So we got into the carriage. There was a boy with us, a cousin I think; there were so many people that me head gets muddled. But I remember being at the cemetery, and I remember that I couldn't find my sister. I remember thinking she was hiding, playin' our game, so I went to seeking. No one noticed; they was all so teary."

He caught a glimpse of her profile, watched her work a knot down her throat.

"I walked around for a long time, calling and calling, 'Ho-ne-sty, come out, come out wherever you are,' because it was part of the game we played. But I couldn't find her. I went back to me mum's buryin' place, but there was no one there. Everyone had left."

"Your family left you at the cemetery?"

"I expect so."

"What did you do?"

Her brow furrowed. "I think I fell asleep. The next thing I remember is a man standing over me. The sun was behind him, and I couldn't see his face. I thought it was my father, so I called out to him. It wasn't my father though."

"Who was it?"

She looked down at their feet. Sand stuck to his toes and to the tips of her shoes.

"A fellow named Cappy. He said that my family didn't want me anymore, and I was supposed to live with him. Only him and his lady didn't want me either. She put me on a ship. I don't remember much after that."

"I'm surprised you remember that much."

"There's some things in life you can't forget, no matter how hard you try." Like him, she squinted into the distance. "Sometimes I can still smell the stench of the hold, though. And I remember the orphan house. But mostly, I remember how

Mama smelled, and how Papa cried when she died."

She looked at him, her expression confused and lost and adrift. So much like he felt at this moment that it was all he could do not to pull her into his arms and never let go. "Why didn't he want me anymore?"

His gut twisted into knots and his heart wrenched. "I don't know, Faith," he answered helplessly, wishing he had the answers she sought. "But I want you."

"I want you, too. More than I ever thought it possible to want a man."

"What if I told you that I've nothing to offer you? Just me. Just now. Would you still want me then?"

She knew what he was asking. It was there, in his eyes, that same need she felt, to simply be accepted for the man he was. What had he told her once? Most only knew the title, not the man?

"With every breath. I have since before I met ye." The acknowledgment should have shamed her. But it didn't. When he'd left her room, she'd been so afraid that, like so many others in her life, he'd just disappear. And she'd never know what it was like to be loved. Deeply. Passionately. Completely.

Without considering the consequences, without examining her reasons, she'd quickly donned her clothes and followed him.

"What if . . . what if I told you that I want you to be the man who makes love to me. The man who feasts upon my lips, buries himself in my body, brings me to the highest of heights?"

He spun around, grasped her upper arms in his,

and drew her against his chest. His breathing came in harsh, labored gasps. For a moment she thought he would kiss her again and her heart soared.

Instead, he hissed, "Go back to your room, Faith, before I lose what little will I have to resist you."

"I don't want you to resist me, Troyce."

"Damn you, I'm trying to be a noble man!"

"Who said I want you to be a noble man?"

She watched the battle wage on his face for just a moment before he tugged her to him and covered her lips with his. Sparks exploded in Faith's head, and her arms wrapped around his neck to keep from sinking. The kiss was not gentle as it had been under the staircase. No, this kiss was wild, hungry, almost desperate. His tongue thrust into her mouth, slewed across her tongue, explored the sensitive recesses with an authority that had her bones melting. Faith could hardly breathe, and she didn't care. He was her breath, he was her heartbeat, he was her dream come true. Every touch, every look, every word wrapped around her and tied her to him with a bind she couldn't deny and no longer wanted to resist.

She pushed herself closer, clung tighter to his neck, plunged her fingers into the soft, midnight hair at his nape. She ached for him in places she'd never dreamed could ache. Just when she thought she couldn't endure another moment of his assault on her senses, he drew back, his chest heaving, his eyes like pitch.

"Will you come with me?"

Anywhere, she thought. Even if it meant being cast away again. The promise she'd made to herself so long ago, the vow she'd made on her mother's soul, seemed so unimportant when he reached out to her. Faith nodded, then took his hand. She had no idea where he meant to take her, or how she followed him. Her legs trembled so badly that she could hardly stand.

He walked backward, his hand clasping hers, his eyes dark as a stormy sky. She couldn't look away. Liquid heat pooled in her belly and that same, mysterious throbbing from before pulsed between her thighs. Every brush of her starched skirt against her skin seemed to set off tiny sparks.

As if sensing her urgency, as if sharing the sudden haste for privacy, Troyce turned on his heel to walk forward along the shore, his stride long and purposeful through the sand. They reached the path that would take them to the cove.

As he led her toward the door to the boathouse, a pang of doubt assailed her. Then she was inside. The door slammed shut, the bolt slid home. And Troyce took her face in his hands and pressed her back against the cool stone wall. She could barely see him in the dimness but she could feel him. His legs flanking hers, his hard and swollen manhood eagerly jutting against the apex of her thighs, his breath ragged and oh-so-sultry against her lips.

And doubts scattered to the four corners of the earth, replaced by need so potent she nearly wept. She wanted to feel his mouth on hers, wild and hungry. She wanted his hands on her body, exploring the most intimate recesses of her body.

But he simply stood there, his hands on her face, his body taut with a restraint she didn't understand. "Please," she, who never begged, then begged him.

"Please, what, princess?"

"Please make me yours."

And that was all it took. His mouth fell on hers, devouring her. Faith wrapped her arms around his waist to keep from sinking. With deft, practiced movements that would make even the most talented knuck cry with envy, he released the buttons of her collar. His fingertips seared her throat, her collarbone, while her breasts strained against the confines of her bodice in eager anticipation of his touch. Then lower he went, to the inner curves of her breasts, his fingers fumbling now, his knuckles brushing the tender flesh of her ribs, then her belly. At last he stopped at the waistband of her skirt.

A breeze blew in through the gap in the fabric, and Faith's nipples tightened.

"I want to see you," he whispered.

"I want to feel you," she whispered back.

His eyes narrowed and a growl rose in his throat. "Keep talking like that and this won't last nearly long enough." He gripped the panels of her shirt and peeled the fabric away. He sucked in. Faith glanced down. Her nipples poked against the sheer muslin of her chemise.

She knew that a proper lady would shield herself.

But then, a proper lady wouldn't be here in the first place, either.

She felt wicked and scandalous and desired. And she loved it. Because she loved him.

She watched as he brought his hands before

him, palm out, and brushed them across her protruding nipples. Faith gasped. Stars exploded behind her eyes.

"Oh, God, you're beautiful."

Again his palms brushed her. She nearly went through the stone. It was torture. Sweet, glorious torture to stand against the cold wall and feel his hot hands against her, touching her. Her clothes became stifling and she wanted them off. At the same time, she wanted him to continue his exploration.

"Oh, Faith . . ." And he opened his mouth against her neck. Her pulse went wild. His chest flattened against her breasts and she whimpered. He suckled her neck. She grabbed the muscles of his back. "Troyce, enough, please . . ."

"What do you want?"

You!

"Do you want this?" He thrust his pelvis against her hips. She cried out, "Yes!"

"Or this?"

He cupped her breast with his hand and squeezed gently. "Oh, God, yes." And a rhythm began, thrust and squeeze, thrust and squeeze. The earth beneath her quaked, the sky above her fell. Powerful currents of sheer sharp pleasure coursed through her body.

She didn't think sensations inside could get any stronger; then he dropped down and wrapped his lips around her nipple.

"I can't, I can't . . ." The back of her head rocked back and forth against the wall. If he stopped, she'd no longer exist, she swore it. Her fingers dug into his scalp. He pulled and tugged with his mouth through the moist material until she thought she'd die if he didn't get her clothes off.

Faith yanked at the ribbon herself then tore at the fabric, sobbing her frustration when it wouldn't give. "Help me, Troyce . . ."

"Is this what you want?"

And with both hands, he ripped the shift down the middle. Her breast spilled free, heavy swollen, needy.

And he was so hungry.

Troyce dropped to his knees, filled his hands with her breasts and, greedy for the taste of her, pulled one distended nipple into his mouth. His palm formed to the curve of her, shaped her, molded her. She writhed and whimpered as he pleasured her, and her reaction drove him wild. When he felt his restraint reach the breaking point, he lifted Faith into his arms and carried her down the path, then up the stone steps before he lost control and took her against the wall. He had no idea how they reached the deck, but once there, he laid her upon the smooth, varnished planks. Her breasts, exquisite, golden mounds, the areolas dark and puckered, remained eager.

He reached behind him, grabbed two fistfuls of his shirt, and tried unsuccessfully to pull the garment over his head. His knee between her legs, lost among the layers of petticoats and skirt, he braced himself above her. "Your turn. Touch me, Faith."

Her hands were tentative at first as she reached for him, then the touch of her palms against his ribs had every muscle in his torso tightening to the point of pain. His nerves quivered and his head spun. A fine sheen of sweat beaded on his brow.

Moving against her, wanting inside her so badly, he longed to hike her skirts up to her waist and drive his sword home. But he held himself in check as she explored the feel of his midsection and chest. Troyce finally could take no more of her sweet torment and wedged his hand behind her and found the button of her waistband. She rocked her body to give him access and the skirt went slack.

Raining kisses upon her breasts, down her belly, he worked the skirt and its accompanying undergarments past her hips and down to her knees. Faith kicked the material away and reached for him, and he laughed huskily at her impatience. Never had he more enjoyed a woman wanting him. And he wanted to savor this moment, savor her.

With his hands on her knees, he let himself feast upon her body. She was still too thin, but not like the first time he'd seen her nude.

She raised up on her elbows and looked at him, her eyes drowsy. The blouse she still wore draped her breasts and waist in a curtain of white, her hair was gloriously tousled, her lips puffy and a deep, cherry red. He could do naught but stare in wonder. That she would give herself to him, no promises, no titles, no fortune, made him dizzy with awe.

Her lashes fell, and she started to pull her shirt closed.

"What are you doing?" he asked, stopping her.

"It's all right, Baron. Ye've changed your mind. I understand."

Bloody hell, was she crying? "Faith?" he leaned

over her and tipped her chin toward him. Her eyes were shiny. "Why would you think I've changed my mind?"

She wouldn't look at him. "Because I'm not—"

"Not what?"

"Not a lady." Again, she tugged at her shirt to cover her nudity. This time, Troyce let her, even though every nerve in his highly aroused body screamed in protest and urged him to take her before he lost the chance. "What does being a lady have to do with what's happening between us right now?"

She didn't answer right away, and when she did, he had to strain to catch her words. "Every man wants a lady. No man wants a guttersnipe."

And his heart fell, shattering into a thousand pieces upon the deck of *La Tentatrice*. "Jesus, Faith. Where do get such ideas?" Then he got angry. At her damnable family, at Jack Swift, and yes, even at Devon. But most of all, he was mad at himself. To see this strong, scrappy street girl broken and cowed . . .

He seized her hand and pressed it to the front of his trousers. Electric shock slammed through his groin. "Does this feel like I don't want you?"

Her eyes widened, her mouth parted. "Then I'm not an amusement?"

"Do I look amused?" he growled.

No, he looked . . . hungry. Powerful. On-the-edge dangerous.

And Faith's heart unfurled. Lucy was so wrong. The baron did want her. With her hand pressed to the front of his trousers, with the iron length of him pulsing against her palm, a boldness infused her, empowered her, awed her. She slid her hand down the proof of his need and smiled when his eyes fell shut and his head dropped back. He moved his grip to her wrist and guided her motion, up nearly to his flat stomach, down between his thighs, groaning when she picked up the rhythm. She'd never known a man could feel so . . . delicious. So hard, and yet at the same time so soft. So firm and so swollen. Touching him, watching him enjoy her touching him, caused her breath to quicken and a damp heat to spread between her thighs. "Troyce, take them off."

He stilled, and his eyes drifted open. Then a wicked smile appeared on his face. "Whatever Her Highness commands."

With a slow, deliberate flick of his fingers, he released the first button of the placket of his trousers, then the one beside it, and the three angled down the thick bulge in the fabric. Faith forgot to breathe. Black hair sprang out from the dark fabric, then taut skin stretched over his manhood. Faith leaned forward and, starting at the bottom, unfastened his shirt. Inch by glorious inch, she laid bare the bronzed skin and rippled muscle of his abdomen, and traced the hollow between his ribs with his tongue up to the formed brawn of his chest.

Troyce gasped, arched, then lost all patience and ripped the shirt off. Faith smiled. This was going to be so much more fun than she'd ever, ever dreamed. "What do you want, Baron?"

He dipped his head and gaze at her from beneath his lashes like a cat on the prowl. Then he moved between her legs and smiled. "I want it all."

Laughing, she opened her arms, and into them he fell, bracing one forearm on the deck so as not to crush her with his weight. The fingers of his other hand began a leisurely stroll up the inside of her thigh to her most intimate spot and sensations poured through her with such power that Faith thought she would go through the deck. When he again touched the moist folds of her womanhood, circling the nub, her thighs fell open.

"No more waiting," she gasped, feeling wanton and wicked and desperately impatient. She knew he would fit himself inside her. At one time, the idea would have frightened her. But now, with her nerves raw and alive, her body wet and hot and ready, she could think of nothing grander than having him inside of her.

And then, he was, just the tip of him, pushing into her tightness. Sliding against her, inside her, enough to drive her mad. She clutched his steely bum with her thighs and pulled his mouth down to hers. His tongue thrust inside her at the same moment as his hips, and Faith went utterly still, shocked by the size and thickness of him.

"It's done—you're mine now," he rasped against her neck. Then he drew back, and pushed forward, stretching her, filling her, skin to skin, pulse to pulse.

"I always was," she whispered, as the slight stinging sensation gave way to liquid heat. He kept his pace slow at first, allowing her to grow accustomed to him. But Faith soon grew greedy for a faster, harder tempo. Her fingernails bit into his back, his chest crushed against her swollen breasts, her hips rose of their own will. Breathing came by sheer nature, fast, heavy, furious. The rhythm increased. Guttural sounds of pleasure matched the beat, and Faith felt herself floating higher. Higher. Higher . . .

The explosion tore through her at the same time Troyce made the last drive home and stiffened above her with a lion's roar. Finally spent, they stayed in each other's arms, with him between her splayed thighs, their legs entwined, their skin clinging. How long they remained that way she would never know.

She only knew that she had never felt so wonderful, so gloriously alive, in her entire life. Her limbs quivered. Her heart slammed against her ribs. Her brain had gone completely numb. "I never . . ." she panted. "I had no idea . . ."

"Nor I . . ." He moved away slightly, careful to keep his weight to the side and drew her against him with his leg. She felt him drag some piece of clothing across their nudity to protect her from the slight chill, then collapse beside her. "Definitely . . . not an amusement."

Faith smiled and cuddled up into the arms encircling her. She closed her eyes, yawned, then just before she drifted off to sleep, she whispered, "I love you, my prince of dreams."

And in the morning when she awoke, he was gone.

*   *   *

Just as dawn was breaking over the horizon, Faith sneaked up the back servants' steps toward her room. If she'd not awakened on the deck of a ship, with only a thin blanket to cover her nudity, she might have wondered if the night she'd spent in Troyce's arms had been nothing more than a dream.

No, it had been no dream. It had been all too wonderfully real. She could still feel the heat of his kiss, the power of his arms, the beat of his heart against hers.

And the emotions swelling beneath her breast grew so large she could hardly contain them.

Every girl should feel like a princess once in her life.

She touched her lips and smiled. But maybe fairy tales did come true. A girl could dream, couldn't she?

Feeling lighthearted and giddy, she raced up the last few steps, then slipped into her room. She startled at the sight of Scatter sitting on her bed.

"Zounds, Fan, where ye been? I've been lookin' all over for ye."

At dawn? She self-consciously smoothed her tangled hair and wrinkled skirt. "I just had an errand to run. Did you need something?"

"Look what I found!" He scooted aside and waved toward the mattress, where a large assortment of glittering gems littered the coverlet. She recognized Lady Brayton's brooch, the one she'd been wearing the day they'd gotten into the pillow fight. And the diamond earbobs she'd worn last night with the red gown. Faith didn't know where the other pieces of jewelry had come from; but at the same time, she wasn't sure she really wanted to know.

"Where did you get all this?" she whispered, even though her heart knew the answer.

"In the stables. I was mucking out the last stall and they were just laying there in this sack. Easy pickin's, huh, Fan!"

She gathered up the treasures and piled them into the bag. "Put it back. I don't care how, but you must put every bauble back where you found it now!"

"Put it back? There's a fortune in that sack! It'd take me months t'score this big on the streets!"

"I don't care. We are *not* stealing from these people. They've treated us well."

"I didn't steal it. I told you I found it."

"Then you won't have any trouble remembering where it goes, will you?"

His shoulders slumped, his head drooped on his shoulders. "Fine, I'll put it back. But if someone else finds my swag, I'm blaming you!"

He wouldn't be the only one.

With the sack clutched in his fist, Scatter started to leave the room. Rapid steps down the hallway had him spinning around.

"Someone's coming!"

Faith tensed. Her attention shot to the door she'd left halfway open.

"What am I gonna do? I'm supposed to be mucking out the stables!"

"Quick, under the bed. And take this with you."

No sooner did Scatter get his long, lanky body under the metal frame than Lucy pushed the door wide open, unannounced. "Ah, so you're finally here."

"What do you want, Lucy?"

"Millie's been calling for you for the last hour." Her gaze swept the room, paused at the bed, then returned to Faith and raked her with disdain. "You might consider making yourself presentable first."

After she left, Faith shooed Scatter out of her room to return the items to wherever he'd "found" them. Then she hastily threw on a clean uniform and hurried toward the kitchen. Breakfast wasn't to be served till eleven, but there were guests to tend, coal bins to stock, bread to bake, and a dozen other tasks to attend to. And the sooner she completed her chores, the sooner she could seek out Troyce.

Her worries over what mischief Scatter might be up to rolled to the back of her mind as she wondered where the baron might be now. She wished she'd been able to wake up beside him, but she also understood the danger in that. Not that anyone ever ventured down to the boathouse; but with so many strangers in the castle, she didn't want to take any chances of discovery. It was bad enough that Lucy had seen her in less-than-crisp form.

Faith had just turned the bend in the hall that led to the kitchens, when a set of voices drifted from an open door, into the hallway. She immediately recognized Lady Brayton's sophisticated lilt.

Remembering the sight of her last night, Faith started toward the doorway, fully intent on confronting her about the mysterious reappearance of her missing red dress when the train of conversation gave her pause.

". . . the most eligible ladies from Brighton to Land's End were in attendance last night, and he showed no interest in any of them."

"You're worrying for nothing, Your Grace."

"I cannot help but worry. If he does not settle on a bride soon, I fear he will leave England again. I could not bear it."

"It's my belief that he is suitably interested in remaining at Westborough."

"It's that girl—the one he dragged home from London. He's been taken with her since the day he brought her into this house, and I'll not have him throw his inheritance away for a girl who—"

"Is suiting a purpose."

"You can't be serious!"

"So what if he amuses himself with her? Lord Westborough knows his duty. You said yourself that no one will invest in his venture, so he must marry a lady of wealth and title. You, my dear, must simply give him a nudge in the right direction."

The conversation turned toward other matters of no interest and yet, Faith was too stunned to move. That . . . Judas! She'd been told the ball was to give him an opportunity to meet with investors. How could the duchess pretend to support Troyce's decision to rebuild his ship and plot behind his back to marry him off?

She had to tell Troyce—what?

What could she possibly say to him? "Your sister is plotting to press you into marriage so you won't leave England?"

He'd never believe her. His trust in her was still too unpredictable, their relationship too fragile. What if he thought that she was trying to drive a wedge between him and Lady Brayton for her own gain? No, it was too risky to say anything yet.

Still, she couldn't just do nothing and let the duchess convince him to take someone else to wife. Not before she had a chance to love him, and he had a chance to love her back, even if only a little.

But what could she do?

Millie. Surely she would have some idea of how to protect his lordship from his sister's wicked plan. But the instant she entered the kitchen and saw Lucy and Millie sitting at the table, their eyes bright and smiles wide, a horrible sinking feeling slowed her steps and dulled her senses.

"There you are, Faith," Millie greeted brightly. "Have you heard the news? Wedding bells will be ringing in Westborough soon."

"Indeed? Who's getting married?"

"Lord Westborough." Lucy simpered. "He put himself on the market last night during the ball."

Faith's heart pitched, her knees went weak. "I didn't realize the bar—his lordship wished to marry."

"Of course he doesn't—no man wants to surrender his bachelorhood, but he's got the barony to consider. 'Tis about time, too, I say."

But what of me? She wanted to cry. What of the sweet things he'd said to her and the feelings he was making her feel? How could he have kissed her the way he had, held her, made love to her, knowing all along he would be taking another to the altar? How could he have taken her heart knowing he'd be giving another his name?

"Faith, are you all right?"

"What?"

"You're looking a bit peaked of a sudden," Millie said, concern etching her brow. "Maybe you should sit down."

"Maybe you're coming down with the grippe like Chadwick," Lucy taunted, glee shining in her eyes.

The grippe. How appropriate she thought, for it felt as if a vise had clamped around her heart and was squeezing all the blood from it. She ignored Lucy's knowing smirk as she stumbled to the door. She didn't know what excuse she made for herself. She didn't even know where she was going. At the moment, she didn't care.

All she knew was that she'd never be good enough for him. She wasn't good enough for anybody.

Chapter 17

Troyce woke up feeling like the hounds of hell had taken up residence in his brain. He rolled over on a prickly bed of straw and immediately regretted the motion when the devil himself started whacking the inside of his skull with a fifty-pound pitchfork. "Ahh, damn," he whispered, pressing his palms to his temples.

He licked his chalky lips and opened his eyes. Chunks of limestone seemed to weigh down on his lids. Each time he blinked, grit scored his eyeballs.

After several tries he was finally able to peer through slits and thanked God for the gloomy gray wedges of light beaming onto the straw-strewn floor. Sunlight would have put him six feet under.

Then again, he figured it was no less than he deserved for drinking himself into oblivion.

He struggled to remember how he'd gotten here, in this state. Hell, he wasn't even sure where *here* was. A stable, he realized, hearing a horse nicker nearby. A vague memory of a country pub formed through the soupy fog of his mind. A bottle of something that tasted like seawater, a pretty barmaid with sienna eyes, red-gold hair, and a wreath of flowers on her crown—

No. Not a barmaid. Princess Faith.

The night before came back to him in a rush. The ball, the moonlight, the boathouse.

Faith.

Ah, God. Had he really gone to her room? Seduced her in her bed? Taken her maidenhead on the deck of his ship? "Bloody hell . . ."

He rolled over on his straw pallet, and his stomach pitched.

Troyce lay still on his side and waited for the wave of nausea to recede before sitting up. Again, the devil stabbed his skull. Again, he cradled his head, and hissed when his fingertips brushed a knot on the back of his skull; he dimly recalled being struck on the head by something quite wicked, but accepted the punishment that was his due.

To bed Faith, to ruin her knowingly when he'd committed himself soon to marry another, was unforgivable. Never had he behaved so abominably toward a woman, no matter what her station in life. He wouldn't have thought himself capable of such a heartless act before last night. Before holding Faith in his arms. He should have resisted her. Should have been more honorable. Should have at least told her. . . .

How was he ever going to explain himself?

He owed her an apology at the very least. Not that she would accept it, nor would he blame her if she threw it back in his face. But he had to try.

His stomach protested viciously when he got to his feet. He weaved in place for a moment or two before he trusted that his wobbly legs would bear his weight without his having to use the stall gate to support him.

He managed to locate his horse after several miserable minutes and led the creature outside. A drizzling rain and flat, gray skies greeted him, an appropriate reflection of his mood. He blinked and lifted his face to the overcast sky, welcoming the cool mist against his face.

The fist caught him unaware.

The blow struck him between cheekbone and jaw. The force spun him around, and he landed on his knees in the mud. "How does it feel, Westborough?" A sturdy boot caught him in the ribs. "Don't feel too ducky, does it?"

Troyce shook his head to clear it and spat out a mouthful of blood. "You've just made the biggest mistake of your life, Swift."

"It's you who made the mistake, Westborough. No one steals from me and gets away with it. Give me my goddamn money. And while you're at it, I want Fanny and the lad back, too."

"Go to hell."

Troyce threw himself to the left and rolled out of the way, narrowly avoiding another kick. The motion made his stomach pitch and bile rise in his throat. Cursing the effects of a hard night of drinking, Troyce willed his insides to settle.

"I'm warning you, Westborough." Swift circled

him like a hawk. "I want my money, and I want Fanny and the boy."

"I don't give a rat's ass what you want." He lumbered to his feet. "If you think I'm just going to hand them over, think again. They suffered enough at your hands."

"Oh, spare me another bloody bleeding heart!" he wailed to the sky. "Now I'm beginning to lose my patience, Westborough."

And Troyce was just beginning to regain his. Thoughts of what Faith's life must have been like with this lanky piece of slime sent wild rage careening through him. He wanted nothing more than to give that rage free rein, charge his target, and pummel him into the mud.

But he'd spent eight years of his life dealing with river scum like Swift. For the most part, they were ignorant slouches, but they were also greedy and without conscience, and therefore should never be underestimated. What they lacked in education, they more than made up for in cunning. One was more apt to find a knife blade sticking out of his back through rash action than calculated thought. Draw them out, Troyce had learned long ago, find their weakness, then strike.

"Now I can make it easy on you, or I can make it hard." Continuing to circle, Swift shrugged out of his macintosh and tossed it aside. "But I'm not leaving here until I get what I came for."

"What do you think you're going to do to me, Swift?" Troyce removed his own coat and began to circle as well. "Beat me? Starve me? Throw me out on the streets if I don't earn my keep? I'm not some desperate kid you can bring to heel."

"The sniveling little maggots need to learn their place. If they want a place to sleep, food to eat, and a roof over their heads, they better bloody well earn it. I don't give handouts to nobody."

"No, you just prey on those weaker and more helpless than yourself. Oh, that makes you a *real* man, Swift." His eyes narrowed, giving Troyce his first sign that his taunting was cracking Swift's control. They were beginning to draw a crowd. Villagers gathered on the outer fringe, their curiosity palpable. "I'll bet it just grated on you that Fanny got away. I'll wager you were mad enough to spit nails, weren't you?"

Swift's mouth flattened.

"She's small, she's quick, and she took risks. And that paid off, didn't it, Swift? What's more, when she outlived her usefulness on the streets, hell, she had something the boys didn't. She had a body to lure the men in. Double the money." His own words sickened him. With herculean effort, Troyce shoved the disgust deep down inside himself and focused on the moment. "Oh, I'll wager that she would have brought in a fortune," Troyce smiled.

"Her scrawny ass? She wouldn't have brought in that much, and she knew it. In fact, most time she's more trouble than she's worth. Always dreaming, trying to put on airs like she's better than everyone else."

"But you threatened her with prostitution anyway."

"She took risks, but she had a wild streak. She needed to learn her place."

Then why was he so insistent on having her back? Why go through all the trouble?

Then it hit him. "How long was she with you? Ten years or so? That must have given her some ranking in the band. The others probably looked up to her." In fact, he'd bet the castle that without her there to rally them, Swift's income was beginning to suffer. "How's the band now, Jack? I'll bet you're losing knucks left and right."

And Troyce knew then that he'd hit the mark. Swift charged, but Troyce was ready. He crouched low, caught Swift around the middle, and threw him over his shoulder. Swift bounced up and charged again. Brawn to brawn, wit to wit, the men wrestled for power, slicing each other with the mutual hatred in their eyes, growling into each other's faces. Troyce managed to push Swift off. He suffered two sturdy blows to his face, before slamming his shoulder into Swift's gut and tackling him to the muddy ground.

And years of pent-up rage poured from his fists. For his parents, his grandfather, the title he never wanted, and the position it had put him in now. For villagers who hated him, a decrepit old manor house that drained his soul, and a marriage he dreaded with every fiber of his being.

But most of all, the rage consuming him was on Faith's behalf, for all she'd endured in her short life. He saw a little girl with amber gold hair, wandering around a cemetery, searching for the family who'd abandoned her. And he saw her at ten years old, selling matches on the street, her stomach pinched with such hunger that it made her easy prey for the wiles of a snake like Swift. And he saw her as she grew from girl to woman, desperate enough to keep herself off the streets that she took risks beyond reason.

And he saw a lovely young woman beneath a staircase, a wreath of orange blossoms in her hair, watching rainbows dance.

I used to dream of being a princess.

His own actions toward her sickened him. He'd been so worried about what Faith might have been trying to take from him that he hadn't given a single thought to what he was taking from her when he'd seduced her on the deck of his ship last night.

She'd promised herself never to become what Jack would have made her. And she'd broken that promise. For him.

A goddamn title. That's what he'd been trying to hold on to.

She'd been trying to hold on to herself.

Gradually, he realized that his fists were no longer making connection with a solid object, and that someone was struggling to contain his flailing blows.

"Lord Westborough, stop! You'll kill him."

He went still and stared unseeingly at the face in front of his. Then the haze slowly receded from his eyes, and Bear's frantic features came into focus. With deep, heaving breaths, his gaze swept the crowd surrounding him, their expressions fearful. Mothers held tight to their children. Crones leaned into burly, middle-aged men. Youngsters stared at him with mouths gaping and brows raised.

Then he looked down at the mess he'd made of the man beneath him and was sickened.

Troyce rose abruptly and backed away. No one said a word as he stood in the midst of them, dragging his bloody and swollen hand down his equally bloody and swollen face. Nor did he say anything to them.

"Bear, I hereby appoint you village magistrate. Your first task is to dispose of *that*."

"Aye, milord." He inclined his hairy head in the first gesture of respect Troyce had seen since stepping foot back on Westborough lands after an eight-year absence. "What do ye want me t'do with him?"

Bear could throw him to the sharks for all Troyce cared. Except, that would be too easy. He remembered Faith's concern over Swift's band, and feared what might happen to any who remained in the tunnels if they weren't cared for. "Lock him up tight somewhere until arrangements can be made to transport him to London." He'd use whatever power he had as a peer to see Swift prosecuted. He wasn't sure what he could do for the rest of the youngsters, but at least he could assure that Swift's days of preying on the weak and helpless were over.

The crowd parted as he made his way back to the livery where his horse waited. He didn't even bother with a saddle; just swung onto his bare back and clucked him into motion.

He arrived at the house a short time later and after washing up in the stables so he'd not frighten anyone else, he let himself into the house.

Millie was in the entryway, dusting the tables.

"Where's Faith?"

"Upstairs, milord." The feather duster went slack in her hand, and her brow creased with worry. "What has she done wrong this time?"

"Nothing—this time it's I who did something wrong." Troyce took the stairs two by two. He passed Devon as she was coming down.

She held up her hand to stop him. "West, I need to speak with you."

"Not now, Devon." Pushing past her, he continued up the stairs.

He found Faith in the tower room, scrubbing the floor on her hands and knees.

Feeling awkward and unsure of himself, Troyce stood in the doorway, his shoulder braced against the jamb. In his lifetime, he'd faced raging storms, violent blizzards, and typhoons powerful enough to make an iron man quake. Yet nothing nature could throw at him compared to the turbulence created in him by one wisp of a woman.

"Faith," he called softly.

She stiffened, but went on as if he hadn't spoken.

"Faith, I owe you an apology."

She dropped the scrub brush into the bucket, wiped her hands down the front of her apron, then after getting to her feet, reached for a folded square of linen. "You owe me nothing, milord."

"Will you look at me?"

She sighed, turned, and gasped. "Crikey, what happened to yer face?"

He smiled at the blunted massacre of vowels. "'Tis nothing, love. A minor squirmish in the village."

"This weren't caused by no minor squirmish. Ye look as if ye been trampled by a team of plow horses!"

He closed his eyes, her touch on his face as close to heaven as he'd ever get. Damned if the temperature of his blood didn't rise—among other things. "Faith, stop." He gripped her hands within his own, drew them away from his skin, and stared at the work-worn palms. "There's something I must tell you. What happened in the boathouse . . ." As he stroked her fingers, the memory of her clutching him in the throes of passion . . . "What happened between us should never have happened."

She went still, dropping her hands, then her gaze. "No, it shouldn't have. Your future bride would be sorely disappointed if she knew her groom was tumbling the hired help the night of their betrothal."

"You know?"

"Servants talk, Baron. Did you think I would not learn of the reason for such a grand affair?"

"I wanted to tell you. If you'll let me explain—"

"You owe me no explanation."

She started to walk away from him, but he pulled her back and searched her eyes. Flat, emotionless, she stared back at him. "I have no choice, Faith. If I do not marry, I'll lose everything."

"I understand."

"Do you?" But he could see that she didn't. And he took responsibility for it.

He let go of her hand and strode slowly to the window. A flock of gulls hovered above the rocks jutting into the Channel below. A sailboat glided through the water. Troyce sighed. "I was barely twenty-one when my grandfather started pressuring me to marry. Twenty-one, Faith. Hell, I'd not even sown my oats yet, why would I want to tie myself down with a wife?

"The pressure continued, and a year later, he issued an ultimatum—marry a woman who met his standards or he would cut me off. She had to be of noble blood, virtuous of character, and wealthy in her own right."

"Why of his standards? Why not marry for love?"

"Because," Troyce turned to face her, sat on the window ledge, and crossed his arms loosely over his chest, "my father had defied him by marrying my mother and lived in misery for the rest of his life. I swore then that I'd not make my father's mistake, but neither was I going to let some crotchety old Frenchman tell me how to live. Hell, I was young and arrogant and quite full of myself. I'd never wanted the title and didn't want the old man's money. I told him so, and vowed then and there to make my own fortune so neither he nor my parents could ever use it as a weapon against me. I went to America to learn of ships. My mother was horrified, my father ambivalent. Miles and I had a grand time." He found himself smiling at the memories.

The smile faded. "Then . . . my mother died, my father grew ill. Westborough fell to ruins. The villagers raided the place, stole everything that might have saved their miserable lives. Most left after that, but some stayed on. They blamed my father for abandoning them and accused me of deserting them. And they were right. I should never have left. I should have accepted my duty. Instead, I ran from it, and I failed them." He silently begged her to understand. "I cannot fail them again, Faith."

"And I would not expect you to. They depend on you."

"Why are you being so damned agreeable?"

"Do you expect me to forbid it? To fall to my knees? Beg you not to break my heart? I won't do it. If I was foolish enough to fall in love with you, it's my own fault. As you've so oft reminded me, milord, I am naught but a servant here, at your beck and whim until I repay the amount stolen from you in London."

For several long moments, neither spoke. Troyce considered telling her that he'd developed feelings for her as well, but he wasn't sure if he would call it love. What was love, anyway? Besides, what purpose would it serve? Would it change anything?

No. Because no matter what he felt, he still couldn't have her.

So he did the only honorable thing he could do. "There's something else I must confess, Faith. Your debt to me is clear." A knot rose in his throat. "You are free to go if you wish."

She choked on a laugh. "I want no favors, Baron. I told you, I won't be your whore."

"It's not a favor, Faith. I told you that when the money that was taken from me was repaid, your debt would be clear. I reclaimed the money from Swift when I went to London."

He watched her calculate the days in her mind and felt his heart sink as her temper rose.

"You kept this from me?" she whispered. "You've had the money for weeks, and yet you let me believe that I was still indebted to you? Why? Why would you do that to me?"

"Because I was afraid you would leave." Because it kept her close. *Kept* her indebted. What a bloody arrogant ploy. When had he become such a pompous ass? When had he sunk to the depths of the Jack Swifts of this world? "If you choose to leave now, I wouldn't blame you. I will not force you to remain here against your will."

"And where the bloody hell am I supposed to go, Baron?"

"Wherever you wish. Maybe you could search for your family."

"I told you, I've no desire to search for them."

"My original offer still stands, Faith. You're welcome to stay here at Westborough for as long as you wish. You could live in the cottage, if that's what you want, and continue working in the manor. I can't pay you now, but until such time as I . . . as I marry, you would at least have food and shelter and clothing."

He expected her to stay on? Watch him marry another woman? Cater to her and the children they would one day have? Go on and pretend as if nothing had happened on the decks of *La Tentatrice*?

He was staring steadily at her, as if waiting for her to decide, when Devon appeared in the doorway of the tower room.

"Troyce, I must speak with you."

"Not, now Devon."

" 'Tis important."

Grateful for the reprieve, Faith started out the door, only to find her way barred by Lady Brayton.

"No, you should stay, Miss Jervais, since this concerns you." To the baron, she said, "This was found in Faith's room this morning." She opened her palm and in it glittered the diamond brooch.

Faith felt every drop of color drain from her face. A roaring began in her ears, dimming the conversation around her.

"She's stealing from us—from me."

"Like she supposedly stole your gown?"

"I was mistaken on that, but there is no mistake now. It was found in her room, on the floor under the bed."

"That doesn't prove she took it."

"Then perhaps you should ask her."

"Faith?"

She forced herself to look at him, at his tight jaw, his tense shoulders.

"Can you explain how Devon's brooch came to be found in your room?"

Look what I found, Fanny!

Put it back, Scat.

Why hadn't he returned the baubles where he'd found them like she'd told him to? Her imagination conjured his young face, white with terror, ghostly screams of help, the clank of iron bars shutting, so vividly that she jerked.

"Faith?"

"It was me," she whispered.

The baron went still. "What?"

"It was me. I st-st-stole it."

The room got so quiet she could hear her heart beating. Ticking. Like minutes on the clock of her life.

"I don't believe you," the baron said.

That she was able to keep her tone calm, flat, amazed her when every nerve screamed in panic. "I said I did it, Baron. Have you ever known me to lie?"

"Then say it again—*without* stuttering this time."

She pinned him with blazing eyes. "Go to hell!"

"I know you didn't take this gewgaw any more than you took Devon's dress. So who are you covering for? Is it the lad?"

The room started to spin. He didn't believe her. The blimey son of a bitch still didn't trust her word, and Faith didn't know if she should laugh in joy or wail in sorrow.

When she refused either to reaffirm or retract her statement, his mouth flattened, and with determination in his stride, stormed between her and his sister, out the door.

"What are you going to do, West?" the duchess cried.

"Something I should have done long before now."

Faith didn't begin to worry until late the next morning when the baron still hadn't returned. She told herself that he was a grown man. That he could take care of himself. But it wasn't like him to leave without a word to anyone.

Hoping to take her mind off the heap of worries

piled on her plate, Faith alternated between pacing the tower floor and cleaning in a frenzy.

"Zounds, Fan, take a look at these!"

She glanced across the baron's study, where Scatter, who was supposed to be helping her dust the frames depicting the de Meir line, was instead reaching for one of a pair of ornamental cutlasses set on brackets attached on the wall. "Don't touch those, Scat. We're in a deep enough pot of boiling water."

He ignored her, as usual, and lifted one of the curved swords from its holder. "Do you think we'll go to prison, Fanny?"

"*You* aren't going anywhere." What would happen to her, she couldn't begin to guess. "It really bothers me how the duchess's brooch could have been found in my room."

"It was in the sack with the rest of the swag when I put it back in the stables."

"And you swear you put it back?"

"I swear on me life. Now the whole swag is gone again. I'm betting someone swiped me spoils, just like I told you they would."

Aye, and that's what really had Faith perplexed. Someone in Westborough was stealing. It wasn't Scatter. And it sure wasn't her.

But someone was.

Sometimes she thought the best thing for all of them would be if she and Scatter just padded the hoof, like in the old days. What stopped her, she couldn't say. Maybe it was the fact that so much still lay unsettled between her and the baron. Or maybe it was that running seemed an admission of guilt. Or maybe it was just the not knowing who—or why—someone wanted her gone so bad that they'd make her look like she was stealing. Whatever the reason, she remained at Westborough, waiting for the lord of the manor to return. Then, and only then, when she could tell him to his face that she was leaving, would she leave.

"Scatter, I told you not to touch those," she scolded him as he stood in the middle of the study, swishing the cutlasses through the air like a swashbuckler. "Now put them away before you get hurt—"

One of the swords clattered to the floor.

"Or they get broke." And she wound up in debt to the baron again.

Sighing, she stepped down off the stool and picked the weapon off the floor.

"On guard!" Scatter immediately struck the pose.

"It's not 'on guard', it's *en garde*, ye little bugger. Now for the last time, put them away."

"Aw, come on, Fan! 'Member when we saw those sword-fighters down in Covent Garden?" He danced from one foot to the other. "*Swoosh! Swoosh!*"

She popped the flailing blade aside with the one in her hand. "Move, ye little leech."

"I see you're no better at sword-fighting than you are at banister-riding."

Faith spun around. "Your Grace!"

Lady Brayton entered the study and stopped beside Scatter. Her hair was perfectly coifed as usual, her gray silk gown immaculately pressed.

She took the cutlass from Scatter and ran two fingers down either side of the dull, curved blade.

Not a word had been spoken between them since Lady Brayton accused her of stealing the brooch, but the woman's animosity hadn't lessened. Seeing her holding the sword, watching her slide her fingers down the curved blade, glimpsing a mysterious glint in her eyes made Faith wonder if, like the baron's, Lady Brayton's anger was the kind that simmered below the surface.

She gripped the grooved handle, tossed it up and down to test its weight. "I haven't held one of these in years." The blade tapped against the one Faith held. "Good heavens, pardon me." Another tap. "Oh, pardon me, again!"

Clutching the grip of her own cutlass, Faith warily eyed the duchess.

"Perhaps you should move aside, young man. I seem to be a bit clumsy with this big knife."

Without hesitation, Scatter moved out of Lady Brayton's way. "That's a good lad," she said.

Then *she* struck the pose. "*En garde!*"

Faith jumped back, both surprised and alarmed. "What are you doing, Your Grace?"

"Avenging my brother's honor."

"I'm not going to cross swords with you!"

One dark brow arced. "Have you no honor of your own to avenge, Miss Jervais?"

And in that moment, Faith understood that, to back down would mean giving up any claim she had to innocence, to dignity, to pride. Aye, even to her place—whatever it was—in Troyce de Meir, third Baron of Westborough's life. And with a tight-lipped, *"En garde"* of her own, she struck the pose.

The clash started out a slow ringing of metal on metal as each woman felt out the other's strengths and weaknesses. Faith knew that her weaknesses far outweighed any strengths, for the closest experience she had with swordplay was with the sticks she and Scat used to use to beat off the rats. Her steps were awkward, her arc often low. But when she struck, she struck swift and accurately.

Lady Brayton on the other hand, was an obviously accomplished—if rusty—swordswoman, with a graceful flair for design and a sure, confident aim.

" 'Tis a pity that you could not attend the ball, Miss Jervais." *One point.*

"Oh, I was there, Your Grace. And I had a glorious time."

One point.

"I thought the roses were an elegant touch, didn't you?"

Faith's cutlass clattered to the floor. Bloody hell. Sighing at the fact that her suspicion had just been confirmed, she picked up the instrument, gave the duchess a silent *touché* salute, then bent her leg and lifted one arm over her head in readiness.

Again, blades rang as they danced about the study. Their skirts dusted the floor, and Lady Brayton's bustle struck several figurines, but their eye contact remained steady.

"Strange how your dress reappeared, isn't it?" Faith thrust, in as close to an accusation as she dared. "And how your brooch simply appeared in my room?" *Two points, with a bonus for audacity.*

" 'Tis nothing less than I expected from a dock-side tart," the duchess parried.

Emotions began to heighten, the rhythm grew quicker. Steel on steel echoed through the cavernous stone halls as the combatants moved from the study to the entrance hall.

"I never asked to be here, you know," Faith said.

"Then why are you?" the duchess demanded from her higher position on the stairs.

"Because it's better than where I was heading."

"I can sympathize with that."

Shocked that the two might actually have something in common, Faith stumbled and nearly lost her grip.

"Careful, Miss Jervais, mistakes like that can cost you the match."

She picked up her footing and crouched. "Does Lord Miles know that you're in love with him?"

It was a cruel blow, one Faith didn't even realize could cripple a woman until she saw the great lady's knees buckle.

"Your Grace!" She tossed the cutlass to the floor and raced up the stairs to help lower her to the step.

For several long, silent moments, only the sound of the battle echoed in the hall.

Then Faith heard a tear drop.

"Forgive me, Your Grace, I did not mean to cause you pain."

Lady Brayton wiped her eye with a lace kerchief she pulled from her wrist. "That's your greatest weakness you know, and it will lose you the battle."

"What's that?"

"Your heart is too soft." Her shoulders lifted, her tears dried. "You are a worthy adversary, Miss Jervais," she said, and Faith swore she'd heard a note of praise in her voice.

"I don't want to be an adversary. I never did."

"Somehow that does not surprise me."

With a sigh, the duchess stood and gathered the cutlasses, then laid them in Faith's arms for her to put them away. For a moment, brown eyes met silver, and Faith felt as if she were being measured.

"You fell in love with him, didn't you?"

"Yes, Your Grace."

A heartbeat passed. Then she asked, "Is there any chance you'll be increasing?"

Softly, sadly, Faith answered, "Yes, Your Grace. There's a chance."

Though Lady Brayton's expression remained neutral, Faith thought she saw anguish flash in her eyes before she turned away. Then, she started up the stairs, chin high, posture proud.

"Your Grace?"

The woman paused and looked over her shoulder, her brow lifted questioningly.

"I'm truly sorry you lost your son."

Chapter 18

❧

Faith returned the cutlasses to their place on the study wall. She wasn't sure what had just happened between her and the duchess. She wanted to believe they'd reached some sort of truce, but it seemed too much to hope for. Not that it mattered either way. Once the baron returned, she'd be leaving anyway. It was for the best. She'd not be able to stay on and watch him make a life with another woman, feeling the way she felt about him. Not when he couldn't trust her.

Still, she wished she knew where he'd gone. It wasn't like him to leave without a word. And hard as she tried, she couldn't rid herself of the image of him lying bleeding on the ground the day of the stoning. She didn't want to think the villagers would hurt him, but neither could she forget how much they despised him.

The sound of horses outside drew her to the window overlooking the front lawn. Faith peeled the curtain aside, dreading and hoping to see his broad-shouldered figure riding up the drive. Chadwick greeted two finely garbed men on lathered horses, neither of whom resembled Lord Westborough. Faith's heart stuttered. *He's a grown man, he can take care of himself.* Yet it was obvious that the visitors had ridden hard.

Aware that they would need refreshments, Faith left the study.

As she was returning to the dining room with a tray of tea, water, and cookies freshly made that morning, a voice traveled down the stone corridor.

"This is Inspector Jones, I am Inspector Riley of Scotland Yard." Faith peered around the doorway and spotted one of the men in the entryway reaching into his coat. He withdrew a square of paper and handed it to Lady Brayton. "We have reason to believe that this woman is employed in this household. Her name is Faith Jervais. She also goes by the name Fanny Jarvis."

Scotland Yard?

He'd called in the authorities?

"What's your business with her?" Lady Brayton asked.

Faith didn't wait to hear their reply. She dropped the tray onto the dining room table and raced up the back steps to her room, betrayal slicing through her breast.

She could hardly believe he'd called in Scotland Yard! Though why it should surprise her, she didn't know; he'd warned her what would happen if she stole from him again, and aye, though she'd known the risks, she'd confessed. Maybe deep down she'd fooled herself into thinking that, in diverting the blame off Scatter, he would be easier on her.

Well t'hell with being honorable. Even if she told him of her suspicions, she doubted it would change anything. He'd already proven that he would believe the worst of her. The bloody coward couldn't even tell her what he'd planned to her face.

She and Scat were getting out of here now.

Focusing her thoughts on escape, she nearly ran Lucy down in front of her room.

"Lucy! What are you doing here?"

"Looking for you. Lady Brayton sent me to warn you that there are a couple of men downstairs looking for you. You must leave immediately."

Why would the duchess want to warn her? Why not simply turn her over to the inspectors? Unless . . .

Had Lady Brayton been behind the "thefts" all along? It made sense. She'd been wanting to get rid of her since the day they'd met and this was her chance, because Faith knew as well as the duchess that once she left, she could never return.

"I can't leave without Scatter."

" 'Tis not him they're after, 'tis you. And unless you want to spend the rest of your life in prison, you must leave this moment."

"I'm not going anywhere without Scatter." Even if it meant getting caught. A promise was a promise. Mates didn't leave mates, and she'd given her word that she'd not leave him behind again.

"Then I'll find the lad and bring him to you."

Footsteps up the front staircase snagged their attention. Panic exploded in Faith's breasts.

"That must be them—they requested to search the house." Lucy grabbed her arm. "Come with me. I know a place where you can hide until it's safe to leave."

Her heart thundering a hundred beats a minute, Faith let Lucy lead her back down the servant's steps. They reached the first floor, then Lucy opened another back door. A set of stairs wound around a stone wall, and a dark corridor stretched before them. She'd never been in this section of the castle before and the dank darkness reminded her of the tunnels of Bethnal Green. "Where are we?"

" 'Tis an underground corridor that leads to his lordship's boathouse."

Lucy lit a torch taken from the wall. They hurried down the hallway, and the crash of water against rocks grew louder the farther they moved. They reached the end of the hall, and Lucy withdrew a set of keys from her apron pocket.

After a moment of fumbling, she found the key that fit the rusted lock. A metallic click echoed through the stones, then the door opened. Lucy placed the torch in a holder near the door. It was a storage room of sorts, home to a collection of ropes, wooden trunks, and small kegs, as well as an assortment of seafaring instruments. Another door was set into the far wall, and Faith assumed it led to the cove housing *La Tentatrice*.

"His lordship usually keeps a store of food in those trunks and there is water in those casks.

That should hold you until I return. Now just stay here. I'll bring the boy as soon as I can."

Before Faith could ask how Lucy knew so much about what the baron kept in the room, the door slammed.

Faith slid down the cold, hard wall, wrapped her arms about her knees, and waited.

"Come on, come on!" Troyce smacked his hand against the roof of the hack. "Driver, what's the delay?"

"Wheel's bogged down, milord. We'll have it freed in a jiffy."

The damned rains! He'd been stuck in London two days longer than he'd planned because of the weather, and now this.

"Never mind, I'll hire a horse."

With the license tucked securely against his heart, he threw open the door to the hack. Rain pelted him in the face. He lifted his collar and adjusted his hat brim.

He knew it was going to cause a scandal, knew he was sacrificing everything, but he didn't give a bloody damn. Faith would be his to have and to hold from this day forward, and if anything or anyone tried to come between them, he'd blacken both their eyes.

He'd known it the instant she'd confessed to taking Devon's broach, when he knew damn good and well that she hadn't done it. Thievery from the peerage was a grave offense. That she was willing to go to prison to protect a boy not even related to her was probably the greatest sacrifice he'd ever seen a person make. Could he do no less?

Hell, he didn't know they would survive. He had no idea how he was going to pay the last of his father's creditors or the taxes on Westborough or even if he could salvage the bloody place. But he did know one thing: As long as he had Faith, he could figure out a way.

"Roses, get your roses!"

The market monger's call across the street from the livery drew Troyce's attention. After leaving instructions for the groom to fetch him his fastest horse, Troyce dashed across the cobblestones.

"Are they all fresh cut?"

"Fresh as the day, guv. We got red uns, blue uns, yella uns—"

"What about silk? Do you have any silk roses?"

"Comin' up!"

Troyce smiled when the man left to whisper frantically to a grubby little boy and send him racing down the wharf. A few more minutes' delay wouldn't matter, Troyce decided. He hoped Faith would see the humor in his token reminder of their dance under the staircase. While he waited for the boy to return, he scanned the boats in the river; one day, God willing, *La Tentatrice* might even join the ranks on the water. In the meantime—

The thought dropped clear out of his head when his roaming gaze caught sight of a man in a black cowboy hat walking across the street, a woman on his arm.

Troyce's heart went numb. He willed her to turn in his direction.

And when she did, his heart turned to stone.

Faith.

No . . . it couldn't be! She'd sworn the last time that she couldn't have been the woman he'd seen in London, and although reluctantly, he'd believed her, because she swore she never lied. And yet, only two days ago she'd lied about taking the brooch.

Or had she?

Well, by God, he would get to the bottom of this once and for all!

Absently, he took and paid for the rose, then started across the street, dodging both hoofed and wheeled traffic in his path. The couple had stopped beneath a canopy in front of the livery and appeared to be waiting for horses of their own.

"I don't know if I can do this anymore," Troyce heard her say in a decidedly American cant.

"Not for much longer, darlin'," the cowboy said.

"It's just so hard keeping up the pretense."

"It won't be for much longer. Think about what will happen if you give up now?"

She caught sight of him. Her eyes widened at his approach and started to turn away. Troyce gripped her by the arm. "Don't even think of running from me . . . !"

"Hey! Get your goddamn hands off my wife, you son of a bitch!"

"Your *wife*?" He spun her around. "You owe me an explanation, and I'm not—"

Anger gave way to shock. The eyes were the same, the features nearly identical. But the difference ended there. The scars of tough living didn't show in this woman's eyes, her face was fuller and there was no lightning bolt scar. "You're not Faith!"

"What? What did you call me?" Before Troyce could answer, a meaty grip wrapped itself around his arm. Instantly, the woman threw herself at the man to stop him from swinging at Troyce. "No! Jesse, wait!" To Troyce, she asked, "What did you call me?"

He shook his head in bafflement. "Nothing. It was a mistake." She only looked like his lady. From a distance it was an easy mistake to make, but up close. . . . "I'm sorry to have troubled you."

"Wait, don't leave!" She wrapped her hand over his sleeve. "You called me Faith!"

"Forgive me. I have confused you with someone else."

"Faith Jervais. Please tell me that's who you thought I was. *Please*."

He stopped in his tracks, his blood went cold. There was something in this woman's voice, a desperation that made his stomach twist and his heart stall. "Who are you?"

"My name is Aniste Jervais McGuire Justiss. Faith is my sister—my twin sister. And if you know where she is, mister, I'm begging you, take me to her."

Dusk had fallen by the time Troyce crossed the stone bridge to Westborough and led his horse to the stables. The lack of horses told him that the last of their ball guests had departed, for which Troyce was grateful. The reunion between Faith and her sister after a sixteen-year separation was a matter best conducted without an audience.

He dismounted and handed the reins to a young village lad just as the carriage bearing the Justisses rolled up the oyster-shell drive. He imagined Faith's reaction when she saw her twin for the first time. She'd be shocked, he knew, and perhaps angry. She'd always believed her family had abandoned her, then sent her away. But once she learned the truth, she'd be just as stunned as he'd been upon hearing the story that morning.

He mustered a weak smile for the couple stepping out of the vehicle. Part of him was glad that they'd been so diligent in their search for Faith and celebrated the fact that the Jervais family would soon be reunited. Another part, however, wished they'd never set foot on English soil. Jervais. It amazed him even now that he'd never made the connection. The name alone resonated with respect, prestige, and wealth, for Anton Jervais had amassed a fortune in shipping and shipbuilding. As one of the most powerful families in the western hemisphere, they could offer Faith everything she deserved, and more.

A whole lot more than a lowly, impoverished baron could offer.

And that, he realized, was the real sinker. She wouldn't need him anymore. Not for a damn thing.

With a heavy heart, he led the couple into the house. Millie greeted them in the entryway. "Good evening, milord," she said, taking their coats. " 'Tis good to have you home."

"It's good to be home, Millie," he replied. "Bring refreshments for our guests to my study, s'il vous plaît. And send Faith to me as well."

"She isn't here, milord."

"Where is she?"

"I don't know, Milord. A couple of men from Scotland Yard came to call yesterday morning. We haven't seen her since."

"Scotland Yard was here? Did they say what they wanted?"

"My father contacted them to find Faith," Honesty supplied. "It's possible that they were the investigators assigned to track her down."

"But Faith wouldn't know that. She has not exactly led an upstanding life before coming to Westborough. If she saw them, she may have panicked." And if she'd left yesterday morning, she could be anywhere. "Millie, who spoke with the investigators?"

"Lady Brayton, milord."

A condemning silence pervaded the hall, and Troyce wished now that he hadn't told the Justisses of Faith's life in his household. "No, I know what you're thinking, and you're wrong." he said. "Devon and Faith have had their differences, but Devon would never wish to see her harmed."

Concern etched Jesse Justiss's rugged features. "I'm not saying she would, but she might know something."

"Will you ask her to join us in the study?" Troyce asked of the housekeeper.

While Millie went to gather a tray and fetch Devon, Troyce led his guests into the library. He hadn't bothered to study Honesty Justiss—just seeing her made him long for Faith—but now, as he slid a glance in her direction to gauge her reaction, he wished he hadn't bothered. She sat on the settee, leaning against her husband. Her face was pale, her features twisted with distress. Without her coat to conceal her, he realized she had a fuller figure, and her clothes were of the finest cut and fabric.

How could he ever have mistaken her for Faith?

"West?"

He tore his attention away from Honesty and greeted his sister. "Devon."

After introductions were made and Devon had seated herself in a chair adjacent from the settee, she said, "Forgive me for staring, Mrs. Justiss. The resemblance between you and your sister is remarkable."

Tears sprang to the woman's eyes. She dabbed at them with the corner of a handkerchief provided by her husband. "Forgive me, Lady Brayton. I'm afraid my emotions are a bit sensitive at the moment. I've been searching for my sister for so long, and to learn that she isn't here as I'd hoped is somewhat of a disappointment."

"I'm sure it is. She left so abruptly that there was no time to stop her. The boy is worried sick. He hasn't been out of his room since yesterday."

Troyce's head snapped up. "Wait, do you mean she left without taking the lad?"

"She took nothing, West. She simply disappeared."

A mate don't leave a mate.

Instant foreboding crept through his bloodstream. "Something's not right. She loves that boy—she wouldn't have left him behind."

"Maybe she thought he was better off here."

"No, she promised him she'd never leave him, and Faith never makes a promise she can't keep. If she'd planned on never returning, she would have taken the boy with her."

"Lady Brayton, could you tell us exactly what happened yesterday morning?" Jesse Justiss prompted, reminding Troyce of his occupation as a Pinkerton Operative.

"Well, Scotland Yard arrived and showed me her likeness. I then brought them into the library, and they told me that her family was searching for her. I believe she may have overheard the detectives and thought they'd come to arrest her for taking my jewels."

"She didn't take them, Devon, I'd stake my life on it."

"I don't want to believe it any more than you, West, especially considering the circumstances, but how else do you explain her abrupt disappearance? If she wasn't guilty, why would she have run?"

"The question is, if she were guilty, why didn't she run sooner?" Troyce countered. "And why didn't she take the boy with her?"

"Who else saw the investigators?" Justiss asked, leaning forward with his arms on his knees.

"Chadwick. And Lucy, of course. I sent her to bring Faith to me. She returned to tell me that Faith was nowhere to be found."

At the mention of Lucy, Troyce's sense of foreboding heightened to a painful level. "Where is Lucy now?"

"Upstairs, I believe," Devon said.

"She went to the village," a muffled voice piped in.

As one, four necks craned toward the window. Brow pleating, Troyce pushed away from the fireplace where he'd taken up his post and strode across the room to peer into the cubby beneath the desk. There, hunched in the near dark, he spotted Scatter. "How long have you been hiding there, lad?"

"A while."

Long enough to hear every word, Troyce suspected. "Then how do you know Lucy went to the village?"

He dropped his gaze, and Troyce imagined he'd crawl under the rug if he could. "She goes ever' night. She's got a beau there."

"Do you know where Faith is?"

"No, suh. But I know she didn't swipe 'er ladyship's baubles."

"You know who did, though, don't you?"

"Aye. But I can't tell ye."

Troyce crouched before the boy, aware of that every ear in the room was centering on his answers and just as aware that if he wasn't careful, this half-wild boy, the only one who might offer a clue to Faith's whereabouts, would bolt. "You can trust me, Scatter. No harm will come to you, I promise."

His face twisted. "She said I'd never see Fanny again if I snitched!"

"She? Do you mean Lucy?"

"Lucy!" Devon cried.

Though his nerves were stretched taut and perched on edge, Troyce kept his tone calm and even. "Scatter, this is very important. I want you to tell me everything you know about Lucy, Faith, and the stolen jewelry. I swear on Faith's life that I will let nothing happen to either of you."

Scatter seemed to weigh his word against his own fears. He leaned his head back, wiped his nose, then sighed. A moment later, he pulled himself out from beneath the desk and lifted solemn eyes to Troyce. "I found a bag of gems in the stables and showed 'em to Fanny. She told me t' put 'em back, 'cause ye were nice folks and we wasn't t'be stealing from ye. So I put the swag back, just like Fanny told me to, and someone took it again. It weren't Fanny who filched it, but I was afraid if I didn't find it, everyone would think she did, and she'd go to prison. Then when Fanny and her ladyship got into the swordfight—"

Troyce's brows snapped up, and he pinned his sister with a look of part astonishment, part reproach. "Swordfight?"

Devon pursed her lips. "Never mind. Go on, young man."

"Well, Lucy was watching from up there." He pointed toward the balcony visible out the doors. "She had this funny look on her face, like she wanted t'run Fanny through herself. So when she left all of a sudden like, I followed her and that's when I caught 'er cleanin' out the chest in 'er ladyship's room."

"*Lucy* stole my jewels?"

"Aye, mum."

"Did she see you?"

"Nay, suh. I padded the hoof right quick, I did. But when Fanny turned up missin', I knew Miss Lucy had somethin' t'do with it, and I told 'er if she didn't tell me what she did t'Fanny, I'd tell ever'one that she swiped 'er ladyship's baubles. She called me a liar. She said Fanny took the lady's things— Lady Brayton knew it, Lord Westborough knew it, and now the coppers knew it. She said if I told, no one would believe me but that I'd best keep me mouth shut else I wouldn't see Fanny ever again."

"Sounds to me like someone isn't so confident that the boy would not be believed," Jesse remarked.

Troyce silently agreed, as the same thought had occurred to him. "I want every able-bodied person in Westborough gathered on the front lawn. We'll split up into groups, half will take the house, the other half scour the village. I want no stone left unturned until Faith and that treacherous bitch Lucy are found."

They searched the village and the surrounding forests by torchlight; they turned the manor upside down. Troyce kept his emotions tightly wrapped in a cloak of numbness, but by the time dawn broke over the horizon with no sign of Faith, the hard shell began to crack. No one had seen Lucy or her beau, a farmer named O'Brien, since the night before, and Faith . . . God, Troyce didn't want to think about what Lucy might have done to her.

"We've searched everywhere," Devon said

when they reconvened in his study. "I don't know where else to look."

"We cannot have come this far for nothing," Honesty whispered. "What if something has happened to her?"

Jesse wrapped his arms about his wife and kissed her temple. "We'll find her, darlin'. I promise you."

And Troyce couldn't bear it anymore. Not the silent glances of compassion Devon threw him, not the comfort Jesse offered his wife, not the intense . . . emptiness of the castle.

He needed Faith. Needed to touch her, see her, smell her sweet scent.

He strode out of the study without a word to her family or his sister and out the terrace doors. By the time he reached the cliffs, he was stumbling. His vision blurred and his chest felt as if each rib was splintering into his heart.

He slid down the cliff path, drove himself along the shoreline, tripped into the boathouse. How he made it to the ship, he didn't know.

He just knew that he had to be close to her.

Reaching the deck of *La Tentatrice*, he lay on his stomach, weary to the marrow of his soul, and pressed his cheek to the cool, damp wood beneath him. "Faith, oh God, where are you?"

And in that moment, he realized that, even if— no *when*—they found her, she wouldn't belong to him anymore.

He'd lost her the minute her sister showed up to claim her.

Chapter 19

She was the most beautiful creature he'd ever seen. Eyes like fine brandy in the candlelight, amber hair glittering with stardust and moonbeams, skin soft as a newborn babe.

She arched into him, the movement sleek and graceful, her breast full, taut, eager for his touch. The scent of her filled him, dazzling his senses, arousing him to fevered heights.

He touched her, and from her came a moan of pleasure.

Then a sneeze.

His eyes popped open. His hand, stroking the polished wood, stilled. Troyce grasped for the moment, for the sensation of feeling Faith, for the dream so close within his reach. But it was only that. A dream.

He clenched his eyes shut and curled his hand

into a fist as the night's events rushed through his mind. He had no idea how much time had passed since he'd sought comfort in the last place they'd been together. Minutes? Hours?

He lifted himself to his knees and sat back on his heels, then reached for the timepiece tucked inside his vest.

"*Achoo!*"

Faith?

Troyce's heart jumped from normal rhythm to triple beats in a millisecond, crashing against his chest so hard it stole his breath. He gave himself a vigorous shake. Was he dreaming still? Or had he really heard her—

"*Achoo!*"

It was Faith! Troyce shot to his feet and strained to detect the direction of the sound. "Faith?"

He raced across the deck and leaped over the railing to the steps. "Faith, where are you?"

Then, weakly, "Troyce?"

"Faith?" He rounded the bow to the starboard side of the ship, following the hollow sound of her voice and pressed his hands against the iron-banded panel of a door shut years ago. His father's old hideaway. "Faith, are you all right?"

"I'm fine," she called through the door. "Just get me—achoo!—out of here!"

He ran his hands over the door. Lichen had taken over the surface and the damp environment had long ago rusted the padlock. "It's locked. I don't have a key."

"Lucy has it."

"Lucy's gone. No one has seen her since last night."

A pause fell, and Troyce frantically scanned the area for something to pry the door open. "Hold tight, Faith, I'll get you out."

A broken claw hammer, a bent piece of pipe and a splintered mallet later, panic began to claw his way through his bloodstream. The wood had swollen beyond its bands and was wedged so tightly against the frame that not even a breeze could make its way past the door. "Bloody *hell*! Faith, I'll be back—I must find a key." Surely his father would have kept an extra one someone among his belongings . . .

"Fetch Scatter," she instructed. "Tell him to bring my rucksack. He'll be able to get me out."

Troyce didn't waste a second questioning her. He made the desperate climb up the cliff path and across the yard. Ten minutes later, he was dragging a groggy Scatter back into the boathouse, Faith's rucksack clutched tightly in his hand, and half the household dogging his heels at a distance.

"Scat, ye lovely little leech!" Faith wept through the door when Scatter called her name.

"I'll get ye out, Fan," he called back, digging through her pack. The tools of her trade spilled out onto the stone, bringing Troyce back to the moment they'd first crossed paths on a London street corner.

Finding what he was looking for, Scatter snatched up a ring of odd-looking instruments. He inserted no less than a dozen of the keylike tapers into the lock before at last, a resounding click made him whoop in glee! Troyce slammed his shoulder against the door several times before the weathered wood finally gave and the portal squealed open.

He wasn't sure who got to Faith first, but as he enveloped her in his arms, he didn't care. Nor, as his mouth covered hers in a soul-searing kiss, did he care that they were nearly crushing the boy between them. They'd found her. She was alive, safe, and unharmed.

And smelling quite strongly of roses.

Half-laughing, half-choking, he pulled back and tipped her chin into the dim light seeping in from the cavern behind him. "Are you sure you're well?"

He barely heard his own words as he stared into her beautiful face. "I am now."

She sneezed again, and he laughed. "What is this pungent thing you're wearing?"

"A cloak—one of your sister's, I suspect. I found it in one of these trunks."

"This was my father's hideaway. Devon and I used to play in here when we were children. It hasn't been used in years. How in God's name did you ever wind up in here?"

"Lucy told me that Scotland Yard was looking for me and that Lady Brayton sent her to tell me to leave before they found me. She said I was to hide in here until she could bring Scatter to me."

"She lied to you, Faith. Devon sent her to fetch you, not send you away. Scatter discovered that she'd been the one stealing and trying to make it look as if you were the one committing the act."

"Scat?"

Troyce ruffled his hair. "He's been quite the champion during this ordeal."

The lad all but crowed like a rooster at the praise.

"But how did she know about this room?" Faith asked.

"She grew up here. She probably knows this house as well as Devon and I. Better it seems. I'd forgotten this room even existed."

Once again, both seemed to realize what would have happened had Troyce not heard her through the door. Troyce swallowed the knot of emotion rising in his throat and pressed her cheek against his chest.

"She was angry with me—she accused me of stealing your affections," Faith softly told him. "She said that if I hadn't come to Westborough, you would have been hers again. I didn't realize how much she hated me until after she locked me in this room. If you hadn't come looking for me—"

He tamped down the swift and fierce sense of vengeance boiling within him and stroked her tangled curls. "Did you ever doubt I would?"

"Aye, I did." She looked into his face. "When the inspectors arrived, I thought you'd sent them. You were gone so long. What was I supposed to think?"

"I can't blame you for thinking I'd sent them here."

"But I didn't trust you. Can you forgive me?"

He brushed a wayward curl from her cheek. "If you can forgive me for keeping the truth about reclaiming the money from Jack Swift."

"Where did you go? Why were you gone so long?"

The license burned a hole through his suddenly hollow heart. "That's not important now. The only thing that matters is that you're safe and well." After ridding her of the cursed, blessed rose-scented cloak and wrapping her in his own coat, Troyce took her hand in his, committing the softness of her skin to memory. "Let's get you out of here. There's someone waiting outside who's been very anxious to see you."

Faith wasn't sure who she expected to see when she stepped out of the old storage room but a mirror of herself was not it.

She stood in stunned silence and stared at the woman staring back at her, gloved hands pressed to her lips, brown eyes so like her own shining with tears.

In a split second, a childhood of girlish songs and hide-and-seek games came back in vivid detail. Pretty bows in tidy hair. Ruffled pinafores and tiny tea parties. Giggles at midnight and laughter in the broad light of day.

And in that split second, the missing half of herself merged as one. Without thought, she took a step forward. "Honesty?" The name she'd so often called her sister as a child came out in a whisper.

"Oh, Faith, it is you!"

Faith started to lift her hands and rush forward. *Honesty, come out, come out, wherever you are. . . .*

The reality hit with the force of a fist to her stomach. She saw herself as a young girl, curled up alone and cold against a grave marker, then in a shoddy house with a slovenly woman and her equally slovenly man, then later, huddled between barrels in the hold of a stinking ship and finally, upon a moth-eaten cot in an overcrowded orphanage with nothing but a cracked Phillip Goldsmith doll to remind her of the life she'd been denied.

And she yanked herself back, rage and bitterness and bone-deep resentment bubbling up in a furious wave. "How dare you show your face here."

Instantly the baron's arms tightened around her shoulder. "Faith—"

"You! Did you bring her here? Did you tell her where to find me?"

She couldn't believe it. She wouldn't believe that the baron, her prince, would do something so utterly and unforgivably cruel.

"Aye, I brought her here."

"You bastard! You bloody, stinking, rotten bastard!" She struck out, not even aware of the blows she was raining upon him until he grabbed her arms and gave her a ferocious shake.

"Stop it, Faith, stop it!"

"Why? Why would ye do this to me? I gave you everything, *everything*!" A sob erupted from the pit of her soul, and her knees buckled beneath her. She would have fallen if he hadn't caught her. "How could ye do this, Baron?"

On his knees before her, supporting her against his chest, he brushed her tangles from her face with the broad of his palm. "Faith, love, listen to me. Aye, you gave me everything. And I, in return gave you nothing, for I've nothing left to give except . . . Please, Faith, let me give you this."

She stared at the stone wall, felt him stroking her hair, felt his steady, sturdy heartbeat beneath her cheek. "I hate you, Baron."

His lips pressed against her temple and his voice was unnaturally gruff when he said, "I know."

* * *

Honesty didn't know how long she stood near the bow of the half-constructed ship watching Lord Westborough rock Faith in his arms. She felt numb down to her being. Of all the scenarios she'd imagined once she found her sister, absolute and utter loathing had never entered the scene.

A touch at her elbow startled her, and she swung a glance at her husband.

"Honesty?"

"She hates me, Jesse." Even as she said the words aloud, she could scarcely believe them.

"She doesn't hate you, darlin', she's just been surprised."

"You heard her, she *hates* me!"

Jesse drew her roughly against him, and Honesty clung to her husband, her vision blurring with unshed tears. "Why? What did I do?" Whatever it was, it must have been *horrible*! No, Honesty couldn't remember, but Faith obviously did. Pulling back from Jesse's embrace, she looked at her twin through a sheen of tears. Lord Westborough was helping Faith to her feet. She wouldn't even look at Honesty.

"Faith," she called as they started down a path leading to the cove entrance. But Faith didn't respond; even Lord Westborough shielded her with his arm, which only drove the stake deeper through Honesty's heart.

"Let me get her up to the house," Lord Westborough told her. "Once she's recovered from the shock, she'll be better equipped to deal with this."

"She's my sister—I only want to—"

"Just—" He stopped himself after that one cutting word and softened his tone. "Just give her some time. She deserves that."

As Lord Westborough led Faith down the pathway and out of the boathouse, Honesty watched the pair, unsure if she should hate the man for taking her sister away or adore him for loving her so much.

She turned to her husband who stared down at her with concern shadowing his green eyes and furrows in his brow. "It's your call, darlin'. What do you want to do now?"

She wanted to scream. Cry. Rail at Fate and shake Faith until her bones rattled.

Jesse pulled her close with his arm about her shoulder. "Well? Do we stay or leave?"

A sudden surge of determination stiffened Honesty's spine and dried her tears. "We stay, for as long as necessary. I did not cross a country, an ocean, and half of England for the last seven months only to be turned away. I don't know what she remembers about that day, or why she holds me to blame for it, but we are not leaving here until I get to the bottom of this."

Jesse smiled, and quipped, "Spoken like a true Pinkerton wife."

Faith stood in the tower room, numb from her head to her toes. She refused to think of the baron and his betrayal, deeper than any she'd known before. And she refused to think of the woman waiting downstairs. Her sister.

She shut her eyes.

She'd have to face her sooner or later. She knew that. There were too many unanswered questions, too many blank years that needed filling in.

And yet, all she could see when she looked at Honesty was a woman so strikingly beautiful that it took one's breath away, a woman in silks and jewels who never wanted for anything, a woman who had known not a day of hunger or desperation or abandonment.

A woman who had been loved by her father.

Faith hadn't let herself think of him in all the years she'd grown up away from him. She'd dreamed instead of the dark and handsome prince of her mother's bedtime stories, the one who would whisk her away from all that was harsh and ugly in the world she'd known.

She'd never have imagined that her prince was really the devil in disguise.

When the knock came and someone entered the room, Faith didn't bother asking who it was. She knew without looking just as she knew how to breathe. It came naturally whether she willed it or not.

"May I speak with you, Faith?"

She sounded as if she'd been crying, but Faith told herself that she didn't care.

"My husband and I will be leaving for London shortly but before we go, I want you to hear me out."

Her shoes tapped against the floor as she moved farther into the room; her skirts rustled as she sat in the crown-backed chair near where Faith stood.

"When we were little girls, something tragic happened. We lost our mother, and we were torn apart. I remember none of it. I did not even remember you until a few months ago. I have berated myself until I'm blue in the face, but it doesn't change the fact that I did not know you existed. Had I known, I would have moved heaven and earth to find you."

Come out, come out wherever you are. . . . Faith closed her eyes, and a tear slipped down her cheek.

"But Papa . . . he never forgot. And he never stopped searching. For him, at least I would hope for your compassion."

"Compassion?" Faith found herself saying. "He threw me away! He kept you, and he threw me away as if I were of no more consequence than a wormy apple. And you, dear, sweet, beautiful Honesty—how dare you come here, into my castle, as if you are some queen to whom I must pay homage! You in your jewels and silks—living a life of ease and comfort while I've had to fight and scrounge and steal for every scrap."

Features so nearly identical to her own gaped in shock. Then Honesty made a strangled sound somewhere between surprise and laughter. "Is that what you think? That I led a life of ease and comfort?"

"Look at yourself. I'll bet Papa made certain that you never wanted for a thing in your entire life. He wanted you. Honesty, the good daughter, while I was nothing but trouble from the day we were born. Growing from child to woman in a house on the cliffs, attending your parties and being courted by your beaus. . . . Do you have any idea what it's like to spend sixteen years running for your very life?"

To Faith's utter astonishment, her sister burst

into peals of laughter that sent her whole body shaking and tears pouring down her cheeks. "Oh, Lord, Faith Jervais, have you got it wrong!" She wiped her face with one hand, and held her ribs with the other. "Dear sister, let me tell you what *my* life has been like for the last sixteen years. . . ."

Over the next few hours, Faith learned the story of her sister's own abduction, her life spent on the run with a man she called "the greatest confidence man in the West," and the story of how Pinkerton Detective Jesse Justiss had tracked her down and won her heart.

By the time she was through, Faith had found herself laughing, crying, and living an adventure she'd never dreamed possible to live—all through the eyes of her twin. She sat on the floor, her back against the window, feeling as if she'd been whacked against a washboard and wrung out of emotion. "To think that I spent all these years thinking that Papa rejected me, when all this time, it's been me rejecting him." She sighed. "What a pair of daughters we make—the liar and the thief."

"True. He probably deserves better than we. But we've been given a second chance to make things right. Not everyone gets that chance."

Faith couldn't agree more. Second chances didn't come around too often, but when one did, it shouldn't be wasted. The baron had taught her that. "There's something I don't understand. What would Phillipe Jervais have to gain by ordering us kidnapped?"

She didn't think she could be any more surprised until Honesty said, "Millions."

Faith's mouth fell. "Millions?"

"Anton Jervais is one of the wealthiest men in the world, Faith. The plan was to drive him insane with grief. With us out of the picture, his son Alex would inherit Jervais Shipping. Except the job was botched. Your abductor was killed, and mine spirited me away."

A downstairs clock tolled twelve times, making Faith aware of the late hour. "I can't believe it's midnight already."

"So it is." Honesty smiled. "Happy birthday, sister."

"It's my birthday?"

"Mine, too. We've just turned twenty-one."

When Honesty reached over to squeeze her hand, Faith did not pull away. Instead, she squeezed back. "Have you a wish for your birthday?"

"Only for a healthy baby."

"You're to be a mother?"

Honesty laid her hand over a barely noticeable bulge of her belly. "I thought it was seasickness. What about you? Have you a birthday wish?"

She hesitated, then confessed, "I think I should like to see my father."

"It's a wish easily granted. If I'm not mistaken, his coach is pulling up the drive as we speak."

Suddenly light-headed at the prospect of seeing her father, Faith swayed when she stood up. Honesty was at her side in an instant, and with her arm hooked in the crook of Faith's elbow, they started for the door. "Millions, eh? I wonder if he holds a fondness for old Spanish galleons?"

"Why, do you have one?"

"No, but I know someone who is looking for an investor."

The old gentleman stood in the open door of the carriage, staring transfixed at the manor. Troyce had heard a pair of girlish giggles just before the front door opened. The following silence told him that Faith was probably standing on the veranda, seeing her father for the first time.

A second later, his heart nearly burst when a flash of gray flew across the lawn and Faith launched herself into her father's arms.

A bittersweet smile played on his lips as he watched the reunion between Anton Jervais and his daughter from the window of his study. They held on to each other as if fearing the other would disappear, and God knew, he understood that fear. He'd felt it only this morning when he'd left Faith to the company of her sister.

A rap on the door drew his attention away from the window, and he turned just as Devon entered the room. "May I come in?" she asked.

Troyce bent over the ledgers he'd been trying to lose himself in and waved absently in the direction of the chair that faced the fireplace.

"I suppose they'll want to take her with them," she said.

The same thought had been parading through his mind ever since he'd realized her family had made themselves known. "It's their right. She belongs to them."

"Are you going to just let her leave?"

"What else can I do, Devon? It's her family.

They can give her so much more than I ever could."

"Except your love."

"My love," he scoffed. "Why would she want me after everything I've done to her?"

"Because you believed in her when no one else did. Not even me. You gave her something to hold on to. You gave her a chance to better herself."

"Better herself? She's a goddamn heiress, and I had her scrubbing chamber pots."

"You didn't know that when you brought her into this house. She was naught but a guttersnipe you found on the docks of London, for God's sake! If you don't do something to keep that girl, then you're a bigger fool than I ever was."

"I think that's it. Our trunks are packed, I've got our tickets, Jesse is checking us out of the hotel— so why do I feel as if I'm forgetting something?"

Folding the last of her gowns, Faith listened to her sister with half an ear. Over the last week they'd spent together in London, she'd learned that Honesty often talked to herself without expecting answers, and in this moment, Faith was grateful for that. Their father had booked passage on a ship for America, which was due to leave port in only a few hours. After sixteen years, she was finally going home.

Except, it didn't feel like home.

It felt like punishment.

As they had nearly every moment of the last seven days, her thoughts turned to Westborough and the lord of the manor. He'd said not a word to her the day she and Scatter had left. He'd simply placed a wreath of orange blossoms on her hair, then bowed over her hand and kissed her knuckles. Then, as now, the gesture had broken her heart.

She didn't know what she'd expected from him. A declaration of love? A promise of forever? Aye, they were silly, fanciful yearnings for her to harbor, yet harbor them she did. For in her heart, she would always be a pickpocket. And he would always be her prince of dreams.

"What is it, Faith?"

She glanced up, startled.

"You sighed."

"Did I?"

"It's your baron, isn't it?" Honesty sat on the bed and clasped her hands in her lap.

Faith shrugged languidly. "He's not *my* baron."

"Does he know how you feel about him?"

"He knows."

"And does he feel the same way about you?"

"A little perhaps. But it doesn't change anything. He still must marry a woman of his grandfather's standards else he will lose everything."

"And what kind of woman is of his grandfather's standards?"

"Virtuous, wealthy, and titled," Faith recalled, flicking the criteria off on her fingers.

"Three out of three isn't bad," she countered her eyes, twinkling.

"'Tis more like none out of three. I'm hardly virtuous, I'm far from wealthy, and I've no title save the 'Miss' at the forefront of my name."

"Oh, Faith, for someone who remembers so much, you've certainly forgotten a lot of things. Our mother was the daughter of Comte LeCroix who scandalized her family by marrying a merchant. They wanted to take us from Mama and Papa and raise us among the aristocracy. Papa adamantly refused and took us to America. But it does not change the fact that we are both *le noblesse* in our own right."

She was a lady, then? A true, blue-blooded, peer-in-her-own-right *lady*?

"Faith, whether you met none of those standards or all of those standards, it should not make a difference. If you love him and he loves you, neither virtue nor wealth nor title should stop you from being together."

"What should I do, then?"

"Well, for starters, you should *not* get on that ship."

"But—"

"No buts. Papa, Jesse and I have been watching you fight to keep a Brit's stiff upper lip, as the saying goes, all week and the three of us are ready to hog-tie you and haul your skinny rear end back to Westborough." She twisted around, and dragged an unresisting Faith down to the bed. "Sister mine, I love you. I would keep you with me till the end of my days if I thought that's what it would take to make you happy, but it's plain as the nose on my face that your heart is here with your baron."

"It cannot be—"

"It *can* be, if you want it badly enough. If I've discovered anything with Jesse, it's that love is the most precious thing in a woman's life, and once found must never be let go. At least not without a fight. You should tell him how you feel."

"And offer him what?"

"The virtue you surrendered to him, the wealth your father bestowed upon you, the title you inherited from your mother, and most simply and importantly, your own precious heart."

For the first time since the night she'd spent with Troyce on *La Tentatrice*, giddy hope blossomed within Faith's breast. She gave her sister a quick hug, then sprang off the bed. "You're right," she said, dragging a gossamer shawl around her shoulders. "I've spent my life running from my fears, it's time I faced them head-on. If he takes my love and throws it back in my face, then I shall find a way to recover. But if he doesn't—"

"If he doesn't, then all your fairy dreams will have come true."

As Faith raced out of the room and down the main staircase of the hotel, she focused solely on finding her father and begging him to take her back to Westborough.

Halfway across the lobby, she came to a stunned halt. "Troyce?" She blinked, certain the sight of the baron standing in the midst of the nearly empty lobby was a dream. Wearing a tailored black suit so much like the one he'd worn the night of the ball, he looked so handsome that her heart stopped beating for a second. "What are you doing here?"

"I warned you about stealing from me."

"Now you wait just a minute, Baron. I stole nothing from you!"

"Ah, but you did, Faith. You stole my heart." His stride was slow, sure, and incredibly sensual as he crossed the lobby.

Faith wasn't certain she'd heard him right. He

came to a stop less than a breath away from her and gazed down on her with those glorious silver eyes. His dark hair had been trimmed and combed back behind his ears. His coat was finely cut grosgrain that accented the breadth of his shoulders, and his cravat had been tied in an intricate knot at the base of his throat.

And in his hand, he carried a perfect red rosebud.

"It's silk, *cherie*," he said, immediately allaying her fears that she would start sneezing all over his chest. "A reminder of the most wonderful night of my life and a token of many more. It will never make you miserable, nor will it ever die . . ." He lifted his gaze from the blossom and gazed steadily into her eyes. "Like my love for you."

He presented the rose to her, and Faith took it numbly. The roaring in her ears was so loud that surely she could not have heard him right.

"My father said something to me the day I left England," he said, his voice gruff. "We'd gotten into a huge row over my grandfather's expectations for me and my father's relationship with my mother. I couldn't understand why he would give everything of himself for her. And he said to me, 'Where there's faith, there's hope. Where there's hope, there's love.'"

Faith could hardly breathe for the pounding of her heart.

Eyes like mist on stone lifted to stare solemnly into hers. "He hadn't lost his faith, and I hadn't yet found mine. Until you. Faith, you gave me hope, and somewhere in it, I learned what it is to love—and how it felt to be loved."

She pressed her fingers to her mouth, and a sob caught in her throat.

And then, there in the midst of the hotel lobby, he dropped to one knee, took her free hand, and brought it to his lips, then pressed it against his rapidly thudding heart. "I can't make you the princess you always wanted to be. But I can make you a baroness, and one day, perhaps, a viscountess. It's less than you deserve, but it's all I've got. Do you think it might be enough?"

"I don't want your bloody title, Baron," Faith answered, so choked up she could hardly form the words. "All I've ever wanted was you."

"And all I will *ever* want, is you."

Epilogue

A salty breeze blew in from the English Channel, where forgotten memories of waves
crashing against jagged rocks became reality.
Faith Jervais, soon to be Lady Westborough, stood
upon the stern of *La Tentatrice*, waiting for the music to begin. The warmth of a September sunset
caressed her face, and the promise of a new beginning lifted her soul.

She closed her eyes and marveled at how drasti-
cally her life had changed in such a short time. Had
it only been three months since she'd been digging
in rubbish barrels for scraps of food? Scrounging
the streets of London for her next mark?

Who would have ever guessed she'd have
bagged the most priceless prize of all?

"Are you ready?"

At the sound of her sister's voice, Faith looked

over at Honesty, glorious in a blue silk gown that barely disguised her pending motherhood. Sixteen years had passed since they'd last stood together. Sixteen years since they'd been stolen from each other by a man with greed in his heart and vengeance in his soul.

"To be truthful, I'm a bit nervous," Faith confessed, clutching the bouquet of silk roses tighter in her fist.

Honesty laughed and linked her arm within the crook of Faith's elbow. "What have you to be nervous about, sister mine? In only a few moments, you will be joined with the love of your life and spend the rest of eternity being blissfully happy."

Maybe that was it, Faith speculated. Maybe, despite every lecture she'd given to herself, there was a frightened little girl afraid to trust her own heart.

Honesty gave her arm a brief squeeze. "He's a remarkable man, your baron is."

"Aye, he is," Faith agreed, her gaze seeking Troyce's lean and powerful figure at the bow of the ship. He looked resplendent in his tailored coattails and creased trousers, the breadth of his shoulders defined, the strength of his body barely contained. "I don't know many who would refuse a million-dollar reward."

"Men do strange things when they are in love."

That, Faith could not argue. The most handsome nobleman in Christendom was about to marry a pickpocket—*former* pickpocket, she corrected herself. "At least he was wise enough to accept Papa's offer to invest in *La Tentatrice*," she said.

"It was a good investment," her father chimed in as he came to stand between his daughters. "Even had it not paid off so well, it was the least I could do for the man who saved my daughter and won her heart."

The first chords of the "Wedding March" cued the beginning of the ceremony, forestalling any reply she might have made and making her heart leap. "It's time," she whispered.

Anton Jervais adjusted the tiara of orange blossoms crowning her curls, then brushed her cheek with his fingers. "It seems hardly fair, my darling Faith." His eyes went damp. "I've only just gotten you back, and now I must give you away."

"I shall never be far away, Papa," she promised, growing misty-eyed herself. "Only as far as your arms will reach." In the next moment, her father's arms reached around her to envelop her in his secure embrace.

The small orchestra paused, then resumed with a crescendo of flutes and harps and violins that beckoned Faith toward the bow of the ship that would soon be sailing toward its new home in Spain.

Pulling back from her father, she drew in a deep breath, then, with a smile, allowed him to lead her along the deck of the ship where a night not so long ago, she and Troyce de Meir, Baron of Westborough, had bound their hearts and souls together for eternity. And as their gazes met over the gathering of their families and closest friends, Faith saw her future in the silvery mists of his eyes, one of unfailing devotion to each other, unwavering faith, and a passionate kind of love that would never, ever be torn asunder. She knew without a single doubt that princes really did come to life and that dreams, no matter how high, really did come true.

Author's Note

Dear Readers,

My earliest memory is of finding a set of baby rabbits orphaned when their mother was hit by a car. I was four years old at the time, and I remember my own mother and me rescuing these tiny, helpless creatures. We'd even taken them to my kindergarten class for show-and-tell once they were old enough to be shown. What is your earliest memory?

For Honesty and Faith, twin sisters separated at a very young age, one had no recollection of the event that irrevocably changed her life while the other remembered it with startling clarity as seen through the eyes of a four-year-old child. Could the special bond between these girls, the liar and the thief, survive the years and miles that had torn them apart?

In *A Scandalous Lady*, I not only had the wonderful opportunity of reuniting these very special women, but of giving Faith a second chance for hope and love. From the moment I "met" Troyce de Meir, I knew he was the perfect man to "rescue" Faith, win her tender heart, and make all of her forgotten dreams come true.

I hope you've enjoyed my sojourn into Victorian England and the world between the underground and the upper class, because like Troyce, I firmly believe that every woman should feel like a princess at least once in her life.

Best wishes,

Rachelle Morgan

Prepare to be swept away by these unforgettable romances from Avon Books

LONDON'S PERFECT SCOUNDREL by Suzanne Enoch
An Avon Romantic Treasure

Evelyn Ruddick knows she should avoid the Marquis of St. Aubyn at all costs, but she is determined to teach the charming, arrogant rake a lesson in compassion. It won't be so easy— especially since his touch is setting her desires aflame, making Evie yearn to submit to *his* passionate instruction . . .

ᴄᴗ

IF THE SLIPPER FITS by Elaine Fox
An Avon Contemporary Romance

Anne Sayer learned long ago that fairy tales don't come true and evil stepmothers do exist. Now dashing and successful, Connor Emory has returned, and this "Cinderella" intends to win back her prince. Because the glass slipper that would never have fit a decade ago, is the perfect size now.

ᴄᴗ

KISS ME QUICK by Margaret Moore
An Avon Romance

The instant Lady Diana Westover spies Edmond Terrington across a crowded room, the lovely, sheltered miss believes she's found the man she's been searching for. Though she knows nothing of men, Diana longs to pen a romantic novel. So she resolves to study the handsome, seductive lord's every move, and to experience the pleasures of his kisses . . .

ᴄᴗ

CHEROKEE WARRIORS: THE LONER by Genell Dellin
An Avon Romance

Black Fox is determined to hunt down the notorious Cat—a thief who robs from the wealthy to give to the poor. But his satisfaction at finally capturing the outlaw turns to shock when he discovers The Cat is a woman! This breathtaking hellion stirs his sympathy and his desire, yet surrendering to a fiery passion could be disaster for them both.

REL 0403

Avon Romantic Treasures

*Unforgettable, enthralling love stories,
sparkling with passion and adventure
from Romance's bestselling authors*

Avon Trade Paperbacks . . .
Because every great bag deserves a great book!

The Boy Next Door
by Meggin Cabot
0-06-009619-5 • $13.95 US • $20.95 Can

A Promising Man (and About Time, Too)
by Elizabeth Young
0-06-050784-5 • $13.95 US

A Pair Like No Otha'
by Hunter Hayes
0-380-81485-4 • $13.95 US • $20.95 Can

A Little Help From Above
by Saralee Rosenberg
0-06-009620-9 • $13.95 US • $21.95 Can

The Chocolate Ship
by Marissa Monteilh
0-06-001148-3 • $13.95 US • $21.95 Can

The Accidental Virgin
by Valerie Frankel
0-06-093841-2 • $13.95 US • $21.95 Can

Coming Soon

Bare Necessity
by Carole Matthews
0-06-053214-9 • $13.95 US

Have you ever dreamed of writing a romance?

*And have you ever wanted
to get a romance published?*

Perhaps you have always wondered how to
become an Avon romance writer?
We are now seeking the best and brightest undiscovered
voices. We invite you to send us your query letter to
avonromance@harpercollins.com

What do you need to do?

Please send no more than two pages telling us
about your book. We'd like to know its setting—is it
contemporary or historical—and a bit about the hero,
heroine, and what happens to them.

Then, if it is right for Avon we'll ask to see part of the
manuscript. Remember it's important that you have
material to send, in case we want to see your story quickly.

Of course, there are no guarantees of publication,
but you never know unless you try!

*We know there is new talent just waiting
to be found! Don't hesitate . . . send us
your query letter today.*

*The Editors
Avon Romance*